Samuel Byron Brittan

Man and his Relations

SALZWASSER
VERLAG

Samuel Byron Brittan

Man and his Relations

Reprint of the original, first published in 1864.

1st Edition 2022 | ISBN: 978-3-75259-112-5

Verlag (Publisher): Salzwasser Verlag GmbH, Zeilweg 44, 60439 Frankfurt, Deutschland
Vertretungsberechtigt (Authorized to represent): E. Roepke, Zeilweg 44, 60439 Frankfurt, Deutschland
Druck (Print): Books on Demand GmbH, In de Tarpen 42, 22848 Norderstedt, Deutschland

MAN AND HIS RELATIONS:

ILLUSTRATING THE INFLUENCE

OF THE

MIND ON THE BODY

S. B. BRITTAN, M.D.

NEW YORK

1864

PREFACE.

IN attempting to classify the phenomena that illustrate the laws and relations of the Human Mind, the Author of the following treatise has only obeyed a natural but irresistible impulse. It is not of course pretended that he was summoned to this work by the commanding voice of a new Apocalypse, and he is quite sure that it was no mere *cacoëthes scribendi* that prompted him to write. It was rather a rational but intense interest in whatever most deeply concerns the true nature and substantial progress of MAN. The preliminary investigation was somewhat protracted; and the philosophical suggestions that accompany the present classification of vital and mental phenomena, are deliberately offered as the result of a long course of observation and numerous experiments in the department of Psycho-physiology.

The Author can only urge the force of his own convictions as a reason for his earnest manner and a somewhat confident expression of his views on questions that may be regarded as unsettled. Had he approached the difficult problems of psychological science with the timid circumspection, that holds itself at a great distance from the themes it proposes to discuss, he would have justly incurred the suspicion of trifling with a grave subject. Whilst he would offer no occasion for such a charge, he is forcibly reminded that a dogmatic spirit is wholly out of place in the philosophical treatment of profound questions.

The facts that illustrate the power of the Imagination and the capacity of the individual Will to influence the functions of other persons— as exhibited in both physiological and psychological effects—are largely derived from the records of the Author's experience; but the results of his own Experiments certainly furnish proper criteria for an enlightened judgment. Whilst the entire course of reasoning, and all the writer's conclusions are cheerfully submitted to the ordeal of the most searching analysis and criticism, he can not acknowledge the right of any one to discredit the facts themselves, especially since they have been repeated, either before large public assemblies, or under the immediate inspection of many intelligent witnesses.

It is not the province of the philosophical inquirer to consider the safety of old systems and popular superstitions. The scientific investigator should make it his chief business to discover and affirm the truth; at the same time, he may very properly leave the schoolmen to look after their own dogmas, and to the profitless task of attempting to preserve a kind of galvanic life in the forms of the dying and the dead.

The labor of arranging the materials for the present volume was undertaken before the commencement of the Rebellion; but the peculiar exigencies of the times occasioned a temporary suspension of the work, and the writer has but just completed his task. It has been emphatically a labor of love, conceived and prosecuted with scarcely a thought of the prospective result, in any commercial sense. Should this treatise awaken in the mind of the reader a rational desire to know himself more perfectly, the labor of its composition will not have been in vain; and the Author will not fail of securing a suitable recompense should the publication of his book promote the cardinal interests of Mankind.

The Author must regard the general subject of this treatise as one of paramount importance. Indeed, natural objects and phenomena become more interesting as we advance from the lower toward the higher gradations of being. Every step upward from unorganized matter presents to the ordinary observer new objects of beauty, while it opens to the philosopher a wider field of investigation. But it is only when we approach the realm of INTELLIGENCE, that we become conscious of standing

" On the last verge of mortal being—

by the enchanted confines of that World where souls exchange their earthly vestments for robes of Immortality. The whole subject is at once supremely solemn and sublime. This unfathomable mystery of thought; this power to grasp the laws of Nature; this majestic play of moral and material forces; these golden memories and prophetic aspirations, that unite the Past and the Future in the Present!—all contribute to deepen the grand mystery of our microcosmical existence, whilst they impressively suggest that our scene of action is the Universe; that Eternity is our opportunity, and that we have Angels and God for our kindred.

NEW YORK, JULY, 1864.

CONTENTS.

CHAPTER V

PHYSICAL CAUSES OF VITAL DERANGEMENT.

CHAPTER VI.

VOLUNTARY AND INVOLUNTARY FACULTIES

CHAPTER VII.

INFLUENCE OF THE PASSIONS ON THE SECRETIONS.

CHAPTER VIII.

THE MIND AS A DESTRUCTIVE AGENT

CHAPTER IX.

RENOVATING POWERS OF THE HUMAN MIND.

CHAPTER XIV.

RELATIONS OF MIND TO PERSONAL BEAUTY.

CHAPTER XV.

RELATIONS OF MIND TO THE CHARACTER OF OFFSPRING

CHAPTER XVI.

THE SENSES AND THEIR FUNCTIONS.

CHAPTER XVII.

PSYCHOMETRIC PERCEPTION.

CHAPTER XVIII.

PHILOSOPHY OF FASCINATION.

CHAPTER XIX.

ANIMAL AND HUMAN MAGNETISM.

CHAPTER XX.

MAGNETISM AS A THERAPEUTIC AGENT.

CHAPTER XXI.

IMPORTANCE OF MAGNETISM IN SURGERY

CHAPTER XXVI.

THE PHILOSOPHY OF SLEEP.

CHAPTER XXVII.

PSYCHOLOGICAL MYSTERIES OF SLEEP.

CHAPTER XXVIII.

INSPIRATIONS OF THE NIGHT.

CHAPTER XXIX.

SOMNAMBULISM AND SOMNILOQUISM.

CHAPTER XXX.

THE CLAIRVOYANT VISION.

CHAPTER XXXI.

THE LAW OF PROPHECY.

CHAPTER XXXII.

APPARITIONS OF THE LIVING.

CHAPTER XXXIII.

STATES RESEMBLING DEATH.

CHAPTER XXXIV.

PHILOSOPHY OF INSPIRATION.

CHAPTER XXXV.

RATIONALE OF WORSHIP.

CHAPTER XXXVI.

NATURAL EVIDENCES OF IMMORTALITY.

MAN AND HIS RELATIONS.

CHAPTER I.

THE TENANT AND THE HOUSE.

Preliminary Observations—Relations of Inward Forces and Essential Laws
to the Forms and Phenomena of the External World—The Kingdoms of
Nature, Material Revelations of the Divine Life—Archetypal Forms of
Nature and Art—Duality of Man—Individualization of the Vital Prin-
ciple—Forms and qualities of Things essentially exist in their Causes—
Formation of the Embryo from the coëxisting interior Individuality—
Supremacy of the Mind over the Body—General Illustrations—Atheistical
Theories—Voluntary Powers of Animals and Man—Descartes' Theory of
the Universe—Man a Kingdom by himself.—Intimate Relations of the
Soul and Body.

LIFE is a spiritual and natural revelation of the Divine
procedure. Not in outward seeming, nor in the changing
phenomena of the terrestrial world, but in their vital principles and essential nature, *all things endure*. Effects are
widely diversified ; they come and go in endless continuity ; but essential causes cohere, and — like divergent
streams — lead back to a common source. The ultimate
springs of being are *one* in the Invisible ; and these great
life-lines that connect external forms with the inward and
central LIFE, are unbroken forever. The organic creation

is preserved and rendered imperishable, in respect to forms,
functions and uses, by the great law and the curious processes of reproduction. It is true that specific forms perish
and are decomposed, so that—in external outlines and superficial aspects—the world is destroyed every day. Yet the
world remains; and, in a most important sense, its forms are
indestructible. The living germs of a creation that is ever
new, take root in the ashes of this vast decay; and the
earth, even now, is far more radiant and beautiful than
when it arose from the slumber of unconscious and shapeless
being,

"In the young morning of Creation."

In every part of the natural world the philosophical
observer recognizes more than is immediately comprehended
in our organic perceptions. The outward processes of Nature
demonstrate the existence of inward forces; specific forms
are the material records of essential laws; whilst the human
body may be regarded as a living revelation of the indwelling soul. These observations will admit of universal application, from the highest to the lowest gradations of being.
Simple elements, chemical combinations and physical forms,
are the elementary and organic revelations of the essential
Life and the inner World. In the process of crystalli-
zation the separate particles assume their places under the
action of inherent forces; the atomic polarities and their
mutual relations being determined — proximately by the
subtile forces of imponderable agents, and in the last analysis by the Supreme Intelligence. The crystal is the con-
crete illustration of those mysterious attractions and affinities whereby the ultimate atoms coalesce, remain united,

and form the worlds. These potencies reside in all matter ; but they are chiefly disclosed to us in the gross elements and ponderable bodies of the natural world, and through the outward avenues of perception ; without which the sensuous observer could neither discover their presence nor their existence. The molecular deposites, chemical processes, and peculiar structure of each separate form, are dependent on the energies inherent in the simple elements, and especially on the great laws of organization and life as illustrated in the external creation. Every atom is a vehicle for the silent but irresistible power that renders it at once an exponent of its own affinities, and the conditions of its association with other elementary particles. Hence the visible world is but the phenomenal exhibition of that superior realm which comprehends the active forces, the primary forms, and the eternal laws of the Universe. The mineral, vegetable and animal kingdoms are succeeding and progressive revelations of those invisible principles that pervade all substance, and pictorial illustrations of the Divine Life that animates the world.

Through all the great kingdoms of Nature the inward force and essential law precede, in the order of time, the outward process and specific form. Hence all visible effects proceed from invisible causes. In the mineral kingdom the aggregation of particles is not determined by outward pressure, nor does cohesion depend on external restraints. The great forces of the natural world act from within—from their centers toward the circumference. The molecular gravitation occurs around the homocentric point of attraction ; and the inward force is at once the immediate source of the material impulsion, and the soul of the particular association of elementary particles. Thus the elements involve the inmost springs of life, and the laws that determine all material combinations and rudimental forms. The acorn contains the oak ; and all the organized forms of the vegetable and animal kingdoms are unfolded from within, by virtue of the forces that inhere in their germinal centers. In speaking of their *development* we distinctly intimate the gradual unfolding of what before existed, but was invisible. It is impossible to form a distinct conception that is not associated in the mind with some idea of *form*. Every work of Art must exist as a mental conception, assuming a more or less definite shape in the human brain. Hence all the objects of beauty and of use, fashioned by human hands, are but objective forms of ideas. In like manner, all natural objects are earthly shadows or reflections of archetypal forms inhabiting eternity, and forever present in the Infinite Consciousness.

The first attempt to look into the Arcana of our own being, usually results in the discovery that Human Nature is at least *two-fold*. The student just entering on this course of investigation may be wholly incapable of making a critical analysis, either of mind or body, and unequal to the task of a scientific classification of vital and mental phenomena ; but he can hardly fail to observe the *duality* comprehended and exhibited in the form and functions of human existence. That the conscious intelligence and the corporeal instrument are, in a most essential sense, *distinct*, while at the same time they are intimately united in the phenomenal illustrations of life, sensation, thought and action, is a truth sanctioned not alone by the philosopher's reason, but by familiar experience and universal consciousness.

It might be interesting to examine the feeble beginnings of our individual existence in the light of modern scientific discoveries. It is true that the subject is still obscure, and all that is comprehended in the accepted theory of impregnation would fail to satisfy the philosophical inquirer. The first visible indication of the new form and individualized life of a human being, is an opaque speck floating in a thick fluid within a vesicle the size of a pea. But I do not propose to discuss the philosophy of this subject. I shall not so much as pause to mark the successive stages of embryonic formation and fetal development; notwithstanding the investigation might prove to be profitable, at least by suggesting reflections calculated to humble our pride.

I have already intimated that the forms, properties and uses of all things coëxist—in a most important sense—with the very elements that enter into their composition and structures. Whatever belongs to the fully developed state of the plant, the animal and the Man must be latent in the causes of their production, and have a vital existence in the germs from which they severally proceed. Thus the embryo contains a man, not yet developed in his faculties and functions, nor complete in organic structure and external outline. If we are right in entertaining the idea that all outward developments proceed from vital principles and archetypal forms within, it may be rationally inferred that our essential Manhood is invisible and spiritual; and that the organic formation results from, and proceeds in harmony with the grand process of interior individualization. It is coherent with the writer's philosophy to ascribe priority of existence to the inward and invisible part of human nature. Each separate organ of the body may be regarded as the appropriate revelation of a hidden faculty of the mind, and a distinct prophecy of the functions it is designed and fitted to perform. The whole organic instrument thus represents that complete assemblage of faculties and affections which together constitute the Human Spirit.

Whatever may be the reader's idea of the nature of the mind, he will be constrained to acknowledge its supremacy over the realm of matter. This superiority is everywhere manifested by the exercise of our voluntary faculties. The body is but the passive instrument of the mind. Moreover, cold and lifeless elements yield to our touch, and take the plastic shapes of living ideas. We mold them into innumerable forms of utility and beauty, and Art has its monuments wherever civilization has found its way. Forms instinct with seeming life, passion and sentiment, start out from the walls of the Vatican and the Louvre, while the sculptured memorials of Genius yet rise like pale specters among the mausoleums of Egypt and the shadows of the Parthenon.

This dominion of mind over matter is not restricted to the more ponderable elements and forms of the physical world ; but it also extends to the imponderables and their mysterious forces, in a degree that is only necessarily limited by our knowledge of the laws of those agents, and the sublime possibilities of human endeavor. Even now we evoke the spirit of the waters to aid us, and it comes forth to move our commerce and our navies against adverse winds and tides. We put a soul in the wheel and intelligence in the shuttle. Remote nations speak to each other with tongues of fire. The finite mind coöperates with the silent forces of the world, and in the voices of Nature we recognize the presence of.the Will in skillful and graceful modulations.

There is a superficial and atheistical philosophy that makes the Universe at most but a vast galvanic pile, and Man no more than an automatic, calculating and locomotive machine. It conceives of the soul as common air, or a transient flame arising from the process of vital combustion; and of all human intelligence as the phosphorescent illumination of the brain. In consonance with this cold and soulless materialism, it is assumed that the suspension of vital motion, marks the termination of all feeling, all thought, all action, and all consciousness; and hence the final extinction of being. This is wholly incompatible with a rational philosophy, nor can it be reconciled with the most significant facts in our experience. We must acknowledge the Mind's dominion over the elements, forms and forces of the Physical World, to be a government only limited in the exercise of its powers by the present standard of knowledge, and the imperfect development of the human faculties. We certainly require no material and metaphysical analyses to enable us to decide a question of this nature. The most grovelling Materialist must accept what is at once so obvious to his senses, his reason and his consciousness; namely, the superiority of the mind over the body; and he must ascribe to the former all those faculties and forces which clothe human nature with more than regal powers.

We have a class of speculative minds who accept the

doctrine of immortality with peculiar modifications. They maintain that men have no souls until some time after their bodies are completely formed, and they have been fairly ushered into the external world ; and hence that the still-born have no existence hereafter. When the animal nature entirely predominates in the parents, it is conjectored that the spirit in the child is not individualized until several months or years after its birth, and in some instances not at all. *This presupposes that men never directly beget their kind; but that brutes are begotten,* and that with occasional exceptions they become truly human at their birth or some-time thereafter. It is perhaps the general opinion amongst this limited class of pseudo-philosophers that we become immortal by breathing the vital atmosphere. It is true that all other animals inhale the same air, and yet never ascend to the plane of human existence. It is difficult to under-stand why oxygen should exert this amazing spiritualizing power over the genus Homo while it has no similar effect on the quadrumana. In fact we discover nothing probable in this singular hypothesis. On the contrary, we may presume that the work of individualizing the intelligent principle in man must commence with, and regulate the process of embryonic formation.

The philosophical mind will not fail to observe in all animated nature something superior to the simple elements and forces of the material world. I refer to those *voluntary powers* which belong to the animal creation. Only lifeless things float on the surface or with the tide. The living tenants of the air, the sea and the mountain streams move at pleasure against impetuous currents and the strongest tides. The acquatic birds, regardless of their relative specific gravity to water, dive beneath the surface, or rise at will above it, into the ethereal regions ; and thus illustrate the superiority of voluntary powers over the innate forces and laws of unorganized matter.

But in Man we are presented with a far more diversified exhibition of voluntary faculties, displayed with sovereign freedom and irresistible force. He is less than our conception of Man who doubts or is disposed to pause at material obstacles. It is Mind that transforms the solid and shapeless rocks into splendid cities, and warms and illuminates them with materials derived from cold and rayless caverns of the mountains, thus bringing "light out of darkness." It is intelligence that renders the most destructive agents harmless. It converts fierce lightnings into faithful couriers, more rapid and sure than the ancient wing-footed messenger of the gods. Thus Man lays his hand on the springs of Nature, and keeps the elements in subjection to his will ; and the vast barriers between continents are converted into international highways, that Civilization may spread the white wings of commerce over every sea.

That creature must be supremely sluggish, if not utterly soulless, whose bleared sense and perverted imagination would make the Mind inferior to the Body ; or who is willing to entertain the idea of such ignoble subordination. But it is illogical and preposterous to admit the superiority of the Mind, and yet maintain that it is only the offspring of our corporeal nature—born and extinguished with the animal fires—that the soul is merely phenomenal, and results from the slow combustion of carbonaceous matter, and the inevitable action of air, light, electricity and other subtile agents on a curious organic structure. To presume that effects may be thus fundamentally *different* from their causes ; or, indeed, that they may even transcend their causes, in degrees that admit of no comparison, is simply absurd. Nor is this assumption rendered more rational or respectable by the constant misapplication of the terms Nature, Reason and Philosophy. And yet popular Material-ism builds its earthworks on the shifting sands of such in-congruous assumptions. Life and all human powers and capabilities are regarded as the product of merely physical causes, that, in themselves, possess none of the attributes of intelligence, and no manifest life. Blind forces may not organize and govern such a world as this ; lifeless elements do not generate and individualize the vital principle ; and the rotary motion of material particles in a vortex never evolved the rational soul.[1]

It is no part of the design of this work to consider Man, anatomically or otherwise, in his relation to the animal creation ; nor do I propose to discuss questions that relate to the origin and distinguishing characteristics of the different races and families of men.[2]   Those who are prone

---

[1] Reasoning from the Cartesian hypothesis and the centrifugal forces, Descartes undertook to account for the formation of the Universe, and the movements of the heavenly bodies. But while his theory was, at least apparently, consistent with the motions of the planets—which revolve in nearly the same plane—it left the comets out to wander, as usual, in every direction through the fields of space, regardless alike of the limits of the Cartesian vortices and the reputation of the philosopher.

[2] If the reader is seeking information in this branch of Ethnology, he is recommended to peruse the "Types of Mankind," and Lyell on the "Antiquity of Man," if he has not done so already.

to consider man as only an animal endowed with superior faculties, have been unable to discover an unbroken connection between human nature and the superior types of the animal kingdom. They have looked in vain to comparative anatomy for a demonstration of their theory. [1] But if instead of confining our observations to the physical department of his complex nature, we have regard to moral aspects and psychological attributes, we shall readily discover that Man is forever separated from the whole animal world by natural lines that are broader and deeper than any that define the limits of the other kingdoms. A great gulf divides the illimitable faculties and rational reverence of Man from the highest development of the brute instincts. Materialism, aided by the most ingenious sophistry, has never been able to bridge the chasm. The grand faculties and achievements which so distinguish Man from all inferior natures, plainly indicate that the Race constitutes a separate kingdom. In a treatise on the Unity of the Human Species M. Quatrefages says that " Man must form a kingdom by

---

[1] " The distribution of the fossil forms of Monkey, from which Man may be supposed to claim a genetic relation, entirely baffles our attempts to associate the existing races of Man with any of the species beneath him."

* * * * * * * * * *

" We believe that all the higher faculties of human nature—all the powers that make us MAN—are visibly independent of that mere structural organization in which,......many of the animals surpass us. Take an animal gifted with the nicest sensuous faculties, and he will not approach in mental capacity the lowest of the human species. Take a man deprived or destitute of all his senses and animal powers ; there is still something in his capacity immeasurably superior to the whole brute creation. There is the gift of articulate language—the power of numbers—the power of generalization—the power of conceiving the relation of Man to his Creator—the power of foreseeing an immortal destiny—the power of knowing good from evil on eternal principles of justice and truth."—*Edinburgh Review*, April, 1863.

himself, if once we permit his moral and intellectual endowments to have their due weight in classification."[1]

In his interior being man presents an organic and beautiful union of many noble faculties and affections, all having a common center in the individual consciousness; while the body is a delicate corporeal machine or instrument, with particular organs corresponding to the several faculties of the mind or spirit, each organ being adapted to specific functions of being. Through this complex organism the intelligent Soul sustains intimate and vital relations to the elements and forms of the Physical World. Thus the immortal powers of our spiritual being all meet, unite, and center in consciousness; at the same time, their mundane instruments belong to the body, and have their organic center in the brain; while the movements of the spirit, as revealed by its action on and through the body, may be appropriately denominated the organic functions.

So intimate is the relation between the body and mind that they act reciprocally and powerfully on each other. Especially does the mind exert a mighty influence, for weal or woe, over the body. The mental and vital action are so inseparable that every silent emotion and unspoken thought leaves an image—dim and shadowy it may be—on the organic structure. The vital fluids flow fast or slow, as the mind is excited, or is permitted to repose. The great thoughts of the poet and the orator quicken the blood in their veins, and accelerate the pulsation in millions of human bosoms. The heart of the poor exile leaps at the thought of his country and the memory of his home. The

---

[1] "Antiquity of Man," page 495.

patriotic deed, and word, and thought even, strike the chords of life till they vibrate with a strange and ungovernable energy. This relation of mental to vital motion must be understood, if we desire to render health more secure, and life a more certain possession. Physiology and Anatomy, as hitherto taught in the schools, only present us with the outward structure, without the inward light that reveals the mysteries of the temple.

It will be conceded that the importance of the present inquiry is in no degree diminished by the obscurity that overshadows the ultimate spring of life and thought. Rather is this an element in the strange and peculiar interest that belongs to the theme. Moreover, the mysteries of human nature are not all inscrutable, and we may yet learn far more of ourselves than is contained in the catechism, or taught in the schools of modern science. And while I shall not attempt, in this treatise, a nice anatomical dissection of the human mind—with a view to those subtile and technical distinctions which the learned and deeply metaphysical inquirer might be pleased to recognize—I shall, on the contrary, without descending to the lower level of the uneducated intellect, aim to present my subject in a clear light to the common comprehension. In the prosecution of this work, I shall regard the distinctions of the metaphysicians, ancient and modern, only so far as they appear to accord with the laws of Nature and the light of a scientific philosophy. It were better to lose our way, occasionally, in the great Unknown, and to take some useless steps in our exploration, than with unquestioning faith and mechanical precision to follow every blind guide.

CHAPTER II.

ELECTRO-PHYSIOLOGICAL DISCOVERIES.

Importance of the Subject—Agency of Vital Electricity in the Organic Functions—Researches of European Philosophers—Galvani—Volta—Aldini—Nobili—Matteucci—Humboldt—Emil du Bois-Reymond—Professor Buff—Alfred Smee—Mesmer—Decree of the French Academy—Distinguished Disciples—Triumph of Truth over Skepticism—Deleuze—Townshend—Georget—M. Foissac—M. Bertrand—Mialle—Baron Dupotet—Dr. Elliotson—Dr. Ashburner and Dr. Esdaile—Homogeneousness of the Nervous and the Electric Principles—Value of the Discovery to the Physiological Investigator and to Science.

AMONG the various departments of scientific inquiry, that which comprehends the laws of vital motion, sensation, and thought, is, perhaps, of paramount importance, inasmuch as it most intimately concerns the nature and preservation of human health and life. Critical observation and profound thought are indispensable to success in this department, and it must be confessed that few persons in this country have attempted the investigation in a scientific spirit. The subject has, however, engaged some of the noblest minds in Europe, and we are permitted to anticipate the solution of its greatest problems.

It is not my purpose to discuss the simple anatomy and physiology of the human body, for the reason that those of my readers who may be in need of information in that department will find what they require in the numerous scientific treatises already extant. But it will be proper in this place to speak briefly of the connecting medium between the Body and the Mind. The sublimated aura that pervades the brain and nervous system, and which is doubtless the proximate cause of all vital and voluntary motion and sensation, *is electrical in its nature.* While Animal Electricity is the immediate agent in the production of all chemical changes that occur in living bodies, it is no less true that the agent itself is generated in all the processes of vital chemistry. The same subtile element is disengaged in all muscular motion, as has been demonstrated by a variety of scientific experiments, some of which I will briefly notice, as they will aid in the further elucidation of my subject.

It is my purpose in this chapter to furnish a concise his tory of the researches and discoveries in Vital Electricity and Magnetism, without which the present treatise would be incomplete. In the latter part of the last century Galvani, a distinguished anatomist and physiologist of the Bologna school, and the celebrated Italian philosopher Volta, made numerous experiments with a view to illustrate the influence of *galvanic electricity* on the nerves and muscles of certain animals. The former discovered this agent, and the latter invented instruments for generating and directing it to scientific and other practical purposes. On this account the agent has been generally known as *Galvanism*, and the in struments as *Voltaic apparatus.* It was especially in the autumn of 1786 that Galvani's experiments, in producing muscular contractions by electrical currents, began to assume a profound significance. In 1791 he published his cele-

brated Commentary, which produced an intense commotion
among physicians, physiologists, and philosophers throughout all Europe, and led to much speculation respecting the
origin of nervous diseases, and the nature of the vital principle. But as metallic rods and other instruments had been
employed in Galvani's experiments, Volta contended that
the phenomena did not result from the presence of animal
electricity, but that the muscular contractions were caused
by a heterogeneous combination of metallic substances. To
meet this objection, Galvani pursued his experiments until
he obtained the same results without the intervention of
metals, and thus demonstrated, apparently at least, the existence of animal electricity and its probable agency in all
vital phenomena.

A bitter controversy ensued ; Volta seemed likely to subvert the claims of his rival, when Humboldt published his
work, entitled, "Experiments on Stimulated Nervous and
Muscular Fibers," etc., in which he favored the position of
Galvani. At length, near the close of 1799, the Italian
philosopher made the discovery of the *Voltaic battery*, which
secured for his opinions a rapid triumph. Nothing further
appeared in support of Galvani's theory of animal electricity, save an essay by his nephew Aldini, wherein the
author recorded the results of many useless experiments,
and attempted to appropriate to himself the honor of his
uncle's discoveries. Aldini's work was published in French,
in 1804, after which no particular attention was paid to the
subject for nearly a quarter of a century. In 1827, Nobili
made a grand improvement in the galvanometer, and demon
strated more clearly than his predecessors had done, the ex-

istence of the electro-magnetic current in the frog. Matteucci experimented on the frog and the torpedo, and soon attracted more general attention to these phenomena. The credit of having made the first really demonstrative experiments in this department is usually given to the author of the " Physical Phenomena of Living Beings." He forced the points of small needles into the muscles of living animals, and then connected their opposite ends with the poles of a very sensitive galvanometer. When the animal moved the muscle, it was observed that the needle of the instrument was deflected, thus showing the presence and passage of an electric current simultaneously with the muscular contraction.

The experiments of Galvani and others, in causing muscular contractions by electricity, artificially generated and applied to the limbs of frogs, and the muscles of other lifeless animals, seemed to afford significant suggestions respecting the homogeneous properties and effects of electricity and the nervous fluid. The observations of the scientific investigators who preceded him, and especially those of Matteucci, furnished a starting-point for Emil du Bois-Reymond, of the Berlin Academy, who constructed still more perfect apparatus, which enabled him to discover not only the muscular current in the inferior animals, but *in the living Man.* The variation of the current by *volition,* in the act of muscular contraction, was also clearly demonstrated by the experiments of du Bois-Reymond, who described his *modus operandi* and the specific results, in a letter to Baron Humboldt, and in a statement communicated to the French

Academy.[1] Reymond's mode of conducting the experiments
in Vital Electricity will doubtless interest the reader :
Taking two homogeneous pieces of platina, he immersed one
end of each in a solution of common salt, contained in two
cups, and then connected the opposite ends of the platina
strips with the needle of his galvanometer. Having arranged his apparatus, he plunged the index finger of each
hand into the solution contained in the two vessels, whereupon he observed a slight deviation of the needle of his
instrument. By alternately concentrating the will on the
two arms, and thus timing the muscular contractions, the
most decided oscillations were produced.

Humboldt repeated Raymond's experiment, and confirmed
(in fact and in the judgment of the scientific world) the
result, by his success and the weight of his powerful testimony. Subsequently Prof. Buff, of Giessen, experimented
with still more extraordinary results. Having joined the
hands of sixteen persons, he caused the individuals at the
extremities of the line to complete the circuit by each dip-
ping the hand that was disengagd into the contents of one of
the cups. The cuticle—on the hands of the persons employed in the experiment—having been previously moistened,
opposed no resistance to a free circulation of the subtile
element. Accordingly, when—at a word—every person in
the circuit—in regular alternation—contracted the muscles of the right and left arm, the galvanic needle was powerfully moved, in opposite directions, and to the extent of
not less than fifty degrees. These results have been further

---

[1] Annales de Chimie et de Physique, 3me série, t. xxx.

corroborated by the experiments and observations of Alfred
Smee of London, the present writer, and others, and they
plainly show that *an electro-motive power pervades the nerves
and muscles of all animal bodies.*[1] This agent is continually
disengaged or evolved in the subtile processes of animal
chemistry, and we have valid reasons for the opinion that
it is the chief agent in all vital and voluntary motion and
sensation.

Phenomena of a very different kind, yet manifestly depending more or less on the distribution and modified action of
the same vital motive power—in other words, on vital electricity and the electro-magnetic conditions of the several
organs—attracted the attention of other minds, and led to
curious and important discoveries. As early as 1774, F.
Antoine Mesmer, a member of the Medical Faculty of Vi-
enna, succeeded not only in reducing the novel processes
and mysterious results of Animal Magnetism to something
like a scientific formula, but in his own extensive practice
he found numerous opportunities to test its value as an auxiliary of medicine. The success of Mesmer, and the singular
power of this new remedial agent excited, among the Faculty
of Paris, a spirit of jealousy and resentment, which was
soon manifested through the Royal Medical Academy. An
arbitrary degree was issued, declaring the use of Animal
Magnetism unprofessional and injurious, and making *expulsion*
from that institution the penalty for advocating its claims.
In 1784 the committee appointed by the French Academy to
examine the subject, having failed to see, feel, taste, smell,

---

[1] See Dr. du Bois-Reymond, " On Animal Electricity," also, Smee's " Electro-Biology."

measure or weigh the subtile, miracle-working fluid which
Mesmer had supposed to exist, reported that there was no
such thing as Animal Magnetism.   But the facts continued
to occur, and to command attention in different parts of
Europe.   Cuvier, Laplace, Humboldt, Coleridge, Dugald
Stewart and many other distinguished names, became identified with the new science.   In 1831 its claims to a place
among the accredited sciences were duly acknowledged in
the report of the scientific commission appointed, if we mistake not, in 1825.   Skepticism reluctantly gave up the
ghost.   The invisible pain-destroying agent was admitted into
the hospitals of Paris and London, and a Professorship of
Animal Magnetism was established in the Medical College
of Berlin.[1]

Several noted experimenters and authors appeared in different parts of Europe, and the phenomena of the magnetic
state were widely and critically observed.   Rev. Chauncey
Hare Townshend, of Trinity Hall, Cambridge, pursued the
subject experimentally with great earnestness, and finally ·
published his work, entitled " Facts in Mesmerism," about the
beginning of 1840.   During his investigations he had an opportunity to witness the effects of the magnetic process on
many persons in England ; also at Rome, Naples, and elsewhere ; and among his subjects were Signor Ranieri, the
historian, Professor Agassiz, and other eminent persons.

---

[1] The discoveries of Mesmer, and his dexterous use of the mysterious
power, gave him an enviable position and a commanding influence.   He had
many distinguished pupils in Paris, received large sums for his course of instruction, and was professionally employed by the principal nobles at the
Court of Louis XVI.

But there were others in this field who are not to be forgotten. For nearly forty years M. Deleuze, a French practitioner and a most conscientious man, was engaged in the experimental illustration of the powers and uses of Animal Magnetism. Deleuze confined his experiments, with rare exceptions, to invalids, and the results of his protracted experience have been given to the public. Several other authors have likewise placed us under obligations for important contributions to the sum of scientific and popular information on this interesting subject. Georget, in a treatise entitled "*Physiologie du Systéme Nerveux*," mentions the result of certain experiments in this species of magnetism, by which he seemed to impart some new properties to water. When highly sensitive persons tasted the water, they could readily distinguish it from that which had not been subjected to the process. M. Foissac manipulated liquids in a similar manner, and Paul Villagrand, a somnambulist, would at once detect the presence of the magnetic influence by the sense of taste. M. Bertrand and others effected cures by the use of magnetized water, and M. Mialle, who at one time could find no repose on account of some painful indisposition. assures us that a piece of magnetized glass, which he placed on his chest—on retiring for the night—had the effect to greatly modify his symptoms, and to induce the presence of

"Tired nature's sweet restorer, balmy Sleep." [1]

Among the practical operators in Animal Magnetism and the earnest defenders of its claims, the Baron Dupotet, Dr.

---

[1] See Dr. Alphonse Teste's Manuel Pratique de Magnétisme Animal. London edition, pp. 208–210.

Elliotson and Dr. Ashburner have long been distinguished. But no man has made a more beneficent use of this agent than Dr. James Esdaile, who was employed in a professional capacity by the British East India Company. His unrivaled success among the people of Bengal, is doubtless in a great measure to be ascribed to his own personal energy, superior skill in his profession, and to the benevolent impulses and aspirations of his heart. Dr. Esdaile found the natives of that country extremely susceptible of this magnetic influence, and in his efforts to meliorate their condition he permitted no occasion to pass unimproved. His surgical operations were generally performed while the patients were in the magnetic trance. Notwithstanding many of these operations were extremely difficult, and such as are usually attended with intense pain, Dr. Esdaile's patients were all the while in an unconscious state, and of course incapable of suffering. Indeed, so effectually were his subjects bound, that not a nerve quivered under the knife, nor was a single muscle convulsed by the burning iron in the process of actual cautery. The coma in some cases continued for hours after the operation was completed, and when the patient awoke he was generally free from pain, and oblivious of what had transpired.[1]

Among the American practitioners in this department, who have occupied the largest share of public attention, Dr. John B. Dods and Laroy Sunderland have published small treatises illustrative of their peculiar views, and the modes they respectively adopted in their experiments. Dr. S. S.

See " Mesmerism in India, and its practical application in Surgery and Medicine ;" by James Esdaile, M. D.

Lyon, and many other respectable physicians, have employed Magnetism as a remedial agent, and as an auxiliary in their pathological investigations. The experimenters who have been attracted by the novelty of the subject, or from mercenary motives, have been very numerous, but they shall be nameless in this connection. With rare exceptions their investigations have been exceedingly superficial. Indeed, Science has nothing to expect from men who have a paramount regard for money, and whose only aim has been to make an amusing and remunerative public exhibition. Such men have a passion for masquerade, and never hesitate to play the harlequin in the abused name of Science, when a promising engagement is offered. The remarkable success which has attended the professional career of Professor Grimes, doubtless entitles that gentleman to the distinction of leading the nondescript army of fantastics, who make grave subjects ridiculous, and even sacred things disreputable.

A few years since, a great number of magnetic and psychological doctors—after pursuing their studies for a few hours—went forth to enlighten the public respecting the mysteries of "Electro-psychology," "Biology," and other kindred subjects. It must be admitted that they secured general attention, and prompted an examination of a variety of significant and important phenomena. While their pretended explanations were generally crude and wholly unsatisfactory, it is doubtless true that their experiments often prepared the way for subsequent inquiries and enlightened convictions.

I have had occasion to observe that Vital Electricity is

the immediate agent in the production of all motion and sensation in animal and human bodies. Hence, the varied and remarkable phenomena, developed in the magnetic states of the system, must depend on the power of the operator to influence the nervous circulation or to control the distribution of vital electricity. The discovery of the homogeneousness of the nervous and the electric power is one of great importance to science, and especially to the physiological inquirer. It lights up the outward temple of our being; it will aid us in solving the problem involved in the circulation of the animal fluids; it suggests a rational philosophy of sensation, and opens the way to a clearer and more comprehensive knowledge of the laws of organic action and vital harmony. In the light of this discovery we shall hereafter survey the outer courts of the temple, and then do what we may to guide the mind of the thoughtful and reverent inquirer toward the inner sanctuary of his being.

CHAPTER III.

CIRCULATION OF THE ANIMAL FLUIDS.

Defects of the Accredited System—Facts in Physiological Science—Amazing Forces and Complicated Functions—Agency of Electricity in the Circulation of the Blood - Reference to Alfred Smee's Work—The Electrical Fishes—Observations of Humboldt and Prof. Beckelnsteiner—Demonstrative Experiment at Saratoga—Generation of Vital Heat by Electric action —Cause of Change in the Color of the Blood.

PHYSIOLOGY, as explained in the class books and taught in schools, furnishes no scientific philosophy of the Vital Functions. Whilst the anatomist maps out the osseous, fibrous, nervous and circulatory systems, and exhibits their organic relations and mutual dependencies, the physiologist contributes his descriptive and technical disquisitions on their respective functions; all of which—with the current knowledge of vital chemistry—is insufficient to satisfy the reasonable demands of the fearless and philosophical inquirer. If the writer may not hope to dissipate the darkness that obscures the way to this temple of mystery, he will at least venture to diverge from the beaten track.

It is ascertained that a well-developed human body contains about twenty-eight pounds of blood, which, by a most perfect hydraulic process, is conveyed from the heart to the extremities at the rate of about three thousand gallons in twenty-four hours ; while, in every year of our lives, not much less than one hundred thousand cubic feet of atmospheric air—passing through the six hundred millions of air cells in the lungs—are required to fan the vital fires. The force necessary to produce the organic action and to carry on the circulation in such a body, has been variously estimated at from fifteen to fifty tons. The attempts to eject fluids into the channels of the circulation—either in the living or the lifeless subject—with other imperfect experiments of the Faculty, scarcely enable us to form anything like an accurate judgment on a question of this nature. That an immense power is required to raise all the valves, and to force the blood to the minute and remote terminations of the capillaries must be obvious to the truly scientific observer. If, however, we adopt as our standard the minimum number, and estimate the vital force at fifteen tons, we shall still be startled and half inclined to dispute the credibility of our own conclusions.

The first suggestion is, that the human frame is *too frail* to resist or endure the action of such an internal force. But it is an accredited fact in science that every square inch of the external surface of the body sustains a column of air forty-five miles high, the weight of which is ascertained to be fourteen pounds. Thus it appears that the whole body supports the enormous weight of more than 30,000 pounds ! The reason why this does not cause an instantaneous collapse, at once extinguishing the life of the body, is because the inside resistance of the electric forces and elastic fluids precisely counterbalances the external atmospheric pressure. When the body is thus acted on by opposite forces *in equilibrio*, we are insensible of their presence. Moreover, this amazing force of fifteen tons, moving within the vital precincts, is so equally distributed, and applied with such precision to the different parts of the organization, that we are quite unconscious of its exercise. We even rest quietly with an electric engine of not less than one horse power at work between our ribs ; at the same time a chemical laboratory—in some sense as extensive as Nature—is all the while in full operation within, and yet we are only disturbed when from some cause the work is partially suspended. Those suction and forcing pumps—that drive the vital fluids through innumerable channels in the mother's breast, at the rate of some 15,000 hogsheads per annum—all operate so noiselessly that the little child sleeps peacefully on her bosom while the vital tide flows close by its ear. The tenant of the house has also a telegraphic apparatus that connects him with every department of the external world, and an inherent active power that destroys and rebuilds his whole establishment once in about seven years—and all of these complicated forces and functions are organically combined and exercised in a space two feet by six !

A power so vast and functions so delicate, complicated and wonderful, must be referred to adequate causes ; and here our physiology is at fault. The teachers of the science leave the beautiful temple of the soul in darkness. Viewed in its external aspects, and from the position occupied by accredited science, the light on the altar is nothing more than the combustion of carbonaceous matter, while there is no divinity at the inner shrine. Science has faith in the reality of so much of human nature as can be seen and handled,

dissected, weighed, and put in a crucible. Beyond this it is
faithless, and many of its professed friends resort to various
shifts and quibbles to conceal their ignorance.

For illustration : The course of the blood—as it flows
from the heart to the extremities and returns—is clearly
enough defined ; but when we ask for the *cause* of this ceaseless motion, we are perhaps gravely informed that the heart
contracts and dilates in regular alternation, and that with
each succeeding pulsation the blood is forced out and
propelled to the remotest points of capillary action, from
which it returns through the venous system to the heart.[1]
But when we push our inquiries, and demand to know *what
causes the heart to contract and dilate* in the manner described, we may be told by some physiological Solomon, who
is content to travel round in a circle, that it may be, or *must
be*, the exciting quality and action of the blood on the nerves
of involuntary motion.   Thus the heart is made to move the
blood while the blood moves the heart, and alleged causes
are taken for effects, and effects for causes *ad libitum*, to suit
the convenience of our blind guides.

The vital electricity generated and evolved in all the processes of human and animal bodies, is an indispensable agent
in the functions of life, motion, and sensation. It is, in fact,
the motive power of the system on which the organic movement constantly depends.   Without the action of electro-
nervous forces, proceeding from the brain as their chief phy
sical center, we have no proximate cause adequate to account
for the distribution of the animal fluids.   In the first chapter

---

[1] The quantity of blood expelled from the heart at each contraction does
not ordinarily exceed two ounces.

it was made evident by the proofs of experimental science, that voluntary muscular motion depends on the transmission of electric currents from the brain. If the evidence be conclusive with respect to all voluntary motion, it is scarcely less so in its application to the involuntary functions. These surely can not be presumed to depend on some other agent. The heart is a muscle, or bundle of compact fibers, possessing strong contractile powers, and its functions obviously depend on the same agent that moves the *extensor communis digitorum*, and all the voluntary muscles in the body.

The electric force from the brain is sent to the heart by branches of the eighth and great intercostal pairs of nerves; thence over the lines by which the nervous energy is distributed along the arterial channels, to be diffused among the capillary termini, where the nutritive elements in the blood are deposited to repair the gradual waste of the body. The arteries also have their fibrous coatings or elastic tissue, the distension and contraction of which is but the continuation of the involuntary muscular motion commencing in the ventricles. The electric quality of the blood, acquired by its contact with atmospheric electricity in the lungs, and the force thereby communicated to the arterial circulation, being at length expended in the wide diffusion of the subtile principle, the blood returns through the *venæ cavæ* to the heart, in obedience to the natural and irresistible force whereby electrically positive and negative bodies and their elemental constituents are everywhere attracted. The whole organic action and the distribution of the fluids is thus perceived to depend on the presence and power of vital voltaic currents.

Alfred Smee, F. R. S., in his valuable works on "Electro-Biology" and "Instinct and Reason," has furnished important illustrations of my subject, contained in many instructive observations and convincing experiments. He has shown that the organs of sensation and motion, in animal and human bodies, are arranged on voltaic principles, and that their respective functions are governed by electrical laws, as modified by the powers of life, sensation, and intelligence. I extract the following paragraph :

"In all cases of sensation the impression is carried to the brain through the nervous fibers, by means of a voltaic current. The nervous fibers consist of tubes, like those of gutta percha, containing a fluid. The mode by which insulation is accomplished is somewhat curious. The nerve-tubes consist of a membrane which is of itself a conductor of electricity. The inside of this membrane, however, is lined with a layer of fat, which is an absolute non-conductor of electricity. In the interior of the fat there is a fluid through which the electricity passes. An entire nerve consists of a number of these primitive fibrils arranged together ; and the whole forms a series of communication precisely similar to the wires which are placed along the lines of railroads, to convey intelligence from station to station."— *Instinct and Reason, page* 41.

That electricity is everywhere employed in the development of vital and muscular motion, and that it is the operative agent in all the processes of animal chemistry, may be further illustrated by a citation of facts. It is well known that the *Silurus*, the *Torpedo*, and the *Gymnotus*, are organized with a kind of *electrical battery*, which for self-preservation, and for the purpose of securing their prey, they discharge in such a manner as to give a violent shock to the nervous systems of other animals. Though this power of the electrical fishes was noticed as early as the time of Pliny and Aristotle, it remained for modern scientific investigators to discover and illustrate the nature of the agent that produced the benumbing sensations. Humboldt testifies that when he was traveling in South America, horses were prostrated in his presence by the Gymnotus, and that he also suffered severe pain in his own limbs, for several hours, in consequence of having accidentally set his foot on one immediately after it was taken from the water. The structure, arrangement, and operation of the vital batteries in these fishes have been carefully examined by several modern philosophers. It is ascertained that in a single electrical organ of the Gymnotus, there are some twelve hundred cells, all connected by nervous channels of communication. These are the receptacles of the electric force. The resemblance of the cells in these fishes to small vesicular organs existing throughout animated nature—united by nerves and secreting mucus—was observed by Prof. Beckeinsteiner, of Lyons. These are plainly discoverable in almost all animals. Moreover, in Man they are found to be most developed in individuals who possess the greatest activity and strength, and at the season of complete maturity, while in old age they are diminished in size and deficient in moisture. All this is confirmed by the well-known fact, that the magnetic powers of the operator are diminished in proportion as the vital and voluntary energies of the system decline. Few human beings can equal the Torpedo in the powerful concentration and disruptive discharge of vital electricity ; and yet the frequent repetition of the experiment has demonstrated the fact, that a highly sensitive person may be temporarily paralyzed, or instantly prostrated, by the electro-nervous shock produced by the strong will of a skillful operator.[1]

That electricity, when it moves in currents, acts powerfully on other and grosser elements, causing the molecules to be violently agitated, admits of several experimental illustrations. For example—if you pass an electric current over a siphon while a stream of water is flowing through it, the water will rush out with an increased velocity proportioned to the strength of the electrical current. That the blood in the arteries is thus acted on by vital electricity is evident from the fact that, in the precise degree that the

---

[1] Some years since, while the writer was engaged in the village of Saratoga Springs, in the delivery of a course of lectures, on his electrical theory of the vital functions, Mr. Cook (an intelligent citizen of that place, whose experimental inquiries in the department of electrical science had been liberally patronized by the government) boldly disputed the theory, and insisted that neither the functions of animated nature, nor the so-called psychological phenomena, depended in any way on the action of vital electricity, either involuntarily applied, or employed as the agent of the will. He was willing to settle that question by the result of "an experiment;" he was quite sure that he could "knock a man down" with a disruptive discharge of electricity artificially generated by his apparatus, and when the gentleman, [the present writer] would do the same with his mental-electric battery, he would believe that electricity had something to do with the phenomena in question.

Mr. Cook was held to his word in presence of the assembly. Two well known and highly esteemed citizens of that place—*strangers to the writer*—were selected for the experiment. After making such manipulations as were conceived to be necessary, I directed the two gentlemen to stand firmly at a distance of twelve or fifteen feet from the position I had assumed. Taking their places as directed, with the muscles firmly braced, and with a strong resolution not to yield to any outside influence, it is useless to say that they had no expectation of falling. The next moment, however, they were both prostrated by the psycho-electric action, and extended at full length on the floor. This experiment, performed in the presence of hundreds of intelligent witnesses, terminated the controversy.

nervous force is unduly directed to any particular part, or concentrated on a single organ of the body, will the arterial circulation be found to increase in the same direction ? Thus the fluids circulate, and the ultimate molecules are deposited in their appropriate places in the process of assimilation. Moreover, that vital or animal heat is evolved by the action of the same electric agent, and that the brain is the principal reservoir from which it is distributed to all parts of the system, is confirmed by the experiments of Brodic on the rabbit. Having destroyed or paralyzed the brain of the animal, he contrived to keep up the respiration by artificial means ; but the temperature of the whole body was steadily reduced to a degree far below the normal standard.

Physiologists tell us that the change that occurs in the color of the blood, in its passage through the lungs, is occasioned by its decarbonization and its union with the oxygen of the atmosphere. But this is rather describing the chemical process than explaining its cause. Or, I may say, such teachers merely seize on one part, or a single aspect of the elemental change, to account for itself, and for whatever else belongs to the whole process. This is leaving a dark subject as they found it, except so far as learned and systematic ignorance serves to render it still more obscure. That the chemical process, involving the change in the color of the blood is produced by atmospheric electricity in the lungs, is confirmed by significant facts and substantial reasons. If we pass an electrical current through a quantity of venous blood, it will instantly exhibit the same change of color that occurs in its passage through the chief organs of respiration.

This seems to justify the conclusion that one and the same agent produces the change in both cases. Indeed, it is by no means apparent that—in the process of respiration—the blood comes into direct contact with the air at all, except when some pulmonary vessel is ruptured. On the contrary, when the lungs are in a sound state, the blood is of course confined to its own appropriate channels—the pulmonary arteries and veins, while the atmosphere alone occupies the air-cells.

I have thus furnished such evidence as the case seems to demand, in illustration of the important office and the mysterious power of vital electricity, as displayed in the distribution of the animal fluids. In the next Chapter the reader will be invited to consider the laws and conditions of Vital Harmony.

CHAPTER IV.

CONDITIONS OF VITAL HARMONY.

Opposite Forces—Illustrations among the Elements—Animated Nature—
Health and Disease—Essential Conditions Specified—The Coöperation of
Nature—A Strong Mind and a Weak Body—Passions and Pursuits as
Disturbing Causes—Our Education Defective—Fashionable Caricatures—
The Ideal Harmony.

THE elements and forms of physical nature are not controlled by a single force acting forever in a direct line,
but by opposite forces *in equilibrio*. The planets revolve, all
Nature moves, and countless living forms are organized
through the harmonic action of positive and negative forces
that govern all the elements of matter. A precise balance
of these forces is indispensable to the uniform and orderly
operations of Nature. When the equilibrium is temporarily
interrupted, motion is sure to become irregular, uncertain
and destructive. The elements furnish familiar but very
striking examples.

When the generation of electricity—no matter from what
cause—is more rapid in one place than in another, the atmospheric balance is liable to be interrupted. Electrical currents first move toward the negative regions of the earth
and atmosphere; the air is put in motion in the same direction; tempests arise, and the wild rush of the elements—in

4

seeking their equilibrium—often spreads ruin like a mantle of darkness over stately forests, smiling fields, and the abodes of men. In like manner, when the explosive gases are suddenly ignited by electric forces and chemical fires, in the deep bosom of the earth, proud cities are demolished ; continents are rent asunder ; islands rise like bubbles in the midst of the sea ; and the great globe itself trembles beneath the terrible pulse and the gigantic tread of the earthquake !

It is well known that two opposing forces govern the movements of the heavenly bodies. Should one of these preponderate, there would be a sudden and awful pause in the music of the spheres. The planets would reel from their orbits and scatter their ruins through the immeasurable fields of space. Annihilate one of these forces, and it is probable that all organized bodies would be decomposed and all matter in the Universe be reduced to its primary elements.

That the forms and functions of animated nature depend on a similar law, must appear exceedingly probable to the mind of the philosophical observer. In the last Chapter it was shown that the existence of positive and negative electrical forces could alone account for the distribution of the animal fluids. If, therefore, the circulation and all the organic functions depend on the presence and equal action of such forces, it will follow that the moment these become *unequal* a functional derangement must ensue, and this would be the incipient stage of disease. But here it may be well to define the terms I must employ as the representatives of ideas.

Health is the natural condition of a living body. I use the word to indicate that equal development and perfect state of the physical system wherein the several organs are sound, and their united action characterized by freedom, precision and harmony. On the other hand, *disease* is any condition of an organized body in which the vital harmony is disturbed, so that the functions are rendered abnormal or irregular. In other words, *disease is the loss of the equilibrium of the forces which produce the vital and voluntary functions of the body.* Whenever this occurs it may readily be perceived by an ordinary observer. The irregular beat of the pulse, the impaired digestion, nervous irritability and general derangement of the secretions, all furnish infallible evidence that the conditions of health have been disregarded, and the laws of life violated. Health being the normal or natural condition, disease, or vital derangement, necessarily presupposes a departure from a true state of Nature. As certainly as all causes produce corresponding effects, health can- not continue where the laws of vital motion and organic harmony are perpetually infringed, nor can disease be developed where those laws are clearly perceived and scrupulously obeyed. To secure health, therefore, it remains for us to adapt our manner of life to the precise requirements of Nature.

The first, and therefore the most essential condition of vital harmony, is *a sound and well developed body.* When the organs are disproportioned at birth, or their subsequent growth is unequal, there can be no certain and lasting harmony in their functions. A perfect organic action is only possible when the organism itself is complete. Precision in the movement must depend on perfection in the vital mechanism. For example, if the vital organs be unusually small, or the space they occupy inadequate to admit of their free exercise and full development, the individual will suffer from constitutional debility; health will be rendered insecure, and the continuance of life uncertain. Again : If the brain be very large, and the cerebral action intense and unremitting, the forces of the system will be unduly attracted to that organ ; this may occasion congestion, insanity, a softening of the brain, or some other local disorder. At the same time the extremities—not being properly warmed and energized by a diffusion of the vital principle— will be cold and weak ; digestion will be slow, respiration imperfect, the secretions irregular, and the enjoyment of uninterrupted health impossible. The opposite extremes in the development and action of the *nutritive system* may produce a Calvin Edson and a Daniel Lambert—the one a suitable subject for the anatomical museum ; and the other a huge mass of carbon, that only waits for a deranged action of vital electricity to set it on fire, when the whole system may be consumed by what the doctors call an intense fever or acute inflammation—familiar terms to represent the process of accelerated vital combustion.

Next in importance to a sound and well-developed organization, is, *the proper application of the force on which the functions of the organs depend.* When this is unequal, or is not so distributed as to supply each organ with its appropriate share, the vital movement and temperature of necessity become irregular. The motive power—which we have ascertained to be vital electricity—can not be unduly concentrated on a particular organ without producing a correspondingly negative state of other portions of the body, and this condition must occasion disorder in the organic action. Whatever, therefore, disturbs the nervous forces, and thus interrupts the physical equilibrium, must produce disease. And yet—disease being an unnatural state of the system—it requires a more potent cause to permanently destroy the vital balance than to restore the equilibrium when it has been temporarily interrupted. For—it will be perceived—when we undertake to derange the forces and functions of our being, we must contend single-handed against Nature; whereas, when we labor to preserve—or to reëstablish if lost—the essential harmony, we have Nature to aid us by her constant and powerful coöperation.

The operations of the mind, state of the affections, exercise of the passions, and our pursuits in life, determine how far the physical harmony may be preserved; also, to what extent it is liable to be sacrificed. The intense action of the mind may weaken all the involuntary functions of the body, and a frail organization is often prematurely destroyed by a mind of unusual activity and power. When a mind of vast capacity is lodged in a frail body, the intellectual faculties should be exercised with great caution and reserve; otherwise the action of the brain will exhaust all the vitality, and the body will rapidly decline. One might as well put an immense engine into a slender vessel, and proceed to test its utmost power in a rough sea, as to give full scope to a strong mind without regard to the capacity of its organic instrument. Yet thousands make this mistake every year, and only realize their error when it is too late to avert the fatal consequences.[1]

Moreover, when the affections are deep and strong—especially when they have been given to unworthy objects—when confidence is lost, and bright prospects vanish like dissolving views ; when friends hold the wormwood to the lips, and Hope disappears or stands in the distance with veiled and averted face; when the heart is crucified, and one is left to wear a crown of thorns for the sake of those he loved!—Oh, then the nerves are swept with a tempest of human feeling ; the brain reels and burns, and the vital flame may be extinguished as the cold floods roll over him !

When the passions are excited to great intensity, and the soul falls amid the darkness of its wild delirium ; then, too,

---

[1] I had a friend—an inheritor of genius. He was of a feeble frame, but his mind was wondrously endowed. He appeared to derive knowledge from spheres invisible and unknown. He was subject to rapt moods, and gave birth to divine ideas. As we have seen the clouds that hovered in the midnight sky suddenly break and pass away—revealing the glorious stars—so did darkness leave the subjects of his contemplation, and thus came the great thoughts to him ! And then, when all the faculties were awake, the action was mysterious and solemn, yet beautiful and musical. To the imaginative observer the mental and moral movement seemed like the music of a great organ—so did the polished dome and every inferior part of the temple shake beneath the action of the indwelling divinity. Like the tolling of a great bell in a frail, crumbling tower, every earnest heart-beat reminded us at once of death and immortality. At length the structure fell ! And when the bell tolled no more in the tower, old men, and beautiful women, and even little children came to watch and weep over the consecrated ruins.

I would have no one disregard his relations to this world, or lightly estimate the boon of the present existence ; but the wrong—if, indeed, there be a wrong—is greatly mitigated when the body is thus made an offering to the higher life of the soul. The deed is characterized by a peculiar grandeur, and I dare not say that Heaven will dishonor the sacrifice.

the vital powers and processes are deranged, and Life trembles in its mortal citadel. Moreover, when our pursuits are of such a nature as to exercise but a single class of the faculties ; when Reason's commanding voice is silenced by the suggestions of a selfish policy; when conscience is immolated at the polluted shrines of Custom and Mammon, the vital balance will soon be lost ; for the individual who has no mental or moral equipoise may not hope to enjoy health, or to preserve the integrity and harmony of his physical nature.

It is greatly to be lamented that our modes of instruction and discipline are so poorly fitted to promote the normal growth and the true life of the Race. They usually cause an abnormal excitement of certain faculties and affections, while others—not less essential to the perfection of human nature—are permitted to remain inactive. These partial aims and defective methods produce various angularities of form and irregularities of function, while they seldom fail to destroy the symmetrical proportions of body, mind and character. If educated for a religious teacher, the man's reverence is liable to be unduly exercised at the expense of his reason ; if trained for the law, his moral sensibilities may be blunted in the process of sharpening his wits; if armed for the arena of political strife, his peculiar training too often renders him regardless of moral obligation, and indifferent to the sanctions of religion ; and, finally, if prepared after the most approved method for society, he becomes the idle votary of fashion, and a servile worshiper at the shrine of Beauty.

Among the multitudes that crowd the great avenues of business, we rarely meet with a man who, in every act of his life, is governed by a clear perception of justice, and an enlightened sense of moral obligation. We should be troubled to find a politician who steadily holds the demands of his party in subordination to the claims of his country. In the palace homes of wealth, and the gilded drawing-rooms of fashionable society, we meet with few women in whom the uncorrupted love of natural grace, simplicity and beauty, predominates over the passion, for the modern, corrupt and frightful distortions of human nature. Instead of men and women, such as God made, with forms and faculties symmetrically developed and harmoniously exercised, we have stuffed effigies of the natural form, and painted caricatures of "the human face divine." Such distorted and diseased images and forms of real life and health, move with artificial grace and automatic precision in all the gay saloons of Paris and New York. Not a few of them, when fairly disrobed, are found to be little else but filthy sepulchers of human hearts and minds.

But when the body is rounded into complete human proportions, the temperaments properly blended, and the faculties and affections equally developed—when the appetites and passions are wisely restrained and truly spiritualized, health is rendered secure ; Man becomes a sweet-toned lyre, and the vital, mental, moral and spiritual powers of the world, all combine to sweep the chords and wake

" The living soul of Harmony."

CHAPTER V.

WE are now prepared to inquire into the physical causes and conditions which dispose the human frame to disease. Here a theme of inconceivable moment is suggested; one that it might be profitable to discuss at far greater length than comports with my present plan. Nothing can be more essential to the temporal well-being of the race than reliable information on this subject; for, if we well understand the general causes of disease, we may often shun or resist the evil by a prudent regard to existing physical states and relations.

It has already been observed that the vital functions directly depend on positive and negative conditions and forces. Now the general states most likely to produce disease—those which comprehend all other conditions and circumstances tending to similar results—will be found to originate in an excess, or from an inadequate supply of this

electric medium—in short, from the too positive and negative conditions of the human body, and the surrounding
elements of the earth and atmosphere. The preponderance
of this vital motor disposes the system to fevers and inflammations ; while a want of animal electricity will naturally
result in such forms of disease as are attended with coldness
of the body, and imperfect sensation, together with a want
of vital power and organic activity.

It is worthy of observation, that Nature—when undisturbed in the exercise of her functions—provides a supply
equal to the necessities of every occasion ; and whenever a
deficiency occurs, we may be sure she has been taxed unlaw-
fully. The vital forces and fluids are unnecessarily expended, and the system rapidly exhausted by a variety of
ways and means ; but I will first point out the general consequences of intense and protracted physical exercise, and
the fearful results of the immoderate gratification of the
appetites and passions. It often happens with persons who
are laboriously employed, that the weight of the body is
gradually diminished. This is a very certain indication
that the vital fluids are not produced or generated as rapidly
as they are dissipated in the various processes of the body.
This condition is unfavorable to health, and such a decline
of the recuperative energies of the system, as compared with
the current expenditure of vital power, can not long continue without causing more aggravated forms of vital derangement. If the conservative powers of the body be
unequal to the task of supplying whatever is demanded to
repair the ordinary waste, it requires no prophet's vision to
enable the rational mind to perceive that—sooner or later—

the system must inevitably suspend its operations. Those who understand the laws of trade will perhaps see the point more clearly in the light of a single illustration.

Suppose that your neighbor has been engaged—during the past year—in some business with which he is but imperfectly acquainted. From an examination of his books, it is made to appear that there has been an excess in the current expenses over the gross receipts. The consequence is, he is involved ; and a fair inventory of his assets awakens a suspicion of his insolvency. If he resolves to continue business under such circumstances, and you have learned to reason from cause to effect, you may infallibly predict the disaster that awaits him. Now, analogous causes inevitably produce similar results in the case under consideration. Unless the production of vitality be equal to the demand in conducting the several operations of the physical system, the man will surely fail, and a final settlement of his affairs will be demanded. Or, to drop the figure, disease will ensue, and death may abruptly close the business of life.

The forces of the living body are expended as they are generated in the performance of the vital and voluntary functions. The proportion employed in voluntary effort is greater or less according to the perfection of the organic structure, combination of the temperaments, the temporal necessities and incidental circumstances of the individual. So long as physical exercise is regulated—as to the seasons and the modes—by an enlightened judgment, and otherwise graduated by the normal capabilities of the constitution, it serves to strengthen respiration, to accelerate the processes of vital chemistry, to increase the measure of animal electricity ; and thus to promote a free, natural and vigorous action of all the organs. But it is no less true that excessive toil diminishes the latent powers of life, enervates the organs, and restrains their appropriate functions; until by degrees the recuperative energies are fairly exhausted, and the whole system sinks under the weight of its unnatural burden.

The intelligent reader will perceive the reasons why too much exercise of the body is liable to interrupt the organic harmony. Whenever we labor excessively—or beyond the limitations which Nature has prescribed for the government of the individual—we make perpetual and unreasonable demands on such springs and resources of vital power as legitimately belong to the involuntary organs and their functions. These drafts are only honored at the expense of health, and, it may be, at the sacrifice of life. When once we reach the proper limit of our powers of endurance, every additional hour spent in physical exertion, extracts some portion of the Life-principle from each separate organ in the vital system, or diverts the same from its appropriate channel. The pulsation becomes labored, digestion is impaired, the liver is rendered inert, the powers of thought languish, the will relaxes its purpose and resigns its object, while the whole man suffers from consequent enervation.

Excessive *alimentiveness*, with rapid and imperfect mastication, is liable to disturb the balance of nervous power and to derange the functions. It imposes an unnatural burden on a particular organ, and hence calls the vital electricity from other portions of the system to the stomach, in an undue degree, to the end that the process of digestion may be accelerated. Several times a day an avalanche descends with fearful momentum—elements gross and ponderable—while mingling torrents, hot and cold, follow in rapid succession. For a while the work goes on without any perceptible interruption. Nature applies all her forces to clear the way and make room for whatever may come next. The secretions are all increased beyond the normal limit, and the whole system is required to perform extra labor, which soon indisposes the individual to voluntary effort. A sluggish state of mind and body succeeds with a tendency to indolent habits. Indolence in turn aggravates the difficulty. At length the oppressed and overburdened organs—so long restrained and obstructed in their functions—lose their vigor, and the reaction prostrates the whole system. The man is ill, and a wise Providence destroys his appetite, that nature may have time for the elimination of the superfluous matter in the body.

Such men resemble mills that are employed night and day to crack, grind and bolt the grain of the neighborhood ; or, they may be regarded as vast receptacles of decaying vegetation, and respectable locomotive sepulchers for the rest of the animal creation! Omnivorous mortals! your greatest triumphs among the elements and forms of matter have been achieved through the concentrated powers of the *gastric juice!* Unlike Bunyan's pilgrim, who had the good sense to *shoulder* the bundle of his iniquities, you impose upon the stomach the enormous and crushing weight of your manifold transgressions.

The appetite for *narcotics and stimulants*, when it exercises an irresistible influence, becomes a prolific source of disease or vital derangement. It is well known that the appetite for food is diminished, and the digestive functions impaired, by the use of tobacco. The peristaltic action of the intestines may be quite suspended, sensation temporarily destroyed, and the faculties benumbed, by the use of powerful narcotics. Moreover, those who are accustomed to the free use of tobacco—no matter in what form—exhibit unnatural restlessness and a morbid irritability when not under the influence of that agent. They may be speedily quieted again by the narcotic spell ; and if their fears have been excited, they are allayed by the subtile influence of the poison. It has been demonstrated by post-mortem examination, that the olfactories, the optic, dental and pneuma-gastric nerves become inflamed and impaired by the use of tobacco.[1] Indeed such agents are all intrinsically at war with the vital principle, and when administered professionally, the practitioner aims to diminish pain and allay the tumultuous action of the nervous system by the very doubtful expedient of destroying nervous impressibility, and hence by a partial suspension of the forces and functions of life.

It was once a favorite hypothesis that all disease originated in *debility*, and therefore *excitants or stimulants* became the most important remedial agents. This notion has been received with great favor by persons of intemperate habits. Such people generally feel weak early in the morning, and frequently through the day ; and as often as they experience this debility, whether in the stomach, the knees,

---

[1] While morphia, belladonna and stramonium produce similar general effects, physicians have observed that each has a specific action on particular portions of the system, which need not be described in this connection.

or in the resolution to reform, they resort to the treatment by taking brandy, or some other positive stimulant. This frequent and unnatural excitement of the vital energies is followed by a reaction, when the life-forces sink as far below the standard of normal activity as they had been raised above the vital equilibrium. At length the organic harmony is permanently interrupted ; the nervous system is unstrung ; the blood on fire ; and fortune, reputation, character and manhood—all wrecked and lost in scenes of wild delirium—are engulfed in a burning sea.

Thousands, by an inordinate indulgence of their passions —whether sanctioned or condemned by the statute—do not scruple to lower the tone of the mind and the character, while they lay the foundations of shame, disease, and death for themselves and their posterity. The *sexual attraction*, when not restrained by reason, leads to fathomless perdition. When not refined and spiritualized by the higher law that forever unites congenial souls, it becomes immoral and adulterous, in spite of all legal enactments and definitions. Lust has a perpetual injunction on the faculties of such people, while their children after them are mortgaged to corruption, and death holds a quit-claim on their mortal bodies. They transgress and repent in regular alternation ; they cry, call on the Lord and the doctor—go to meeting and take physic—and then—sin again.

The conditions of the human body are liable to be materially influenced by the existing electrical state of the earth and atmosphere. When thunder-storms are of rare occurrence, in the summer months, indicating an unusual absence of atmospheric electricity, this agent passes imper-

ceptibly from the living body—rapidly if the atmosphere be
in a humid state—until the electro-vital power is so far
reduced that negative forms of disease everywhere prevail.
Cholera Asphyxia is well known to involve a cold or very
negative state of the system.   In this leading characteristic
it is the opposite state to a fever.   It is attended with a
slow, feeble pulse, general lassitude, and a rapid decline and
suspension of all the vital functions.   It is a well known
fact that the year 1832—in the summer of which the cholera
raged so fearfully in this country—was distinguished fo᠁ an
almost total absence of electrical phenomena.   Nor is it less
a matter of fact and of history that during that season there
were no fevers, or at least the cases were of rare occurrence.
About the first of September there were violent electrical
storms in different parts of the country, and the cholera
speedily disappeared.

That opposite electrical conditions produce fevers and
inflammatory states of the body, is doubtless true, and might
be illustrated at length—did our limits permit—by the citation of numerous facts and reasons.   I will, however, observe, in this connection, that those phases of vital derangement, which I denominate the *positive forms of disease*, are
wholly different in their symptomatic aspects from the class
previously described and characterized as *negative diseases*.
The disorders which result from an excess of vital electricity
in the body, as a whole, or from an undue concentration o
this agent on some particular organ, are accompanied with
a higher temperature, an accelerated pulse, and a general
irregularity in the organic action.   The extent of this derangement may be estimated by observing the perisystole as

the electro-thermal currents rise and fall. Moreover, the diseases of this class are most general and fatal when the atmosphere is in a highly electrical state, as evinced by frequent and violent thunder storms. The results may admit of some modifications from individual peculiarities and local conditions ; but it is presumed that the general correctness of our position will be confirmed by every careful observer. [1]

How shall we prevent the recurrence, or effect the removal, of the disorders already described ? My answer must necessarily be brief and general. Whenever the first of the several causes of vital derangement, indicated in the foregoing specification, does actually exist, or is likely to transpire—when vitality is or may be expended more rapidly than it is generated—measures should be taken to augment the vital resources ; or, what may be easier of accomplishment, to lessen their expenditure. If the individual has been accustomed to severe and protracted physical labor, it will be necessary to diminish the time and intensity of his efforts. If the derangement be caused by the excessive indulgence of the appetites, the subject should seriously engage in an investigation of the laws of health, and in the contemplation of such exalted subjects as will set

---

[1] As a popular author of philosophical and spiritual books—who has long been familiar with the writer's views respecting the relations of certain diseases to the positive and negative conditions of the human body and the surrounding atmosphere—may have expressed similar opinions, I deem it just and proper to observe that the present writer long since developed his whole theory of the essential causes of vital derangement, and the positive and negative forms of disease, in a course of lectures, which were prepared about twelve years since, and delivered in many large towns and cities as early as the year 1849.

him free from their foul dominion. If inordinate sexual indulgence be the cause of vital inharmony, the individual must learn to discipline his passional nature, and subdue his erratic and delirious impulses by the exercise of Reason. And, finally, if the organic harmony be interrupted by intense and continual mental application, he must leave the study and wander in the fields, that a variety of objects may divert the mind from any laborious process.

It becomes all who would guard against unnatural weakness and deformity, premature decay of the faculties, and an untimely departure from the sphere of their earthly relations, to be careful that the physical energies are not wasted in unlawful pleasures and pursuits. Every violation of the laws of vital and organic harmony, is a blow aimed at the root of the tree of life ; and when at last by repeated blows we have interrupted its connection with earth and time, no power can arrest its fall.

CHAPTER VI.

VOLUNTARY AND INVOLUNTARY FACULTIES.

The Mind and its Agent—Voluntary and Involuntary Faculties distinguished
—Relations of Mind to the Organic Functions—Its influence in Vital
Chemistry—Agency of the Will—Power to resist Pain—St. Augustin and
the Priest—The Italian poet, Marini—Remarkable powers of Charles W.
Lawrence—Influence of Mental Excitement on Sensation—Case of Nathan
B. Gates—How timid natures suffer and the brave endure.

> " Who reigns within himself and rules
> Passions, desires, and fears, is more than king."
> MILTON.

THE human economy presents at once the most beautiful
organic arrangement, and the most complicated modes of
action. Here, indeed, we find the perfection of organic relation and dependence, and the very " poetry of motion."
When we ascribe the corporeal functions to vital electricity,
as a proximate agent, we are quite sure that the alleged
cause is adequate to produce all effects, though these are such
complex and amazing revelations of inward power, as to require the most subtile and potent principle in Nature.
Nevertheless, the electrical element is but the subordinate
agent of *Mind*, in which all motion has its origin. Whether
as it relates to the human system, motion be voluntary or involuntary, the active power belongs to the spirit, and has its

material residence in the brain ; while the chief office of the
heart appears to be to regulate the vital momentum, or to
measure the quantity, and to determine the rapidity of the
circulation.   The heart beats not of itself; the nerves
vibrate only as they are pervaded by a subtle energy that
is disturbed by outward causes, or swept by the invisible
powers of thought and feeling.   Within the vital precincts
of this ingenious mechanism, is the enshrined and unap-
proachable presence that moves the whole—the

"Immortal Spirit of the chainless Mind."

But what has the mind do with the pulsation, and how can
volition influence the involuntary action of the vital organs ?
There are times when the mind is apparently at rest ; seasons
when the judgment is powerless ; when Reason, like an un-
faithful sentinel, slumbers at his post, and—to our consciousness—not a single thought moves in the silent halls of the
soul.   And yet, at such times, the vital motive power is at
work, and the necessary functions of being are still performed.   Here I may observe that *the Mind has its voluntary and involuntary powers, and these are related as causes
to the voluntary and involuntary functions of the Body.*   The
passions and affections, in which the very rudiments of
motion, form, life and sensation appear to have their incipiency, are *involuntary*.   We can neither love nor hate at pleasure ; nor do we believe or disbelieve from choice.   But the
ability to recall past events, and to trace the relations of external objects, may be—within certain natural limitations—
voluntary powers.   It is no less true that whoever has the
capacity may reason or not reason, according to his inclina-

tion. A plain distinction here finds a foundation in a fundamental difference. All the functions and processes that may
be prompted or suspended by the will, are voluntary. Of
this class the powers of locomotion and speech afford familiar examples. There are other organic functions which do
not depend on volition, such as the action of the heart, the
process of digestion, the assimilation of foreign substances,
and the secretions. These functions may be produced by the
spirit acting (unconsciously to the external mind,) on the
physical organs, through electric currents in the nerves of
involuntary motion. Thus the involuntary powers of the
mind doubtless govern the involuntary functions of the body.
By this silent, involuntary, and unconscious agency, the
human heart pulsates more than one hundred thousand times
in twenty-four hours ; and yet this motion continues, in some
instances, more than one hundred years. Mysterious, beautiful and wonderful, indeed, are the phenomena of life ! We
are amazed that an organism so delicate and complicated
should keep in repair so long, and that it is even capable
of sustaining a power so vast in degree, and so multiform in
its modes of action.

But the involuntary functions of the body may be strongly
influenced, if they can not be absolutely controlled, by voluntary mental effort. Some of the more familiar illustrations of this point may be seen in the effects which intense
and protracted thought and feeling are liable to produce on
the functions of respiration, digestion and secretion. In
proportion as the forces are unduly attracted to, and expended by the brain, the supply demanded by other vital
organs is necessarily diminished. Hence, a vigorous and

continued exercise of the mind will weaken the digestive function, and retard all the vital processes. While the organs of respiration move involuntarily, they are likewise provided with nerves of voluntary motion, and their action may be temporarily suspended by the executive power of the mind. But in certain mental states the respiratory organs are directly acted on, and their functions at least partially arrested, when the individual is wholly unconscious of any voluntary effort. It is well known that intense thought will almost suspend respiration ; hence the familiar observation that public assemblies, when deeply interested, listen with fixed and *breathless* attention. Determined mental or physical effort immediately after eating, renders the process of digestion labored and imperfect, because it diverts the electrical currents from the stomach, where an increased measure of vital electricity is demanded to facilitate the chemical process. For this reason, authors and other persons whose minds are too constantly exercised, are especially liable to suffer from indigestion, as well as from a general decline of nervous energy.

It has been observed already that the mind acts directly on the electrical, or nervous circulation, and through that governs the distribution of all the grosser forms of matter in the body. Thus the molecular deposits are increased or diminished, in the several parts of the human system, in proportion as the different faculties and affections of the mind are called into action, and their appropriate organs are correspondingly exercised. It follows, therefore, that the action of the mind may derange or equalize the vital forces. The organic movement may in this manner be accelerated or retarded, and the whole body wasted or renovated. This power of the mind is supreme. When misdirected or improperly applied, it is not only capable of disturbing the vital harmony, but it is liable to produce the most terrible forms of disease, and may suddenly suspend the vital functions.

When the voluntary faculties of the mind are properly disciplined and fully developed, their superiority over the powers of involuntary motion is strikingly displayed. Nervous impressibility may be greatly diminished by a resolute effort of the will, and the convulsive action of the nerves and muscles of involuntary motion may be resisted by a strong and unwavering purpose. In this manner a violent cough may be checked, and the paroxysms in hysteria greatly modified or wholly subdued. In certain deranged states of the nervous system, the patient is irresistibly disposed by turns to indulge in passionate weeping and immoderate laughter ; and these symptoms are most prevalent among females, who are ordinarily more inclined to yield to involuntary impulses, at the same time they are less distinguished than men for executive capacity, or for strength and continuity in the exercise of the will.

But there are more striking illustrations of the power of the mind over the forces and functions of involuntary motion, and in which the superiority of the rational mind over the natural operations of a merely physical agent will be clearly seen. Many persons have the power to drive pain from the different parts of their own bodies, while some are able to infuse new energy into a feeble organ by the voluntary agency of the mind. It is possible for a man of heroic disposition to resist—by the force of his will—the reflex nervous action, and to calmly submit to the lash or to the most painful surgical operation without so much as moving a muscle. The brave man, who thus bears the trial without shrinking, really suffers but little in comparison with the timid mortal who instinctively recoils at the sight of the scourge or the knife. This problem in human experience admits of an easy solution. The firm and resolute man, fortified by his own unflinching courage, braces his nerves against the shock. By the power of his will he prevents the nervous forces—when they are agitated at the extremities or on the surface—from rushing impetuously toward the seat of life. He feels but little pain, because the electrical currents, through which impressions are conveyed to the brain, are but slightly disturbed. The vital balance is preserved by the firm and steady action of the mind. On the other hand, the irresolute and cowardly man—by the subjection of his will and the recoiling action of his whole mind —permits the nervous circulation to rush with great violence from the seat of the injury to the sensorium, causing every smitten and tortured nerve to writhe in the intense agony of the hour.

The voluntary power of the mind to resist pain, and to influence the involuntary functions of the body, like every other faculty, may be augmented by appropriate exercises. The soul may be so far withdrawn from the outward avenues of sensation, as to render the physical organs entirely inoperative. It is well known that a person in a complete state of magnetic coma will not suffer from a corporeal injury. But this state of physical insensibility may be self-induced.

St. Augustin refers to the case of a priest whose power of abstraction was so great that his body could be subjected to torture without his being conscious of the injury inflicted. It is also alleged respecting Marini, the Italian poet, that while engaged in a revision of his Adonis, he became so deeply absorbed that he put his foot in the fire, and kept it there for some time, without the slightest consciousness of his exposure to the devouring element. The Fakirs stop respiration, seemingly without injury, and in some instances vital motion is wholly suspended for an indefinite period. Mr. Charles Lawrence, with whom the writer was for several years on familiar terms, possessed a remarkable voluntary power over sensation and vital motion. He could so paralyze the censor nerves that his skin might be punctured without causing pain, and a violent blow did not occasion the least suffering. By the power of his volition he could immediately accelerate the pulsation in a surprising degree ; and he could also entirely suspend the heart's action in three minutes ! These effects were repeatedly produced in the presence of the writer, before public assemblies, and to the satisfaction of several committees composed of members of the medical profession..

Brave men seldom speak of their pains, and they are cravens who suffer over much. Whenever the powers of the mind are all engrossed in the contemplation of a great subject, or concentrated for the achievement of some noble purpose, the nerves of sensation lose their susceptibility. We close the gates that open into the citadel of our being, and assume a defensive position and attitude. We resist all impressions while the whole electric force is being concentrated on the nerves and muscles of voluntary motion through which the mind aims at a free, forcible and effective expression. As all sensation belongs to the spirit, a man is not likely to experience pain, in consequence of a bodily injury, when all his faculties are otherwise and elsewhere employed. This suggests the reason why men do not suffer from physical violence when they are under the influence of a strong mental excitement. The writer has a nephew who has an intense passion for hunting. While pursuing his game, on a certain occasion, a companion in the chase discharged the contents of his gun into one of his lower limbs, neither party being aware of the fact for some minutes ; nor was the injured man the first to discover the accident. Moreover, those who are wounded in battle are often wholly unconscious of the fact until they faint from loss of blood.

The history of the Church presents many examples of the supremacy of intense emotion, or holy passion, over all the powers and susceptibilities of mind and body. There were illustrious examples of patient endurance among the early Christian martyrs ; in the ranks of the followers of Peter the Hermit ; and before the bloody tribunals of the *Auto de fé*. Archbishop Cranmer—prompted and sustained by intense feelings of mingled penitence and devotion—held forth the hand, employed in the indorsement of papal doctrines and unrighteous authorities, and exclaiming— repeatedly and with a firm voice—" *This hand has offended !* he deliberately held it in the fiercest flames until it was literally consumed. It is also recorded of James Bainham that he appeared to be exalted in spirit beyond the possibility of physical suffering. When his limbs were partially consumed, he called to the spectators to witness the miracle of his death; and then, while the forked flames coiled around his whole body, he said—in a voice that indicated at once · his amazing power of resistance and the deep serenity of his spirit—" THIS FIRE IS A BED OF ROSES TO ME !" Others clapped their hands and shouted aloud for joy, until the devouring element stifled their utterance, and their enfranchised spirits ascended in fiery chariots to heaven.

I have learned from personal experience, as well as from long and careful observation, that the mind may so act on the sensorial medium of the nervous system, as to produce many strange and startling physiolological effects. Invisible spiritual powers may likewise be brought to bear on the earthly objects of their guardianship, in the temporary suspension of feeling; so that any violence done to the mortal body may cause neither pain nor inconvenience. In view of these facts, we may rationally infer that those who have all their faculties excited to action, and focalized in some mighty endeavor, may be quite incapable of suffering. Many a nervous woman has doubtless endured more pain while seated in the dentist's chair, than the most illustrious martyrs of Liberty and Religion have suffered on the scaffold or at the stake. The historian has chronicled the names and deeds of moral heroes who were seemingly so elevated in soul as to be far above the reach of their persecutors. In their serene happiness and sublime integrity; in the generous enthusiasm of a great, unselfish purpose, and the fervor of intense devotion, they walked in holy triumph before God —wearing mantles of consuming fire—up to their great IMMORTALITY.

CHAPTER VII.

INFLUENCE OF THE PASSIONS ON THE SECRETIONS.

Nature of the Passions—Opinions of Philosophers—The classification by
Plato and Aristotle—Influence of the Passions on the processes of vital
chemistry—Effects of intense Sensuous Love—How certain Passions produce particular forms of Disease—Influence of Fear in changing the color
of the Hair—Philosophy of the process—Professor Beckeinsteiner's experiments on Animals—Singular experience of a Telegraph Operator—Irregularity of the change in persons of unequal mental, temperamental, and
organic development—Illustration from the records of the writer's observations—Further summary of the Electro-chemical and Physiological effects
of the Passions.

THE faculties and passions of the human mind, like the
organs of the body and their functions, depend on suitable modes of exercise and discipline for the measure of
their strength, and the capacity to perform their normal operations. We come into existence with vast latent powers
of action, and immeasurable capacities for improvement;
but these remain concealed and inactive until the circumstances and conditions of the outward life, or the more subtile powers of the inward world, awaken the unconscious
possessor from the state of oblivious repose, and he is summoned, by the very laws and necessities of his own being,
into the wide arena of human activities. Thus we all enter
on the career of our endless existence and progress. From

its obscure beginning on earth, the great spiral of ascending
Life opens up to man through all the intermediate stages of
corporeal and spiritual growth, into the celestial degree of
his nature, and the highest heaven of the immortal life and
world.

In the earlier stages of human development, we find the
most powerful incentives to action in the excitements peculiar to the emotional nature.   Philosophers have entertained
different opinions respecting the source of those strong and
impetuous mental emotions which we denominate *the Passions*.   Advocates of the material philosophy are of course
disposed to locate them in *the corporeal system*, where they
profess to find everything that essentially belongs to man.
Des Cartes entertained and inculcated this opinion, while
Mallebranche conceived that they are " agitations of the
soul," proceeding from the rapidity of the arterial circulation, and the impetuous flow of the animal spirits.   This
philosopher's materialism is clearly enough exposed in the
simple statement of his opinion.   He mistakes effects for
causes when he ascribes the soul's action to the momentum of
the fluids in the body.   The rapid motion of the animal fluids
does not precede the excitement of the Passions, but, on the
other hand, the circulation is powerfully influenced by every
tempest of passional feeling.   While the mind may be composed, and free from any tendency to such excitement, the
pulsation may be accelerated, and the blood flow with abnormal rapidity, under the intense electric action of a fever; but
the Passions are never aroused without communicating the
excitement to the circulation and the whole organic action.

The Passions may be defined to be those strong exercises

or movements of the spirit which are often rendered abnormal and dangerous by their suddenness, irregularity, or intensity, and which are chiefly caused by the contemplation
of outward objects, and the occurrence of unexpected events.
In the inferior or superficial mind the Passions may be rela-
tively active and strong ; but such persons seldom exhibit
the depth of feeling which characterizes their superiors.   In
a mind of great natural endowments, the Passions—if they
obtain the ascendency over the Reason—exhibit corresponding intensity and power ; sometimes rising to the sublime
extremes of desperate daring, and to almost supra-mortal
achievements.   The records of War furnish memorable examples ; and when the Passions excited are intense hatred
of oppression, and earnest love of Humanity, the contest is
sanctioned by the common sense of the civilized world ; while
the triumphant actor becomes, in some sense, a moral hero,
whose deeds are approved, and whose name and memory are
long and reverently cherished.

The Passions have been variously classified by different
authors.   Plato comprehended all under love and hatred ;
while Aristotle, by maintaining that each one of the passions
is productive of either pleasure or pain, thus virtually reduced them to two general classes.   As viewed by physicians and physiologists, they have been divided into *the exciting and the depressing passions ;* and this classification has
been determined by their specific effects on the organic functions.   Whether each particular passion is to be regarded as
an essential, innate disposition of the mind, or as the modified action of the faculties, resulting from their peculiar combination in the individual, is a question that has given rise

to numerous theories and conjectures which scarcely require our attention, since they are rather curious than instructive.

The substances or varieties of animal matter, chiefly separated and combined from the elements of the blood, in the processes of secretion, are, according to Bostock, aqueous, mucous, albuminous, gelatinous, fibrinous, oleaginous, resinous and saline ; all of which are comprised and classified in the brief statement of Magendie as exhalations, follicular and glandular secretions.

The influence of mental emotions on these processes in animal chemistry now demand our attention. No matter how many passions may be embraced and named in a precise classification, they are comprehended in desire, love, joy— fear, hatred, sorrow—all others being compounded of such as are included in this specification. Now, as the circulation of the animal fluids is directly dependent on the distribution of the electro-nervous force, it follows that the passions—by their direct action on the nerve-aura—must powerfully influence all the secretory processes of the system.

Ethical as well as scientific writers have observed that those states of passional excitement, in which love exerts a strong influence on the mind, are more compatible with the laws of vital harmony than such as spring from resentment and exhibit malevolence. This is doubtless true ; and yet when love is not refined and intellectual, but sensuous or passionate—exhibiting far less of rational affection than of animal desire—it has an immeasurable and dangerous power over the vital forces and fluids. It causes protracted and tumultuous action at the nerve-centers, with such an excessive determination of the electric forces to certain portions

of the delicate and complicated glandular structure, as often
results in constant abnormal excitability, and a total suspension of the natural functions.   Many pious and passionate
people—who respect "the statute in such cases made and
provided," at the same time they religiously obey the Ten
Commandments—have no proper control over their desires.
Their conventional ideas of fidelity are about as good for
body and soul as a slow but fatal poison.   Love—though in
a true sense it is one with Life—becomes a destroying flame
that dissipates the fluids, interrupts the organic harmony,
blunts the mental faculties, obscures the moral and spiritual
perceptions, and enervates the whole man.   Such people
often kill themselves and others in a most reputable way,
and thus illustrate the relations of suicide and homicide to
the legal standard of propriety and virtue.

The domination of a single passion over the mind and
character—especially when it stimulates the secretions in a
particular part of the body—is liable to interrupt the proper
action of the glandular system, and thus to prevent the appropriate distribution of the fluids.   There are certain states of
feeling and habits of life which may increase the action of the
exhalent vessels, and diminish that of the absorbents, causing
an effusion of serum.   This diseased state of the system, and
unnatural accumulation of water, is ordinarily denominated
dropsy.   If the aqueous accumulation be about the brain,
it is known as *hydrocephalus*, and it is also distinguished by
various other names, which are determined by the organs or
parts of the system affected, and by its complication with
other forms of disease.   When, from the influence of the
passions, or from other causes, the normal action of the ab-

sorbing and secreting vessels is permanently disturbed, the
waste or effete matter of the body is liable to be deposited
at the points of electrical convergence, producing a variety
of morbid states and affections. When the processes of secretion are thus deranged, the proper elimination of the
several forms of animal matter is rendered impossible. If
obstructions occur in the sacs and ducts of the glandular
system, so that the matter—to be modified for the purposes
of animal life, or to be expelled from the body as useless—
is not properly prepared and absorbed, or *excreted*, as the
case may require, the derangement may result in *adipose sarcoma*, a variety of glandular swellings, or tumors, strumous
tubercles, or a diseased state of the system generally, if the
morbid matter be more widely and equally distributed. Thus
a vital organ—on account of its original disproportion, or
from incidental causes—may become a point of electrical
concentration, or a magnetic center, to which the elements
may be unduly attracted. Fluids, which should have been
elsewhere secreted, or expelled from the body through appropriate channels, accumulate, by an electro-hydraulic process, beyond the utmost capacity of the absorbing vessels,
and the excretory processes of the system, to remove them ;
and thus the vital harmony is disturbed, and the organic
action may be fatally deranged.

The power of the Passions to influence the processes of
vital chemistry is strikingly displayed in the change that
occurs in the color of the hair, in consequence of intense
feeling or strong cerebral excitement. Though this change
is generally gradual, it is sometimes sudden and almost in-

stantaneous. Our observations on the relations of electricity to vital force and chemical action, suggest the probable causes of all similar phenomena. A chemical analysis
of the hair discovers—among other important constituents
—phosphate and carbonate of lime, iron, oxide of mangan-
ese, and *sulphur*. The substance last named enters very
largely into its composition, and its presence is doubtless indispensable to this curious phenomenon, which I will here-
undertake to explain. Any physical derangement or mental
excitement, producing a strong determination of the vital
forces to the brain, is liable to develop an electro-chemical
action, in which the oil containing the coloring matter of the
hair may be absorbed by the sulphur, which is then perceived
through its transparent envelope. Thus hair of all colors
and of every conceivable shade, assumes the same appearance. It is well known that extreme fear, or, indeed, any
violent passion that occasions an undue determination of the
nervous circulation to the head, is liable to produce this
mysterious change. It has also been observed that fear sometimes causes the hair to stand on end, and we are obliged to
refer this fact to the same cause. Every novice in electrical
science knows that electricity will produce this effect. It is
only necessary to insulate a man, and pass an electric current
through or over him, and each separate hair will assume an
erect position. Now, if powerful cerebral excitements develop the same results, we may reasonably infer the presence
and action of the same agent. This inference derives additional confirmation from the fact, that if you pass the hand
over the cranium of the man, or along the spinal column of

a cat, while the nervous forces are thus excited, electrical sparks may be distinctly perceived.[1]

There are other facts which forcibly illustrate the writer's theory, and the following extract from an influential public journal furnishes a striking example :

"A most extraordinary effect, produced by electricity, lately happened at one of the electric telegraph stations in France. A gentleman—employed in one of the principal offices—was in communication with one of his colleagues, when the electric wire he was using happened to relax, and to come in contact with his arm. The current was passing through it, and the *employé* sustained a violent shock, which raised him from his chair and threw him violently through a window opening on a garden. When he recovered his senses he could not recollect his adventure, and could only be convinced of it by perceiving that his hair and beard, which were formerly of a beautiful jet black, had become in various places as white as snow."

In this case the chemical action and the consequent change in the color of the hair resulted, perhaps, from the electrical discharge from the battery through the telegraphic wire ; and yet, it must be admitted, that it may have been produced by the sudden and powerful determination of *vital* electricity to the brain, occasioned by the shock.   Whether it was

---

[1] Professor Beckelnsteiner's directions respecting the mode of experimenting on animals, and the surprising results of his own experiments, are thus described : " When the temperature is below thirty-two degrees, the wind north and the sky clear, expose a cat to the cold until his fur lies close to the skin and appears greasy ; expose your hands to make them equally cold ; then take the animal on your knees, apply the fingers of your left hand on its breast, and pass your right hand down its back, pressing moderately ; at the fifth or sixth pass you will receive a slight electric shock. At first the cat appears pleased, but as soon as it feels the shock it jumps away, and will not endure the repetition of the experiment the same day. After the experiment the animal looks tired ; some days after it loses its appetite, seeks solitude, drinks water at rare intervals, and dies in a fortnight. The same experiment succeeds with rabits, and they die the same day."

the external or internal current, or both, that wrought the change, we may not absolutely determine ; but the relations of electricity to the phenomenon are sufficiently obvious, whatever hypothesis we may be pleased to adopt.

The truth of my general idea is still further supported by the fact, that this change in the color of the hair is first manifested over those portions of the brain which are most exercised.   Hence the change is unequal in all persons who are subject to violent impulses, or distinguished for angular mental developments; at the same time the process not only occurs at a later period in life, but it is gradual and uniform among persons who possess a calm unruffled disposition. When the cerebral development is harmonious, and the vital forces are equally distributed, the change never occurs at an early period in life ; but with the victims of religious mono-mania and of hopeless love, it is usually very rapid, while the raven locks of certain terror-stricken ones have become white in a moment.   I will here cite a single additional fact in illustration of my theory.   While the writer was giving lectures in Worcester, Mass., on the general subject of this treatise—some ten years since—a lady who was suffering from severe physical derangement came to ask advice re-specting her health.   She was a total stranger.   Glancing at her head, I discovered that the hair over those portions of the brain wherein the phrenologists locate Veneration and Marvelousness, were almost white, while in the region of Hope it was still dark as the plumes of the raven.   Madam, I observed, *you have been fearfully excited on the subject of religion.*   She gazed at me a moment with a feeling of evi-dent astonishment, and then proceeded to say that she had

been greatly disturbed by the doctrines and preaching of
" Father Miller," and, on this account, that *she had formerly
been in the lunatic asylum !*

Admitting the general correctness of this philosophy, it
will appear that the hair undergoes this change in old age
because the vital electric forces are gradually withdrawn
from the extremities—from all external surfaces and portions
of the body—and gathered up at the brain, where the life-
principle remains to the last.

It must be sufficiently obvious to every observer of vital
phenomena, that the passions act directly on the nervous
forces, or the animal electricity of the body ; and hence all
the delicate and mysterious processes of secretion must be
immediately and powerfully influenced by the passions.   But
of their specific relations to such electro-chemical changes,
I can not treat at greater length ; nor would the larger number of my readers be likely to be interested in the minute
details of the subject.   I will, however, further suggest, by
a brief and imperfect statement, some of the more obvious
effects of the passions on the secretions.

Jealousy, by its tendency to increase the biliary secretion,
is liable to overburden the hepatic duct and its tributaries ;
grief so acts on the lachrymal gland, that tears are secreted
and profusely discharged ; while excessive joy, and other
strong mental emotions, sometimes produce the same or similar effects.   The functions of the skin are often strongly influenced by the Passions.   In this manner the insensible exhalations from the body are increased and diminished.   Pro-
fuse perspiration sometimes accompanies or succeeds violent
mental emotions.   The urinary secretion is thus varied in

quantity, and, doubtless, in its chemical constituents, by the influence of the Passions on the electrical forces that deter mine all the changes in the subtile chemistry of the living body. It is a well known fact that the misdirected action or improper excitement of the mind, immediately after parturition, has resulted in the sudden suppression of the lochia, and a repulsion of the lacteous secretion from the breasts. Indeed such is the power of the Passions to produce electrochemical effects, in this direction, that a sudden fit of anger in the mother has produced violent spasms in the child at her bosom.

In the light of the foregoing observations, the importance of restraining the Passions, and giving them a wise direction, can not be too highly estimated. If, in this respect, we fail in the government of ourselves, we may extinguish the vital flame with a flood ; we may dissipate the life-fluids and be consumed by inward fires ; or, at least, the tempest of uncontrollable passion is left to break the essential harmony of our being, while Discordia—daughter of Night and sister of Death—smites and snaps the chords of Life.

CHAPTER VIII.

THE MIND AS A DESTRUCTIVE AGENT.

Influence of Mind over the Vital Forces—How it deranges the Functions and destroys Life—Its Relations to Congestion, Paralysis, and other forms of Disease—Fatal Consequences of false Impressions—Hydrophobia produced by the Mind—A fatal Bleeding without the loss of a drop of blood—Examples cited by Dr. Moore—A Man shot dead with blank cartridges—Death of another on the block—How a Pestilence may be arrested—Three fatal cases of Cholera as the result of the Mind's action—An illustrative Fable—A Man killed by an ungovernable Temper—Irritable Children and weak nerves—Mistakes at Coroners' Inquests—The Broken Harp.

THAT the mind exerts a mysterious and wonderful control over the body, must be obvious to every one who has observed the relations of its faculties and affections to physiological phenomena. The electro-chemical changes that occur in the vital laboratories are rendered irregular or uniform by the prevailing states and incidental exercises of the Mind. The most destructive elements in the physical world, when left to spend their whole force on the unprotected human body, are scarcely more disastrous in their effects than the misdirected action of its powers ; at the same time the life-forces may be augmented and equalized, and the wasting form mysteriously renewed by the appropriate exercise and right direction of the Mind.

The fact is thus confirmed by universal experience, that

the functions of life are influenced—accelerated, retarded or
arrested—by the mental action on the bodily organs. And
as disease has its origin in a disturbance of the vital forces,
and consequent derangement of the circulation, we at once
discover the vast importance of mental harmony to physical
health. Many persons become diseased from believing they
are so already. In a highly nervous organization the action
of mind may be so intense, and the body so easily impressed
as to generate any conceivable form of disease in this way.
Any powerful mental impression will generally leave its
image, more or less perceptible, on the physical constitution.
Thus a jealous, unsocial, or melancholy disposition, will be
likely to occasion bilious derangement. Extreme fear, anger,
or any other violent passion, will expose the system to spasmodic attacks ; while an anxious, sympathetic and restless
state of mind will inevitably induce nervous diseases.

   Among the causes that act on and modify the electrical
conditions of the body, there is not one that exerts a mightier
influence than the Mind itself. Having a direct control over
the immediate agent of vital motion, it affects the distribution of all the fluids, and determines many of the physiological changes that occur. The mode of this connection,
between the mental and vital action, will admit of a philosophical explanation. It is well known that electricity ac-
celerates the motion of the fluids. If you discharge an
electric current through a siphon while a stream of water
is passing, the water will be driven out with great force,
moving in the direction of the electric current. That the
distribution of vital electricity—by the voluntary and involuntary powers of the mind—has the same effect on the blood

in the arteries, and on the circulation of the animal fluids
generally, is equally true, and is confirmed by a long course
of observation. A single fact will suffice to illustrate this
point. In all surgical operations performed while the patient
is in a state of physical insensibility, whether induced by
magnetic coma or otherwise, the loss of blood is inconsider-
able. In such cases, the mind's action being measurably suspended, the electrical forces are not disturbed, and the equilibrium of the circulation is not materially interrupted. But
when the same operation is performed on a conscious, sensitive subject, the mind is of course concentrated at the seat
of the injury ; the nervous forces and the blood necessarily
exhibit the same tendency, and the patient is liable to bleed
copiously, and, perhaps, may lose his life from excessive
hemorrhage.

I am not unconscious of the power of the elements on
man. I know that the fluids of animal bodies may be suddenly dissipated by the frost and the fire. But the Mind,
when misdirected, is not less powerful and mortal in its
action. When, for example, a person is suddenly startled
and terrified, the motive power is driven back from the surface and the extremities to the brain, which is so powerfully
surcharged as frequently to cause dizziness, sometimes temporary insanity, and we have well-authenticated accounts of
persons who have instantly expired, so terrible has been
the shock occasioned by this violent determination of the
nervo-electric forces to the brain. That precisely this
physiological change does occur, is evident from the following considerations : First, the partial or total loss of
muscular energy in the extremities, appears to demonstrate

the absence of that electric agent on which all muscular power is made to depend. Second, increased motion in the region of the heart and the brain. The accelerated arterial action, and the intense cerebral excitement as evinced by the hurried and irregular character of the mental functions, furnish evidence not less convincing that the motive power is concentrated at the seat of life. [1]

Having proved by repeated references to scientific experiments, that what is usually denominated the nervous fluid in animal bodies, is a subtile form of electricity, and that the same is evolved from all parts of the system where there is either chemical or mechanical action, I shall now appeal to facts to illustrate the irresistible influence of this electrical medium—agent of the Mind—in the production of the greatest physiological changes of which the human body is susceptible. The facts illustrative of this point are numerous and conclusive, only a few of which can be comprehended in the present citation.

The writer's views respecting the power of the Mind over the electro-nervous currents and the arterial circulation, will receive strong confirmation from the further examination of the subject. To the careful observer it will be obvious, that mental and moral disturbances produce corresponding physical derangements. As intense love, violent hate, sudden jealousy, extreme apprehension, or any powerful mental impulse, will instantly interrupt the vital equilibrium,

---

[1] That the cerebral action is greatly increased under such circumstances, is rendered evident from the experiences of persons rescued from drowning, who assure us that, under the apprehension of immediate death, the mind acts with such incredible rapidity that the whole history of the drowning man passes before him in a single moment.

it follows that the most aggravated forms of disease may have their origin in the Mind. If the individual is more distinguished for vigor of thought than for intensity of feeling, the unbalanced tide of the circulation will flow to the brain, and be accompanied by a strange cerebral excitement and a flushed countenance. If, on the other hand, the person be characterized by blind, unreasoning passion, the vital torrent may rush to the heart, leaving the visage pale, and causing an accelerated arterial action. Not only a momentary functional derangement is thus produced, but congestion, paralysis, insanity and death, often occur in consequence of this direct power of the mind over the elemental principles and organic action of the body.

To insure uniform health and a protracted earthly existence, the corporeal development should be commensurate with the increasing mental activity and power. Any great disproportion will be found to be incompatible with mental and vital harmony. The capacity and intensity of the Mind's action is not unfrequently the cause of increasing physical debility, and a premature dissolution of the body. Like powerful machinery in a frail building, the Mind shakes the slender fabric in every part. At length in some great emergency—when the storms of life break over us with terrific power, calling for herculean effort—the mind suddenly breaks away from its frail and mortal fastenings, and the startled voyager finds himself beyond the vicissitudes of Time—floating at ease and gracefully in his immortal argosy —with an Angel at the helm, and the great ocean of the limitless Life before him.

The intimate connection of the Mind with the vital principle is forcibly illustrated by innumerable cases of disease, and many deaths, occurring coincidentally with the previous anticipations of the victims. Whenever such fears and expectations are fostered, they are liable to acquire a dangerous influence over the mind, and, in the end to produce the apprehended physical results. Strong mental impressions are sure to leave their images on the body, more or less distinctly, according to the active power of the one, and the intrinsic susceptibility of the other. The membranes are delicate chemical surfaces, and the Mind—by the forces at its command—*electrotypes* the forms and shadows of its thoughts and feelings. It is possible to produce any physiological change or condition which may be comprehended in a distinct mental conception or impression. Let a number of persons meet the same individual during the day, and—without exciting a suspicion of collusion or mischief—assure him that he appears to be ill, and he will soon be seriously indisposed. This action of the mind has, in several instances, been carelessly excited and manifested by such startling and painful results as should suffice to admonish the ignorant and thoughtless operator that all similar experiments are, at least in his hands, attended with extreme danger to the health and life of the subject.

This power of mental action and association produces many surprising effects. Impress the mind of the magnetic sleeper that he must wake from his trance at a particular hour, and the vital force will so react on the body—under the mental impression—that it will be impossible for him to sleep beyond the prescribed limit. Moreover, while it requires a powerful effort to drive a man out of his earthly house, so long as he is determined to remain therein, it is quite impossible to restrain or keep him when he has once resolved to depart. The system can in no way be more speedily and fatally deranged than by fixing in the mind a settled and intense conviction that the body is exposed to the impending evils of disease and death. Indeed, a dose of arsenic in the stomach, or a rifle-ball deposited within the pericardium, would scarcely be more fatal than a positive impression that death is inevitable.

Physicians and others often speak of those who merely *fancy* or *imagine* that they are ill. If they mean that physical disease, in such cases, originates in the disordered action of the mind, the writer has already expressed his concurrence ; but if, on the contrary, such forms of expression are intended to imply that the disease, in all similar examples, *has only an imaginary existence*, I must dispute the assumption, because the most terrible forms of vital derangement are induced in this manner, and even death suddenly evoked by the action of the Mind. Many a business man has been prostrated by a violent nervous or bilious attack, in consequence of having his note protested. The rates of exchange often influence the appetite, while a rapid decline in the price of stocks may occasion a loss of flesh, or have something to do with a chronic diarrhea. Large payments—especially when money is worth " two per cent. a month"—have a tendency to relax the system, while " bank credits" and " bills receivable" possess wonderful tonic properties.

Many persons have died only because they thought their time had come. Dr. George Moore mentions the case of a woman who had her dress torn by a dog ; she imagined that the animal was rabid, and that the virus had been communicated to her ; and, strange to say, her death occurred soon after, and was preceded and accompanied by symptoms of hydrophobia, so marked and unmistakable that the Medical Faculty could find no occasion for so much as a technical distinction. He also records the fact that John Hunter, a distinguished anatomist, ascribed an affection of the heart, which finally terminated his life, to an apprehension that he had received the poison into his system while employed in dissecting the body of an individual who had died of hydrophobia. [1]

The reader has doubtless been informed of the nature and the results of an experiment made on a man in France who had been condemned for a capital offense. Having his arm concealed so that it was impossible for him to make observations through the sense of vision, the cuticle was slightly scratched, without, however, drawing so much as a single drop of blood. At the same time warm water was poured over the arm into a receptacle. Thus the senses of feeling and hearing were made to aid in the deception ; and under the impression that he must inevitably expire from the loss of blood, he actually fainted and died. It is also said of a man who was doomed to be shot, that he instantly expired when a number of soldiers—at a word—discharged *blank cartridges* at him ; and I have somewhere read of a person who died on the block, though the executioner's axe fell without disturbing a hair of his head.

During the prevalence of epidemic diseases, multitudes

---

[1] See Dr. Moore's treatise on " The Soul and the Body."—p. 228.

doubtless fall victims to their own morbid apprehensions. Nothing can be more important under such circumstances than to *create a new excitement* in the common mind. When the black banner of the Destroyer is unfurled in the sluggish atmosphere of the doomed city, the currents of thought and feeling all tend in one general direction, and they act with startling and terrible force on the public health and the very springs of life. On such an occasion a threatened invasion, or the shock of an earthquake, might check the pestilence and save the lives of thousands. Any event that would occasion a sudden reaction of the universal mind would tend to produce a vital equilibrium, and hence to change the electro-chemical and physiological conditions to a more normal standard.

The destructive power of the Mind is strikingly exhibited in the results of an experiment performed, some time since, on four Russians who had been condemned to death for political offenses. The reader may have seen the account that originally appeared in the London *Medical Times*. It is, however, too important as an illustration of my subject to be omitted in this connection. Under the supervision of distinguished members of the medical profession, the convicts were permitted to occupy beds whereon persons had died of epidemic cholera. They were not, however, aware of their exposure in this instance, and not one of them had the disease. Subsequently, they were informed that they must sleep on beds which had been occupied by cholera patients. But in this case *the beds were new*, and had never been used by any person ; nevertheless, under the more potent action of the mind, *three of the four took the disease—in its most malignant form—and died within four hours!*

Thus we perceive that absolute contact with the very elements of infection were powerless to injure the body, while under the more certain and fearful action of mind the disease was generated—death suddenly evoked, and his mission accomplished. Numerous cases of a similar character may be found in medical books and in the public journals, while innumerable examples occur whereof no record is made. Verily our boasted culture and the advantages of modern civilization are turned to a poor account if they do but expose us to unnatural ills, and thus render us more miserable. It is impossible to disguise the fact that among savages and wild beasts disease is comparatively unknown, while civilized man is cursed with a thousand mortal maladies. It will be found at last that most of these are born of the Mind. Ever does each passing thought move like an incarnate spirit over the chords of life, and horrible discords or beautiful harmonies awaken the soul as they echo through the mystical courts of its temple.

Sometimes an important truth obtains expression in the form of an ingenious fiction; and I find a significant illustration of my subject in an Oriental fable. It is represented that the Spirit of the Plague once met an Eastern Prince, and informed him that, during the year, he should remove ten thousand of his subjects. Before the close of that year *one hundred thousand died.* Meeting the Prince again, the Destroyer reminded him of the fulfillment of his prediction. " But," said the Prince, " you have taken one hundred thousand." "Nay," rejoined the other, "I removed only ten thousand—*Fear took the rest.*"

Men are startled when Death approaches suddenly, and they pause to consider the reason of his coming. But few are conscious that in the thought and deed of every day, men solicit his untimely presence. The evil of which we speak—the influence of mental disturbances on the functions of life—is not most terrible where it is most strikingly displayed. To a certain extent—a fearful extent too—this evil is well nigh universal. Millions lay the foundations of wasting disease by yielding perpetually to violent impulses. A thousand trivial circumstances in the common affairs of life are permitted to disturb the equilibrium of mind, and the angry thought strikes harshly on the vital chords until the instrument is unstrung, and Life's song on earth is hushed forever.

How strangely are we conquered by little things! The man who stood firm under the great calamity—braving the stormy elements like some great rock in the midst of the troubled sea—now, in an unguarded moment, bows low beneath the slightest breath of misfortune. Things so small that he would be ashamed to mention them, are his masters, and he their slave. I have seen a being in human form, raving as though he were possessed of a devil! and, on drawing near, I learned of the bystanders that Nature had not made his horse strong enough to bear the burden he imposed ; and for this cause he was mad. An angry spirit breathed over the fountains of life, until the vital tide rose in a crimson flood and submerged the brain—*He died of congestion !*

7

I have been in many a domestic circle where the woman—whose mission should be to calm the little discords that break the harmony of social life—would lose the command of her temper every hour in the day. The most trifling incident was sufficient to arouse the war-spirit in the little citadel; and small missiles, in the form of angry looks and words—possibly deeds—were hurled at any one, as though *all* had offended. Much the good woman wondered that *the children were cross*, and that she was herself *troubled with weak nerves!* And yet seldom indeed has any one lived thus, to the age of thirty-five years, who was not hopelessly diseased.

Anxiety, like an omnivorous worm, gnaws at the root of our peace; Care, like an ugly old hag, stirs the fires of life to put them out; false Pride and a selfish Ambition contribute to waste the nation's health, and lead to a fearful prostitution of the noblest powers. Some die of chills brought on by a cold and comfortless faith; others are consumed with the burning fever of a too intense devotion; while many take *a melancholy whim*, and give up the ghost as honorably as those who take a rope, or prussic acid. Thus thousands perish every year, the victims of spasmodic emotions, and the abnormal operations of a disorderly mind. Many of them expire *suddenly;* and, at the coroner's inquest, it is reported that they died of disease of the heart, congestion of the brain, excessive hemorrhage, or sudden paralysis. But the truth is, the primary causes are back of all such physical effects. Some die from extreme fear; others from intense anger; others still from fits of jealousy, or from a deep and silent sorrow; many are killed by *an all-conquering idea,* and not a few from that ungovernable yet hopeless *love* that, like accumulated electric forces in the midnight sky, *must rend the cloud,* that it may follow its attraction and find its equilibrium.

There is no security for the earthly tenement when the reckless occupant kindles a destroying fire within, and suffers the flames to run through all the apartments. If a man allows himself to be led by every wild impulse and erratic fancy, or if his disposition be like gun-cotton, he is never safe. His body becomes a kind of magazine in which the passions frequently explode and shake the whole building. That man's house will not be likely to last long, and he should pay an extra premium for insurance. The importance of preserving a calm and equal frame of mind will be sufficiently apparent, if we but know and remember that the most frightful physical maladies result from disturbed mental conditions. Look at any person of ungovernable temper, who has reached the meridian of life, and you will find the body a wreck. The nervous system resembles a broken harp, hung in a tree that has been scathed by fierce lightnings. The harp is still swept by every wind of passion, and, in the fitful vibrations of each untoned string, a dismal spirit utters its mournful wail !

CHAPTER IX.

RENOVATING POWERS OF THE HUMAN MIND.

Unreasonable confidence in Drugs—The Renovating Principle in Man—The restorative process—Its relations to the Mind—Influence of outward conditions—Consequences of Opposite Mental States—Total relaxation and inactivity dangerous—Faith superior to Physic—Relation of Amulets, Prayers, Incantations, etc. to physiological effects—Importance of giving a right direction to the Mind—Health found in a pleasant Aromatic—Disease removed with a hot Poker—The Paper-cure—A Psychological Emetic—Jesus observed the Psycho-dynamic Laws—Absurdity of the theories of popular Materialism.

THE true philosophy of disease, comprehending its causes and their action within the sphere of organic relation and dependence ; also the relative efficacy of physical and mental agents in its treatment, and the natural methods of physical restoration, have been but very imperfectly understood From reading of the wonderful virtues of certain nostrums, as well as from the avidity with which thousands swallow pills and powders, one might almost fancy that health, and life, and perhaps *immortality*, are to be purchased at the drug shops. This state of things does not indicate an intelligent perception of the laws of life and health.   On the contrary, it evinces a profound and almost universal ignorance of the whole subject, notwithstanding its intimate relations to the most vital interests of the present life.   .

Here, I apprehend, is an evil as strongly rooted as the pernicious customs of our imperfect civilization, and as mischievous as the perverted habits of the people. Perhaps I can not render a more essential service, in this connection, than by exposing this evil, while, at the same time, I offer some suggestions concerning the nature of the restorative principle and the renovating powers of the mind.

Let me observe, *in transitu*, that the reader must not expect me to practice the peculiar circumspection which prompts certain writers to stand at a great distance from a difficult theme.   I shall hope to be forgiven if I do not approach the subject with all the caution and reserve which may seem to be appropriate to the occasion, seeing that, in its discussion, so many scientific men have already exhausted their learning, and ignorant ones have exposed their folly.

The renovating principle, or restorative power, has no place in medicine: IT EXISTS IN MAN, *and is manifested in and through the living organization.*

It is well known that when any part of the body is impaired, by accident, or otherwise, Nature, without delay, commences to repair the injury.   If, for example, you lacerate a muscle, an unusual tendency of the vital forces to the injured part will at once be perceptible.   This determination of the electric forces of the living body increases the molecular deposits which finally unite the dissevered portions of the muscle as firmly as before.   When a bone is fractured, Nature employs substantially the same process, and generally with similar results.   If one organ of sense be destroyed, or rendered inoperative, the other senses are usually quickened, so as to afford at least a partial compensation or indemnity

for the loss sustained. Thus it it will be perceived that *the
renovating power is in Man,* and that it constitutes one of
the essential laws of his constitution.

Nature, I know, may be assisted—by various extrinsic
means and measures—in her efforts. to recover the normal
exercise of her powers. But the bandage, applied to a flesh
wound, only serves to protect it from the action of the atmosphere ; an internal vital power is required to make the
wounded member whole again. The appendages applied by
the surgeon to a broken limb, subserve no higher purpose
than to keep it in place, while nature performs the more
important office of uniting the bone. In like manner, when
any internal organ becomes diseased, or a general functional
derangement occurs, we employ remedial agents in vain,
unless Nature summons her forces to the work of expelling
the evil. All that she requires at our hands is, that we aid
in removing the obstacles we have thrown in her way. And
when the resources of modern science and art are fairly exhausted, the doctors are obliged to leave Nature to conquer
the disease, and she often accomplishes her task, not only
without their aid, but in spite of their opposition.

The power of the mind, as exhibited in the application of
the vital forces to the organs of the body, has already been
variously illustrated. Moreover, that the mind's action, when
misdirected or greatly intensified, is capable of producing
physical effects of the most startling and fatal character, is
rendered obvious from our investigation of the laws of vital
motion, and especially by the illustrative facts contained in
the last Chapter. That disease, in its most aggravated
forms, occurs from mental as well as from physical causes,

will not be questioned ; and that Death often approaches
suddenly, or gradually retires from our presence at the mandate of the kingly Mind, is scarcely less apparent to the
thoughtful observer.   Indeed, no mere physical agent can so
powerfully influence the distribution of the electro-nervous
forces, and, consequently, the health and life of the body.

But if the abnormal exercise and the misdirected action
of the human faculties and affections involve such disastrous
consequences to the body, it will necessarily follow, that
where the mind acts consistently with the laws of life and
health, rightly distributing the vital motive power, it must
inevitably become the most efficient agent in the treatment
of disease, and in the removal of all the causes of vital
inharmony.   I hazard nothing in affirming that many forms
of disease may be far more effectually treated by the application of mental forces than by the use of physical agents.
If the mind, when misdirected, occasions an irregular organic
motion and diseased condition of the body, it can only be
necessary to *reverse* or change its action, while we preserve
the strength and intensity of the mental function, and the
disease will be arrested and removed.

There are certain states of the public mind which exert a
great sanitary influence.   When the season is fruitful, and
the hopes of the husbandman are more than realized ; when
the spirit of a living enterprise is in all the wheels and springs
of our complicated mechanism ; when Commerce spreads
her snowy pinions over all the rivers and seas ; when the
laborer goes to his toil with an elastic step, and returns with
a joyful song ; when the world is at peace, and every im-

7

portant branch of national industry is stimulated, inspiring
confidence in the universal mind and heart, there will be less
business for physicians, nurses, coroners and undertakers.
Comparatively few persons are likely to be sick, so long as
they are successful, and the world smiles upon them. Moreover, most people manage to live about as long as they con-
trive to make life profitable, by living truly in respect to
themselves, and with a wise reference to the common welfare.

A state of mental depression acts with a destructive power
on the body. Restless and unhappy people are almost always
lean and sickly. The animal fluids are dissipated by the
inward fires ; the nerves become morbidly impressible and
the mucous surfaces are rendered dry and feverish ; the
acidity of the stomach is increased by the asperities of the
disposition ; the outlines of feature and form leave Hogarth's
line of beauty to be supplied by the imagination ; while the
muscles of the face are *underscored* by care, and all life is
gravely accented. But the man of aspiring hopes, who perpetually looks on the sunny side of life, will seldom suffer
from disease. Agreeable emotions stimulate the functions of
the nutritive system, at the same time the power of assimilation is sure to be greatly diminished by the dominion of
such passions as exert a depressing influence on the mind.
It is worthy of remark, that the digestive function is usually
strong in those persons who have large mirthfulness, and
whose acute perception and lively appreciation of the
ludicrous phases and aspects of human character and life,
incline them to "the laughing philosophy." Indeed, that
fleshy people are uniformly good-natured, is a suggestive text

from our proverbial philosophy. It is not, however, their flesh that determines their dispositions ; but, on the contrary, the state of mind and feeling that induces flesh.

Whatever strengthens our confidence in mankind, and inspires our hopes of future happiness, must energize the powers of life. The faculties of the mind require proper stimulants, and when these are employed with a wise discrimination, they exert an invigorating influence on the organs of the body. Our powers all decline when there are no strong incentives to action. It is hardly possible for one to live long who has no purpose in life. The man who has realized all that Fame and Fortune promised, and with laureled brow sits down to enjoy his possessions, experiences a sudden and powerful reaction of all the forces of his nature. From that reaction—consequent upon the existing state of the mind—few entirely recover, while thousands pass away. They remain so long as they have an object to live for, and only expire when life becomes vain and purposeless.

Life and death furnish many impressive illustrations of my idea. While visiting in a large New England town, not long since, a gentleman who resides there called my attention to several costly mansions, whose wealthy owners, having retired from active business, died soon after they were fairly settled in their new and splendid abodes. Having accomplished their own great object in life—*making princely fortunes for themselves*—the chords of being were suddenly relaxed, sinking far below the standard of a natural tension and a healthful activity. True, there were thousands of homeless wanderers all around them in the world, and

millions more whose lives have been a desperate struggle
with " outrageous fortune ;" but all such were left to terminate the fierce conflict with life itself. When no selfish
object remained to invite the exercise of their powers, and
the narrow aims and interests of a false pride and a heartless
ambition were all fully realized, the dwellers in princely
mansions had, perhaps, no object for which to live and act.
Accordingly, they sought rest, and found a lasting but
ignoble respose. Thus life, to the selfish man, is but a poor
and profitless investment, even when

> ———" they whose hearts are dry as summer dust,
> Burn to the socket."

Among the agents comprehended in our eclecticism, Faith
is doubtless far more potent than Physic. In fact, the
articles embraced in the *materia medica* often derive all
their remedial powers from the patient's preconceived idea of.
their curative properties. When faith in the efficacy of any
agent, however powerless in itself, is sufficiently strong, the
anticipated physical results are quite sure to follow its administration. The protecting and renovating powers of Amulets
and the fancied occult influence of charms, (so much in use
in past ages,) employed by ignorant people to shield their
bodies from disease, and their souls from the assaults of
satanic agents, are doubtless to be ascribed to this action of
the mind within itself and on the body. No matter what the
material instrumentalities may be, in any given case, since
the results are not so directly and essentially dependent on
these as on the mind's action. Papal prayers and Pagan
incantations will serve equally well at the exorcism of

imaginary demons ; at the same time, a string of berries
from the mountain-ash, the dry bones of a departed saint, or
any one of the ingredients of the witches' caldron, will cure
a devout, ignorant man whose disease had its origin in the
mind.

The most accomplished practitioners are ordinarily those
who use the least medicine, and depend most on giving a new
and right direction to the patient's mind.   Those who disregard the relations of the mind to the body, and are ignorant
of the psychical laws, can never be eminently successful.
Where nothing is done to inspire the patient with confidence,
very little will be accomplished by our efforts to remove his
disease or to mitigate his sufferings.   The specific effects of
the most valuable remedies are often neutralized by the
repulsive manner of the physician, while the patient's doubts
respecting his capacity are often stronger than ordinary
tonics and strengthening plasters.   On the other hand, when
the patient's faith is established and unwavering, bread-pills,
sugar-powders, or Dr. Townsend's sweetened-water, will
readily accomplish amazing psycho-physiological effects   It
may be necessary to disguise the real condition of a sick man,
in order to save him from the fatal consequences which an
actual knowledge of his case would be likely to produce.
For similar reasons, and from the best motives, the discreet
physician may resort to a seemingly innocent deception, in
order to realize the most beneficent results.

The writer was once called to visit a lady who had suffered
from protracted indisposition and a long confinement.   She
was so seriously ill that her case had baffled the skill of
eminent physicians.   Her physical infirmities, originating

mainly in disordered mental states, reacted with most depressing and melancholy effects on her sensitive mind. She was strongly inclined to the opinion that her case was hopeless. The number of her chronic difficulties was only limited by her knowledge of the infirmities of poor human nature. She readily concluded that only those understood her case whose diagnostic readings confirmed her own preconceived opinions. The writer, of course, indulged her whimsicalities, (that is an essential part of the treatment,) but with an air of unusual gravity assured her that the case was, nevertheless, one that could be most successfully treated. At first she was incredulous, but at length confidence was fully established. Taking from my vest pocket a box of " Hooper's Cachous Aromatisés," I removed the label without attracting her attention. Having described in a most particular and emphatic manner the specific action of *my electrical pills*, (the description comprehended the precise physiological changes necessary to a healthy action,) I handed her the box with minute directions, and the positive assurance that the contents of a single box would suffice to restore her to perfect health. The lady pursued the treatment with the strictest fidelity, and was *completely restored!* Since her recovery she has repeatedly importuned the writer for several boxes of those electrical pills, which she desires to present to friends whose cases are similar to her own.

It is said that Pliny recommended the warm blood of an expiring gladiator as a remedy for epilepsy; and not more than two hundred years ago the lichens which grew from human skulls were the best remedy for that disease known to the medical faculty of England. Alfred Smee, in a note to his "Instinct and Reason," (page 270,) mentions a cure which resulted from the directions given by the doctor to the nurse, who was instructed to apply, if necessary, a *red-hot poker to the patient's back.* A physician with whom the writer is on familiar terms, affirms that he produced a powerful cathartic action by the use of *flour, moistened with saliva,* and made into pills. Some days since I heard of the case of a German, who being seriously indisposed, applied to one of our American physicians for professional aid. The doctor wrote a prescription, and handing the paper to the patient, said, " *There, take that,*" presuming that he would go at once to the apothecary for the medicine. Meeting his patient some few days after, he inquired after the state of his health, whereupon the German replied that he was quite well, but that he found some difficulty in getting the doctor's prescription down, as *he was not used to taking paper !* [1]

When this vigorous and renovating action of the mind can be otherwise induced and directed, the same results may be produced without the use of ordinary remedial agents, or other material means. Some years since, while the writer was employed in delivering a series of lectures on mental and spiritual science—in Springfield, Mass.—the statement was made, that whenever the mind's action can be controlled

---

[1] The following fact is related by Dr. George Moore :—

During the seige of Breda, in 1625, the garrison was on the point of surrendering from the ravages of scurvy, principally induced by mental depression. A few vials of sham medicine were introduced, by order of the Prince of Orange as an infallible specific. It was given in drops and produced astonishing effects. Such as had not moved their limbs for months before, were seen walking in the streets—sound, straight and well.—*The Soul and the Body,* p. 225.

agreeably to psychological laws, the specific action of any medicine may be produced by the direction given by the mind to 'the electro-vital forces. This was boldly disputed by the Medical Faculty ; and the experiment of administering a *psychological emetic* was accordingly made in the presence of a large public assembly—on a healthy Irishman—which in less than three minutes resulted in his discharging the contents of his stomach.

The great Physician of the Jews recognized this action of the mind as possessing a great renovating power over the body.   Two blind men came to him on a certain occasion to have their sight restored.   Jesus said to them, " *According to your faith* be it unto you ; and their eyes were opened." To the woman who " touched the hem of his garment," he said, " *Thy faith hath made thee whole.*"—[Matthew, ninth chapter.]   These and other similar forms of expression clearly indicate that the cures wrought by the Divinely-gifted Man of Nazareth were not arbitrary exhibitions of an independent power, but that they were in consonance with the psychodynamic laws.   Cures are now daily accomplished when the material agents employed have no specific action on the system, and also when no such means are resorted to by the patient or the practitioner.   In either' case the cure must be ascribed to the action of the mind.   So important is this concentration and application of mental forces to the diseased body—so essential is *faith* on the part of the patient, that without it the chances of recovery, in any serious case, are few and small.   Few persons afflicted with chronic diseases are ever cured without strong confidence in the physician or his remedies.   On the other hand, when all the energies of the soul are summoned to the work of deliverance, disease is straightway forced to resign its usurped dominion.[1]

The idea that diseases may be removed and the body restored by the agency of the mind alone, involves—in the judgment of many people—a great tax on human credulity. They have no hesitation in believing that a small blue pill, a little tincture of lobelia, or an *infinitesimal dose of the fortieth dilution of some impotent drug* will accomplish the work of organic and functional renovation, whilst *Mind*, with all its immortal powers and Godlike capabilities, is regarded as an inadequate cause of similar effects.   This is the worst conceivable form of Materialism.   It invests the smallest quantity of inorganic matter with a power greater than the soul is admitted to possess.   It utterly denies the supremacy of Mind over the realm of material forces, forms and elements ; while it virtually disputes the healing power of the great Physician, because he did not give physic to the Jews, but removed their maladies by the mightier energies of MIND.

The remarkable cures wrought—in the early part of the last century—at the tomb of the Abbé Paris, appear to have depended far more on the faith of the devotees themselves, than on the miraculous energy ascribed to the dry bones of the departed Saint.

CHAPTER X.

MENTAL AND VITAL POWERS OF RESISTANCE.

The Inward Forces—False views of the nature of Disease—Conditions of the Earth and atmosphere—Man's positive relation in the outward World—How the Citadel may be defended—Experiments of Dutrochet—Structure of the membranes of animal and human Bodies—Relations of Mind to the powers of physical resistance—The Sisters of Charity—Strong mental excitements may fortify the Body—Power to resist Heat and Cold—Reference to Dr. Kane, the Arctic Explorer—Col. Fremont's Expeditions—Painful Experiences among the passes of the Sierra Nevada—The Colonel's Inspiration—Conquests of the Positive Man.

> ———" All declare
> For what the Eternal Maker has ordained
> The powers of Man ; we feel within ourselves
> His energy divine."

IN the external economy of Human Nature—in its best estate—we are presented with a most majestic and beautiful earthly form ; with vital forces and organic instruments the most subtile and complicated, and with functions of being the most delicate, mysterious and wonderful. Nevertheless, we should be wanting in the most significant and convincing illustration of the Divine wisdom and benevolence, if Man, with his exquisite susceptibility and transcendent powers, were surrounded by destructive agents, whose presence he was unfitted to perceive, and against whose secret assaults he could oppose no adequate resistance. But we are not thus defenseless.   On the contrary, there exists no outward cause of vital derangement for which Nature has not provided a sufficient inward protection.   Man has only to comprehend his nature and relations, and to wisely apply the forces at his command, to insure his personal safety.   When his latent powers are fairly called into the outward arena, being normally exercised and rightly directed, he will be strong in the integrity of his nature, and may walk forth amidst a thousand dangers, with none to make him afraid.

Many persons seem to entertain the idea that diseases have an *independent existence*, and that they are individualized in the atmosphere.   Those unphilosophical observers, in whose uncultivated minds idle fancies, and the most improbable conjectures, assume the dignity and authority of an enlightened judgment and scientific conclusions, may readily imagine that the vital air is but the broad highway through which invisible forms of Evil—the ministers of infection and disease—go down to the carnival of Death ; and that an indignant Providence unchains the viewless winds, arms them with numberless poison shafts, and sends them forth to smite and to destroy.   Such notions evince as little reason as reverence.   The truth is, disease is only a deranged state of the vital forces and functions, or a temporary condition of an organic form induced by an infringement of some existing law.   As disease has no separate existence outside of organic forms and relations, but is wholly dependent on the violation of vital, physiological or other laws for its development, it follows, that to escape disease, we have but to live and act with a wise reference to the laws of our com-

8

mon nature. Neglect those laws, and earth has no asylum where the enemy will not find and punish the offender.

But are there no conditions of the earth, and especially of the atmosphere, that may diminish the vital forces of the human body, or otherwise derange the organic action? Obviously such conditions are liable to occur, at all seasons and in every part of the world. But when the body is in a perfectly normal state, it so readily accommodates itself to the electrical and atmospheric changes, that it suffers no injury from their occurrence. Occasionally a person lives eighty or one hundred years, in the enjoyment of complete and uninterrupted health. Such men must inevitably have been exposed, more or less, to the influence of the elements, and to all the ordinary vicissitudes of life ; and yet they are strangers to the physical infirmities of mankind. The examples of this class may not be very numerous, but they indicate with sufficient clearness the inherent capacities of Man. The powers necessary to vital harmony and a protracted existence—still latent in the great body of Humanity —are here and there obscurely revealed in individuals, as prophecies of still nobler achievements for the Race, as we go forward to realize the great destiny and the sublime possibilities of human nature on earth and in the heavens.

The capacity to resist the outward causes of disease mainly *depends on the positive nature and relation of man, as compared with the unorganized elements, and the surrounding forms of the organic creation.* The human body is perpetually generating and disengaging the vital electric element that constitutes the circulating medium of the nervous system, and the vital motive power. The several processes of respiration, digestion, circulation, secretion, and the powers of molecular attraction, chemical affinity and muscular motion, are all employed in the evolution of the subtile principle, which is constantly passing off from the healthy body in inappreciable currents to pervade the material elements and objective forms of the external world. As these processes are uninterrupted in the healthy body, the gradual waste is constantly supplied ; and so long as the inward forces and subtile elements continue to flow out from the vital centers to the circumference of our being, we can not be injured by the outward agents that induce disease. This determination of the electric forces from the center to the surface, not only carries the effete matter out of the body—thus cleansing the channels and purifying the elements of the circulation—but so long as this flow of the vital tide is not interrupted, the agents that disturb the electrical equilibrium, and the organic movement, are driven away, and the normal condition of the body is preserved. It is only when the vital forces are diminished at the seat of life, or when the electric currents set back from the external to the internal surfaces, that the avenues leading to the citadel are left open and defenseless.

This point will admit of a clearer elucidation. When two bodies in opposite electrical conditions, or sustaining positive and negative relations, are brought together, there is an instantaneous effort on the part of Nature to establish an equilibrium between them. The subtile fluid emanates from the positive body and goes out to pervade the other. If the bodies be composed of homogeneous elements, in similar proportions, and hence have equal capacity as conductors, they

will be reduced to the same electrical condition. If we charge
a leyden jar, and a negative body that will serve as a conductor be placed in suitable relations to the same, the accumulated electricity will be discharged from the jar to the body
thus presented. Now, in a less sensible, though not less
certain manner, the same phenomenon is constantly recurring
from the contact of the human body with external objects.
But the discharges occur on the *inductive* principle, and are
not, therefore, perceptible, as in the *disruptive discharge* from
the jar, or from the clouds, when summer showers are accompanied by electrical phenomena.

It has been observed that the human body, while in a
healthy state, is positive to the inorganic substances, and, I
may add, to the forms of organized existence below man. I
need not pause here to discuss the nature of the outward
agents and specific conditions which induce disease in any
given case ; but it may be clearly shown, that while the
system preserves its natural or positive relation to the external elements, it can not be materially injured by their action.
So long, for example, as the body continues to sustain this
relation to the atmospheric changes, we can not take cold,
nor are we liable to suffer from exposure to contagion. The
invisible arrows of the destroyer fall without the walls of
the fortress in which the forces of life are entrenched. The
enemy is kept at bay by virtue of the resistance which his
positive relation enables man to exercise. While the normal
condition is preserved, he is perpetually sending out electrical
emanations, which pervade the surrounding atmosphere and
the objects with which he is most intimately connected. On
the contrary, when the relation is changed—when the body

becomes negative in the sphere of its outward relations—
the corporeal organs and their functions may be impaired
and deranged by the general state of the elements, or by the
specific properties of surrounding forms and substances.

Agreeably to this positive relation of living bodies, we
find that the skin and other membranes are adapted to the
exhalation rather than the inhalation or absorption of particles. It was Dutrochet who demonstrated, by his experiments in *Endosmose* and *Exosmose*, the great exhaling capacity of the membranes of animal bodies. At the same
time his scientific investigations render it equally evident
that the outward elements do not readily enter the body
through the cutaneous envelop. While substances in a liquid
state would easily pass out—from the inner to the outer
surface—through the pores of the skin, no similar hydraulic
pressure would suffice to force them through the perspiratory
ducts in the opposite direction. The result of the experiment suggests the cause of this difference. When the force
is applied from within, the valves of the epidermis are naturally thrown open ; but when the pressure is on the external
surface, the oblique valvular openings—numbering some
2500 or 3000 to every square inch of the surface of the body
—are closed as a means of protection. I am aware that some
authors have maintained that certain substances in solution
can be introduced into the system through the cuticle ; and
it is even asserted that life has been preserved for some time
by the absorption of nutrition. But these statements must
be regarded as extremely improbable in the light of Dutrochet's experiments ; at the same time other scientific observations contribute to establish the fact, that the absorbing

power of the membranes bears no proportion to their exhaling capacity.

On this peculiarity in the membraneous structure and functions of the skin, the natural power of the living body to resist the outward causes of disease must in a great measure depend ; for not only is it thus qualified to expel—in a summary manner—the impurities that would otherwise remain and generate disease, but it is likewise enabled to resist the influx of foreign elements that might impair the organic functions and render life insecure. Thus the body is fitted by Nature to expel disease, rather than to imbibe the elements that generate the evil. So long, therefore, as the normal condition is faithfully preserved, and man sustains proper relations to the elements and forms of the physical world, he is invulnerable to cold, to miasma, and to all the subtile agents of infection.

It is well known that there are certain mental states that greatly increase and others that materially diminish our susceptibility to sensorial impressions, and to the influence of such agents as are liable to disturb the organic harmony, The *activity* of the mind is not merely an indispensable condition of its own growth, but it is necessary to physical health, inasmuch as the body is liable to become negative when the mind is wholly inactive. A proper mental excitement imparts an additional stimulus to the organic functions. In the hours of rest we are entirely passive or negative, hence the increased liability during sleep, to take cold or imbibe disease from contagion. Whatever renders the body negative, in the sense here implied, exposes it to injury from outward causes. But as the mind is capable of sending the electrical forces to every part of the system, it follows that the walls which surround the powers of life may be strongly fortified. When the whole surface is electrically charged there is no opportunity for the admission—from external sources—of the elements which produce disease. They are driven off, and the body is protected by the spontaneous flow of the electric forces from the center toward the circumference of our physical being.

The phenomenal illustrations of this part of my subject are as significant and forcible as they are numerous and diversified. The timid watcher who goes reluctantly to the bedside of a sick friend—filled with the apprehension of a mortal danger—will so withdraw the electro-nervous forces by the recoiling action of his mind, that every avenue leading to the seat of vital power will be left open, and he will almost inevitably fall a victim. On the contrary, the physician, who with firm purpose and unshaken nerves, walks through the wards of the hospital, is seldom injured by the foul atmosphere of disease and death. The Sisters of Charity, whose devotion to the interests of Humanity and the claims of their Religion prompt them to brave the secret agents of destruction, are very rarely sacrificed to the Southern pestilence. Let a negative man sit still for two hours on a cold stone, where the autumn winds chill the blood as they hymn their *requiem* to the dying year, and he may lose his own life in consequence; at the same time, a live member of the Democratic party—if under the influence of strong political excitement—may stand at the corner of the street and quarrel with a Republican all night, without suffering from exposure to the frosts and storms of winter. A delicate and susceptible lady who would take cold from a moment's contact with the damp ground, or from a slight exposure to the evening air, when the mind is in a state of repose, may escape unharmed when she is under the influence of intense mental excitement. Let her be told for example that her child has fallen into the river, and the agitation of mind occasioned by the startling intelligence will enable her to expose her person to the fiercest action of the elements with impunity. The strong impulse of the soul sends the forces to the extremities, and so diffuses the electric aura over the whole surface of the body as to furnish a complete protection.

The normal temperature of the body, among the human species, varies in different races and individuals from 96 to 100° Fahr.; and is but slightly modified by the circumstances of geographical position and the vicissitudes of the Seasons. In Summer and Winter—in the frigid and the torrid zones, it remains the same. From this fact we may infer that the vital power to resist the variations of temperature is almost unlimited ; and this is one of the most essential laws in the economy of all Animated Nature. This inherent capacity to endure sudden changes and the greatest extremes of heat and cold, is often essential to the preservation of health and life. In certain persons this power has been exercised and developed in a surprising degree. Blagden was able to endure the atmosphere of an oven in which water boiled while the surface was covered with oil, and when the mercury stood 257° Fahr. We have also an account of two girls in France whose experiments demonstrated their capacity to resist a still higher temperature. Francisco Martinez, a Spaniard, who made an exhibition of his powers at

Paris—some thirty years ago—did not hesitate to go into a large stove heated to 279°.

Moreover, it appears from the testimony of a number of reliable witnesses, that the *Convulsionaries* at the grave of Saint Medard, in France, were no less distinguished for their ability to resist extreme heat. La Sonet, surnamed the Salamander, in the course of two hours subjected her body to the action of fire for more than half an hour ; and during the time she was so exposed fifteen sticks of wood were consumed ; the flames at times uniting above the woman, and thus encircling the whole body. La Sonet manifested no signs of pain, but appeared to be sleeping. A certificate —attesting the actual occurrence of the facts in this case— was signed by several enlightened witnesses including a brother of Voltaire and a Protestant nobleman from Perth. [1]

In the year 1832 the writer witnessed some masterly illustrations of this power by a Frenchman, who was known as the " Fire King." Monsieur could enter a heated oven and remain long enough to boil eggs or cook a steak, without any apparent inconvenience to himself. In his public exhi- bitions he was accustomed to take his place on an elevated platform, over which an iron frame was erected, and where he was surrounded on all sides with light combustible materials, including several hundred blank cartridges. When his ar- rangements were completed he applied a lighted match to a fuse, and in a moment he would be so completely enveloped in flames as to be almost or altogether concealed from the spectators. His outside garments were always consumed, but the devouring elements left no signs of its power on the

---

[1] See Blake's Encyc.,—Art., Animal Heat.

person of the Fire King. It would be difficult to find more extraordinary illustrations of this amazing power of resistance, if we except the alleged miraculous experience of the three Hebrews, who were unharmed by the fiery ordeal of Nebuchadnezzar's furnace.

The power to resist *Frost* chiefly depends on the condition and action of the mind. The chemical elements in all human bodies are essentially the same, and, when mental and vital motion are suspended, they will freeze at about the same temperature. Nevertheless, among living men one may be invulnerable—with respect to cold—while others are doomed to perish. It would not be safe to baptize a faithless man —having small vital powers—in the winter ; but the young convert—all glowing with the enthusiasm of his first love— with the fire of a deep and earnest devotion burning in his heart and warming his whole being, may experience no injury from immersion in the icy flood. We have a striking illustration of this point in the case of Dr. Kane, whose explorations have contributed so much to science and to secure for himself an honorable and lasting fame. If he was not endowed by Nature with robust health and great powers of physical endurance, he doubtless possessed gifts which invest the individual mind and character with something more than kingly power—he possessed an enlightened mind, a strong will, and withal a magnanimity of soul that rose with the dignity of his purpose, and was equal to the necessities of the most trying emergency. Through the long Arctic night he braved the tempests that vailed the boreal heavens and swept the glacier steeps around him. Others, less resolute and noble, were entombed in icy sepulchers ; but the eternal frosts of the polar regions could not chill the blood that was quickened by a passion for adventure, warmed by an enthusiastic love of knowledge, and impelled by the strong incentives of a lofty and worthy ambition.

I find other-illustrative examples—not less instructive and convincing—in the history of Col. Fremont's expeditions. When his less ambitious companions froze their limbs and their faces, gave up in despair and perished from cold, hunger and fatigue ; when others—rendered insane by long suffering—wandered away from the party and were lost ; and even the hardy mules—huddling together—one after another froze, tumbled down, and were buried in the deep snows among the tributaries of the Rio Del Norte, the brave leader of the party was unharmed by the frost.[1] Whether encamped among the snowy peaks and dangerous passes of the Sierra Nevada, or exposed to the remorseless fury of the wintry storms—as they swept over the lofty summits and through the deep defiles of the Rocky Mountains—Fremont was always resolute and always safe ; and through all the exhausting labors, intense sufferings, and hair-breadth escapes, of his five expeditions across the continent, he seems

[1] On one occasion when Col. Fremont was encamped among the rugged mountain passes, 12,000 feet above the sea, it became necessary to send several of his men to the Spanish settlements of New Mexico to obtain provisions and also to purchase mules to aid in the transportation of his baggage. After the departure of his men he became anxious for their safety, and with several of his brave companions traveled 160 miles, in the snow and on foot. At length, on the evening of the tenth day—when the four men who had undertaken to reach the Spanish settlements had been out twenty-two days—he found three of them exhausted and ready to perish—King, the leader of the little band, having already expired from hunger and fatigue. In speaking of this incident, Col. Fremont says : *I look upon the anxiety which induced me to set out from the camp as an inspiration.* Had I remained there waiting the arrival of the party which had been sent in, every man of us would probably have perished.—*Upham's Life of Fremont,* p. 287.

to have been shielded by an armor more impenetrable than steel. The soul is mightier far than strength of nerve and muscle, armed with all the implements of war ; and the hero who first unfurled the banner of his country from the loftiest summits of the Great Sierra and the Rocky Mountain ranges was *strong in spirit ;* he was illuminated by *a conscious inspiration* and armed with the all-conquering forces of his own unyielding will.

Thus the active, the resolute, the positive man—the man who walks forth with a firm step, and an intrepid spirit, is invested with an armor more invulnerable than the heavy mail of the days of chivalry. The dangers which have proved fatal to others, leave him unharmed. If he meets his enemies in the way, they retreat before him. The miasmatic exhalations which sometimes pervade the atmosphere are powerless to invade the walled citadel of his being. He walks with the pestilence, but an invisible protecting power is around, above, and beneath him.

Nothing, therefore, can be more essential to health—more deeply inwrought with all that renders life secure and pleasurable—than the preservation of the relation which Nature has assigned to Man. To this end, dear reader, observe the laws which govern the human organization. Be free in thought ; be firm in purpose ; be energetic in action. If you are beset with dangers, never—as you value health and life—relinquish your self-possession. If fortune frowns, be calm and you will conquer. The man of great physical and moral courage, if guided by wisdom, is well nigh immortal now. The negative man—the coward—dies a thousand deaths, while the brave man dies but once.

CHAPTER XI.

EVILS OF EXCESSIVE PROCREATION.

The higher Law—What things are pure and beautiful—Writers on the Philosophy of Impregnation—Rapid Propagation among the lower Classes—The Problem and the Solution—Destruction of the Unborn—Excessive Procreation at war with Nature—The evil Consequences—Legal and Conventional Morality—The Cannibalism of Lust—Infidels in the temple of the Affections —Indifference to momentous Consequences—A solemn Responsibility— Fearful self-sacrifice—Disease at the Baptism, and Crime at the Communion.

THAT man is an Atheist who does not recognize the existence and the supremacy of the Divine natural law in and over all. The essential springs of our common life, the natural relations of the sexes, and the inevitable and lasting consequences which attach to every purpose and succeed every action, admonish us that, higher than the constitutions and court circulars of States and Empires, supreme over all legislative enactments, civil tribunals, and imperial decrees, are the laws of the Creator, as enacted and recorded in the very rudiments of our common nature. The laws of nations, and the civil policies of human governments, are wise—and they conduce to the progress and the happiness of the people —only so far as they are faithful translations of the statute-book of Nature into the living language of human speech and action. Moreover, in the precise degree that our legislators

depart from the Divine requirements, as expressed in the
fundamental laws of Nature, the government becomes oppressive and degrading ; at the same time, so far as the political
institutions, the civil policy and the social life of a people
are based on essential principles, and in unison with the
inherent laws of universal hamony, they may furnish incentives to individual enterprise, or otherwise promote the col-
lective interests of the race.

The will of Heaven, in respect to this world, is conspicuously revealed *in the economy of the world itself*. Before
that august tribunal all things are pure and beautiful—are
intrinsically true and good—in proportion as they conform
to the essential life, the organic laws, and the normal relations of our being, and are thus adapted to actualize the
heavenly harmonics among men. Thus alone we may hope
to realize the appropriate answer to the prayer : " Thy kingdom come, thy will be done in earth as in heaven."

I do not expect to unfold, in this Chapter, the philosophy
of *impregnation ;* nor will it be proper, in a popular treatise
on a profound subject, to even attempt a subtile analysis and
comprehensive exposition of the conditions, laws and processes involved in the reproduction of the species. The obscure beginnings of our organic formation and life are vailed
in mystery ; and no one should undertake to enlighten the
public mind on a subject of this nature who has not been
favored with extensive and varied oportunities for the most
delicate experiments in vital electricity, and for minute and
critical observations in the subtile chemistry of animal life.
The writer's opportunities for a microscopic inspection of
these vital mysteries have been quite too limited to justify

the expression of an opinion ; and as this field is far removed from the sphere of ordinary observation, I will leave it to some future author, whose capacity for critical investigation may be equal to the task, and whose opportunities may be commensurate with his desires and the peculiar claims of the subject. In the meantime, those who desire to become better acquainted with the physiological theory of impregnation, may, if they please, peruse the works of Blumenbach, Velpeau, Spallanzani, Dutrochet, and other writers on Embryology.

Under the influence of our corrupt civilization the propagation of the species is so rapid, that extreme poverty becomes the common inheritance of millions. Among the poor and laboring people the population increases with the greatest rapidity. This is not, of course, to be mainly ascribed to the superior strength of their vital energies and animal passions ; nor, on the other hand, chiefly to the enervating influence of a life of indolent pleasure and luxurious indulgence, on the part of the wealthier classes. It does not require the vision of a seer to enable the discerning mind to suggest other sufficient reasons for this difference, the particular elucidation of which may not be appropriate in this place. Suffice it to say, thousands of embryotic forms of humanity are every year destroyed by professional men and methods. Multitudes thus perish in secret which no man can number. Precisely where Nature develops the germs of new life, and God unfolds immortal entities, they find their sepulchers. If the poor are not restrained, in this respect, by reason and conscience, they may be by their ignorance of such destructive arts as have prevailed among the more polished, fashionable and affluent circles. Those who possess wealth and influence, but whose false or superficial culture may have obscured the moral perceptions, are often the first to shrink from the most solemn responsibilities, and they have not been the last to pollute their own souls by the foul sin of fœticide, now so prevalent even among the polite and professedly pious circles of modern society.

The circumstances of the laboring classes, more especially in great cities and populous manufacturing districts, are such that parents who have a numerous progeny, can scarcely provide adequate food and clothing. Under these unfavorable conditions, the education of the young is of necessity sadly neglected ; and if soul and body are kept together for awhile, it is that the former may be vailed in darkness, and the latter clothed with rags. Both are almost inevitably engulphed in the great maelstrom of social wrongs and popular vices ; and thus vast multitudes ignobly perish—

"Unwept, unhonored, and unsung."

They are all unnoticed and *unknown* while living, except those who, with desperate energy, inscribe their names on the rolls of infamy, leaving their frightful record in lines of blood.

These monstrous evils, which so enfeeble, debase and scourge our country and the civilized world, are not to be removed by sheriffs, nor can they be shut up in prisons and kept out of sight. Moreover, they are not likely to be greatly diminished so long as we are surrounded by the present imperfect social conditions, and our ideas of virtue and humanity are not elevated above the legal and fashionable standards. These evils, great as they confessedly are, under the most auspicious circumstances, are liable to be frequently aggravated by the commercial and financial revulsions which occur in this country, from what incidental causes it is not my object to inquire. It is at least apparent to all observers that the great forces and interests of the business world are often temporarily deranged or paralyzed so that many are reduced by extreme want to some fatal alternative. Thus thousands are every year driven to desperation and ruin by some dire necessity. If we do not find an efficient remedy for these evils in the wholesome restraints of a higher moral science, and the realization of a purer and nobler life, it must follow—as our country becomes more populous— that these evils will naturally and inevitably increase, until—in the United States as in the Old World—millions will be chained from the hour of their birth to the low sphere of degrading servitude, famine feed on multitudes, and despairing souls, with their necessities like a millstone about their necks, be swallowed up in the abyss of hopeless suffering and rayless oblivion.

That the multitudes, however imperfect and deformed, will wholly restrain their natural, and especially their *unnatural* impulses, our knowledge of human nature does not authorize us to infer. We are not visionary enough to even dream that ordinary mortals can be suddenly transformed into angels of the celestial degree, by the total annihilation of their animal instincts. No such merciless crucifixion of human nature is demanded ; nor is such a state of etherealization, for the present, to be desired. For, if it were fairly inaugurated, propagation might be suspended ; or, to say the least, the race become so ethereal as to be unfitted for the

9

present state of the natural world. But I would have *men* obey the *dicta* of Reason and Nature. Moreover, the present rapid indiscriminate, and lawless propagation of the species *is not natural;* on the contrary, it is at war with Nature. At the same time, the sense of moral obligation is perpetually violated, and thousands are virtually put to death by those who should be their natural preservers. Who does not know that, in a state of nature, offspring are far less numerous 'than they are under the influence of our corrupt civilization. We have only to look at the facts developed in the character and history of the North American Indians, to perceive that, in this respect—as well as in other characteristics of civilized life—*we are aliens from Nature*, who rashly trample down her institutions, and yet murmur because we are appropriately arraigned before her tribunal, and punished as her righteous Lawgiver decrees.

We have a miserable conventional morality, sanctioned alike by the ministers of Religion and Law, and withal fatally fashionable. It leaves Virtue to wander about slipshod, and sends Chastity on an exploring expedition into ideal regions; while it covers lust and crime with fine linen and *a marriage certificate.* The votaries of this legal morality—*who can conceive of nothing higher*—are ragged and filthy as the *lazaroni.* Such men are virtuous according to the statute, and as pure as the legal definition of chastity requires. The law provides that they shall only be allowed to debase and destroy one fair object at the same time. One after another they may defile the white shrines; commit sacrilege in temples consecrated to Love by the presence of the Holy Spirit; and like ruthless iconoclasts, may disfigure the images of beauty, or shiver the finest symbols of the angelic creation. It is only necessary to procure a license from a civil magistrate. Against the violence of such criminals the law interposes no barrier. At the same time, conscience has leave of absence when the State asserts the paramount dignity and authority of the Constitution and the Courts. The innate sense of delicacy—so natural to the female in her virgin state—is seldom respected by sensuous men, who, like the *carnivori*, live on flesh, and with whom the restraints of the criminal code determine the precise limits of virtuous indulgence.

Men are often grave and thoughtful about trifles, while they are disposed to be thoughtless and trifling over the most important interests and solemn realities of life. A respectable mechanic will exercise far greater caution in tempering *a cheap jack-knife* than most people display in determining the tempers of their own offspring ! That the predominant feeling and general tendency of mind existing in the parents at the time of conception, and—so far as the mother is concerned—during the successive stages of gestation, may determine the mental characteristics and prevaling disposition of the child, is confirmed by facts which are quite too palpable to be overlooked or denied, and of too significant and momentous a character to be lightly regarded. The demands of this essential law of our being will never be duly respected so long as the generation of human beings is left to accident (?) sudden caprice, or unconquerable passion. Millions of unwelcome children are forced into the world, and left unarmed to grapple with a cruel destiny. The advent of each is viewed as a misfortune, or, perhaps, regarded as a Providential affliction. Children generated and born under such unsuitable conditions are liable to carry with them life-long consequences of the thoughtlessness or depravity of their progenitors ; especially when the unhappy state of feeling in the mother, during the whole period of gestation, has contributed to fix and deepen the impression. They are liable to be quite destitute of filial affection, and often possess an inherent feeling of opposition to parental influence. It is criminal in the extreme to assume this high responsibility without a wise reference to the natural and spiritual relations of the parties, and a due regard to existing physical, mental, and moral conditions. As no act in life is, or indeed can be, productive of more important and lasting consequences of weal or woe, it must be obvious that no human transaction demands a stricter observance of the laws of nature and the dictates of reason, or a more devout respect for the suggestions of conscience and religion.

I have intimated that the legal morality is *defective.* Indeed, if it were brought to trial by a Divine standard, under an enlightened interpretation of the laws of Nature, it would be perceived to be *grossly immoral.* Many women have drunken husbands, and by the stern demands of the law are forced to live with them ; and, moreover, to submit to the foul dominion of morbid lusts, excited and corrupted by unnatural stimulants. Children are consequently begotten when the husband's wits are out and Reason has resigned her throne to Rum. To submit to the loathsome embrace is sufficient to shock all the finer sensibilities of woman ; but when there is added to this, the fearful apprehension that she may

bear children when love is not in the act that determines
their existence—that the offspring may be conceived in the
wild delirium of unbridled lust and intoxication—oh, then,
how sadly must all true human feelings be outraged and conscience violated!   Even life with such corrupt and corrupting concomitants is rendered more terrible to a sensitive
mind and a benevolent heart, than death with all its real or
imaginary horrors.   But even this does not reveal the deepest shade that darkens the legal standard of morality.   That
is manifest in the disposition the law makes of those who are
born out of wedlock.   It often robs them of their inheritance,
and thus loads them with legal disabilities and with the
world's reproach, as if it were a crime for the young and
innocent ones to live.

Consumption, Scrofula, Insanity and other frightful mala
dies, are known to be congenital diseases in many families ;
and by an irresistible law these evils are transmitted from
one generation to another.   Disease poisons the currents of
vitality ; the blood of nations is corrupted, and death is mirrored in the very fountains of this vitiated life.   Is there no
remedy for these stupendous ills ?   Must they be perpetuated
and augmented *ad infinitum* under the shallow and blasphe-
mous pretext that Providence thus decrees ?   Shall foul corruption continue to be generated in high and low places,
dressed in fine linen and taken to church to be baptized ?
Must deformity, suffering and death be immortalized in the
flesh that doctors may be supported ?   These are grave questions which humane and rational men are in conscience bound
to answer.   There is at least one sure way to arrest this tide
of wrong and ruin.   *Men and women whose original constitu-*

*tions or habits of life unfit them for assuming such a responsi-
bility, should not become parents.* The streams of evil which
have corrupted society so long must be cut off at their source;
and this can only be done by suspending the processes of reproduction wherever the conditions are such as to render
their continuance either inhuman or unwise.

They are not common offenders against Humanity and
Heaven who legalize great wrongs and make iniquity re
spectable; who polish the chains of low desire and gild the
soul's dungeon walls; who—worse than all—(in the form of
a comely personality) lead foul lusts and secret crimes to the
baptism and the communion. Nay; such are not vulgar
sinners; nor will an ordinary atonement suffice for these.
A righteous retribution will doubtless banish them from
Heaven, and leave them to wander afar—until, like the lost
Peri, they move the crystal bars of Paradise by tears of
penitence.

CHAPTER XII.

MENTAL ELECTROTYPING ON VITAL SURFACES.

Relations of Light and Electricity to Vegetable Chemistry—Prismatic office of the Flowers—Electrotyping on the body of a living Man—Philosophy of marking Children – Relations of Poetry and Pictures to Ideality and Beauty – Influence of a Mouse and a Minister—Reproduction of the Golden Locks, and Reflection of the Violet Ray—John the Baptist and the Boy with one Suspender—A mournful Case—Results of Obedience to the Law

IN the organic chemistry of the living world Electricity and Light are the ever-active agents on whose subtile powers the most delicate processes in Nature constantly depend. We are assured by curious scientific experimenters that the growth of plants has been immensely stimulated by electrical currents artificially generated, and directed to their roots. When this agent is thus set free, it moves the grosser elements through which the currents are transmitted, or as far as the electric excitation extends, stimulating molecular attraction, changing the polarities and the relations of the ultimate atoms, modifying and determining chemical affinities and combinations—so that the assimilation of foreign particles i. greatly accelerated, and the vegetable organism correspond ingly enlarged. It is also worthy of remark, that such trees as have *pointed, needle-shaped leaves*, like the pine, are invariably *evergreens*. This fact suggests the idea that possibly

the innumerable points which such trees present may so attract the atmospheric electricity as not only to preserve the
fluidity of the sap in the lowest temperature, but also to
prevent its receding from the exposed surfaces of the branches
when the mercury falls below the freezing point.

That light is indispensable in the chemistry of the vegetable
kingdom, must be apparent to every observer. The meanest
shrub, or the humblest wayside flower makes silent but significant proclamation of this truth. The germs that are buried
in the soil all sprout upward toward the ethereal regions of
the atmosphere, and never downward toward the center of
the earth. By a law of Nature they all reach out after the
light. The flowers open with the morning, and close when
day retires beyond the evening star. The rich verdure that
clothes the fields and forests is fresh and beautiful, as if, at
the world's baptism, an emerald sphere had been fused in the
sun; and all the gorgeous colors of the floral empire are born
of LIGHT! The flowers are the living prisms in whose delicate and beautiful structures the primal rays are mysteriously
separated, variously combined, and reflected with such purity
and intensity as admits of no successful imitation by human
effort, aided by the most accomplished art.

The rays reflected from the outlines of an object to the
eye leave its image on the choroid membrane; or, passing
through the camera, produce a semblance of its form, with
appropriate lights and shadows, on any delicate surface made
sensitive by a suitable chemical preparation. In a similar
manner the forms and, to some extent, the colors of objects
may be *electrotyped* on the external surfaces of living human
bodies. I believe there are several well-authenticated facts

illustrative of this singular susceptibility. It is not long since it was stated in the public journals that a man who was standing near a tree when it was struck by lightning, immediately presented a vivid picture of the tree on the exposed side of his body. While he was not fatally injured by the shock, it would nevertheless appear that the passage of the current so near him acted on the chemical constituents of his body with such power as to electrotype the nearest object on the cuticle. It is also alleged that the bodies of several persons killed by lightning have exhibited a similar phenomenon.

The singular effects produced on the unborn child by the sudden mental emotions of the mother are remarkable examples of this kind of electrotyping on the sensitive surfaces of living forms. It is doubtless true that the mind's action, in such cases, may increase or diminish the molecular deposites in the several portions of the system. The precise place which each separate particle assumes in the new organic structure may be determined by the influence of thought or feeling. If in the mother there exists any unusual tendency of the vital forces to the brain, at the critical period, there will be a similar cerebral development and activity in the offspring. A lady who, during the period of gestation, was chiefly employed in reading the poets, and in giving form to her day-dreams of the ideal world, at the same time gave to her child (in phrenological parlance,) large *Ideality* and a highly imaginative turn of mind. Some time since I met with a youth who has finely molded limbs and a symmetrical form throughout. His mother has a large, lean, attenuated frame, that does not offer so much as a single suggestion of the beautiful. The boy is doubtless indebted for his fine form to the presence of a beautiful French lithograph in his mother's sleeping apartment, and which presented for her contemplation the faultless form of a naked child.

Any object of intense desire, or that occasions sudden surprise or extreme fear, is liable to be impressed on the fœtus. These effects are most frequent among women whose minds and nervous systems are most active and impressible. By this psycho-electrical action external objects are instantly pictured on the delicate surface of the living form. This sudden involuntary action of the passions of the mind on and through the forces of the body, has produced many startling effects, and thousands of human beings carry with them through life the living illustrations—sometimes mournful in the extreme—of this mysterious power. On one occasion, after the delivery of a lecture in a small town in Central New York, I went to the house of Mr. K——, to pass the night. My theme had been, the power of the mind as exhibited in the organic formation and vital action of the body, and also in the various expressions of which the human face is susceptible. Mrs. C——, who was a member of the household, intimated a desire to exhibit a marked illustration of the subject. Accordingly, calling her little son, of the age of three years, to her side, she exposed his back to the inspection of the company. Between his shoulders there was a most perfect representation of a mouse. The mark—which was elevated somewhat above the surrounding surface—was literally covered with a thick coat of fine hair, like that of the animal represented ; and, what was still more surprising, the cuticle also precisely resembled the skin of a mouse.

This was the mind's work of an instant ; and while such facts demonstrate its supremacy over the elements of matter, they also indicate the danger—under like circumstances—of yielding to sudden impulses, and the importance of a supreme self-control.

The operation of this psycho-physiological law has subjected more than one innocent woman to grave suspicion.[1] Mere admiration of a person—if the emotion be continuous and strong—may suffice to impress the image of the admired object—more or less perfectly—on the offspring. That remarkable effects are produced in this way, the intelligent reader will not be disposed to deny ; and surely the philosophical observer will not be the first to indulge in uncharitable suspicions of female infidelity, should his children resemble some one else rather than himself. Some years since the writer was acquainted with a married lady, who lived in Fairfield county, Conn., and was universally respected and esteemed for her exemplary life and unblemished character. She was strongly attached to her church ; and her pastor—who was an earnest and forcible speaker—realized her ideal of early and uncorrupted manhood. The lady was accustomed to listen—on each succeeding Sabbath—to his eloquent discourses, with reverent and wrapt attention. She possessed a lively imagination, and a strong, but doubtless a strictly legitimate interest in the young clergyman ; and the image so often presented to the eye and the mind, was transmitted to another. During the second year

---

[1] It would seem from the account given in Genesis, (chapter xxx,) that the patriarch Jacob understood this law, and that it enabled him to practice a pious fraud, whereby he secured to himself the flocks of Laban.

of the ministry of Mr. ——, in that place, the lady referred to became the mother of a son, who, from his birth, was observed to resemble the minister ; nor is the likeness less apparent since the child has become a tall and graceful youth.

A gentleman of our acquaintance, who has very dark eyes, hair and beard, is wedded to a lady with brown hair, and a complexion not lighter than his own. Of nine children—the offspring of their marriage—six are living, and, with a single exception, they all have dark, straight hair and hazel eyes. Indeed, for several generations, not a single member of either family has had curly hair. The exceptional case is a fair youth with large, blue, expressive eyes and golden locks, with a natural tendency to curl. Some time before his birth the parents had occasion to spend a month with a family in Boston, where there was a radiant child with delicate skin, mild blue eyes, and a profusion of sunny curls. The lady visitor became deeply interested in that beautiful child, and often gazed at it with rapturous admiration and delight. The strong impulse of the mind thus *electrotyped the image on her own offspring*, so regulating the subtile processes of the vital chemism, as not only to determine its general complexion, but also the precise color of the hair, and even blending the sublimated elements in the organic chemistry of the eye with such nice precision as to fix and reflect the violet ray.

The human mind thus leaves a multitude of images— beautiful and terrible—not only on the delicate organization through which it perpetually manifests its powers—and which doubtless contains the mystical records of all its feeling, thought and action—but the mental impulses, when sufficiently intensified, are reproduced in those who come after. If such external objects and scenes as occasion the mental excitement, leave no visible outlines on the face or form, they may still be expressed in another way, and be no less distinguishable. A gentleman who resides in Le Roy, N. Y., in an interview with the writer, some time since, related a singular fact, that may be appropriately introduced in this connection. His wife had a beautiful picture of John the Baptist hanging in her room. The figure was in a nude state, except the loins, which were encircled with the girdle of camel's hair, supported by a single strap passing over one shoulder. The lady being in delicate health for some time, (antecedent to the birth of a son, now some sixteen years of age,) had occasion to spend much of her time on a couch from which the picture was constantly exposed to view. The youth referred to presents one of the greatest novelties in the category of psychological phenomena. It is a curious fact that *he will never wear but one suspender!* If commanded to put on *a pair,* he will obey ; but he is quite sure to have them *both over the same shoulder that supports the strap and the girdle in the picture.*

I well remember a young man, whose earth-life, of some thirty years' duration, was the frightful embodiment and expression of one terrible scene. He had not opened his eyes to behold the light of the natural world, when a desolating tornado passed over his native town. The tall oaks, which had braved the storms of centuries, bowed low as the slender grass bends in the summer's breeze ; or, rather as the grain is leveled by the reaper's sickle. It was a fatal hour ! The sufferings of many years seemed condensed into one awful moment of unspeakable horror, and the terrible scene cast its dark shadow over the whole life of a human being. That tempest was reproduced in that man. For nearly thirty years—and until the close of his mortal existence—his eyes rolled in their sockets with a strange delirious expression. Ever and anon he sighed heavily, as the winds sigh through the tall trees ; and his head and all his limbs swayed to and fro, perpetually, as the forest boughs are moved when the breath of the tempest sweeps over them. Poor mortal! his melancholy life is over, and he has found rest at last where the storms of earth and time shall disturb his repose no more!

This case graphically illustrates the action of a law that operates as irresistibly as gravitation throughout the realm of our organic existence, and which is scarcely less manifest in its ordinary effects. By disregarding this law our children may be monsters in their physical conformation ; or, with respect to mind and character, they may be the breathing, conscious shadows of gigantic wrongs—for all moral, social, and political evils are but the reflected images of the imperfect conditions under which we "live and move and have our being." On the contrary, let that law be wisely respected, and those who shall succeed the present generation—in the drama of practical life and the records of authentic history—will present superior types of womanly grace and manly perfection ; and thus the Race may advance, in all that imparts a real value to life and true dignity to the human character, until the glory of a moral transfiguration —like a mantle of light and a crown of joy—encircles the universal Humanity.

CHAPTER XIII.

INFLUENCE OF OBJECTS AND IDEAS
UPON THE MIND AND THE MORALS.

Definition of Beauty—The Views of Kant, Burke, Hogarth, Alison, Dugald Stewart and Goethe—Influence of Music—Its action on the nervous circulation of Animals—As a Remedial Agent—Case of Saul—Melodies of Nature—Irresistible power of Gentleness and Love—Miss Dix in the Maniac's cell—The Apostle John, Fenelon, Oberlin and Howard—The Mystical Book of the Recording Angel—An essential Law of Organized Existence—Assimilation of Moral Elements—How we are transformed by our Ideals—Materialism of Modern Utilitarians—Material Symbols of Religious Ideas—The Goths in Italy—Grecian and Roman Art—Lessons from Nature—A Poet's Vision—The Visitor in White Raiment—Fashioning the Angel Within.

"A Thing of Beauty is a joy forever."

ACCORDING to Kant, Beauty is the regular conformation of an object of Nature or Art, in which the mind intuitively perceives this configuration, without reflecting upon its ultimate design or purpose. Burke seriously supposed that beauty consisted in small forms, smooth surfaces and delicate structures. The celebrated Hogarth, in his Analysis, found it in curved lines, whilst Alison insisted that " if there were any original and independent beauty, in any *particular form*, the preference of this form would be early and decidedly marked, both in the language of children and the opinions of mankind." While acute critics and great artists have disagreed respecting the sources of beauty, as well as the philosophy of its effects on the mind

and character, I may be allowed to discover this supreme
excellence wherever they respectively found it, and also
where they did not so much as look for it at all.

It will be observed that the definitions already cited,
virtually restrict the application of the term to visible outlines and material proportions ; and to such other superficial graces and aspects as the mind perceives through the
direct agency of the senses. We can scarcely accept such
definitions so long as the very *sources* of all outward beauty
are internal, invisible and divine. If the harmony of the
several parts of the human body, and of all external forms,
constitutes physical beauty, there must also be intellectual,
moral and spiritual beauty ; and these consist in the symmetrical development, harmonious union, and esthetic action
of all the human faculties and affections. To be sufficiently comprehensive, the definition of Beauty must apply
to all physical, intellectual and moral excellence. The
Universe is its majestic temple, adorned with expressive
symbols, and consecrated by a pure and perpetual ministry.
Every splendid creation of God in Nature and of human
genius in Art, is an altar before which men admire and
adore the indwelling Divinity. This is no profane adoration. The mere Mammon worshiper may, indeed, be regarded as a miserable idolator ; but Life—Genius—Love
Beauty—all these are earthly revelations of the Absolute
Perfection. The glory of the Shekinah shines out from the
material forms of the world, as through a diaphanous vail,
and in the light of this perpetual transfiguration we

　　　—" Look through Nature up to nature's God."

If we restrict the application of the term to the works

of Nature or Art, Beauty must nevertheless be understood to comprehend many of those lofty attributes and qualities which the word *Sublime* is especially used to distinguish. But the terms are by no means synonymous. The one may be properly applied to whatever is fitted to produce pleasurable sensations; on the other hand, the scenes that inspire the deepest awe, and the objects and events which excite the greatest terror, may be replete with the elements of sublimity. It was observed by Dugald Stewart that the distinctions of several authors are not usually warranted by a fundamental difference. While Beauty and Sublimity have many attributes in common, it will be perceived, that each is characterized by peculiar elements which distinguish it from the other. Several writers, including the eloquent Burke himself, feeling at times that any definition of Beauty that restricts it to symmetry of form, harmony of color, and " poetry of motion," is too contracted to express the whole truth, have been constrained to admit in fact, at least, if not in words—that Beauty consists in all such qualities as awaken emotions of tenderness, affection and delight. [1]

---

[1] Goethe's perception of beauty was too exquisite to be expressed ; and in his judgment the divine charm was so intangible as neither to admit of precise description nor logical explanations. The Poet of Weimar—regarded by a princely admirer as " the third in the great triumvirate with Homer and Shakspeare"—thus illustrates the subject :

"Beauty is inexplicable. It appears to us a dream, when we contemplate the works of the great artists. It is a hovering, floating. and glittering shadow, whose outline eludes the grasp of definition. Mendelssohn, and others, tried to catch beauty as a butterfly, and pin it down for inspection. They have succeeded in the same way as one succeeds with the butterfly ; the poor animal trembles and struggles, and its brightest colors are gone ; or if you catch it without spoiling the colors, you have at best a stiff and awkward corpse. It wants that which is most essential, namely, life—*spirit*, which spreads beauty on every thing."

The word beauty is not ordinarily restricted to things cognizable by the vision alone. By a very natural transition it is applied to musical sounds, and also to whatever either addresses the imagination, the reason or the moral sense, in such a manner as to gratify the human faculties and affections. The sense of beauty is expressed with great delicacy and irresistible power in harmonic combinations of sounds ; or, more properly, by a succession of atmospheric vibrations occurring in consonance with the laws of Acoustics. The gentle undulations of the air, occasioned by the regular vibration of a sonorous body, produce astonishing effects on the nervous systems of men and beasts. The inferior animals are never wholly insensible of the mysterious influence of Music. Even the *Reptilia* yield to the irresistible fascination. The native Americans and the serpent charmers of India have this singular power in a remarkable degree. When the Indian juggler sings a slow tune, or blows gently on his instrument made of reeds, the serpents raise their heads and move to suit the measure of the music.

---

[1] The following curious illustration of the mysterious influence of music on the nervous circulation, and consequently on the functions of animals, is extracted from one of Madame Bretano's letters to the German poet, Goethe :

"This winter I had a spider in my room ; when I played upon the guitar it descended hastily into a web, which it spun lower down. I placed myself before it and drew my fingers across the strings ; it was clearly seen how it vibrated through its little limbs. When I changed the cord it changed its movements—they were involuntary ; by each different arpeggio, the rhythm in its motions was also changed. It cannot be otherwise—this little being was joy-penetrated or spirit-imbued, as long as my music lasted ; when the strain was ended, it retired.

Another little play-fellow was a mouse ; but he was more taken by vocal music. He chiefly made his appearance when I sung the gamut ; the fuller I swelled the tones, the nearer he came......My master was much delighted

This subtile and masterly power over the mind and nervous system of Man has been observed by physicians, physiologists and philosophers, in almost every age ; and so remarkable have been its effects, and withal so beneficial, that it has been employed as a remedial agent in certain forms of disease. There may be different opinions respecting the influence of music on the general character ; but all agree that it serves—temporarily, at least—to subdue the baser passions, and to awaken emotions of serene and intense joy. The Biblical student will recall the case of Saul, king of Israel, who being subject to a species of madness, was recommended to have recourse to music as a remedy for his gloomy hallucination. Accordingly, he sent for the Hebrew poet and musician, the tones of whose lyre subdued the nervous tension and mental agitation of the king, as the minstrel's skillful hand unbound

" —— the sleeping soul of Harmony.

There are few who have not felt the power of Music. The restless child falls asleep on its mother's bosom with the sweet lullaby sounding in its ear. The worshiper in the Cathedral service feels the fire of devotion kindling in his heart, and a subtle influence running along every nerve of sense, as the lofty arches echo the solemn strain. All Nature is God's temple ; and every reverent soul worships in the groves or by the waves while the elements chant their wild melodies among the boughs and in the shells. The pin-

---

with the little animal ; he took great care not to disturb him. When I sung my songs and varying melodies, he seemed to be afraid ; he could not endure it and hastened away."

nacles and the caves are tuneful, as if Euterpe had inspired
the Geni of the mountain and the sea. We feel a mysterious sense of a divine presence when music gently rocks the
cradle of the atmosphere. Under this mysterious influence
the destructive passions seek repose, and the wild delirium
of feverish and brutal desire is subdued. Even the furious
maniac, whom no man could bind, has been chained by a
harp-string. Music is medicine for madness ; and whoever
would at once restrain and restore the madman should go to
him with a gentle voice and Moore's Melodies. Twine
musical chords around his troubled spirit, and his captivity
will only make him gentle and joyful. If wild beasts are
thus tamed, rude savages made civil, and the fierce maniac
rendered harmless as a little child, who shall resist the
saving power of Music ?

> " Who ne'er hath felt her hand assuasive steal
> Along his heart—that heart may never feel.
> 'Tis hers to chain the passions, soothe the soul,
> To snatch the dagger and to dash the bowl
> From Murder's hand ; to smooth the couch of care,
> Extract the thorns and scatter roses there."

I am not in error in ascribing a divine efficacy and redeeming power to that moral beauty which is displayed in
gentle words and righteous deeds. The triumphs of the
celebrated Pinel amongst the inmates of the mad-house in
Paris, afford striking illustrations of the majesty and divinity of that power. But we have at least one conspicuous example at home. It is recorded that Miss Dix, on one
occasion, visited the cell of a maniac who was so wild and
violent that he was kept constantly chained. She commenced reading the Sermon on the Mount, in a voice modu-

lated with great delicacy and irresistible pathos. In the gloom of that lonely cell, a gentle woman—frail in form but divinely strong and beautiful in the purpose of her heart and life—communed with the common Father. By her side was one whose soul was dark as the dismal precincts of his own dungeon. The smile that in youth illuminated those features was soft and radiant as the clear light of a spring morning without clouds. But the midday glory of his life was lost in a deep eclipse. Through the mournful gloom the fierce lightnings of disordered passion gleamed out like electric flames in the midnight sky; while the tangled locks floated wildly over the terrible brow that once had been the throne of Reason!

But the madman was not yet beyond the influence of the divine harmonies. The words of the gentle minister were like oil poured over the troubled waves of feeling. His paroxysms gradually subsided. The tender sympathy and spiritual beauty of the being before him softened his expression and subdued his frenzy. She was to him an Angel walking on life's troubled sea, whose influence was silent yet sublime as the power that stilled the waves of Galilee. The wretched man bowed his head and wept; and when at length the modest suppliant arose to depart he attempted to embrace her, and declared that she was an angel sent from Heaven to comfort him in his solitary despair. Such are the significant illustrations of the poet's sentiment:

> —" Mightier far
> Than strength of nerve, or sinew, or the chains,
> The heavy bolts. and bars and dungeon walls,
> Is Love."—

Love, however manifested, is a great moral harmonizer, whose polyglot is comprehended by all races of men ; whose inspirations, like sunshine, clothe the moral world with perennial beauty, and filling even the wildernesses of human life with fresh flowers and immortal fruits. The words and deeds of some men are characterized by a grand harmony, that renders existence itself a sweet symphony or a solemn psalm. It is never in vain that such men strive to harmonize the moral elements, for the world must feel their power. When we are tempest-tost, they stay the restless "tides in the affairs of men"; they span the darkness of the retiring storm with the illuminated symbol of a great promise ; and when the deluge of unholy passion subsides they open the windows of the ark that the dove may return. The name and the precepts of Jesus have been all-powerful over the disciples of every period and country, chiefly because his nature and his life were characterized by the highest elements of moral excellence and spiritual beauty. The Apostle John, Archbishop Fenelon, and John Fredrick Oberlin gave illustrations of the highest types of beauty ; while the life of Howard was a pathetic overture to the great unwritten oratorio of the Captives Redeemed. Such men banish discord from the scale of being, and make life musical in spite of those who live.

We are now to consider the influence of external scenes and objects in the development of the human mind and the formation of character. The forms and phenomena of Nature make their impressions on the sensories and leave their images in the consciousness. Owing to the prominence of present objects and events, they may seldom or never be awakened in the external memory. Indeed, they appear

to come and go in endless succession. To the merely sensuous mind they are swept away like names or figures traced
in the sand on the sea-shore. Each passing wave of time
and sense obliterates the previous impression, however the
images remain in the soul forever. The consciousness is the
Book of Life wherein our thoughts and deeds are recorded.
Those mystical records are imperishable as the deepest lines
that mark the separate individualities among men, and in
the great Hereafter they will be recognized as the spirit's
immortal possessions.

By a law of association those images are sometimes revived, when forgotten thoughts, and the shadowy forms of
things perished from the earth, glide through the silent halls
of memory. Occasionally, they come out in bolder relief;
chiefly in some great emergency, when a sudden shock jars
the material connections of the spirit; and we realize, for
a moment, that we are standing on the confines of the invisible life and world. At such a time, in the ordeal that tries
the soul, images of all the past start out—sudden and
specter-like—from the shadows, and appear in the vivid
outline and startling detail of solemn reality. Thus, when
the vail of flesh shall be removed, our souls will stand forth
as living monuments, inscribed with the records of all feeling
—all thought—all action, which we have sensed, conceived,
or performed from first to last, to be reviewed in the all-
revealing light of eternity.

This is neither a mere fancy nor an idle speculation; but
a truth of inconceivable importance in its bearings on the
development and destiny of the Race. The poet's idea that
we become a part of whatever is around us, and the decla-

ration of an ancient author that, " as a man thinketh *so is he*," are manifestly true as philosophical propositions ; for all things that occasion sensation or awaken thought, become incorporate elements in our individual character and social life. Our physical, intellectual and moral individuality is but the sum of all our experiences, organically combined and endowed with personality. Thus the Revelator and the poet discovered and announced one of the grand essential laws of human nature, and of all organized existence. Plants and animals are known to partake of the nature of the substances they assimilate ; nor can man be unlike the elements which nourish his body or serve as food for contemplation. All surrounding forms and substances contribute to supply his physical and spiritual necessities. In one way or another they enter into the composition of the body ; they awaken sensations, mold the forms of thought, or otherwise influence the manner and the issues of life.

Men are ever transformed into the essential spirit and express images of their Ideals, by a law that operates as uniformly as gravitation. In those wild, inhospitable and desolate regions, where Nature assumes her roughest garb, and Art exhibits only rude and ungraceful forms, we find men either savages or inclined to barbarism. The images of frightful objects and terrible events are like themselves, and hence they darken and disfigure the mind. Surround a man with horrible imagery ; place objects on every side which excite apprehension, resentment and disgust, and their terrible outlines, deep shadows and vivid colors, will be represented with fearful fidelity in his soul.

In the Pacific Isles where men are cannibals, every child

inherits a life of disgusting brutality. The images impressed on the young mind vitiate the springs of being, distort the infant visage, and brutalize the deeds of manhood. Men never think of going to the Cannibal Islands to complete their esthetic acquirements ; for the reason, doubtless, that every person endowed with common sense has some perception of the effect of surrounding objects on human development. In India and other unfavored portions of the earth, where the most imposing exhibitions of Art consist of clumsy idols whose open jaws, glaring eyes and monstrous forms shock the nerves of the civilized world, we find that the human mind and character are fashioned after such brutal ideals. Even the religion of the people is of the same general character. Juggernaut is the principal divinity, and his worship is celebrated by obscene rites and exhibitions of shocking barbarity. Travelers have assured us that, the road leading along the coast of Orissa to the temple of the great Idol, was paved with the bleaching skulls of millions who have perished by the way. Thus when hideous forms and corrupt ideas cast their shadows on the senses and the souls of men, they are—by a physical and moral necessity—incorporated with the essential elements of the human constitution. This immutable law is thus revealed in the mournful illustrations of its power.

But wherever Nature puts on her robes of light; where Art consecrates temples, and the ideal perfection is recognized ; there the elements of beauty —by a natural process of assimilation—become essentially our own. There, also, we find the instrumentalities of human progress, and the work of intellectual culture and moral refinement actually

going on. It is important, therefore, that we associate—as
far as possible—with beautiful forms and divine ideas, that
we may imbibe their essential spirit, and grow into their
likeness in outward form and actual life. Such ideas and
objects as disturb the mind, and hence not only darken the
soul, but interrupt the harmony of its natural life and physical relations, should be promptly and forever dismissed, *so
far as this course does not involve a neglect of individual responsibilities and the public welfare.* If we desire to escape
contamination we should cease to observe and think of such
things as defile the man. Reading the lives of traitors,
pirates and other abandoned criminals; witnessing public
executions, and listening to inflammatory and vindictive
appeals to the baser passions—all belong to the same category. They inevitably quicken and strengthen the brute
instincts in human nature, and hence they positively pervert
the faculties of the mind, excite the destructive propensities,
and degrade the whole character.

If these views of human nature, and especially of one of
the essential laws of its development are admitted to be
well founded, it will appear that the subject, in its moral
aspects, is of vital importance. The wide publicity given
to the details of crime, by the newspaper press, is a most
fruitful source of evil. It imposes no salutary restraint
on those who are already shameless and abandoned; but
the young mind and heart are constantly darkened and
depraved by perusing the frightful catalogue. Indeed, the
community is thus constantly corrupted by a practice which
the calm judgment and enlightened conscience must condemn. It is very questionable whether the ends of justice

are in any way promoted by publishing all criminal transactions, since the perpetrators are thus admonished to keep
out of the way of the ministers of law. In this respect we
can conceive of no adequate compensation for the manifold
evils consequent on the course and conduct of the secular
press. The conservation of the peace and safety of society
will scarcely be accomplished by such means. On the contrary, a common benefit would be conferred could the confessions and convictions under the criminal code be confined
to the courts. For this reason we would seal up the annals
of crime, and shut out from the rising generation the scenes
that darken and defile the young mind and heart. Hew
down the gallows, and wash the bloody stains from the
magisterial ermine and the priestly robe! Let the record
of the law perish, and the memory of the execution and its
infernal engine be blotted out forever!

Kant observes that the pleasure inspired by the elements
of beauty does not depend on any idea of utility ; and it is
for this reason that our modern utilitarians insist that it is
a useless possession. But the simple fact that the pleasure
derived from this source does not arise from any association with the idea of material uses, sufficiently indicates its
unselfish and spiritual nature. It is only because the elements of essential beauty can not be coined into dimes, exchanged for merchandise, or otherwise made subservient to
the corporeal appetites, that they are thus lightly esteemed.
The vulgar conception of utility is the offspring of the
grossest materialism. Those who still cherish it are unim-
aginative and sensuous mortals, who would either buy or
sell the Elysian Fields for a cotton plantation! They would

recommend the Muses to learn and teach agriculture. If
an Angel should visit them, they would expect him to report the state of the stock market on " the other side ;" and
they are prone to prize Heaven chiefly as an office of insurance against destruction by fire! O, ye sensible and
practical men, who never waste your time in dreaming—
who never make an investment where it does not pay—is
there no god but gold? Can no power break through
the concretion of sensuality that covers your souls? And
is there nothing in Beauty and Divinity to divert your attention from the world, ye whose god is Mammon, and
whose treasures are laid up in deep vaults and iron safes?

In this commercial age we are not likely to over-estimate
the Fine Arts as instrumentalities of individual development
and general progress. We should rejoice to witness anything like a proper appreciation of their silent ministry and
irresistible power on the mind and the life of a people.
Show us a tribe that has no love of beauty, or a country
destitute of Art, and we need look no further for a barbarous people and scenes of disgusting brutality. Coarseness,
vulgarity and crime, are even more frequently associated
with the rites of Religion than with the ideal conceptions
and artistic creations of essential Loveliness. It is a significant fact that the religious sentiment may coëxist with a
depraved moral sense, and is often strongly manifested
by persons of perverted passions and an abandoned life.
At the same time the elegant Arts not only contribute to
subdue the savage nature, to promote civilization and a
higher mental culture, but they also help us to recognize the
Divinity whose presence is veiled in every form of Beauty.

The uncultivated mind has no power to recognize essential principles and abstract ideas. Hence the multitudes require some sensuous image or representation of whatever is to be apprehended, admired or worshiped. The Roman Catholic Church, realizing the necessity of its disciples, annually circulates millions of prints and plaster casts, representing the most touching and impressive scenes in the lives of Christ and his Apostles. Everything that reminds the disciple of his Master has a sacred significance, and the memorials of imprisoned and martyred saints at once inspire his reverence and soften his heart. Every Catholic has a picture of the Virgin, or wears the cross as the expressive symbol of fidelity and patient suffering, and the assurance of his salvation. The reader may not require such material emblems of moral truths and spiritual realities. It is the province of the highly developed mind to dispense with the shadows of its thoughts, and to lay aside the perishable symbols of its faith and worship, while it reverently walks into the very Pantheon of the gods.

But the time has not come when even the more enlightened classes can profitably part with the physical forms of the objects of their affection and adoration. The worshiper still claims the symbols of his religion, and the lover sighs for something tangible to embrace. Perhaps we all prefer—at least in some qualified sense—to find and to grasp the substance *in the shadow.* There is a kind of universal language in Painting as in Music ; and no oral speech can better portray the delicate shades of feeling, or give to the stormy passions a more forcible expression. Pictures are mute but eloquent teachers. Forms, apparently instinct

with life, passion, and sentiment, seem to start out from the
silent walls of our dwellings, or they gaze at us through the
dim light of ancient galleries and deserted mansions. Each
is the embodiment of an idea, rendered more captivating
and impressive by the manner of its expression.   We recognize Painting, Sculpture and Music as the graces whose
triple influence surrounds the impersonal presence of Beauty ;
and we find in their purest creations the distant but radiant
images of the Divine Perfection.   Their ministry softens the
ruder features and aspects of this world ; it restrains and
spiritualizes the passions; it inspires purer impulses and
nobler motives, and elevates the world's common thought
and practical life.

There is a tradition that when the Goths were masters
of Athens they preserved the public Libraries, because they
were presumed to "contribute to the effeminacy of the citizens."   Had those barbarous tribes been refined and en-
nobled by the contemplation of the more perfect creations of
Genius, they would certainly have spared the great monuments of Art when they overran Italy in the fifth century.
It was a false religious idea that kindled the fiery zeal and
nerved the strong arms of those ruthless iconoclasts.   They
led a life of warlike adventure, and even coveted death on
the bloody field that they might be honored with the society
of heroes in the great palace and the presence of Odin.
With such religious conceptions they did not hesitate to de-
molish the civil institutions of the Roman Empire, and to
bury Literature and the Arts in a common grave.   But the
languages of the Greeks and Romans were immortal ; and
those who brought out from their national sepulchres—after

the lapse of centuries—the splendid remains of Grecian and
Roman art, revived the love of Beauty, and awakened the
slumbering spirit that subsequently gave birth to Michael
Angelo, Raphael, Correggio and Titian, and that still inspires the living masters and the true lovers of Art in every
part of the civilized world.

Outward objects are often suggestive of spiritual ideas.
Our first and our deepest religious impressions are inspired
by the grand and beautiful forms and phenomena of Nature.
Nor is this inspiration less divine because an observation of
natural scenes and objects affords the occasion. The ancient revelators were perhaps most frequently and highly
inspired when engaged in such reflections. The Hebrew
Poet was both humbled and exalted by the grandeur of the
Universe. In the midst of his sublime contemplation, he
exclaimed, " When I consider the heavens, the work of thy
fingers, the moon and stars which thou hast ordained, Lord,
what is man?" And considering " the lilies of the field,"
Jesus declared with emphasis, that Solomon in all his glory
was not arrayed like these. Indeed, Nature is never wanting in religious suggestions to the enlightened and reverent
soul. Thus the earth and sea—the transparent ether—the
shining worlds, that sentinel the heaven of heavens—all great
and solemn and sublime—naturally dispose the mind to devout meditations.

Nature is a most eloquent preacher, and he is cold at
heart who does not realize the divinity of her ministry.
Those whom the world has not corrupted are never insensible ; and in childhood, especially, we feel her power.
When Morning like a chaste virgin goes forth in robes of

light to walk on the tops of the mountains, the soul of
Youth follows her like a spirit of prayer. Spring comes and
breaths above the graves of the sleeping germs ; they spring
up and blossom ; and their resurrection to more abundant
life, is an assurance that being and beauty are immortal.
The rose that blooms by the cottage door blushes when it is
kissed by the sun-beams, and loving inspirations kindle in
the mind and warm the heart.   And when the skylark sings
in the morning, at the windows of heaven, his song. is a
sweet suggestion, that Nature is full of music, and that the
objects and aims of life should be above all groveling and
earthly things.   It is with a feeling of profound adoration
that we gaze at the stars ; and if we meditate by the sea,
where the winds and waves discourse of the Supreme Majesty, we hear divine voices in the unrestrained elements ;
and solemn reverberations, swelling

" Over each isle and continent and sea,
Waking, enrapturing earth's down-trodden nations,
With God the Father's great command—Be Free !"

If the foregoing illustrations present at best but a feeble
expression of an intense conviction, it is because language
furnishes only a narrow and clumsy vehicle wherein Truth
rides with difficulty.   However, the influence of physical
objects and earthly scenes in the development of the human
mind and the formation of character, must be so obvious
as to render further elucidation unnecessary.   That men are
transformed into the moral and material likeness of the
forms they observe, the natures they contemplate, and the
ideal conceptions they entertain and cherish, will scarcely
be denied ; and we may, therefore, dismiss this part of the

subject with a single additional illustration. I find the suggestion in a little poem entitled, " Robin Gray."[1]

> " He dreamed that the angel Gabriel came
> And stood by his cottage door,
> And a wondrous light from his raiment fell,
> And shone on the sanded floor."

Robin gazed at the celestial visitor with deep amazement and silent admiration ; and when the vision departed—and while the illuminated shadow yet lingered in his soul—he felt an intense desire to preserve the image of that divine personality. Inspired with the thought, he commenced to mold the form of the Angel in marble. In the early morning he went to his task and toiled until the evening shades appeared. Thus he labored, day after day ; and ever and anon the Angel came and stood by him in visions of the night to revive the waning impression.

But Robin grew thin and pale, and a strange light—like the mysterious glory of transfiguration—shone out through the sweet solemnity of his countenance. The vigor of his arm was impaired day by day, and yet the marble remained rough and cold in his hands. The divine form did not appear in the stone ;

> " But the Angel within his breast each day,
> More luminous grew and bright."

One morning an early visitor found Robin prostrate on the floor of his little cell. He was pale, passionless, and pulseless as the marble that, even in death, he still grasped with the energy of a living purpose. The materialist gazed on the scene and he said, alas, it is a failure ! He lived for

---

[1] Contributed to the Shekinah by Mrs. S. S. Smith.

a single purpose to which he consecrated life and all his powers ; but this is the end of life, and his work is unfinished ! Nay ! not so in the poet's vision, nor in fact. *That was not the end of life.* In one corner of that little cell— invisible to mortal eyes—stood Robin Gray, clad in the robes of a great immortality ; and stamped on every lineament—with such vivid distinctness as face answers to face in the untroubled waters—was the image of the Angel.

If we may accept the poetic idea, that a beautiful statue is concealed in every block of marble which may be discovered by the skill of the sculptor, we may at least entertain the thought that an Angel reposes in the rudest human form, which some skillful moral artist may awaken and exhibit *en alto relievo.* In this work no one can labor sincerely and yet labor in vain. It is true our objects may be misinterpreted or disregarded by others ; and after long forbearance, earnest effort, and patient suffering, we may not develop the Angel where we waited and watched for its advent. But the failure, at most, can only be apparent ; since every such effort must serve to mold our own natures into the likeness of the grand Ideal that stands revealed in the temple of the soul. A Christian Apostle recognized this principle when he would have formed in the disciple, " the hope of glory," in the image of the Divine Man. If, then, our attempts to develop in others the celestial form and life on earth are not crowned with visible results, we may yet be accounted worthy of a sublime success. When the veil that obscures the moral vision is removed, and we stand at last in the clear light of the great Hereafter, all will be well if we shall have FASHIONED THE ANGEL WITHIN.

CHAPTER XIV.

RELATIONS OF MIND TO PERSONAL BEAUTY.

General Observations—The Fine Arts and Civilization—The Magic Isles—Influence of Ancient Greece on Modern Ideas—Value of Personal Beauty—The Author's Analysis—Prevalence of false Views—Reference to Headley's Letters from Italy—The Conceptions of French and Italian Ladies—Influence of the Mind on the Muscles—The History on the Wall—Expression as an element of Beauty—Creations of Ludovico Caracci, the Cyclops of Timanthes and the Cartoons of Raphael—Illustrations from practical Life—Desolating power of the Passions—Glory of a great Character.

> " Wt y tinge the cheek of youth ! The snowy neck
> Why load with jewels? W by anoint the hair?
> Oh, morial, scorn such arts ! but richly deck
> Thy soul with virtues."—Greek Poet.

OUTWARD Beauty is the sensuous image of a spiritual and divine Reality—the visible, though imperfect, expression of the invisible and absolute Perfection. The mind that is liberally endowed by Nature, and refined by culture and the contemplation of the most perfect ideals, is never insensible of the presence and the power of Beauty. Indeed, the inability to perceive this supreme excellence implies a radical defect in human nature, that is wholly incompatible with the highest intellectual, moral, and spiritual attainments. The love of Beauty adorns the earth with innumerable creations to delight the senses and the soul. It plants the myrtle and the rose in the wilderness; it makes the barren moors and desert solitudes blossom; it cultivates Oriental gardens, and rears splendid temples and palaces;

it inspired the great masters of Grecian Art, and they left
their carved memorials and pictured thoughts in the world's
Pantheon to awaken the esthetic sense in the barbaric mind;
to refine the taste of every succeeding age, and to redeem
the common life of the world from its grossness and sensuality. The truly spiritual mind—gifted with an acute perception of beauty—surveys the immortal images on the canvas
and the shadows cast in marble, and finds in them a revelation of the hidden, spiritual and divine excellence. From
the invisible Perfection the great artist derives his inspiration, and to that unseen Reality his aspirations constantly
ascend. Nor is the attempt to realize his prayer in the
embodiment of his Idea ever in vain; for he is a common
benefactor who invests the world with new attractions.

The love of Beauty is the worship of God. Nature and
Art—every fair and glorious creation of earth and sea
and sky—the human form and face divine, instinct with
life, passion and sentiment, or smiling in marble or on the
canvas—have all a sacred ministry—to inspire a love of
the Perfect and to fashion a Divine Ideal in the conscious
soul. Thus all beautiful things exert a redeeming influence
on Man. They refine the passions of our common nature,
while they lift us above the deformities of this present
world. All Nature is the revelation of a Spiritual Presence
in material forms, and the clearest elucidation of the Divine
perfections. There are enchanting melodies, eloquent sermons, sublime philosophies, great poems, and a Gospel of redeeming power—all embodied in the forms of the outward
world. These are expressive symbols of the everlasting
Life and Thought. There are also sweet lessons on the

cheek of innocence, in the bosom of love and in the eye of
genius, that we should learn and cherish. We can never
study them in vain, nor can it be irreverent to *imitate them*,
as far as we are able, for thus we approach the radiant foot-
prints of the Divine Artist, ' who made everything beautiful
in his time.'

The influence of the Fine Arts on our civilization and
the relations of all the forms of Beauty to the intellectual
development and moral elevation of the people, have seldom
been wisely estimated. It is quite certain that we are
indebted—in no small degree—to ancient Greece for an
acquaintance with the sources of Beauty, and for some of
the means of modern growth and refinement. Those magic
Isles—

"Where burning Sappho wept and sung,"

were consecrated to all that was most beautiful in Art. It
was in that charmed region that letters were invented ;
there the strings of the lyre first vibrated to harmonic
numbers ; there Homer sang his immortal song ; there lived
Solon and Lycurgus, and the fathers of theatrical tragedy.
A popular author has denominated the Grecian architecture an "artistic revelation," and the same may be said of
its sculptured forms, which have never been excelled.
While the philosophers and law-givers of ancient Greece
doubtless continue to exert a wide influence in molding the
Theology and the Legislation of all modern Christendom, it
is certain that her inspired masters in every department of
the Elegant Arts have for centuries contributed to foster a
love of the Beautiful, and human nature has been refined
and exalted. The noblest forms of Art have perhaps done

more to redeem the world from savagism, than all the religions on the face of the earth, Christianity alone excepted.
It would be a moral impossibility for a man to look at the
Graces every day for one year and remain an awkward
clown; nor would even a Barbarian think of offering human
sacrifices to Venus or Apollo.

We have defined Beauty to be, in the most comprehensive sense, the light and glory of the Divinity shining
through the material forms of the World. With such a definition, even *personal beauty*—of the sources of which I am
now to treat—is by no means to be lightly esteemed.[1] It
certainly inspires pleasurable sensations in every beholder,
and cannot, therefore, be a worthless treasure in the estimation of others. It unbars our doors to the stranger, and
gives him a passport to the confidence of his fellow-men,
and hence can never be useless to its possessor. We all
naturally associate the peculiarities of form, feature and
expression, with certain mental and moral characteristics;
and we seldom or never find the man—in his essential character—unlike the image he presents to the world. A
careful personal inspection for half an hour may reverse the
judgment founded on the most important testimony. It
will be found that even those who profess to disregard
personal appearances, generally form their own estimate of
the individual's mind and character from what they observe
in his exterior; nor are the greatest and most discerning

---

[1] Socrates called Beauty a short-lived tyranny; but Plato viewed it as a
privilege of Nature. Theophrastus said it was a silent cheat, whilst Aristotle affirmed that it was better than all the recommendations in the world.
Homer regarded it as a glorious natural gift, and Ovid esteemed it as a
favor bestowed by the gods.

minds frequent exceptions to the rule. The great dramatic Poet has said, respecting a beautiful human form,

" There's nothing ill can dwell in such a temple."

And all admit that *he* was a profound interpreter of human
nature. True, we may misinterpret the signs of character ;
but we can scarcely overlook them. They are too conspicuous to be readily concealed, and withal too deep and
lasting to be obliterated even by " Time's effacing fingers."
When the essential elements of beauty are harmoniously
blended, in one who is thus divinely commissioned to sway a
scepter over the realm of the affections, the attributes of the
celestial life are tangibly revealed on earth.   Milton thus
sings of such a being :

" Grace was in all her steps, heaven in her eyes,
In every gesture dignity and love."

The elements of personal beauty are chiefly comprehended
in symmetry of form and feature, in an agreeable association and blending of colors, in mingled softness, vivacity
and force of expression, and in the grace and " poetry of
motion." It is worthy of observation, that those who attach
the highest value to personal attractions, often make the
most fatal mistakes in their attempts to secure the coveted
boon.   In this country, especially, thousands vainly attempt to make up for their natural defects of form by the
most ludicrous efforts to conceal them, rather than commence and pursue such a course of physical exercise and dis
cipline as must inevitably give elasticity and vigor to the
different members, and rotundity to the whole body.   Instead of directing the latent energies of Nature to the full

accomplishment of her appropriate work, too many employ
the *costumer* to make up the form agreeably to the latest
decrees of imperial Fashion. They trouble themselves to
restrain and fetter their own natural powers, and then
make great sacrifices to patch up their imperfections. Such
persons—while they live and when they die—are but poor
effigies of human nature, which the sage and the savage
alike must regard with pity or derision. [1]

The same miserable infatuation is exhibited in the at
tempts to produce and to preserve the particular combinations of color necessary to the perfection of personal beauty.
Fair ladies pass their days in listless inactivity, in darkened
parlors, without the inspiration of the free air, and away
from the purple glories and the golden rays of the morning.
Their nights are spent at the rout, and in crowded banquet-
ting halls, until from the loss of natural repose at proper
seasons, the intoxication of unnatural excitements, untimely
and immoderate gratification of the appetites, the nervous
system is unstrung, the digestion impaired, the skin becomes

---

[1] In form the Italians excel us. Larger, fuller—they naturally aquire a
finer gait and bearing. It is astonishing that our ladies should persist in
that ridiculous notion, that a small waist is, and. *ex necessitate*, must be, beautiful. Why, many an Italian woman would cry for vexation, if she possessed such a waist as some of our ladies acquire only by a long and painful
process. I have sought the reason of this difference, and can see no other
than that the Italians have their glorious statuary continually before them
as models ; and hence endeavor to assimilate themselves to them ; whereas
our fashionables have no models except those French stuffed figures in the
windows of the milliners' shops. If an artist should presume to make a
statue with the shape that seems to be regarded with us as the perfection of
harmonious proportion, he would be laughed out of the city. It is a standing objection against the taste of our women, the world over, that they practically assert that a French dressmaker understands how they should be made
better than Nature herself.—*Headley's Letters from Italy.*

sallow, and the roses on the cheek wither in the night air
or fade in the glare of the gas lights. When the weak
votary of pleasure has thus sacrificed her personal charms,
she vainly attempts to supply the lost treasure by the use of
powder, rouge, and a species of enamel that closes the pores
and suspends the functions of the skin. The same superficial arts are employed alike in the palace-chamber and in
the bordello. For a proud lady who values her beauty,
thus to destroy all the freshness of spring, and extinguish
the ruddy glow of the morning which once shone in her
countenance, is lamentable enough ; but when she transforms her delicate frame into *a portrait painter's easel*, and
makes of her fair cheek a mere *pallet* for a very poor
amateur, she presents for our contemplation one of the most
ridiculous illustrations of human weakness and folly.

> " Lo, with what vermil tints the apple blooms!
> Say, doth the *rose* the painter's hand require ?"

We have often been surprised that persons of large means
expend so much for wardrobes, which are neither elegant
nor convenient ; for carved furniture and costly equipage ;
for jewels and other personal ornaments. It is a vulgar taste
that is fed and satisfied with such an exhibition of elaborate
trifles, and the useless attentions of a long retinue in gilded
liveries. The esthetic sense is scarcely awakened in persons
of this description. The more cultivated mind requires
higher forms of Art and types of Beauty. It is the peculiar
province of the Poet and Musician, the Painter and the
Sculptor, to minister to those who find in their purest creations the distant but radiant images of the absolute Perfection. Such souls need no gilded accessories. Whilst they

yet walk on earth, they wear crowns of light and the robes
of a great Immortality.

The free and harmonious exercise of the human faculties
and affections is indispensable to a complete and symmetrical development of the body. Moreover, it has been rendered evident, by other portions of this treatise, that mental
and moral harmony are productive of physical health. Thus
the mind—when rightly exercised—by producing a normal
condition and action of the whole system, may illuminate
the deep azure of the eye, and cause the rose and the lily to
bloom together on the cheek and the brow. Expression—
which is but the action of passion, thought and sentiment, on
the muscles of the face—of course depends on the states and
exercises of the mind ; and—to use the expressive words of
another—"grace doth take therefrom its own existence."
Thus the chief sources of personal beauty are perceived to
be within, and the outward form, features, expression and
action, must generally constitute a reliable index to the
mind, the heart and the life.

The power of the mind over the body, and the influence
of sensation and thought in forming the features, and determining their expression, is worthy of careful observation.
So completely and indelibly does the mind stamp its image
on the form, that in every lineament of the face we may
trace the revelation of some moral attribute or mental possession. The spirit of kindness wreathes the countenance
with smiles Hatred can never conceal its ugly visage
behind a wall of flesh, but hangs it out for the world's inspection and instruction. While the man—shut up in his
earthly dwelling—vainly imagines that his real character is

unknown, and will remain concealed until his mortal habitation is destroyed, he is unconsciously tracing his secret history on the outer walls of his house, where it may be read by all men. The eyes, especially, are the windows of the mortal tenement, through which we perceive the disposition of the occupant, and the character of the guests he is wont to entertain. The predominant idea, ruling passion, and governing sentiment of the individual are usually made manifest, even to the careless observer. Some nerve vibrates at the gentlest touch of a thought, or trembles beneath the tread of fairy-footed sunbeams, as they come up from all the forms of the world to track the mystic halls of vision.

> "Some chord in unison with what we *hear*
> Is touched within us, and the soul replies!"

And thus all the senses present avenues through which Nature—by her outward forms and physical phenomena—appeals to the conscious soul. From day to day the spirit leaves a visible and impressive transcript of its history in the yielding clay. Thoughts have an influence over the nerves of motion, and our secret emotions are incarnated in our muscles. Thus the contracted, selfish, and bigoted man presents you with a diagram of his lean, dejected soul in the acute angles of his visage. The poor miser who only lives to grasp yet more firmly what he has, and (if possible,) *what he has not*, will be quite likely to form his face after the fashion of a *steel trap ;* while in the curved lines that arch the expanded brow, and in the frank, generous and joyful expression, we recognize the genuine certificate of Nature, bearing the seal of Divinity.

Many faces present to the critical reader of character, a

terrible record of the exercise of perverted faculties; of
golden hours and opportunities squandered in indolence and
dissipation ; of the indulgence of secret and wasting vices ;
of bright hopes blasted in the morning of life, and eloquent
promises of future usefulness, already forgotten and never
to be redeemed. Oh, who would become the author of such
a history ! Who would thus illustrate his life and times by
frequent exhibitions of depraved and ungovernable passion,
and the deep furrows which lust and crime leave on the
darkened visage ! Alas, how many, with bright skies above
them, begin life with clean hands, pure hearts, and good resolutions, and yet seemingly live but to cherish the unwelcome thought, that the world is faithless and life is vain !
And yet the world—in an important sense—is precisely
what we are pleased to have it. Only those who make
grave mistakes in life, find the green earth desolate and the
moral heavens darkened at mid-day. When the brand of
conscious *wrong* is not on the brow, we walk erect and look
the world in the face ; when the fair cheek is unsullied by a
blush of shame, Hope hangs her bow of promise over
against every storm of life. When our moral atmosphere
is unclouded, we see clearly that this world is a living
revelation of Beauty, basking forever in the light of the
Divine love, and inspired with conscious and perpetual joy.

It is especially in *expression* that the mind exhibits the
most direct, manifest and masterly power over the nervous
and muscular systems ; and here, also, it doubtless contributes most essentially to personal beauty. No face can be
said to be really beautiful that is devoid of expression,
while the *features* are often redeemed from their obvious

irregularities by combined delicacy and force of expression. A face in which every thought reveals its image—wherein the sentiments and passions appear as if endowed with personality and reflected in a mirror—becomes a living and moving picture, which is mysteriously changed by every wave of feeling, as well by the soft, gentle and compassionate emotions of the loving heart, as by the stern, aggresive and terrific passions of the enraged avenger. Those who would realize how much may be revealed by the silent language of the passions, as exhibited in expression—even on the canvas—may study the Cyclops of Timanthes, the works of Ludovico Caracci, and the Cartoons of Raphael. For a vivid conception of the bold and striking contrasts presented in the living revelations of the tender and terrible passions of human nature, we may contemplate the humble penitent who seeks forgiveness at the Cross ; the Samaritan who bends in compassion over the fallen stranger ; the conqueror in the hour of his victory ; and the maniac, whose brow has been scathed by the fierce lightnings of disordered passion, and whose eyes—

> "——— like meteors in eclipse,
> Cradle their hollow emptiness."

Man, in respect to his body, is the chemical and organic embodiment of all the substances he has assimilated, or made a part of himself. By a law that governs every department of the human constitution, and the whole organized world, we become like the elements we feed upon. To render the mind vigorous and the character illustrious, it is necessary not only to become familiar with great thoughts and noble resolutions—by means of the ordinary commerce of ideas—

but *we must assimilate them*. If they become a part of ourselves, by a gradual process of passional, intellectual, moral
and spiritual assimilation, they never fail to fashion the
character ; at the same time, they leave indelible impressions on the outward form and in the actual life. There is
much of organic deformity and functional inharmony in the
world ; we are imperfect in ourselves, and surrounded, at
least, by temporary evils on every hand ; but these may not
overcome a great and resolute soul. Moreover, the world
is radiant and glorious with the elements of Divine light
and beauty, and it remains for us—by this power and process of assimilation—to make them our own. Those who
would be truly beautiful in feature, expression and motion,
must be pure in feeling and elevated in thought. They
must appropriate all generous and noble sentiments, and all
living and beautiful ideas. Thus the mind becomes a splendid temple, at whose pure shrine the Graces minister, and
wherein the images of all glorious forms have an abiding
place. By the dynamics of the mind and muscles those images will reappear in the face. The interior illumination is
visible through the half-transparent shade, and the countenance is transfigured in the light of the spirit. How
strangely deformed, repulsive, and soulless do the patched
and painted harlequins of fashionable society appear, when
viewed in contrast with a character that is truly great, and
a face whereon ineffable sweetness, unsullied honor and
sovereign majesty are enthroned together !

The human form and face, when shattered and blasted by
the violence of perverted appetites and destructive passions,
may be compared to some feudal castle on which fierce bat-

tle-storms have spent their fury ; over whose ruined turret
the raven flaps his sable pinions, and in whose deserted halls
the owl and the bat, and even slimy reptiles, find a congenial dwelling-place.   The guests of such a man are lean, hungry demons ; lascivious satyrs ; many nameless monsters,
and the embodied representatives of every vitiated sense
and depraved imagination.   When the depressing and destructive passions are permitted to have unlimited sway, they
are fatal to personal beauty, as they are to health or vital
harmony.   As the billowy flames sweep over the broad
prairie, consuming the tender herbage, and leaving the wide
expanse a blackened waste, so the more fearful and destructive flames of intense and disorderly passion sear and darken
the human visage, consuming the fresh blossoms of Spring,
and leaving no trace of the beauty of youth or the glory of
life's Summer time.   Whoever thus submits to the foul dominion of the baser appetites, will ere long be scathed by
internal and unquenchable fires, until every flower of beauty
withers where it grew, and the human face is made to resemble those cheerless deserts which the burning sirocco
has blasted and made desolate forever.

But while some men thus live and die to admonish the
weak and the unworthy, others who are guided by Reason
—who rule the world in love—contribute to redeem mankind by the truth and power of a noble example.   The man
who thus combines the elements of true greatness, is at once
powerful in his gentleness, and gentle in the exhibitions of
his power.   His soul is the fit temple of the Virtues, and
the living symbol of the Divine presence.   In him great
thoughts are vital realities that take form in glorious deeds.

He goes forth to meet the human world as Summer comes to
the waiting earth—

"Sowing rich beauty over dens and tombs,
And barren moors, and dismal solitudes."

The transcendent light of one such character can neither
be extinguished nor concealed, for the elements of common
earth, out of which our bodies are fashioned, are not imper-
vious to its rays. Such a man is, indeed, an epitome of the
Universe. The sun himself rises and shines in his soul, and
over the full-orbed world that revolves within the orbit of
his mind. Time, that destroys proud empires and wastes the
pyramids, makes his soul more perfect, day by day, and its
outward revelations ever more expressive and beautiful.
And as the Years let fall their golden sands upon his head,
the spirit absorbs and concentrates their light, that by reflection it may illuminate the world. Even in his old age, the
man who answers this description is never associated in the
mind with mournful and deserted ruins. We rather look
upon him as a venerable temple of the PARACLETE, unspoiled
by profane hands, and within whose consecrated courts no
ruthless iconoclast has defaced the sacred images. Over
those walls the ivy twines its tendrils in loving embrace;
beneath that illuminated dome the invisible soul of the
Harmonies yet lingers; and within the open portals the
white-robed Spirit stands gazing, with unclouded vision, at
the Sun—which seems "largest at his setting."

CHAPTER XV.

RELATIONS OF MIND TO THE CHARACTER OF OFFSPRING.

An Organic Law—Natural Imperfections the Causes of Social and Moral Evils—Conditions and Laws of Vital and Moral Harmony—Law of Hereditary Transmission applicable to the whole Man—The Family Character and the Family Face—Apparent Exceptions to the Law—Mental and Moral States of Parents reproduced in their Offspring—Illustrative Examples—A Melancholy Instance—The Question of Responsibility—Injustice of Criminal Tribunals—Obliquities of Reason and Conscience—Barbarous Spirit of Popular Opinions—The Church Contaminated—Deliberate Murders under the Sanctions of Law and Religion—Members of Congress Honorable Exceptions—Moral Blindness—A Mischievous Doctrine—One Law works ruin to Transgressors, while it redeems the Faithful.

THE whole world of organized existence is subject to the action of one great Law. The particular forms and special qualities of all things are determined by the intrinsic nature and peculiar characteristics of the remote and general, and the immediate and individual, sources of their organic life. The operation of this law may be traced through the entire vegetable and animal kingdoms. The man who sows good seed in his field will be sure—other things being favorable—to reap an abundant harvest. On the contrary, if the grain be imperfect, the germs will be defective, and the plants being sickly will, perhaps, wither and die before the season of maturity. Under the same general law, the organic and other essential characteristics and specific dispositions of animals and men are transmitted to their offspring. It would be unphilosophical and absurd

12

to expect the children of diseased and weakly parents to be
constitutionally sound and vigorous. No more can we
rationally expect that the offspring of ignorance, indolence
and vice, will be distinguished for mental strength and virtuous activity. The imperfections transmitted from one
generation to another are never restricted to the body.
The whole man falls under the operation of the same law ;
and thus the bodily health, intellectual capacity, and moral
character are alike determined. These considerations warrant the inference that there is much in the corporeal, mental, moral and religious condition of man, that results from
antecedent causes, against which—in the very nature of the
case—the individual can oppose no adequate resistance.

The causes that determine human feeling, thought and
action, are not, in all cases, subject to the control of the
individual ; much less do they exist by his volition or appointment. It may be said in truth of any man, that *his
original constitution was not in all respects perfect;* also that
the multifarious circumstances and conditions of his outward
life are not precisely adapted to promote and secure his
greatest usefulness and his highest happiness. No one, however refined and exalted in all things that pertain to the
physical, mental and spiritual life of the world, has yet
reached the sublime moral altitude from which the illuminated soul

" Stoops to touch the loftiest thought."

But the capacity to ascend to the highest heaven is latent
in the soul. The power to break away from our mortal
restraints, and to rise above earthly ills and encumbrances
—revealed in our aspirations—will be realized in the great

Hereafter, as we rise from the present imperfect actual up through the infinitely unfolding Ideal of human existence.

Men do not create their own faculties nor, *consciously*, fashion the organic medium through which they act. The individual is not responsible for the blending of mental and temperamental qualities in his constitution ; he did not institute the social order and the political systems of the world ; nor bring with him the unfavorable conditions and false relations which inevitably—in a greater or less degree —determine the manner and the issues of his life. To find the causes of these evils, and to account for the wide diversity in the characteristics of men, and the aspects of human existence, it would be necessary to go back beyond the dawn of consciousness in the individual. There we might, perhaps, discover the reason why one man is from his birth free from any organic defect, or constitutional infirmity, that may predispose him to sickness and death ; while, in many others, life is poisoned at the fountain. We might also discover that outward conditions often make human destiny on earth a painful problem, to be solved on the moral blackboard of perverted faculties and a misspent life.

It has been observed that organic perfection is indispensable to vital harmony. If one organ be defective, the action of the whole system may be irregular, and its continuance uncertain. A man may constantly observe the organic laws, and in nothing disregard his relations to the physical world ; but if the body and the vital movement be incomplete or irregular, all his efforts may be inadequate to secure permanent health and protracted existence. Improvement in such cases is certainly not impossible ; on the contrary, a faithful observance of the laws of our being cannot fail to secure comparative health and happiness. The mental and moral faculties, not less than their corporeal instruments, acquire new strength by *right action*. By this means we may escape many of the ills from which others suffer. We may fortify ourselves in such a manner as to guard against outward foes ; by which I mean, various maladies and causes of vital derangement, *not involved in the laws of procreation*, and to which we have no constitutional predisposition. But when the foe is in possession of the citadel—*which he holds by a hereditary title*—when disease has its origin and its seat in the very rudiments of human nature. and its deadly virus is transfused through every vein and artery ; when its consuming fires dissipate the fluids, torture the nerves, and the tissues shrivel like parchments cast in flames—then, indeed. we may strive earnestly, but strive in vain, to dislodge the enemy or to resist his power. Many persons live just long enough to sow the seeds of misery, and then depart, leaving others to reap the fearful harvest of pain and death. Wherever the elements of a congenital disease exist, and are transmitted, the subtile destroyer will sooner or later manifest his presence—if not otherwise—in the pale countenance, the frail, attenuated frame, the bloated limbs, or the demoniac expression. Thus the blood of generations is polluted and set on fire ; and the fair forms of thousands fade and pass away in life's morning hours.

There are abrupt and painful contrasts in life, and it is impossible to overlook the deep shadows and startling colors combined in the picture of *the world as it is*. But if there are organic imperfections, which inevitably result in

an irregular vital motion, uncertain health and premature
dissolution ; so, also, there are many people in whom the
cerebral development and action are no less unequal and
irregular, and such persons are liable to be imbecile in mind
or unstable in virtue.   If, in the one case, there is a natural
predisposition to disease and a speedy disorganization of
the system, there is in the other an equally forcible manifestation of such mental and moral infirmities as lead to a still
more fearful ruin of earthly interests and human hopes.   If
one person is rendered sickly by hereditary infirmities,
which he could neither remove nor successfully resist, it is
quite as obvious that another may be depraved and vicious
from a similar cause.   There is not so much as the poorest
semblance of reason in the assumption—whether expressed
or implied—that one part of man's nature is thus subject to
the law of hereditary transmission of forms and qualities,
whilst other departments and attributes of his being are not
so influenced and determined.

Thus the original constitutions of some people are rendered as truly incompatible with strict moral rectitude, as
others are with the laws of vital harmony and the realization of sound health.   The child is as sure to resemble the
parent in its moral characteristics as in its mental faculties
and physical form, features, expression, complexion and
other distinctive qualities.   Hence the family character is
often quite as perceptible—through succeeding generations
—as is the family face.   If it be objected that some individuals, in respect to character, are altogether different from
their progenitors, my reply is—the child does not, in all
cases, resemble the parents in form, feature and complexion.

These apparent exceptions to the universal law, doubtless, result from peculiar combinations of opposite personal qualities—thus united in the same organization—from the operation of the psychical laws, and in part, perhaps, from causes which are neither accurately defined nor clearly understood. However, that the law I am endeavoring to elucidate really exists, no intelligent observer will be disposed to deny ; nor can we reasonably presume that any portion of human nature is beyond its dominion, or exempt from its influence.

It will be perceived that the mental faculties and moral states of men and women are reproduced in their offspring. We are familiar with a gentleman of high respectability—the father of nine children, six of whom are living—who assures us that he is able to trace in each one the existing states, personal habits and general pursuits which characterized his life at the time they were respectively generated. At one time, having just commenced his labors in the ministry, his mind was for some months most solemnly impressed with the weight of his new responsibilities. Though naturally buoyant in spirit and somewhat inclined to mirth, he seldom smiled, rarely conversed on trifling topics, but devoted a large share of his time to silent meditation. During that period his second daughter was born. The child was well organized, bright and intellectual ; but in her childhood was not disposed to talk, and was never known to laugh aloud until *she was more than four months old*.

Some time since the writer spent several days in Western New York, at the residence of Mr. C——, an honest and a generous man. Some twenty years ago he was employed in making extensive additions and repairs to his house. The

work occupied a long time, having—from various causes—
been repeatedly suspended. The premises were in a state
of confusion all the while, and Mrs. C——, though an excellent lady, was not one who could feel settled in mind so long
as everything around her was in disorder. Possessing a
most active temperament, acute sensibilities, and withal a
large love of order, her discordant surroundings kept up an
unpleasant excitement of mind, and increased her nervous
irritability. There was no place where she could feel at
rest, and she sighed in vain for the solace of undisturbed
repose. Mr. and Mrs. C—— have a son who was conceived
and born under the influence of this nervous and mental agitation. The young man is constitutionally restless, dissatis-
fied and unhappy in a surprising degree. In his waking
hours he seldom remains longer than a few minutes in one
place, and during his whole life he has been constantly
"seeking rest and finding none."

A miserable man—who often shocked the delicate sensibilities of his wife by staggering into her presence in a state
of intoxication—has not only transmitted his insatiable
thirst to his unfortunate son, but even reproduced (either
directly or through the action of the mother's mind) his own
irregular locomotion, so that *the youth could never walk
straight*. It is but a few years since such a melancholy example came under the writer's observation. The boy was
then some fifteen years of age, and in other respects an interesting youth ; but, alas! he is the moving, lifelong and
appalling record of the great error of his sire! A lifetime
spent in penance, as an atonement, could never obliterate
the fatal consequences of one such deplorable mistake.

Such mournful records do reckless men and thoughtless or abandoned women leave behind them to testify that they have lived!

But how does our general course of reasoning affect the question of individual responsibility? It may be objected that if a man inclines to evil, on account of some original defect in his mental and moral constitution, it follows that he acts from an irresistible *necessity ;* that he is in no way responsible for his conduct, and we can do nothing to reform him. But our argument surely does not authorize the conclusion that man is a mere machine, destitute of voluntary powers, and wholly subject to the control of foreign agents. The objection—which is based on a false inference—is in itself rather specious than sound. If a man be of a consumptive habit, it does not thence follow that he has nothing to do to preserve health. On the contrary, it is the more important for such an one to exercise the utmost caution. A well man may venture to inhale the night air, he may brave the storms, the floods and the frosts ; but for a sick man to expose himself in a similar manner would be rash and perhaps inexcusable. This will equally well apply to man as a moral agent. If there exists a constitutional inclination to evil, or a perverted exercise of the faculties, it is the more necessary for the individual to be strictly guarded against every cause or circumstance which may favor his downward determination. It is the more important that all good influences be brought to bear on him, for in this way we may restrain and strengthen him, and in the end give him a moral momentum from which he will move onward and upward.

However, from our investigation of the laws of human nature, and the present imperfect conditions of society, it is rendered obvious that many transactions in this world are properly referable to such a predisposition of mind, on the part of the actor, as fairly places him without the pale of ordinary responsibility. Legislators and jurists may be slow in the legal and practical recognition of this truth ; but the enlightened moral philosopher can entertain no doubt on this point. The man who is *absolutely impelled* in a wrong direction, should not be fiercely censured and rudely condemned for yielding to an irresistible impulsion. A moral obliquity *may be* as excusable as a spinal curvature. If, in respect to his moral nature, a man is lame, he must have extrinsic aids and supports to assist him through the world, *and he should no more be sent to perdition for limping than any other cripple.*

Whoever inherits diseased appetites and perverted passions may find them stronger than either the reverence for law or the love of liberty. Indeed, so long as life lasts they may defeat the best resolutions, and in every conflict conquer the man ; though all the while, with an inward desire for a purer and nobler life, he continues to

" Resolve and re-resolve, then dies the same "

And even when life is over, according to the proverb, " the ruling passion may be strong in death."

Now, in my judgment, a man is entitled to quite as much sympathy and compassion, if the defects of his constitution belong to the moral economy of his being, as if they were the more superficial evils which chiefly effect the body. Yet, strange to say, so far as congenital evils merely influence the

vital functions, or the operations of the intellect, they are
regarded as *blameless misfortunes ;* at the same time, in
every instance where they involve the moral constitution
and action, they are viewed as *criminal offenses.* It will be
perceived that the ordinary treatment, in cases of moral disease or derangement, derives no sanction or support from our
course of analogical reasoning.   Moreover, the common disposition of offenders against the laws is at war with the
essential principles and the benign spirit of a true moral and
Christian philosophy.   Sick people—even when disease is
the result of careless exposure, or a conscious violation of
some known law—are tenderly nursed.   The deaf, dumb
and blind, as well as idiots and insane people, are all kindly
cared for ; but if one be morally incomplete, or some terrible malady has its origin in the very rudiments of his moral
nature, he is savagely treated even by the professed ministers of justice.   How is humanity crushed and trodden under
foot, and language perverted, when *justice* is but a softer
name for cruelty and revenge ; and we are obliged to go,
for the world's definition, to the whipping-post and the gallows ; or to loathsome dungeons—fit sepulchers for dead
men's bones—where lizards copulate and multiply !   Even
in this model Republic the high places of authority and responsibility are often occupied by petty despots, and licensed
criminals, who sit in judgment on their fellows.   Professing
to be human, to be civilized, and, withal, to be *Christian ;* (?)
they yet disfigure men's bodies with the lash, or break their
necks on the scaffold, in a formal manner, and before vulgar
crowds.   The judgment of the court, the writing of the
death-warrant, and the foul work of the executioner, are all

done under the high sanctions of Law and Religion ; and
accompanied, too, with the solemnities of prayer ! In the in-
sulted name of Jesus—who "came not to destroy men's lives,
but to save them"—some professed minister of his Gospel
pronounces a benediction, and thus ends the horrid tragedy;
and this is *justice*—according to the fashion of this world !

> "Earth is sick, and Heaven is weary,
> Of the heartless words that States and Kingdoms utter
> When they talk of justice !"

It may be said that much that is abnormal and wrong in
human conduct cannot be traced to hereditary and organic
predispositions to evil. This is very true. Many persons
become depraved and vicious from the influence of corrupt
examples, and from a variety of other causes. But we have
looked in vain to the exponents of Law and the teachers of
Religion for a wise discrimination in this matter. The degree of moral turpitude, in the individual, is measured and
determined by the abstract nature of his act, and not at all
by the man's power or his incapacity to have acted otherwise. He may be as incapable of perceiving a moral distinction as a blind man is of discerning colors, or a hole in
the wall ; but this will avail nothing in extenuation. Physical blindness, to be sure, is a great misfortune, and those
who suffer from this disability are very properly sent to
some asylum to receive a polite education ; but *moral blindness* is regarded as a crime, for which the poor victim may
very justly be sent to prison here and to hell hereafter.
Neither his natural constitution and temperament, nor his
education and early associations, are competent to materially
modify the legitimate course and bearing of the law. Yet

men who are imbecile in mind, and whose moral perceptions
are obscure and therefore unreliable, often fall because unable to see clearly, or to preserve their moral equilibrium.
They have not the strength to stand erect in truth and virtue, and—in numerous instances—they are no more to be
blamed for falling than the traveler at night who stumbles
over a precipice.

However, if any unusual clemency is manifested, it is
generally reserved for those who, perhaps, least deserve it.
Our tribunals are sometimes merciful to the enlightened
transgressor—the man who has had the advantages of a superior education and refined society, and who may therefore
be presumed to have clearer perceptions of right and wrong.
If any indulgence is granted, it is to this class of genteel
offenders, while all legal and deserved penalties are reserved
for vulgar sinners, who have no influential friends to shield
them.   Even a coarse, blundering saint, is less respected in
our modern fashionable society, than a polite and accomplished knave ; and by common consent men of great wealth
and members of Congress are entitled to *the special privilege
of shooting people and going unhung !*

Punishments, to be salutary in their influence, must be benevolent in their design, and of such a nature as to increase
the moral strength of the subject.   In all cases we should
keep in view the legitimate objects of government and the
true dignity of Man.   Moreover, those who blindly seek and
consummate their own ruin do not thereby forfeit all claim
to human sympathy and the Divine regard.   If a naturally
sound and vigorous man should lose his health in consequence of his own imprudence, it would still be our duty to

watch over him in sickness and to minister to his wants. Or, should he pluck out his own eyes, he would certainly deserve as much sympathy as an ordinary blind man. Nor is this remark untrue in its application to the moral nature. What if thy fellow be willing to exchange an Eden of light and joy for a wilderness of darkness and despair! To be thus morally insensible, is, of all other misfortunes, the greatest and the most deeply to be deplored. The world and the church may leave such to perish ; but the great Father will remember and watch over his wayward child.

If we consider how much the life, character and condition of the individual are made dependent on preëxisting causes, over which he can exercise no possible control, we shall become more charitable in our judgments, and more humane in our treatment of the abandoned and criminal classes. To reform the offender we must lift him up from his fallen condition. The wise husbandman who finds in his nursery a tree that is inclined to take an oblique direction, never treads it into the dust. On the contrary—if he designs to have it upright—he gently raises it up, and secures it in its proper place, until its original downward tendency is overcome, and it is prepared to stand erect in its own strength. Then let no one trample his fellow to the ground because he is morally bowed down. If he has "fallen among thieves" who ·have stolen the divine loves from his heart, stripped him of the robes of innocence, and robbed him of his peace of mind ; be thou to him neither the priest nor the levite, but *the good Samaritan.* Have compassion and lift him up again ; minister to his necessities, and he may yet stand upright in the dignity of a divine Manhood.

Reader, if thou art strong in the integrity of mind, and heart, and life ; let not that superior strength prompt thee to despise thy brother of lower degree. He may have some constitutional weakness ; some unfortunate tendency of mind ; some obliquity of reason or perversion of the affections, against which he is struggling night and day—struggling, perhaps, in vain, yet with the sincerity and heroism of a martyr. If he is no better than St. Paul, there may be " a law in his members warring against the law of the mind, and bringing him into captivity." On the other hand the constitution of thy nature may be more fortunate. Moral powers and intellectual capacities, which have not fallen to his lot, may happily be thine. But " who maketh thee to differ from another, and what hast thou that thou didst not receive" ? Be not high-minded. If thou art great and strong, it is well. True greatness will neither minister to a vain pride nor foster a selfish ambition ; but will cause its possessor to be humble and grateful. Come, O Spirit of Light and Charity ! Come quickly ! Speak to the listening world in that deep prophetic voice that thrilled the soul of the Poet :

> " When through the silence overhead
> An Angel with a trumpet said,
> Forevermore, Forevermore,
> The Reign of Violence is o'er:
> Then like an instrument, that flings
> Its music on another's strings,
> The Trumpet of the Angel cast
> Upon the heavenly lyre its blast ;
> And on—from sphere to sphere—the words
> Reëchoed down the burning chords,
> Forevermore, Forevermore,
> The Reign of Violence is o'er !"

It may be objected that our philosophy of the moral ob-

liquities of human nature is opposed to the Divine justice
and benevolence, since it presumes that the innocent sometimes suffer for the guilty. It is written in an ancient Book
that the iniquity of the fathers is, or may be, visited on the
children to the third and fourth generations. It is true that
the influence of our actions never can be restricted to ourselves, nor even to the times in which' we live. From our
intimate and indissoluble connection with the Race, it will
extend to those around us, and in some degree to all who
shall come after us. The doctrine, therefore, that the sovereignty of the individual entitles him to disregard his relations to others and to society at large—gives him the right
to do wrong, under the shallow pretense of taking the consequences to himself—*is a selfish and mischievous falsehood*.
Such an individual sovereignty does not exist, and this in-
sidious and corrupting philosophy has no fellowship with
Reason and Humanity. The institutions of Nature are not
merely adapted to men in their individual circumstances,
capacities and relations. They are parts of one universal
system, and must be regarded not as separate and independent forms of being, but they should be viewed in the light of
that Wisdom which comprehends all things in their true relations, and with a wise reference to their ultimate results.

The very law whereby the distinctive attributes and specific tendencies of one individual are transmitted to another,
forms no exception to the benevolence and wisdom which
characterize the whole economy of Nature. It is granted
and insisted that, through the operations of this law, men
sometimes propagate disease and multiply murder. Millions
are borne down the polluted stream of Time to perish on

the Stygian shore. But with our limited knowledge we should be slow in our disposition to impeach the Divine wisdom. I think I perceive the justice of this law. True, if we disregard its requirements, our children may be more frail and imperfect than ourselves. Nevertheless, I feel assured that this very law is at the foundation of our highest hopes, and inwrought with the imperishable glories of the immortal life and world. In the absence of such a law, the succeeding generations of men would occupy much the same position. At least, there could be no improvement in the natural constitutions of men resulting from obedience to the principles of natural rectitude ; hence, the general condition of society, from age to age, would exhibit little or no improvement in the Race. The same law that involves the retrogression and ruin of transgressors, is the law of PRO-GRESSION to those who observe its requirements. To all such it is the ladder on which they ascend to Heaven. Obey that law, and it shall be a lever to raise the world. Thus the whole Race may advance in intellectual, moral and spiritual excellence until Man shall rival the Angels, and become, in the highest and holiest sense—THE CHILD OF GOD. The earnest prayer of Humanity will then be answered, and the sweet prophecy of a Divine Kingdom on earth fulfilled. The Philosopher will have found the *New Atlantis ;* the Poet's dream of *Utopia* will be realized ; and the fraternal nations will meet at the open gates of a vast Commonwealth more glorious than Campanella's *City of the Sun.*

> " Then shall the reign of TRUTH commence on earth,
> And starting fresh, as from a second birth,
> MAN, in the sunshine of the world's new spring,
> Shall walk transparent like some holy thing."

CHAPTER XVI.

THE SENSES AND THEIR FUNCTIONS.

Number of the Senses—The Faculties and Organs—Sight—Hearing—Smell ing—Tasting—Feeling—Estimated number of nerves in a single Organ— General diffusion of Sensibility—Philosophy of Vision—Views of the Platonists, Stoics and Epicureans—Mariotte's opinion respecting the seat of Vision—Sir David Brewster and M. Lehot—The Sensorial Processes—Alfred Smee's experimental Illustrations.

Through all these faculties ablaze with light
From God's infinitude I looked abroad,
And each according to its form, its place,
Its function or its element, received
A separate splendor from the All in All.

Lyric of the Golden Age.

THE Senses are the faculties whereby we perceive the existence of the objective creation ; and become acquainted with the precise outlines, relative positions, comparative dimensions, and—to some extent—with the intrinsic properties and existing states of material forms and substances. Several metaphysical writers, who were quite as much distinguished for the originality as for the accuracy of their speculations, have maintained the existence of *six or seven distinct Senses ;*[1] but the commonly accepted classifica-

---

[1] Dr. Thomas Brown of Edinburgh, and also Whewell, in his Philosophy of the Inductive Sciences, maintained the existence of what they denominated the *muscular sense.* Moreover, several writers have spoken of the *moral sense,* and likewise of the *esthetic sense,* as if they were separate faculties of the mind, and to be included in the category of the other senses.

tion of our perceptions resolves them into *five*, namely, sight, hearing, smelling, tasting, and feeling. The Latin *sentio*, to *feel*—in its application alike to all the external phases and instruments of perception—is not misapplied ; for, in a general sense, *feeling* may comprehend them all.

From our inquiry into the nature of the Senses, as well as from all ordinary observations of their organic functions, we readily perceive that in their corporeal relations and external aspects, they belong to the whole animal creation as well as to Man, while—in a very limited degree—certain plants seem to exhibit a participation with animated nature in the mysterious powers of sensation. Nevertheless, in human nature— as will be more clearly perceived hereafter—all the Senses converge and have their ultimate seat in the individual consciousness—*in the spirit*—as the several organs of sensation all center in the physical sensorium.

Sight is very generally regarded as the most important of the five Senses. It is through the eye that we obtain the clearest perceptions of the particular forms and relative positions of all outward objects. Destroy the vision, and the panorama of the living world would be rolled up—the spectator left in the darkened halls of space, and the stately procession of the stars would retire, to be present to our cognition no more. Sight is the only sense from which we derive any proper conception of *color*. Without the faculty of vision darkness of all things would be most substantial, for day with night (in our experience,) would alternate no more. The beauty of the green earth ; the waters, as they dance and shimmer in the sunlight ; the azure deeps, vailed with gold, crimson and purple draperies ; and the refulgent dyes, diffused from the great alembic of Nature, making the flowers more beautiful than "Solomon in all his glory"—all these with the forms of human beauty, and the smiles of joy and love, would be intangible and unknown. It required a great, inspired genius—overshadowed by the misfortune that hides the world—to give us Milton's graphic picture :

> " Thus with the year
> Seasons return ; but not to me returns
> Day, or the sweet approach of eve or morn,
> Or sight of vernal bloom, or Summer's rose,
> Or flocks, or herds, or human face divine ;
> But cloud instead, and ever-during dark
> Surround me ; from the cheerful ways of men
> Cut off, and, for the book of knowledge fair,
> Presented with an universal blank
> Of Nature's work, to me expunged and 'rased,
> And wisdom at one entrance quite shut out."

Through the sense of *Hearing* we become acquainted with the peculiar motions of material bodies and the corresponding vibrations of subtile elements which produce the diversified phenomena of sound. Strictly speaking, sound is only a *sensation*, and hence an elastic medium of communication between the moving object or sonorous body and the acoustic organ, is indispensable to its production. This was demonstrated by the experiments of Hauksbee and Biot. When they suspended a bell in the exhausted receiver of an air pump, no sound was transmitted. It will be perceived that hearing is intimately related to the laws of acoustics, as sight is to the whole science of optics and chromatics. Some knowledge of those branches of physics may therefore be necessary to a clear understanding of the subject ; but the

writer can not occupy the space allotted to this Chapter with
a disquisition on collateral issues, or the particular sciences
to which the general subject is so obviously related.

The sense of hearing contributes very much to the proper
education of the mind, and to the real pleasures of our social
existence. We can but imperfectly conceive of its uses, even
while they are a constant revelation to the consciousness;
and when the mournful contrast—suggested by the depri-
vation of this sense—is presented in living forms before us,
we seldom realize the truth, that the perpetual darkness that
shrouds the sightless mortal is scarcely more intolerable, or
more to be deplored, than the unbroken silence that reigns
above, beneath, and around the man who is deprived of
hearing. To him the elements are all dumb; earth and air
respond in no measured resonance—loud or soft. The birds
are voiceless in the trees; the grand quartette of the Winds—
that made the mountain pines tuneful from sympathy—is
hushed forever; the liquid melodies of the rippling waters
no more

"On bubbling keys are played;"

even the deep, mysterious voices of the sea become inaudible, while the soft tones and the sweet speech of Love
expire together on the lip. To all such the world is silent,
indeed, and existence is solitary.

The sense of *Smell* is far less important to man than sight
or hearing. It is also much less acute in the human race
than in several species of animals. The dog will follow a
fox or a hare for hours without once seeing the game, but
wholly, it is presumed, from the peculiar odor that remains

in the invisible footprints. Perhaps no other sense is so frequently defective or so liable to become impaired from slight causes; and it is worthy of observation that there is not one which may be suspended with so little inconvenience to ourselves or others. Its loss does not unfit a man for business, and it can not materially embarrass his intercourse with the world.

But when this sense is so perfect as to detect the presence of the most delicate aroma, it becomes a source of the most exquisite pleasure. In tropical climes the whole atmosphere is often pervaded by precious odors that daily rise with the ambrosial dews from Nature's great censer. Those who inspire the perfumed atmosphere of Ceylon, or are fanned by breezes from the orange groves and spice fields, may conceive how much of pleasure comes to Man on the viewless air, and through one of the lesser avenues that lead from the outward world to the conscious soul. It is worthy of remark that while the sense of Smell may not be so indispensable to the business and the happiness of life as the other senses, it is far less likely to corrupt the character and the life. While sight, hearing, tasting, and feeling, may offer frequent occasions to the tempter, and perchance furnish the incentives to evil, this sense has done least of all to corrupt the fountains of our moral life, or to impair the integrity of our physical and spiritual being.

It is true that all the Senses are equally pure when uncorrupted by any abnormal exercise, or excessive indulgence; but it does not follow, on the one hand, that all are equally essential to our mental growth and moral elevation; or, on the other hand, that all are equally liable—by being corrupted—to impair the health of the body and the integrity of the soul. If in the general economy of our physical being, *Taste* is more important than the sense last named, it is also more likely to be perverted, and thus to become a prolific source of evil to ourselves and others. Indeed, no one of the senses has ever furnished half so many occasions for the violation of the laws of health and life as this one ; nor is there one among them all whose dominion over human nature is at once so extensive and so degrading.

In some important sense *Feeling* may be regarded as the basis of all our special sensations. While the other senses have particular organs through which their functions are performed, this alone is so widely diffused that every part of the body has its electro-nervous lines of communication with the brain. The nervous papillæ, of the skin, though somewhat unequally distributed over the entire body, are numerous in every part ; and to the number of impressible nervous fibers some authors have ascribed the *complication* as well as the delicacy and intensity of our sensations. Alfred Smee, in his work on " Instinct and Reason," expresses the conviction —as the result of a deliberate calculation—that the human capacity to appreciate the sounds in a range of twelve and a half octaves, requires more than 3000 nerves to convey the impressions to the brain. This may be a speculative opinion ; but doubtless every one of the innumerable sensitive filaments—communicating with the centers of nervous energy and reaching the surface at the proper point—has its peculiar function as well as its particular place ; and for aught we know to the contrary, the complexity of our sensations may depend on the number of the papillæ to which the electrical excitation from whatever cause is communicated.

This wide diffusion of sensibility over the whole body serves as its most efficient protection. It is the shield that enables us to ward off the shafts of the destroyer, without which we should be in constant danger from heat and cold, as well as from many other causes, visible and invisible. Moreover, if feeling, like the other senses, were confined to some particular organ, other parts of the body might be exposed to injury without our knowledge. But by a wise arrangement of the physical economy of our being, we are enabled to anticipate the evil. Pain, like a trusty sentinel, guards every avenue leading to the citadel of life, and we are faithfully admonished whenever danger is approaching.

It will be perceived that the nervous system is a most delicate and complicated telegraphic instrument, communicating in all directions—and in the most perfect manner—with the elements and objects of the external world. Respecting the ultimate seat of sensation, and the philosophy of the effects produced on the organs, diverse opinions have been and are still entertained. Among the ancient philosophers, the Platonists as well as the Stoics, maintained that vision depended on rays proceeding from the eye to the object; while the Epicureans supposed the process to be reversed, and that the sensorial phenomena were produced by the images of corporeal things reflected to the eye. In respect to this part of the process, there exists a more general agreement among modern philosophers. But the precise seat of the sensation, or the part of the visual organ in which the images are formed and retained, is still a controverted question. The common opinion that the retina arrests and holds the images of outward objects, has been boldly questioned since Mariotte accidentally discovered that the optic nerve, at its base, is insensible to light. This discovery led the author to the conclusion that the seat of vision is in the *choroid coat ;* and as that is opaque, while the retina is transparent, his conclusion has been favored by other philosophers, and by certain observations of Sir David Brewster. M. Lehot held that the *vitreous humor* is the seat of vision, but without furnishing such evidence in support of his opinion as scientific observers require to establish a rational conviction.

Without proceeding further with the citation and discussion of the opinions of material philosophers, whose minute dissection of the organs, and classification of their functions, have failed to determine the ultimate seat of any one of the senses, I will now offer some general suggestions toward an explanation—on electrical principles—of the sensational *processes*, as they occur in animal and human bodies. In some of the preceding Chapters, the writer had occasion to show that Vital Electricity is the circulating medium of the nervous system, and the active agent in the processes of organic chemistry, and in all vital and muscular motion. The facts cited to prove that animal electricity performs this important office in the organic functions, need not be repeated in this connection. But it should be observed that if this subtile principle is the circulating medium of the nerves, it is the proximate agent of *sensation*, as well as of motion. This conclusion is rendered probable by the nature of our sensations, and confirmed by various experiments in vital electricity, some of which have already been cited in the present treatise on Man and his Relations.

I have only space sufficient for a very brief, general, and necessarily imperfect statement of the electrical theory of sensation. The rays of light reflected from the surfaces of outward objects to the eye, disturb or move the sensorial medium on the optic nerve, through which the electrical excitation is instantly conveyed to the sensorium. The undulatory motion of the air—or the vibrations of some more subtile medium that pervades the atmosphere—occasions a similar electric action on the minute terminations of the auditory nerve, which are freely distributed over the delicate membrane that lines the internal cavities of the ear. Odors in like manner excite the electric aura that pervades the nervous filaments of the olfactory surfaces. We determine the presence of certain properties of matter by the sense of *Taste*, the electro-nervous excitement in this case occurring on the delicate papillæ of the tongue, and are thence communicated to the brain. Moreover, each papilla in the true skin marks the termination of some sensatoïy nerve, and a point from which impressions from the external world may be electrically transmitted to the mind.

Alfred Smee, in the course of his biological experiments, observed that the voltaic force was moved in the nerves of animals when a proper stimulant was applied to the organs of sensation ; and he maintained that by the use of an instrument, designed for that purpose, he could readily convey "a knowledge of the presence of an odor to an adjoining room." He also made an artificial *tongue*, by filling a V-tube with a solution of salt in water, and placing a platinum wire in the solution at each end of the tube. With this simple instrument, the savor of meat, and other articles of diet may be conveyed through the metallic nerve from one apartment to another. The same writer gives the results of similar experimental illustrations of the sense of Feeling. A brief extract will more clearly indicate the nature of his claims, founded on the results of his curious experiments :

"The sense of tact is a sense of bodily changes ; but the nerves which carry the knowledge are probably placed close to the skin. * * There is no experiment more easy in Electro-biology than to prove that the mechanism for this transmission of impressions is *voltaic*. I have ascertained the fact in cats, rabbits, eels, birds, and other creatures, over and over again A physical mechanism may be readily made (upon voltaic principles) which shall be excited by variations of temperature, and which shall convey the impressions to a distance." [1]

I have thus briefly discussed the nature and the organic functions of the Senses, in their relations to the body and to this world. As their higher relations to the spirit, and to the immortal life and world, do not properly belong to the present volume, it will be perceived that we have reached the appropriate termination of the present Chapter.

---

[1] Instinct and Reason, p. 40.

CHAPTER XVII.

PSYCHOMETRIC PERCEPTION.

Atmospheres of Worlds and of all Living Beings—Physical Elements and Moral Forces—The Soul-measuring power—Characteristics discovered in the subtle effluence from the Human Mind—Dr. Buchanan's earlier Investigations—How Psychometry was regarded by the Faculty—Discovery of Crimes and detection of Criminals—Important experiments on the brain—The Author's experimental tests—Psychometric powers of Mrs. Mettler—Miss Parson's graphic pictures of distinguished characters—Translation of Ancient Mysteries—Consecrated Places—Revelations to the Inward Sense.

" And shadows of all forms of life and thought,
Moved through the solemn temple of the soul."

A VARIETY of curious phenomena contribute to establish the general fact, that both animals and men leave subtile emanations from their bodies in all places which they have previously occupied. Every object they have touched is pervaded by the invisible effluence, and every sensitive nature feels its presence. Thus the dog is enabled to pursue the deer for hours without once seeing the game, following all the while by scenting, or otherwise perceiving the aroma from his footsteps. In like manner he finds his master in a crowd, or pursues him with an unerring certainty when he is far from home. Doubtless the dog discovers traces of other animals and of men by subtile emanations from their bodies, which pervade the earth and air. These aromal essences appear to reach the animal sensorium through the olfactory surfaces, though this is by no means certain, inasmuch as the instincts of some animals likewise enable them to perceive *danger*, when the causes are but indirectly, and, perhaps, very remotely related to living men and beasts. The dog has been known to exhibit great uneasiness when his master was exposed to accident from secret snares and pit-falls. In places where bloody deeds were long since perpetrated, animals have been known to manifest signs of extreme fear. In these respects it is alleged that the instinct of the horse is scarcely less mysterious and reliable than that of the dog. From the Scriptural account of Balaam's peculiar experience, it would appear that even the stupid beast on which he rode was endowed with clearer perceptions than many men, and that he was a far better discerner of spiritual things than the false prophet himself.

All worlds have their atmospheres ; and the more sublimated elements in the organic forms of the living creation are *exhaled* like the incense of flowers. Those ethereal essences are invisible ; but they are not less substantial in their essential nature, while they are far more powerful in their silent action. Indeed, all the more potent agents in the natural world are invisible save in their effects. Every one of the simple elements is represented in the great atmospheric sea that surrounds our orb ; and even the densest forms of matter are susceptible of being so widely diffused and so finely attenuated, as to become impalpable and imponderable. Immersed in this ethereal ocean—composed of the subtile emanations from the earth and its inhabitants—we are constantly liable to be influenced by intellectual powers and moral qualities as well as by physical elements and forces. A man with an infectious disease certainly can not appear in our streets and other public places, without endangering the health of many citizens, by the morbid and pestilential emanations from his body. Nor are the principles and laws which govern the mental and moral economy of human nature less potent and unerring. We may be sure that, whenever a moral pestilence—endowed with personality and locomotion—is permitted to appear in the marketplace, the social circle, or the sanctuary, there is an accompanying influence that inevitably lowers the general tone of society, and the moral health of the community is impaired. The electro-magnetic emanations from such persons possess all the qualities of the constitutions from which they proceed ; and the unfortified ones, who come within the physical, mental and moral atmospheres of such people, are liable to be corrupted. The capacity for original and vigorous thought, the common sentiment, and all noble resolutions may thus be enfeebled and depraved.

Persons of acute mental perceptions and exquisite moral sensibilities, detect the essential attributes and peculiar characteristics of others as soon as they are fairly within the charmed circle of their atmospheric emanations. Most men and women of cultivated minds and refined habits have an intuitive consciousness of the fundamental differences in the minds and morals of persons whom they meet in social life and in the transactions of business. Every public speaker is conscious of being influenced by the subtile emanations from the multitude. These are so dissimilar, at diverse times and

places, that on one occasion the orator may experience an
unusual mental illumination—enabling him to rise into the
highest heaven of thought—while under other circumstances
an oppressive influence, like a leaden weight, rests on all his
faculties. Sometimes the mere presence of a stranger, with
whom we have never spoken, inspires the mind and heart
with serene and pleasurable emotions, while others make
us restless and unhappy. Some people carry along with
them a strange suggestive power, whereby they impregnate
our souls. Under their influence the mind suddenly becomes
prolific ; our faculties are excited, and we are drawn out in
conversation ; while at the approach of other persons, we
instinctively retire within ourselves. Their frigid or fiery
natures shut up the avenues to the sensitive mind and heart,
as the cold night winds close the flowers ; or we are made
to feel that they come but to consume us with their burning
breath, and the desolating storm of unbridled passions.

The atmosphere is a principal vehicle whereby not only
the pure aromas of the flowers, but also the grossest exhalations from diseased bodies and unhealthy locations, are
widely diffused. The impregnation of the vital air, by un-
wholesome emanations from corrupt forms and miasmatic
districts, renders this great fountain of life and health the
most efficient agent in spreading contagion and death. The
invisible agents of infection are carried in every direction
by the atmospheric currents. Thus certain maladies become
epidemic, and great cities are devastated by the pestilence.
In like manner every human being who has a sound constitution and unimpaired health, contributes to energize the
springs of life in all who approach him. Sensitive persons

immediately feel the sustaining magnetism of his presence. This is sometimes sufficient to relieve severe pain ; to make the weak man suddenly strong ; and not unfrequently has this normal magnetic power equalized the vital forces, and thus harmonized the organic functions of persons who were completely prostrated by disease. If we reflect that a single grain of musk, or other diffusible aromatic, may completely permeate an immense volume of common air—so as to be perceived through an outward avenue of sensation—we shall scarcely attempt to determine how far the invisible emanations from men and angels may extend ; nor shall we presume to fix limits to their subtle influence on the faculties of the human mind or the functions of animal existence.

Moreover, the principles involved in this part of my subject might be forcibly illustrated by appeals to ancient history and modern experience. But it is not my purpose to occupy space and the reader's attention with a citation of accredited facts, though many such might be derived from the annals of the Church. It is recorded that a surprising virtue went out from Jesus of Nazareth, and restored a woman who merely "touched the hem of his garment." We have witnessed cures that were scarcely less remarkable, and it is time for us to attempt something like a rational estimate of the importance of these subtle principles in the present economy, and the ultimate issues of human existence. The subject is not only interesting to the metaphysical philosopher, but viewed in its moral and practical relations and aspects, it is one of vast importance. The man who passes along the highway, changes the vital elements of the very air we breathe by the emanations from his body and mind ; the persons who prepare your food or share your couch, modify all the conditions of being ; while the friends at the table and the fireside each exert a power for good or ill that remains long after the guests have departed.

The capacity of certain impressible persons to perceive, by an exquisite power of cognition, or semi-spiritual sensation, the general and particular characteristics of distant and unknown persons, by merely holding their autographs in the hand, or against the forehead, has been demonstrated to the satisfaction of numerous experimental observers. It was about the year 1842, that Joseph R. Buchanan, M. D., widely known as a free, fearless, and philosophical investigator—commenced his public lectures on Psychometry and other subjects embraced in his neurological system of Anthropology. He was, unquestionably, the first really scientific man who attempted to commend the revelations of the psychometric sense to the schools and the several learned professions. But in his intelligent and noble efforts to enlighten alike the learned and the ignorant, he derived but little encouragement from the former. Professional pride often stands in the way of honest convictions, and rarely permits a generous coöperation. Even the members of the Medical Profession—among whom Dr. Buchanan is a conspicuous light—were little disposed to treat the subject with the respect it deserved, and the candor that will be found to characterize every disinterested seeker after truth. But in the late Dr. Samuel Forry of New York, Dr. Caldwell of Louisville, Ky., and the Faculty of the University of Indiana, Dr. Buchanan met with honorable exceptions. While many independent minds became interested in his psychometrical experiments, our recognized authorities in science, with rare exceptions, thought too much of reputation and ease, and too little of the truth, to venture into new fields of investigation.[1] Among those who manifested at that early period a becoming interest in the subject, were several literary and scientific gentlemen in the city of New York, who served on a committee of investigation, and reported through their chairman, Dr. Forry, that "they had sufficient evidence to

---

[1] The Utopian anticipation that any great truths would be received at once, merely because they had been logically or practically demonstrated, is speedily annihilated by experience and observation. Under our unphilosophical systems of education, pure reason is but little cultivated ; and in the daily course of life there is so little dispassionate reasoning, compared with the great number of acts proceeding from habit and the impulses of feeling, guided only by simple perception, that an appeal to pure reason is well known to be a very inefficient mode of guiding or convincing mankind. Prejudice, association, example, and a misconceived self-interest, will blind the leading classes of society to the most palpable truths. The facts of Animal Magnetism, and especially clairvoyance, after being demonstrated before scientific medical committees, in Paris, and before tens of thousands, if not millions, of intelligent observers, throughout the civilized world, are still contemptuously ignored or rejected by the leading medical authors and reviewers, without any conscientious inquiry into the reality of such facts. They are simply dismissed, with a sneer, without honest argument or inquiry, with a vehement scorn of human intelligence and human veracity, which might be appropriate in a convict steeped in vice, but which is inexcusable in the members of a scientific profession, and still more in those who aspire to be the leaders of human thought. That demoralizing and soul-hardening philosophy which treats the human race as a vast assemblage of knaves and fools, from which no word of truth should be expected, and whose testimony is utterly inadmissible in science, has so long ruled the high places of the medical profession, that it is vain to expect its abolition in the present generation ; and under such a system it is vain to expect, in the authoritative quarters of the profession, the recognition of any wonderful facts when their supporting testimony is rejected, and the parties who reject conclusive evidence either totally refuse to make any investigation themselves, or enter upon it with a dogmatic and stubborn party spirit, determined to sustain their own foregone conclusions.—*Introduction to Buchanan's Neurological system of Anthropology.*

14

satisfy them that *Dr. Buchanan's views have a rational experimental foundation, and that the subject opens a field of investigation second to no other in immediate interest, and in promise of important future results to science and humanity.*"

While Dr. Buchanan's observations and experiments constitute the more important elements in the early history of Psychometry, it must be conceded that the fundamental facts and laws which the subject involves were discovered some time before the commencement of his investigations. The early experimenters in Animal Magnetism did not fail to observe that persons of acute sensibility were enabled to establish a sympathetic *rapport* with others at a distance, by holding a lock of hair, an article of clothing, or a finger-ring which the absent party had worn; or, indeed, by taking in the hand any small article of personal property that had been in contact with the body. While the impressions made on the mind of the sensitive investigator, in such cases, were perhaps mainly derived from the organic, physiological and pathological conditions of the person under examination, still it can not be denied that a mysterious *soul-measuring faculty* was frequently displayed. The diagnosis sometimes comprehended the mental and moral, as well as the physical conditions of the subject. Crimes and criminals were occasionally discovered in this way. The smallest fragment of a cravat, worn by a thief, would hold him fast; a shirt was a better means of detection than a sheriff; and an old shoe would suffice to put the sensitive explorer on the track of those who were either concealed, absent or lost. When the search resulted in finding the object, not only physical conditions and specific localities could be described

and pointed out, but the memory became an open book, that
could be read in the darkness of midnight ; the unspoken
thoughts of men were mysteriously revealed ; and the most
secret purposes were disclosed before time had afforded an
opportunity for their actual accomplishment. This capacity
to discover the measure and to define the limits of the
mental and moral powers, did not necessarily depend on information derived from autography. Similar information
was otherwise conveyed to the mind through the channels of
psychometric perception ; and thus the organic combinations,
the peculiar moods, and the superficial aspects of the human
faculties, affections and passions, were clearly revealed.

The fact that accurate pathological information was conveyed through the processes already described, was quite
sufficient to warrant the presumption that a knowledge of the
mental exercises and moral qualities of the individual might
be obtained in a similar manner. If the ordinary emanations
from the body indicated the existing states of the several
organs, it was reasonable to infer that a ' *thought*, expressed
through the nerves of voluntary motion, would possibly carry
along with it to the paper a subtile principle which might
serve as an index to the whole character, or a key to all the
treasures of the mind. And this amazing suggestion has
been literally verified by numberless experiments! Dr. Buchanan claims to have demonstrated the fact that a subtile
aura, in some respects distinct and peculiar, proceeds from
every separate organ of the brain, and records in invisible
but ineffaceable lines, the essential nature and precise measure
of each mental manifestation. Having placed one end of a
metallic conductor in the hand of a very sensitive subject, he

proceeded to touch the different organs of the brain of another person with the opposite end of the conductor, through which the influence—proceeding from the organic action of the separate faculties—was transmitted with such force and distinctness as to be clearly perceived by the psychometer, though he was not allowed to see what portions of the brain were touched.

When the multitudes are divided between unreasoning skepticism on one side and blind credulity on the other, the friends of a recently discoverd truth are fortunate if they have a representative qualified by nature and education, to conduct a scientific investigation of a new subject with candor and discrimination. Dr. Buchanan did not fail to exhibit the requisite qualifications—neither rejecting facts when they were new and strange, nor yet rashly accepting results because they were specious, while there remains a chance to prove that they may have been chimerical.

The ability to discern the real character of persons, by merely holding a letter against the forehead, certainly reveals a faculty that may be frequently employed with great practical advantage. Language is often used to *conceal* the essential character and real intentions of the speaker or writer; but the psychometrical power penetrates the frail disguise. With the aid of a simple autograph the soul-measurer lifts the moral visor, strikes down the glittering hield, and reveals the naked falsehood that lurked behind. As the subject does not appear to call for a statement of illustrative facts and experiments, recorded at length, the circumstantial details may be omitted. A brief reference to the following examples will suffice to show that, not only the general character and habits of thought are revealed by the psychometrical process, but the temporary moods of the mind, the existing thoughts and the present action are liable to cast their shadows over the sensitive soul. While Mrs. Mettler was holding a sealed letter from Dr. Buchanan— who was at that time editing the *Journal of Man*—she declared that the chief study of the writer was "Man, *in his whole nature.*" When an envelope inclosing some stanzas written by a convict, was placed in her hand, she observed that the author had a double character—the sphere was unpleasant, but that the person could "*write poetry tolerably well.*" A letter written by Kossuth, immediately after the delivery of a powerful speech in St. Louis, *caused her to ges- ticulate as if she were addressing a multitude, and this was followed by a feeling of extreme exhaustion.* The letter of an insane man, who had killed his own child, occasioned sympathetic delirium and convulsions. Some irregular pencil lines and scratches, traced by the hand of an infant child *gave no impression.* A very delicate picture on silk— painted by Miss Thomas, of Edwardsburg, Mich., and pre- sented to the writer—was handed to Mrs. M., under the cover of a sealed envelope, whereupon she affirmed that the author of the contents of the envelope had *painted her idea,* instead of expressing it in words.

Twelve years since the present writer published a number of mental and moral portraits of distinguished persons in the *Univercœlum.* They were living pictures, drawn with re- markable strength, beauty and fidelity, by Miss Parsons, of Boston. When a letter, written at Chelsea, England—by Thomas Carlyle—was handed to Miss P., she said, " The

sea is not far off; or a thought of the sea is in his mind."
When her hand was unconsciously resting on the autograph
of Washington Allston, she pronounced his name. A letter
from Ole Bull produced great exaltation of feeling. For
some time she appeared to be immersed in a sea of music, as
a few lines from her word-picture of the inspired Norwegian
will plainly indicate. On clasping the letter in her hand,
she at once exclaimed :

"Impetuous and enthusiastic !   *   *   He seems to me to be all soul, yet
all expression. I would be breathless and listen—I would have perfect silence about me. I can not bear to hear my own voice, it is so discordant.
Language is so stiff, and cold, and harsh ! Oh ! could you but hear the stars
as they roll to music—the flowers as they grow—the rythm of the streams and
birds ! This exquisite music calls up such adoration ! *This man worships.
At first he is absorbed in prayer ; then he is silent and solemn ; and self is
lost in the Infinite."   *   *   *

While Thomas L. Harris was employed in the improvisation
of his "Epic of the Starry Heaven," I made an experiment
in Psychometry (in the presence of several witnesses), which
was attended with surprising results. Mr. H. was one day
under a foreign intelligent influence, purporting to be spiritual, and was irresistibly impelled to write the name, Dante.
The slip of paper, bearing the name of the great Florentine
poet, being properly inclosed, was placed in the hands ot
Mrs. Mettler. At first she exhibited emotions of sadness and
grief. Then rising and walking toward a remote corner of
the apartment—her eyes being closed—she appeared to hold
converse with invisible beings. She paused and seemed
looking at objects beneath. Her whole frame shook spas-
modically, and the facial muscles were distorted and convulsed, as if frightful images were presented to her vision.

At length she spoke with uncommon emphasis, and in a strain that led those of the company who were acquainted with Dante's history to think that she was literally immersed in the poet's mental atmosphere ; and that visions of his earth-life and of the *Divina Commedia* were passing before her.

But the historic and other extraordinary characters are not the only ones that exert an influence on human affairs, long after the earthly drama of life is over. Every man leaves a record that time can not obliterate. Every work of the individual heart and hands is an enduring monument of his soul's ideal ; and his moral image is indelibly stamped on everything which his thought, affection or passion have prompted him to touch. The conclusion is startling, but inevitable. It is, moreover, full of beautiful suggestions, useful instruction, and solemn warning. Every secret act is recorded, and may be openly reviewed by those who shall come after us. It has been proved by experiment that the vital and mental influences which emanated from the actual life and thought of the buried nations, still lingers about the enchanted ruins. The psychometer may decipher the hieroglyphics on the ancient tombs and temples, and thus interpret the spirit of bygone ages. In this way we may yet learn respecting the ancients what History did not chronicle. While we are daily preparing the life record, that to-morrow may be submitted to this searching ordeal, it may be profitable to consider that wherever we go, and in all that we do, we either grope in darkness, among the thorn we have planted, or we walk in light, scattering fresh flowers by the wayside, to cheer and bless those who may succeed us in the journey of life.

The idea of the ancients, that certain localities were especially consecrated, was not all fanciful. It is well known that in those places where spiritually-minded persons are accustomed to meet frequently for social and sacred purposes, certain invisible powers manifest their presence with far greater freedom and in a more tangible manner. Where true hearts meet and are united in pure affection ; where great thoughts shine out from the temples of the mind; where the aspirations of congenial souls mingle and ascend in spiritual worship, then, and *there*, will kindred natures from the Inner Temple assemble, and the place will be consecrated by their presence. Their divine emanations fall on the altar of the heart and quicken the latent powers of the worshiper. Thus, by the law of spiritual attraction, the powers of the immortal world may assemble in such places as are consecrated by pure love and devotion, by noble deeds and sacred associations. They walked by the haunted streams ; they met the old Druids in the solemn forests, and appeared in the lonely mountains by the altars of the ancient Prophets.

When one is gifted with a keen psychometric sense, he at once perceives the nature of the emanations from his visitors, whether they are visible or invisible. If he enters the haunts of deception and vice, clouds darken the spiritual vision, and he finds the trail of the serpent in his way. Those who are distinguished for their exquisite susceptibility, seldom fail to perceive the general sphere of the houses they enter. Not unfrequently are these psychometric impressions, or intuitive revelations, made as soon as they cross the threshold. Sometimes harsh discords fall on the inner sense, and the nerves vibrate under the painful pressure of domestic and social antagonisms. But the mansions of domestic peace and true fidelity of soul, disclose Elysian fields of the affections, where the Angels walk in light, or recline amid scenes of blissful repose. The senses are all refined and exalted by a pure moral and spiritual atmosphere. Every object seems to be pervaded by a subtile, mysterious power, that gently sweeps the inmost chords of being. We feel that we are in one of the consecrated places. The lively sense that elsewhere revealed the serpent's trail, here finds the radiant footsteps of celestial visitors and heavenly emanations that make the place holy.

"The pure in heart" meet and dwell in heavenly places. Angels stand by them in their transfigured beauty, and surround the loving heart with a sphere that is full of light and melody. They come to lead the weary pilgrim from the rude scenes of outer life and consciousness, to mansions of inward rest. They leave their pure emanations behind when they depart. Every earthly object they have touched is made luminous, and continues to scintillate with star-like radiations. To the spiritual eye their very foot-prints are visible in the light on the floor. The glory of their presence dissipates the darkness of the world; their smiles dissolve the frosts of years; they restore the spring-time of the affections, and make life's barren wastes bloom like the gardens of Paradise. While I write I am insphered in music, soft and soothing as the gentlest strains from Æolia, when the expiring winds whisper their last benison to the trembling chords of the Lyre.

CHAPTER XVIII.

PHILOSOPHY OF FASCINATION.

Isolation impossible—The democracy of Nature—The Elements impressive Teachers—All bodies have their Atmospheres—Reciprocal interchange of Elements—Universal Relations, Causes and Effects—Power of Fascination directed to specific Objects—Examples of Charming—Birds fascinated by Serpents—Case of a Child near Gilbert's Mills—An illustration from Vaillant's Travels in Africa—Opinion of Dr. Newman—Serpent Charmers of India—The Laplander's power over his Dogs—Sullivan and Rarey, the Horse-tamers—Fascination of Birds by a Belgian Beauty—Man the Governor of the World—A lecture at Putnam—A Canine illustration.

COMPLETE isolation is never one of the conditions of being. The elements exist together, and are modified by mutual association and action. Ultimate particles, by a natural coalescence, unite and form the worlds. The great kingdoms of Nature—rising in orderly succession, one above another—have no absolute independence. Each sustains intimate relations to the others, and the whole resembles a vast pyramid. whose base is broad as *terra*, and whose common vertex is Man. The forms of the organic creation all exhibit intimate relations, and are mutually dependent ; nor can man, with all his boasted freedom, separate himself from his natural relations, or break away from his appropriate place in the complex web of existence. Every day his pride is humbled by some lesson of painful experience, and he is made to feel the force of a natural law of democratic equality. Providence permits inferior natures to share with him the common elements of the world. The same earth nourishes man and every meaner creature, and the same atmosphere moves the lungs of every living thing. The prince has small reason to frown on the beggar, or the philosopher to despise the savage, since those who consume most of the products of the earth are of all men most dependent. Before God the artificial distinctions which elevate the inheritors of wealth, and power, and royalty, may only serve to reveal their intrinsic poverty and the most abject dependence. The fire that consumes their dwellings and their goods, the frost that chills their blood, and the tempests that destroy their harvests, alike admonish them that Nature resorts to no special legislation in their behalf. Even the pestilential vapors from the loathsome hovels of the great city—borne along by the free winds—often become ministers of justice and equality, to teach the rich and the proud the unwelcome truth that they belong to the same fraternity with the wretched outcasts of St. Giles.

This intimate relation of all the forms of the natural world to each other, involves a perpetual commingling of their subtile emanations and forces ; hence their reciprocal influence and all the phenomena of action and reaction. But I will be more explicit. Doubtless all material bodies have their atmospheres, composed of the more ethereal portions of the simple substances and organizations which constitute the forms of the material creation. Moreover, the mind that is gifted with acute and delicate powers of perception—from the conscious influence of these refined elements on the phases of thought and feeling—may determine their respective sources, inasmuch as the essential nature and specific qualities of the emanations from all bodies must resemble the grosser elements, thus held in chemical and organic union by the power of cohesion and the mysterious principle of life. The ponderable and imponderable substances of the physical world are chiefly dissimilar in the existing *states* of the simple elements, and the conditions of organic and inorganic combination. It follows, therefore, that the material and spiritual worlds and their elemental principles, the earths and their organized forms, the souls of men and the hosts of heaven, all have atmospheres which combine and represent the essential attributes and qualities of their respective natures and peculiar states.

The forms of organized life are constantly influenced by the existing conditions of the unorganized elements. The varying degrees of light and moisture, and the thermo-electrical changes constantly occurring in the earth and atmosphere, all modify the states and processes of vegetable, animal, and human existence. It is well known that plants and animals, by a natural and constant reciprocation, furnish each other with the essential elements of their mutual life and growth. Each is necessary to the normal existence of the other. Moreover, they exert an influence on man under all circumstances, and in every period of his mundane career. Gorgeous colors, harmonic sounds, delicate aromas, and exquisite flavors, all feast and delight the senses. But the invisible emanations from inanimate forms produce other and less agreeable effects. Invisible agents of infection are evolved from the decomposing processes of the organic world. The smoke arising from the combustion of certain poisonous plants and trees, diffuses their deleterious properties. Moreover, the natural exhalations from the Upas, in the forests of Java, and, to some extent, from trees that grow in our own country, are said to infect the atmosphere by their poisonous effluvia.

A comprehensive law unites all things in one universal economy, embracing every orb and every atom. All receive their mysterious quickening from the same incomprehensible Center of life and motion ; and whatever antagonisms may appear on the remote surfaces of being, there is UNITY at the Heart. This relation of all things to a common source, involves a corelation of the several parts, one to another, and each to all. Hence the universal sympathies of Nature, as illustrated in the laws and processes of molecular attraction, elective and chemical affinity, and the natural gravitation and cohesion of simple elements in worlds, and suns, and souls.

If, then, a subtle influence emanates from every orb, and even from each ultimate particle which is irresistible as the gravitation that balances the Universe, and all the potencies of Nature, reside in sublimated invisible elements ; if every inanimate object sustains relations to all others, and each simple substance is thus surrounded by its own peculiar emanations—influential as far as its atmosphere extends— we need not be surprised to learn that similar influences proceed from all the forms of animated nature ; and that by voluntary effort they may be greatly intensified and easily directed to particular objects. While the absence of life and locomotion leave all inanimate things to preserve the

same relative positions, the inhabitants of the animal kingdom—by the power of voluntary motion—are enabled to
change their positions in respect to fixed objects and geographical lines, and thus to change their relations to each
other at pleasure. It will be perceived that the sphere of invisible, commingling elements, that surrounds the animal and
the man, can scarcely remain unchanged during any two
days in the whole existence of the individual. Hence the
influences which excite and determine feeling, volition and
action, are susceptible of an indefinite number of changes
and combinations. Everything that lives and moves in our
presence, modifies the very atmosphere we breathe. A man
may not so much as speak or lift his hand—not even *feel*
deeply or *think* earnestly—without moving the electro-magnetic aura that surrounds his person. In this manner we
unconsciously modify the conditions of being as far as our influence may extend. And who shall define the ultimate limits
of individual influence? It is not without some show of
reason as well as fancy, that certain ingenious theorists have
maintained that the ripple occasioned by dropping a pebble
into the midst of the sea moves the surface to the distant
shore; that the reverberations of sound have no limit in
space; and that the great globe itself—in some inappreciable degree—trembles beneath our footsteps.

The mysterious forces of life, as developed through the
agent of sensation, and of vital and voluntary motion, are
essentially the same in all animal and human bodies. This
electric agent, on which the functions of animated nature
are perceived to depend, being homogeneous in all the forms
of the living world, it is but natural that they should—

through this refined and all-prevading medium—exert a powerful influence on each other. This being the proximate agent in all the functions of animal and human bodies, it is only necessary to control the distribution of this principle, in order to influence the voluntary and involuntary functions of all living beings. Whenever this refined aura is sent out from one animal or man to another individual of the same or of a distinct species, the creature to which it is directed may be influenced in a degree that varies according to the measure of executive force in the operator, and the degree of susceptibility in the subject. If the active force be strong, properly concentrated, and directed with unerring precision ; and if, at the same time, the recipient be in a passive condition, or quiescent state, so that the vital effluvium may be absorbed, or otherwise permitted to pervade the channels of nervous energy, the effects produced on the functions will be at once decided and wonderful. The subtile effluence from animals and men appropriately belongs to themselves, and may be influenced by them after it has been made to pervade other living forms. In proportion, therefore, as this homogeneous agent of sensation and motion is *infused* by one living being into another, the two become—temporarily, at least—associated or conjoined. When this relation has been fairly established, and the common medium of electro-nervous communication flows uninterruptedly, the one acquires a mysterious and irresistible power over the sensations, affections and movements of the other.

The examples of the exercise of this power—when they occur among animals of the lower orders, and between man and inferior creatures—are ordinarily distinguished and

characterized by the terms *fascination and charming.* The
phenomenal illustrations are numerous, but a few examples
will suffice in this connection. That beasts of prey and
serpents frequently exercise this remarkable power over
other creatures, and that reptiles, birds, and quadrupeds are
susceptible of the influence, are facts established by the concurrent testimony of many conscientious observers. The
writer once witnessed the results of this species of enchantment. I was one day angling along the bank of a stream
in Spencer, Massachusetts, when my attention was attracted
by the wild, unusual notes and the rapid gyrations of a
robin. The bird was moving in concentric circles about a
little tree, and around a principle branch of which I espied
the coil of a large black snake. The head of the serpent
was elevated, and his eyes apparently fixed on his prey, while
the bird was every moment drawing nearer to destruction.
The natural enmity of man to all snakes, which (according
to the theologians) I inherited from the common mother of
mankind, prompted a resolute assault on the serpent, broke
the spell, and the affrighted bird escaped.

In like manner serpents and cats charm mice, squirrels,
and other small animals ; and instances are not wanting in
which human beings have been spell-bound by this subtile
magnetism. Dr. Newman, in his work on Fascination, refers
to two or three persons who were fascinated by serpents ;
and several well-authenticated cases have appeared in the
newspapers. Among the number of recent examples, I am
reminded of the case of a small boy—five years old—son of
a Mr. Martin, who lives near Gilbert's Mills. The little
fellow was observed to be very quiet, uncommunicative, and

apparently failing in health. From day to day he was wont to leave his companions and spend some time alone, at a little distance from the house. One day a person, who was thus led to watch his movements, followed him to the bank of a creek. When the child had seated himself and commenced to eat his dinner, a large snake made his appearance, and coiling itself about the lad in the most familiar way, shared the child's repast, licking his fingers and rubbing against the cheek of the charmed boy, as if caressing him with the fondest affection. The snake was killed, and the child soon recovered his normal health and disposition. If such examples do not render the Hebrew story of Eve's seduction more than probable, we must leave the skeptics in the hands of the theologians.

It may not be safe, in all cases, to abruptly destroy the reptile under such circumstances. When the operator and the subject are both human, it is often found that there is such a complete blending of the nervous forces of the two bodies, that any injury inflicted on the former is instantly felt by the latter. Indeed, the magnetized subject will often sense the least violence done to his magnetizer, when he is not sensible of the injury done to his own body. Vaillant, in the account of his Travels in Africa, relates that on one occasion he shot a large serpent while the reptile was in the act of charming a bird. He was surprised on observing that the bird did not move as he approached. On a closer inspection the reason was obvious—*the bird was dead.* In the opinion of Dr. Newman, either fear or this strange power of fascination destroyed its life ; but in the judgment of the present writer the death of the bird is not to be ascribed to

15

the one or the other of the causes named. Doubtless the same shot that killed the serpent destroyed the life of the bird also, owing to the intimate blending of the nervous or vital forces of the two bodies.

While few men have been fascinated by snakes, the serpent charmers of India all possess this remarkable influence over the reptillia of their country, and nothing is more common among the barbarous African Tribes than this power of fascination. Travelers inform us that the natives handle scorpions and vipers with the greatest freedom, and without the slightest injury or apprehension, placing them in their bosoms or throwing them among their children. According to Mr. Bruce, who had abundant opportunities for personal observation, the venomous creatures close their eyes, and appear to be rendered powerless by handling; and he affirms that they make no resistance when the barbarians devour them alive.

When the serpent exercises this power, either over the animal or human subject, the head assumes an erect position, and the eyes, which are directed to the object, exhibit an unusual brilliancy. The electric forces are most intensely focalized about the organs of vision when the attention is thus concentrated, and the subtile influence is projected in invisible shafts while the gaze continues to be fixed. This is substantially the method adopted by the human operator, while the whole process and the actual results are fundamentally the same. By this influence the Laplander at once subdues his furious dogs, rendering them perfectly harmless and docile in a surprising degree. We have lion and tiger tamers in our own country, before whose fixed gaze and resolute will the ferocious beasts quail and become submissive. Other men tame wild horses. Townsend gives an account of one James Sullivan, who was familiarly known as the *whisperer*. He would enter the stable alone with the most vicious horse, and in half an hour the animal would be completely subdued by the fascinating spell of Sullivan. Rarey has quite recently attracted general attention in this country and in Europe by his truly masterly exercise of the same power.

Birds are susceptible of this power of fascination ; but from among the illustrations of this class I can only cite a single example. Some time since Mademoiselle Vandermeersch, a beautiful young lady from Belgium, created a peculiar interest by an exhibition of her learned birds. Some may be inclined to ascribe the results in this case to an ordinary educational process ; but it was apparently under the action of her will that the birds were impelled to answer various questions correctly, by drawing cards on which the appropriate answers were inscribed. When the beautiful charmer demanded to know the hour, her goldfinch would hop out from his cage and look about among the cards, apparently engaged in serious deliberation. At length he would lay hold of the right card, and tossing it to the company in a cavalier manner, would return to his perch in the cage. In this way a great number and variety of questions were answered with surprising accuracy.

That Humanity possesses this inherent power over the brute creation, the writer has no doubt. The facts cited in this chapter are incidental illustrations occurring under a great law, that is broad and comprehensive in its scope as the nature and relations of animal and human existence. Had that law been everywhere perceived and universally acted on, it is quite likely that all inferior creatures would have recognized man's right to the scepter of the world. But through his ignorance and his cruelty he has trampled that law under foot; and, as a natural consequence, the stronger animals have manifested a determined resistance to his authority.

I can not omit some reference in this connection to an interesting incident in my own experience. I was on one occasion illustrating this idea of the natural supremacy of man, in the course of a public lecture, delivered in the Village Hall, Putnam, Conn., when I observed that a strange dog was laying at full length on the floor, at a distance of not less than thirty or forty feet from the platform. The noble animal—a large one of his kind—appeared to be asleep, and no more interested than other drowsy hearers. The speaker was insisting, with some earnestness, that had man strictly obeyed the natural law, designed to regulate his relations to the animal kingdom, *the whole brute creation would probably have yielded instinctive obedience to his authority.* Just at that point in the discourse the dog, without any apparent cause, was suddenly disturbed. Rising from his recumbent position, he walked slowly to the front of the speaker's stand. Looking steadily in my face for a minute or two, he deliberately ascended the stairs and stretched himself at my feet, at the very moment the argument was concluded ; thus presenting a most interesting and impressive illustration of a curious and profound subject.

CHAPTER XIX.

ANIMAL AND HUMAN MAGNETISM.

Introductory Observations—Assumptions of Superficial Investigators—Testimony of the late Dr. Gregory—Philosophical Suggestions—Lawless Speculators and scientific Babel-builders—Criticism of the Great Harmonia—Amazing production of Mechanical Force—Timely discovery of a common Error—Professional Fallacies—Science defined and Medicine found wanting—Phenomenal aspects of the Magnetic Sleep.

A S electrical forces develop and regulate the processes of organic chemistry, the functions of voluntary and involuntary motion and sensation, and the circulation of all the animal fluids, it will be no less apparent, that all forms of vital and functional derangement originate—as to their organic incipiency—*in electrical disturbances of the nervous system*. By a natural and necessary sequence we therefore conclude, that any method or process whereby the practioner, in the healing art, is enabled to directly govern the electrical forces, or materially influence the distribution of this subtile agent, at once invests him with a masterly power over the various forms of disease.

It was observed, in the former part of this treatise, that all disturbances of the vital forces, and consequent irregularities in the organic action, may be comprehended in two general classes, namely, *the positive and negative forms of disease.*

Every departure from the normal standard involves either an excess or a deficiency of the electro-vital motive power. Moreover, the positive and negative states of the body, and of the particular organs, are invariably accompanied by a correspondingly increased or diminished electro-thermal, chemical, vascular and organic action. To accelerate or to retard these processes and functions—as circumstances require in the treatment of diesase—we must of course act on and through the very agent on which they severally and collectively depend. Vital electricity being the operative agent in animal chemistry ; in the generation of vital heat and organic force ; in the circulation of the fluids ; and in all the functions of sensation and voluntary motion, it follows of necessity, that the power to control the circulation and action of this agent qualifies its possessor to determine the physiological action and the pathological states of the system, and hence to subdue all the curable forms of disease.

Among the pretenders to a knowledge of the Magnetic Mysteries of the living world, very few have pursued the investigation of the subject in a truly scientific spirit. Even those who set up the most imposing claims to public confidence, often expose themselves and the subject to derision, by their large faith in the infallibility of their own desultory speculations and impressions. With such pretended philosophers the observation of a new class of phenomena is at once presumed to confer something more than a hypothetical existence on a hitherto undiscovered imponderable. Some animal ' Magnetic Fluid," " Ethereum," or " Od Force," is alleged to exist and to be the operative cause in the production of the newly classified phenomena. Vain and superficial

investigators are quick to herald their discoveries and slow
to learn that they were only imaginary. Such men are
accustomed to treat the whole ideal family *auras* as if they
belonged to the category of demonstrated realities. If one
can not derive instruction from such weakness and credulity,
he may at least be amused to see with what readiness certain
grave and distinguished persons mistake a specious hypothesis for a scientific deduction, and promptly pay their respects
to the whole retinue of imaginary agents ; at the same time
they indorse the paper of every last discoverer of a "new
fluid" until it passes current with the people.

If in order to avoid a too frequent repetition of the same
words in similar relations, different terms are employed in
the same general sense—or to denote the same thing—it may
be all very well, and the only question likely to arise would
relate merely to the proprieties of speech ; but if each separate term be understood to represent some new principle or
force in Nature, distinguished by essential qualities, from the
one agent on which the phenomena of life, sensation and
motion are known to depend, the error assumes a grave
character, and should be exposed. Not only do the experiments of Galvani, Matteucci, Reymond, Humboldt, Buff, Smee,
and others demonstrate that the vital, sensorial and voluntary functions of human and animal bodies *are electrically
produced ;* but other distinguished electricians, chemists and
physiologists — without pursuing a similar course of experiment—have adopted their conclusions. To the list of
scientific authorities—already referred to for confirmation
of the writer's views—I will only add the name and testimony of the late Dr. Gregory, for many years professor of

Electricity and Chemistry in the University of Edinburgh. I extract the following passage from his chemical science :

" The existence in all parts of the body of an alkaline liquid, the blood, and an acid liquid, the juice of the flesh, separated by a very thin membrane, and in contact with muscle and nerve, seems to have some relation to the fact, now established, of the existence of electric currents in the body and particularly to those which occur when the muscles contract. The animal body may therefore be regarded as a galvanic engine for the production of mechanical force......A working man, it has been calculated, produces in twenty-four hours an amount of heating or thermal effect equal to the demand in raising nealy fourteen millions of pounds to the height of one foot. ...But from causes connected with the range of temperature, he can only produce, in the form of actual work done, about as much mechanical effect as would raise three million five hundred thousand pounds the hight of one foot in twenty-four hours."

If vital and voluntary motion and sensation thus depend on the presence and motion of a subtile fluid known as animal electricity—the actual existence of which no scientific observer pretends to dispute—it must be obvious that the various chemical, physiological, and psychological changes which result from the magnetic manipulations directly depend on the influence exerted over this known and acknowledged agent of feeling, thought and motion. If the excitation of the electric fluid that pervades the sensories occasions sensation, there is no valid reason for presuming that some other agent—not absolutely known to exist—is acted upon when the avenues of sensation are closed, as in the magnetic sleep, or opened to the phantom throng of psycho-sensorial illusions. It must be obvious that whenever feeling is either increased, diminished or suspended, the effects must be produced through the unequal distribution or abnormal action of the very agent on which the sensation, in all its phases, proximately depends. Moreover, the medium of vital motion must be the subtile principle through which we operate when the organic functions are accelerated, retarded or otherwise influenced by the manipulations of the magnetizer or the will of the psychologist. The assumption that a fluid, distinct from vital electricity, is either imparted or withdrawn from the subject in the production of these effects, derives no confirmation from the record of scientific discovery. Nor is it logical to infer, from the facts themselves, the existence and action of some undiscovered imponderable, so long as an agent already known to exist will suffice to account for all the phenomena.

Certain undisciplined minds are extremely liable to mistake a peculiar looseness of statement for remarkable freedom of thought. Such men discover only useless landmarks and arbitrary restraints in the ordinary demonstrations of science, while the best evidence that they are independent thinkers is to be found in their mental recklessness and irresponsibility. We have teachers who insist that Magnetism is a subtile *fluid;* that it exists essentially as well as phenomenally ; that Magnetism is warm whilst Electricity is cold ; that the one is the agent of sensation in animal and human bodies, while muscular motion directly depends on the other; that Magnetism is the positive force in the vital constitution, and Electricity the negative force ; that in producing the magnetic state we must withdraw the positive force from the subject *by the still more positive power of the operator.* In the name of Philosophy all this and much more is very freely offered and as promptly rejected.

The foregoing assumptions, taken together, do not constitute a comprehensible thesis, but an unintelligible jargon,
with no better foundation than the erratic and lawless speculations of the uneducated mind. I may be pardoned if I
do not understand true mental freedom to consist in a total
indifference to natural law, in the absence of rational
restraints, and in ignorance of scientific discoveries. It is
quite natural for those who have been enfranchised to this
unlimited extent, to feel that they are entitled to " the largest
liberty." They may permit the imagination to " take a
spree" in the new realms of thought; the nobler faculties—
for want of more serious, orderly, and profitable employment
—may each in turn play the harlequin ; and even Reason—
intoxicated with self-love—be allowed to appear in perpetual masquerade. But instead of a mere repetition of this
species of "ground and lofty tumbling" (for the further entertainment of those who are, for the most part, convinced and
interested by the mere prestige of certain proper names,) an
indestructible basis—natural forces, accredited facts, and
discovered laws—is here offered as the foundation of a
rational philosophy. By logical deductions from such premises we shall proceed to the final conclusion, leaving such
speculators in fancy stocks as are determined to build the
whole temple of Science on visions and impressions, to

    " Dive at stars and fasten in the mud."

While there may be no such " *magnetic fluid*, universally
diffused" in Nature, as is presumed to exist in the thesis of
Anthony Mesmer, and in the faith of his willing disciples.
still the phenomena under discussion are neither unreal nor

unimportant. In respect to animated nature, therefore, the term *Magnetism* may properly represent a variety of curious and instructive phenomena, all depending on certain electro-physiological conditions and changes in animal and human bodies.

The popular notion that the so-called magnetic phenomena depend on the agency of a fluid, distinct from the animal electricity evolved in the processes of vital chemistry, and disengaged in the organic functions of the system, rests on nothing better than a very common assumption. It is neither sustained by a single principle nor illustrated by a solitary fact in science. Moreover, it will be time to consider the *temperature* of Magnetism when it is fairly demonstrated that such a *fluid* has anything more substantial than an imaginary existence. The kindred assertion that " electricity is *cold*," is not illustrated in a very clear and convincing way by the results of its action, as seen in the sudden combustion of buildings, in the fusion of metals and solid rocks, and in the evidences of intense heat found on the barren plains of Silesia and Persia, where the sands are often melted and formed into vitreous tubes of several yards in length, by the disruptive electrical discharges from the atmospheric batteries. [1]

But I have not done. That the nervous medium of sensation is essentially distinct from the agent of vital and voluntary motion, is not even supported by a remote probability. We are not authorized to infer that the nervous fluid is one thing, when it is excited at the papillary terminations—by

---

[1] See Webster's Elements of Physics, London edition, page 470.

outward elements and external objects—and something essentially different, when it is disturbed at the source of the
motors, or at the nervous centers—by some involuntary emotion, or the action of the will. Nor is this all. The notion
that, in order to produce a state of coma, the magnetic or
positive force of the body is withdrawn by the still more
positive power of the magnetizer, does not appear to be according to the natural law ; for since positive and negative
objects and forces, only, exhibit attraction, it would follow
that if the positive force of the subject be extracted at all, it
would seek and find its equilibrium alone in a union with
what is negative in the operator. [1]

The nervous system is a most delicate, complicated and
beautiful electro-telegraphic machine. The intelligent operator—the SPIRIT—has his chief residence and principal station in the physical sensorium, from which the lines of
communication diverge to all points. He has one large and
many smaller batteries with corresponding reservoirs, together with suitable machinery, alkalies, acids, etc., for the
generation of the electric force required on all the lines of
communication, and for numerous other important purposes.
The whole realm covered by the infinite ramifications of the
nervo-telegraphic network, is one splendid workshop, and the
property of the same individual. The proprietor employs
electro-hydraulic and caloric engines of small dimensions but
of great power. Beside a force—estimated at fifty tons—
expended in blowing the vital fires, in driving the engines,
working the forcing-pumps, in the transportation of liquid
and solid substances to every part of the industrial domain,

---

[1] The reader is referred to the Great Harmonia, Vol. III, Lecture XI.

and in frequently moving the whole concern from place to place, the owner—under favorable circumstances—is sure to have a surplus electro-thermal power—applicable to mechanical purposes—which, (according to the calculation of Dr. Gregory and other scientific authorities) *is sufficient to annually carry seventeen hundred tons from the foundation to the top of St. Paul's in London !* Such parts of the business as do not require a constant, intelligent supervision, proceed uninterruptedly through the night. *The whole* business of the establishment is prosecuted, on an average, some sixteen hours in twenty-four, during which time the superintendent keeps his office doors and all the windows open ; but generally he drops his curtains at regular intervals, bars the doors, and retiring to an inner chamber, rests for several hours without interruption.

As the writer does not belong to any school in Medicine, and is not otherwise employed in the practice of the healing art, he may reasonably expect to escape the suspicion of writing to advertise his claims as a practitioner. Other motives and objects demand a reference to my own experiments in this department, and to these I shall devote the succeeding Chapter. I am reminded that when one undertakes the advocacy of new views, calculated to unsettle the general confidence in existing systems, the public has a right to demand the best evidence the case will admit of, and may justly withhold so much as even an implied indorsement in the absence of all tangible proofs. Mere theorists and philosophical speculators, who support their fanciful and improbable notions by no substantial evidence, can not reasonably expect to inspire confidence, either in the value or the correctness of their peculiar ideas. Moreover, no intelligent, fair-minded man will be disposed to cling to his preconceived opinions when once they are plainly disproved by the discovered laws of Nature and the results of scientific experiment.

It was only after suffering for years the painful consequences of my error, (the very common and often fatal mistake of supposing that health is to be sought in nostrums and purchased of apothecaries, rather than found in an intelligent perception of, and a strict obedience to, the laws of vital harmony,) that the fallacies of the Profession were fairly uncovered and comprehended, and the use of medicine —as ordinarily administered—was perceived to be the trial of doubtful expedients, rather than a truly scientific adaptation of means to ends. I can not be unjust toward others without impoverishing myself ; and I have certainly nothing to gain by undervaluing the learned professions. I am well aware that the Medical Profession has already furnished a long list of illustrious names of men, whose discoveries occupy a large space in the scientific records of our country and the world. Perhaps no profession is now dignified by a greater number of free, enlightened and noble minds ; and it is precisely for this reason that I shall not be accused of treating the subject unfairly. It will doubtless be conceded that *Science properly comprehends not merely a classification of particular facts, but likewise an explanation of the essential laws on which such facts depend.* Wherever this definition is accepted, it will be perceived that Medicine does not answer the description. It is readily granted that we are supplied with the necessary classification of the phenomenal effects of Medicine and the superficial aspects of disease ; but we wait for the discovery of *the essential laws* under which all physiological, pathological, and therapeutic effects occur ; and until those laws are clearly recognized and duly respected, the practice of Medicine, at best, is but a course of doubtful experiment which may destroy the constitution with the disease.

In returning from this digression, a brief summary of the phenomenal aspects of the Magnetic slumber will conclude this Chapter. When sleep is induced by magnetic manipulations, the avenues leading from the outer world to the soul are closed ; the process of telegraphic communication is suspended, and the physical and mental functions—so far as they depend on voluntary effort—are temporarily arrested. These effects can only be produced by the direct influence exerted over the known and accredited agent of sensation and motion. By the concentration of that agent at certain points, and by the wide diffusion of the subtile principle ; by its equal and unequal distribution ; by its sudden dissipation from particular organs and the centers of electro-nervous energy ; by alternately interrupting and restoring the electrical equilibrium of the brain and other vital parts ; and by changing the polarity of the organs—all of which effects the skillful operator may develop, agreeably to certain physical and psycho-electrical laws—we produce all the mysterious changes in the processes of animal chemistry ; in the varying phenomena of sensation ; and in the organic action of the whole body, which are known to occur under the hand, the eye, and the will of any person who is skilled in vital magnetics.

The condition of the magnetic sleeper is usually one of serene and profound repose. He gradually becomes unconscious of time and space, and, in a greater or less degree, regardless of his relations to external objects. When all the outward avenues, through which the soul is wont to receive its impressions, are thus closed, a temporary paralysis rests on the physical medium and instruments of sensation A leaden slumber weighs down the eyelids ; the ear is dull and insensible ; and the delicate " nerve spirit," that like a fleet courier ran through and along each sensitive fiber, and every nerve of motion—keeping the soul in correspondence with the external world—like a weary traveler rests by the way. Thus the portals of our mortal tabernacle are closed for a season ; the conscious and voluntary faculties of the mind are held in subjection by a spell that finds its most striking analogy in death ; while the immortal dweller in the temple retires alone—to the inner sanctuary—for the sweet solace of calm repose and silent communion.

CHAPTER XX.

MAGNETISM AS A THERAPEUTIC AGENT.

Absurdities of a routine Practice—Cosmological Changes—Progressive refinement of Human Nature—Modes of equalizing the Circulation—A System founded on Natural Law—Confirmation a Cure for Rheumatism—Observations by the Author—Mrs. Gardner cured of Asthma—Case of Catalepsis at the City Hotel, Springfield—Medical skill ineffectual—The young Lady suddenly restored—Asphyxia from a fall—Mrs. Mills cured of pleurisy—Rheumatic Fever and Inflammation immediately subdued—Philosophy of the Effects—Case of Miss Sarah Elizabeth Lockwood—Spinal Disease accompanied by loss of Speech and Locomotion—Testimony of the *Stamford Advocate*—Letter from the Patient—Instantaneous cure of Symptomatic Derangement—The Lunatic clothed and in her right mind.

THE remedial agents employed with success in one case may totally fail in another—and even prove to be injurious—owing to the endless diversity among men, in respect to physical organization, combination of temperaments, states of the mind, and varying degrees of susceptibility to physical mental and moral influences. Hence the same medical treatment in all cases—for the same general type of disease —without such modifications as the individual constitution may require, can never be uniformly successful. Much less can a routine practice, founded on ancient medical author ities, be pursued at this day with any reasonable hope of beneficial results. The constitutions of men ; our manner of life ; our pursuits and habits of thought ; and even the

16

earth and atmosphere, have all changed. We are becoming
sublimated by the progress of civilization, the influence of
Literature, Art, Science and Commerce, and the development of the mental and spiritual faculties and forces of
human nature.

Moreover, the same kinds of food that once were readily
digested and assimilated—thus freely contributing to augment the vital energies—are now burdensome to the stomach
and wholly unsuited to promote either physical health or
mental activity. Similar changes have occurred in the
specific forms of disease. All these should be carefully
observed, and their relations to the fundamental laws of
being comprehended. The wisest physicians already perceive the necessity for corresponding changes and modifications in the professional modes of practice ; and hence they
administer medicine with caution, in alterative doses and
sublimated forms. Some centuries ago, when men were less
human, and far more gross and animal than now, they survived the action of powerful drugs and a thorough course of
depletion, such as would now be followed by a complete and
hopeless prostration of the system. It is barely possible that
the inhabitants of Central Africa and the South Sea Islands
might still be benefitted by such treatment, but it is absolutely
certain that the more refined nations of Europe and America
require it no longer.

When the physician is called to attend a sick man, his first
object is to *equalize the circulation*. If this purpose can be
accomplished by the use of the doctor's remedial agents, the
patient will be sure to recover. But with rare exceptions
the means and modes adopted by the Faculty are neither the

most direct nor the most effectual. Attempts to sustain the
vital principle by the use of deadly poisons ; to equalize the
forces and to restore organic harmony by causing a general
insurrection in the stomach, followed by fierce, intestinal
tempests ; removing pain by the administration of opiates
that deaden and destroy sensation ; diminishing the systolic
and diastolic action by tapping the tributaries of the *vena
cava* ; and sending *mercury* like a swift sheriff to arrest the
disorderly vital forces and, perhaps, to transform the physical man into an instrument for barometrical observations
for the remainder of his natural life—all these are the
clumsy, unnatural, and dangerous devices of scientific ignorance and titled empiricism.

But I am to present the claims of a more rational and
effectual treatment, founded on the existence and recognition
of a fundamental law in the vital economy, and the discovery
and adaptation of natural means to the most beneficent ends.
Some of the simpler phenomena in this department occur so
frequently as to be matters of common observation. It is
well known that severe pain is often greatly alleviated or
wholly removed, by gently passing the hand a number of
times, over the affected part. A similar motion of the hand
from the brain, along the spinal column of an animal, will
produce a state of unusual passivity ; and cats, dogs and
other quadrupeds, not unfrequenly fall asleep when thus
subjected to the influence of even the inexperienced and
unskillful experimenter. Fifteen minutes in a barber's chair
—with the manipulations of the tonsorial operator about the
cranium—may suffice to cure a headache. By a similar
process, and agreeably to the same general law, nurses—

almost unconsciously to themselves—subdue the nervous
irritability and restlessness of children ; and it often
happens that the moral and physical resistance of older
persons is overcome by the magnetism of the hand. I find
a humorous illustration of the subject in an anecdote that
recently appeared in the papers. An ignorant old lady,
who had but recently received confirmation at the hands of
the Bishop, presented herself a second time as a candidate,
saying, she wanted to be confirmed again—*because it was so
good for her " rheumatiz."*

Though little understood, this natural mode of treating
diseases is far more effectual than the means and methods
prescribed by the scientific authorities in medicine. It is
practiced with success among heathen nations and savage
tribes, often accompanied by mystical ceremonies, the invo-
cation of occult powers, conjurations and incantations—all of
which may be useless in themselves. In the common judgment of more enlightened nations, they sustain no relations
to the physical result—*the restoration of the patient*—except
as their influence is exerted on the body through the excited
reverence and increased faith of the ignorant being in whose
behalf they are practiced. Many cures, thus wrought by
the imposition of hands—*by manipulations that equalize the
electrical forces, and thus harmonize the organic action*—have
led multitudes to suppose that the successful practitioner was
endowed with preternatural and superhuman powers.[1] In
all such cures the electro-magnetic operator should come into

---

[1] The idea that the most benighted Pagan *may be* aided by kindred spiritual beings, is not to be wholly discredited by any one acquainted with the
laws of the mental and moral world.

tangible relations and mental rapport with the patient. When the relation is fairly established—with a wise reference to the fundamental law, and the specific conditions of the parties—the most astonishing results are speedily produced. Violent pains are suddenly removed; acute inflammations rapidly subdued; the vital energies excited and augmented, sensation and muscular motion restored, while strumous tumors and other swellings gradually disappear under the hands of the magnetizer. Moreover, the world has yet to learn that this species of natural magic—in other words, the art of so directing the subtile elements and invisible forces of the natural universe as to develop apparently supernatural results—may coexist with a positive philosophy and a Spiritual Rationalism, as well as with ignorance and the most degrading superstition.

Before entering on a course of practical experiment, I was led, by reading, observation and reflection, to the conclusion that all forms of disease commence in the nervous system, by a disturbance or unequal distribution of vital electricity; and that the organic, functional and symptomatic effects all resulted from this derangement of the electro-motive power of the organization. Having satisfied myself on this point, it was but natural to conjecture that the specific effects of all remedial agents occur under the action of the electro-nervous forces, and agreeably to the laws of vital electricity. I had observed the surprising results produced by magnetic manipulations—had often produced those effects. Acute pains were readily removed; extreme nervous irritability was rapidly subdued; sarcomatous and encysted tumors, rheumatic and other swellings, had mysteriously disappeared

under the hands of the operator. I had also marked the
salutary results of the Hydropathic treatment in fevers, and
the beneficial effects of poultices and other moist applications
in subduing local inflammations. I had no doubt that these
and all similar effects occurred agreeably to an electro-vital
principle. Regarding inflammation as proceeding from a
highly electrical state of the parts affected, it could only be
necessary—provided I had really discovered the fundamental electrical law—to adapt the treatment to that law in its
relations to the human system, and the conditions would be
rapidly changed; so that in every case, where no destruction
of the organs or tissues had occurred, a normal state would
necessarily and almost instantly supervene. These general
observations, respecting the philosophy of the subject, may
be more clearly elucidated by a citation of particular facts.
As my limits will only admit of the introduction of a few
experimental illustrations, I shall endeavor to select such
examples from my own experience as will combine the largest possible variety of causes and effects.

In the early part of my investigations—some fourteen
years since—I became acquainted with Rev. Charles H.
Gardner and his family. Mrs. G. had suffered long and
severely from a distressing asthmatic affection. As medicine
afforded no certain relief, and promised no permanent cure,
she expressed a desire to test the efficacy of Magnetism, and
at her solicitation the writer made a trial of his powers.
Mrs. Gardner proved to be a highly susceptible subject ; a
state of complete coma was readily induced, and the first
experiment resulted in a thorough cure of the asthma.

In December, 1849, I made an experiment at a public house

ın Springfield, Mass., the result of which occasioned no little interest at the time.   Having just completed a protracted course of lectures on vital and mental phenomena, I had accepted an invitation to pass the last evening I designed to remain in town, with a select company at the house of a friend.   I left the old Hampden at an early hour, without informing any one where I might be found, should my presence be demanded in the course of the evening.   The incident 1 am about to relate occurred at the City Hotel.   At about the hour of seven o'clock, P. M., while a number of young people—assembled in the parlor—were engaged in an animated and playful conversation, a young lady, of remarkable beauty and accomplishments, was seized with catalepsis in its most frightful form.   Voluntary motion, sensation, respiration and consciousness, were all instantly suspended.   The report was rapidly circulated that the young lady was dying ; and as she was widely known, and had many friends and admirers, the excitement soon caused a crowd of two or three hundred people to assemble in and about the hotel.   Three physicians were called in, whose united efforts to relieve the patient were unavailing.   At length, in the course of the evening, some earnest friends of the lady—whose faith was not exactly restricted to the ordinary anti-spastic agents employed by the medical profession—having ascertained the writer's whereabouts, came to solicit my presence and assistance.   It was half-past ten o'clock when I reached the City Hotel, and the young woman had been in the cataleptic state more than three hours without exhibiting the least indication of returning consciousness and animation.

I felt assured that this abrupt and complete suspension of

the functions had resulted from a sudden loss of the electrical equilibrium—that some constitutional cause, or incidental circumstance, affecting the vital forces through the agency of the mind, had occasioned an instantaneous determination of the nervous circulation to some vital organ—probably the brain or the heart, and that an observation of the relative temperature of different parts of the body would enable me to ascertain the precise point of the electrical concentration. An examination at once settled this question in my own mind, and without a moment's delay I commenced making appropriate manipulations in all directions from the supposed point of electrical convergence. It was very soon apparent that I had not misjudged. Visible signs of a speedy restoration of all the faculties immediately followed the application of the treatment, and *in fourteen minutes after the writer entered the apartment, the patient was fully restored, and employed in adjusting her hair before the mirror.*

Some years since while on a visit to Greenfield, Mass., I chanced one day to be present when a young man accidentally fell from an elevated platform or scaffold, striking on his head—the weight of the blow being directly over and under the left eye. I was instantly at his side, and found him completely insensible. Though the shock was so powerful as to produce temporary asphyxia, he struck the ground in such a manner as to occasion no abrasion of the skin. Knowing that the electro-nervous forces would naturally rush to the seat of the injury, and that the arterial circulation—being graduated by the distribution of vital electricity would immediately follow in a corresponding degree, causing irregular vascular action and congestion, I instantly set myself to work to prevent any unpleasant result. Applying cold water to the surface—chiefly with a view of rendering the cuticle a good conductor, so that the accumulated vital electricity might readily escape, and the blood be removed by *resolution*,—I commenced, after the magneto-electric method, to dissipate the forces. I soon succeeded in producing a strong counter action and an increased determination of the electrical circulation to other points. Consciousness and all the voluntary powers were rapidly restored. The operation occupied half an hour, and resulted in the complete removal of all the consequences of the accident. The next day there was not the least soreness felt, or discoloration visible, to indicate which side of the head had been injured.

I need not record the details of the next case, a brief comprehensive statement being all that is required. Mrs. Anna Mills was an acutely sensitive person, with a finely wrought nervous system. She frequently suffered from acute inflammation of the thoracic and abdominal viscera, and the vital forces were often deranged by the slightest causes. At the time the writer's services were demanded, a professional diagnosis disclosed an extreme inflammation of the pleura. It was a critical case, that did not yield to the action of medicine in the least possible degree. In this instance *the most perfect relief was afforded in fifteen minutes*, and the next day the patient was moving about the house, and apparently quite well.

In the year 1852 a gentleman who lived in Newark, N. J., and had there listened to several lectures on the electrical theory of the vital functions, called on the writer and described the case of a young woman, eighteen years old, who belonged to his circle of acquaintance. The patient was vitally strong and ordinarily enjoyed the most vigorous health ; but at the time she was represented as suffering intensely from acute inflammation in one leg. Her friend was extremely anxious that I should personally attend to her case ; but as my sphere of action was the platform rather than the sick room, and especially as my time was much occupied, I perseveringly declined the responsibility. Several times in the course of one week the gentleman came to me and urged the peculiar claims of the case, until at last I reluctantly yielded to his repeated solicitations and called on the patient. I found her suffering from a rheumatic fever and intense inflammation of one lower limb, extending from the extremity to the hip, and affecting the joints, tendons, and all the fibrous textures. The limb was stretched at full length, and in a horizontal position. It rested on a pillow placed in one chair while the patient was seated in another, which she had constantly occupied during the preceding seven days and nights, without one hour's sleep or a single moment's freedom from pain. The leg was swelled to an amazing size, and about the joints the venous congestion gave the entire surface a dark purple appearance.

On inquiry I learned that the physician—in his attempt to reduce the inflammation—had depended chiefly on the application of a liniment, that appeared to be composed of origanum and other vegetable oils. Feeling assured that the application of such an oleaginous compound must of necessity check the insensible perspiration—which always facilitates the escape of vital electricity from the body—render the cuticle a non-conductor, and thus increase the inflammation, I did not hesitate to express the conviction, (without an intimation from any one respecting the actual facts in the case) *that the inflammation had greatly increased since the first application of the liniment.* My observation was instantly confirmed by the concurrent testimony of the whole family, though all had attributed the aggravated symptoms to other causes than he doctor's prescription. The case afforded an excellent opportunity to test the reality of the supposed discovery, to which reference has already been made. If a cure could be effected—agreeably to the electrical law involved in the theory, developed in this treatise—I had no doubt of its speedy as well as its certain accomplishment. It was only necessary to render the cuticle a good conductor of vital electricity, and then—by the proper application of an electrically negative body—the excess of the subtile element would be set free, its rapid diffusion inevitable occurring on the conductive principle.

I will here give the simple treatment and the surprising result. Adding an ounce of spirits of ammonia to a pint of cold water, I sponged the limb thoroughly, and until the oily substance was entirely removed from the surface. Then relaxing the muscles of my own arms and hands, by withdrawing the nervous forces as much as possible—thus rendering the extremities electrically negative—I commenced manipulating lightly—making the negative passes from the highest point to which the inflammation extended, to the ends of the toes. As often as the surface of the patient's limb became dry by the rapid process of evaporation, occasioned by the unusual heat, the wet sponge was again passed lightly over the surface, thus restoring and increasing the conducting capacity of the cuticle—which is always suspended in proportion as the skin is deprived of its natural humidity.[1] Thus the manipulations over the moist surface were continued without interruption for forty minutes. The inflammation was greatly reduced, and after the first operation the patient could move her limb and had the partial use of all the joints, not one of which had been moved in the least during the seven or eight days next preceding the application of this treatment. At the expiration of twelve hours I repeated the operation, occupying some forty minutes, when the patient was relieved of all pain and could support the weight of her body on that limb. Once more, after a similar interval the same treatment was again applied for half an hour, whereupon the patient ran up and down stairs without the least pain or inconvenience. On the evening of the next day she walked to Library Hall, a distance of half a mile, to attend a lecture delivered by the writer—walked home again—and from that time had not the slightest symptom of inflammation.

The reader's attention is now invited to a case of a wholly different nature. MISS SARAH ELIZABETH LOCKWOOD, of Stamford, Conn., a young lady some twenty years of age, had suffered long and fearfully (according to the physicians who had treated her case for several years) from *a spinal*

---

[1] It is well known that when the insensible perspiration is arrested by cold, or from any other cause, leaving the surface dry, it occasions *fever;* the electro-thermal, chemical, and organic action, are all rapidly increased ; and this derangement of the vital forces may result in an acute inflammation of some internal organ or membrane. When the natural process—whereby animal electricity is disengaged or set free—is thus suddenly suspended, the vital motive power inevitably accumulates, and it is but natural that the molecular and organic motion should be correspondingly accelerated.

disease, which had resulted in a suspension of the peristaltic motion of the intestines ; suppression of the catamenia; a total paralysis of the lower limbs, and complete loss of the voice. The treatment had been topical bleeding, blisters, setons in the back, etc. ; and every inch of the cuticle, from the medulla oblongata to the lower extremity of the spinal column, gave evidence of the faithful application of the professional treatment, which of course had subserved no good purpose. Indeed, the poor victim of disease and malpractice—like the woman whose case is reported in the practice of Jesus—" had suffered many things of many physicians . . . . and was nothing bettered, but rather grew worse."—(*Mark* v., 26.)

When the writer first called to see Miss Lockwood, she was in many respects more helpless than an infant. She had no power to move her lower limbs at all, or even to hold up her head, and she had not spoken above a whisper in eight months. I have not space to describe the precise method adopted in her case. Suffice it to say, the application of the treatment was in strict accordance with the principles involved in the writer's theory. Concerning the result, the patient may very properly be permitted to speak for herself. The following introduction to the statement of Miss L. is from the pen of Mr. Hoyt, the intelligent and gentlemanly editor of the *Advocate*, in whose paper the letter was originally published, in July, 1850 :—

FROM THE STAMFORD (CONN.) ADVOCATE.

" Mr Brittan has not only been successful in explaining the philosophy of his subject, but eminently so in the practical application of the principles to the treatment and cure of some of the most aggravated forms of disease. By perm'ssion of the parties, we publish the following communication from Miss

Lockwood. It is a strong case ; the facts are generally known in this community, and may be said to have occurred within the sphere of our own observation :—"

PROF. BRITTAN :—*Dear Friend*—Actuated by a lively sense of the great benefits conferred by your treatment, I am constrained to make the following statement :—

In the Spring of 1846, while at school, I began to be troubled with a pain in my side and head, and extreme general debility. During the ensuing year I was treated by two physicians of different schools, with very indifferent success. In May, 1847, another physician was called to attend me ; but for some months I was absent from the vicinity of this gentleman's residence, and his visits were only occasional till the autumn of the same year, when, on my return home, very much reduced in physical energy, and dejected in spirits, it became necessary for him to attend me constantly. I was confined to my bed for some fifteen or eighteen months, during the period from 1847 to 1850. Four or five other physicians saw me at different times, but I received no permanent relief from their prescriptions.

I was virtually given up, my case not admitting of a rational hope of recovery. I continued in a perfectly helpless condition until April, 1850. It was impossible for me at this time to hold up my head, for a single moment, or to change my position in the bed. Added to the feebleness of infancy, I was unable to find much rest or sleep. I suffered constantly the most acute, burning and painful sensations in my head and spine. My circulation was so terribly unbalanced that my limbs were almost as cold as death. In this situation you found me, and justice requires me to add, that from this prostrate and seemingly hopeless condition you have succeeded in raising me. For the last three or four weeks I have been visiting my friends, and you can not imagine how delighted I am that I am able to go out once more. If it had not been for you, doubtless I should have passed many more wearisome weeks and months, buried from the world and all its enjoyments.

When I think how perfectly helpless I was, when you first saw me, it seems to me almost a miracle that you relieved me so soon. I can not find words to express my gratitude to you. I think if physicians would adopt your mode of treatment they would be more successful than they are now, in curing some diseases, at least. It is to be very much regretted that you will not devote your time to the sick. That you personally may be blessed with health, the greatest of all blessings, is the wish of your friend.

SARAH E. LOCKWOOD.

P. S.—For the information and encouragement of others, I will further remark :—While I do not profess to understand the principles of Mr. Brittan's electrical system, I may venture to speak with confidence of the results in my own case. The third time he called to see me, I was made to speak in a full voice, which I had not done for eight months ; to support myself on my feet, and to walk across the room. All pain and nervous irritability now rapidly subsided, and I began to feel the energy of new life in every part of my frame. During the past month I seem to have entered on a new existence. My sleep is sound, unbroken and refreshing ; my appetite good, and I am rapidly gaining strength.

I shall not cease to hold in the most grateful remembrance the kind Providence that placed me in his care ; nor shall I neglect to commend his treatment to others who are afflicted. With much respect, yours,   S. E. L.

Stamford, Conn., June 24, 1850.

With a brief citation of one other case I must leave this department of my subject. I was once called to the bed-side of a young girl of some seventeen summers, who was raving with the wildest delirium. For two days and nights it had required two or three persons constantly to keep her on the bed. With my right hand I grasped both of her hands, and placed my left hand on the patient's forehead, thus forming an electro-vital circuit, by which I hoped to equalize the electric forces of her brain and nervous system. The violence of the paroxysm was subdued in less than one minute. The patient was soon quieted ; the pupil of the eye contracted, and the countenance rapidly assumed a natural expression. The eyelids began to droop, and in five minutes she slept. I thereupon disengaged myself, and occupying a seat, at a distance of two or three yards from the bed, I watched the patient attentively. She slept fifteen minutes without stirring a muscle, when she opened her eyes in a perfectly sane state ; and immediately she *was clothed, and remained in her right mind.*

CHAPTER XXI.

IMPORTANCE OF MAGNETISM IN SURGERY.

Magnetism in the treatment of Disease—Its use in the practice of Surgery—
Removal of a Cancerous Breast by M. Cloquet—Singular ground of opposition to Magnetism—Stupidity of Dr. Copeland and a Scotch divine—Dr.
James Esdaile's practice in British India—Seventy-three painless operations
at Hoogly—Case of Teencowrie Paulit—Removal of a Tumor weighing
eighty pounds—Decisive Experiments—Opinion of Dr. Esdaile—Magnetism
prevents excessive Hemorrhage and subsequent Inflammation—Further observations—The Author's Experiments—Application of Magnetism in
Dental Surgery—Saving a finger that had been off nearly half an hour—
Scientific authorities mistaken—The Doctors mortified instead of the Patient's finger.

NOT only are the magnetic processes of the utmost importance in the treatment of all neuralgic affections, every
phase of inflammation, chlorosis, anchylosis and paralysis,
and likewise in removing sarcoma and anasarca, together
with all abnormal obstructions and morbid secretions, by
increasing the electro-anastomotic action ; but it may also be
employed, with most beneficent results, in the practice of
Surgery. The modes whereby we influence the distribution
of vital electricity, enable the skillful operator to control
sensation in the subject ; and hence the most difficult, protracted and painful surgical operations may be performed
without pain. Moreover, that the danger from hemorrhage,
and from subsequent inflammation, is greatly diminished by

Magnetism—when a complete state of coma has been induced —will scarcely admit of a rational doubt in the mind of any one who has witnessed the results of its application.

It is now more than a quarter of a century since M. Cloquet, an eminent surgeon, removed a cancerous breast from a woman while in a magnetic trance, and whose insensibility to pain during the operation was demonstrated to his entire satisfaction. Indeed, the use of Magnetism was, for a time, opposed in Europe *on account of its pain-destroying power*— opposed by certain doctors, who probably loved to see their patients shrink from the knife, or writhe under the process of cauterization. It is said that the Royal Medical and Chirurgical Society of London received, with implied approbation, the absurd assumption of Dr. Copeland, that "*patients ought to suffer while their surgeon is operating.*" He appears to have regarded pain, not only as a wise and necessary provision of Nature, but also *as an agreeable pastime* for those who are duly commissioned by the authorities of science and law to inflict it on their hapless victims. The science of Dr. Copeland was about as remarkable as the piety of a stupid old Scotch divine, who, not long since, opposed the use of chloroform, in obstetric cases, as an unholy and profane attempt to subvert the Divine law, woman having been visited with a special curse because she took the initiative in the transgression[1]

Isolated cases, illustrating the use of the magnetic processes in the alleviation of human suffering, have occurred in the experience of many practitioners, both in this country and in Europe; but the application of this beneficient agent,

---

[1] See Genesis, Chap. III., 16th verse.

in the practice of Dr. James Esdaile, as surgeon in the service of the British East India Company, perhaps affords the clearest experimental demonstrations of its paramount importance. He found the natives of Bengal extremely impressible, and a few trials, by himself or his assistants, generally subdued their natural powers of resistance, leaving them in a state of profound coma, and insensible of pain. In the short period of eight months he performed, at Hoogly, no less than *seventy-three painless operations in surgery*, embracing among others the dissection and amputation of different members of the body, operations for scrotocele and hydrocele, removal of scrotal and other tumors : actual and potential cauteries, etc., etc. In these operations the subjects were entirely deprived of physical sensation ; with rare exceptions, they were altogether unconscious, and often expressed the greatest surprise on learning what had been done to them during the interval of oblivious repose. The operations were seldom followed by much pain or inflammation, and the process of cicatrization generally occurred by the first intention.

In order to give the reader—who may not have access to Dr. Esdaile's book—some idea of the difficult and painful nature of some of his surgical operations, and also of the benign influence and salutary results of Magnetism in such cases, I will here refer, in a more explicit manner, to two cases. Teencowrie Paulit, of the age of forty years, had been " suffering for two years, from a tumor in the antrum maxillare," which—in the language of the doctor—had " pushed up the orbit of the eye, filled the nose, passed into the throat, and caused an enlargement of the glands of the neck." Respiration was rendered so difficult that he had slept but very little for five months. After repeated and fruitless trials on the part of Dr. Esdaile's assistants, the doctor himself at last made the effort, and succeeded, in about forty-five minutes, in producing the state of magnetic catalepsy, when he at once proceeded to remove the tumor— the operation being one of the most protracted and painful in surgery—and the patient being all the while in a comatose and unconscious state. The following extract is from Dr. Esdaile's description of the operation :

" I put a long knife in at the corner of his mouth, and brought the point out over the cheek-bone, dividing the parts between ; from this I pushed it through the skin at the inner corner of the eye, and dissected the cheek back to the nose. The presence of the tumor had caused the absorption of the anterior wall of the antrum, and on pressing my fingers between it and the bones, it burst, and a shocking gush of blood and brain-like matter followed. The tumor extended as far as my fingers could reach under the orbit and cheek-bone, and passed into the gullet, having destroyed the bones and partition of the nose. No one touched the man, and I turned his head into any position I desired, without resistance, and there it remained until I wished to move it again. When the blood accumulated, I bent his head forward, and it ran from his mouth as from a leaden spout. The man never moved, nor showed any signs of life, except an occasional indistinct moan ; but when I threw back his head, and passed my fingers into his throat to detach the mass in that direction, the stream of blood was directed into his wind-pipe, and some instinctive effort became necessary for existence ; he therefore coughed, and leaned forward, to get rid of the blood ; and I supposed that he then awoke. The operation was by this time finished, and he was laid on the floor to have his face sewed up ; and while this was being done, he for the first time opened his eyes."

The man subsequently declared, in the most unequivocal manner, and with peculiar emphasis, that he experienced no pain during the operation ; and it appeared that not only the coughing, but even the forward movement, to prevent suffocation by discharging the blood, was involuntarily and unconsciously performed.   When the wounds were dressed—on the third day after the operation—it was found that the parts were united throughout by the first intention, and the man could both breathe freely and speak plainly.[1]

The case of Gooroochuan Shah, a native shop-keeper, is perhaps the most extraordinary of its class on record.   He had a tumor of almost incredible dimensions.   *For years it had served him as a " writing-desk."*   This enormous mass, weighing eighty pounds, was removed by Dr. Esdaile while the man was in a death-like sleep that suspended all the powers of sensation.   When the patient was restored to consciousness, he affirmed that " nothing had disturbed him." Had the tumor been removed while the man was awake, and the voluntary powers of his mind actively employed, it is not probable that he could have survived the operation.   On this point Dr. Esdaile expresses his opinion as follows :

" I think it extremely likely that, *if the circulation had been hurried by pain* and struggling ; or, *if the shock to the system had been increased by bodily and mental anguish, the man would have bled to death ;* or never have rallied from the effects of the operation.   But the sudden loss of blood was all he had to contend against ; and, though in so weak a condition, he has surmounted this, and gone on very well."[2]

In five weeks Gooroochuan Shah was so far recovered that he was permitted to leave the hospital and return home.

Skepticism on a subject of this nature was excusable in the

[1] American edition of Mesmerism in India, pp. 146–49
[2] Ibid, pp. 221, 222.

time of Mesmer, but at this late day it is only compatible
with a most incorrigible indifference and a mournful destitu-
tion of all knowledge on a subject of great moment. The
domain of accredited science comprehends no phenomena
more real, or more susceptible of a clear and triumphant
authentication and defense, than those developed by the magnetic processes; and we shall look in vain for any that
more deeply concern the vital interests of mankind. To
say nothing of the psychological phases of the phenomena,
the physiological effects are such as can neither be counter-
feited nor mistaken. Sensation and voluntary motion are
often wholly suspended; the limbs become rigid, preserving
any position in which they may be placed by the operator;
and sometimes the thoracic movement is completely arrested.
Those who are suffering from a serious derangement of the
nervous forces, and in consequence experience extreme pain,
or a partial suspension of the power of voluntary motion, in
certain portions of the system, often find that the magnetic
sleep results in an equilibration of the vital motive power,
and hence of the entire circulation. The arterial action and
the respiration are invariably diminished by the magnetic
processes, and the temperature of the body falls in the same
proportion. Hence the efficacy of magnetic manipulations
and the consequent state of coma in subduing fever and
inflammation. Under the mysterious spell, the eyes roll
wildly about the orbit as the magnetic needle oscillates when
suddenly acted on; the iris loses its contractibility under
the strongest hydro-oxygen light; neither muriatic acid nor
a hot iron applied to the flesh occasions the slightest pain;
the strongest fumes of liquid ammonia make no impression

on the olfactory surfaces; and the discharge of heavily loaded firearms close to the ear, will not in the least disturb the unconscious sleeper. It will be in vain to look for the *experimentum crucis* elsewhere, if it may not be found in these various and wonderful phenomena.

That all the effects produced, on and through the motive and sensorial medium of the living body, are occasioned by the irregular distribution and consequent action of vital electricity, we have no room to doubt. While Dr. Esdaile does not to attempt to furnish a philosophy of the facts, developed in his interesting experience, he drops occasional observations from which it appears, that he more than suspected that all the magnetic phenomena depended on the capacity of the operator to give a new direction to the nervous circulation, and thus to either increase or diminish the action at the centers of nervous energy. On this point he thus suggests the view he is inclined to entertain:

"It seems to me that irregularity in the distribution of the nervous energy is at the bottom of all the mesmeric symptoms, however produced, whether naturally or artificially; and I suspect that the same effects may follow a state of exhaustion or repletion of the nervous system."[1]

When the patient is conscious during the performance of a surgical operation, and the voluntary faculties of the mind are fully aroused and painfully excited, the mental forces will inevitably be concentrated at the point where the injury is inflicted. The electrical currents are thus increased in that particular direction, and their action greatly intensified; and as the distribution of this agent graduates the measure

---

* Mesmerism in India, p. 134.

and the motion of the blood and all the animal fluids, it follows of necessity that the arterial tide is augmented in the same direction, and in a corresponding degree, producing excessive hemorrhage ; while this concentrated electrical action, at the seat of the injury, increases the subsequent tendency to inflammation.

But the loss of blood, and the danger of inflammation in all surgical operations, must be greatly diminished by the magnetic sleep. No careful observer of the facts in the case will be disposed to question this, and whoever discerns the laws that regulate the vital action, and the circulation of the fluids in animal and human bodies, will be able to comprehend, at least in part, the philosophy of these effects. When the patient is insensible of pain, and unconscious of the injury inflicted, the general circulation is undisturbed by any excited action of the mind. There is no sudden agitation of the fountain of life ; the arterial currents move through their channels with a steady, rhythmical flow, under the normal play of the electric forces on the vital organs. All this is confirmed by the following observations of Dr. Esdaile, founded on the results of his numerous experiments. Having in view the importance of Magnetism in the practice of Surgery, he says :

" The benefits are not confined to the extinction of pain during the operation, but are of the greatest general and particular advantage in the after-treatment of surgical diseases. The nerves and brain have not been shattered by bodily and mental anguish, which generally excites an irritative fever in the system, wasting the powers of life, and rousing local inflammation in the injured part ; thereby often destroying all the hopes and precautions of the surgeon. In the mesmeric sleep, only the necessary local injury has been inflicted ; and on awaking, the patient sometimes feels *no pain whatever*, and generally only a slight smarting in the wound ; and the constitution sets about repairing the breach of substance quietly, and under the best possible circumstances. If local pains follow, they can be easily removed by topical manipulations."[1]

Of necessity the writer's own opportunities to witness the application of Magnetism in practical surgery, have been very limited ; and yet I am not without a small experience even in this department. On one occasion—some years since—I magnetized the wife of a clergyman, who had nine decayed teeth extracted without once breaking the spell. On the restoration of sensation and consciousness, she was most agreeably surprised to find that the cause of long and severe suffering had been completely removed, without in-flicting upon her sensitive nature a single pang. Indeed, all persons who are susceptible of this state of complete coma, may have the sensories temporarily paralyzed at the pleasure of the magnetizer. The skin may be punctured and the flesh lacerated, and yet the sleeper will feel no pain ; though it is worthy of observation that he is keenly sensitive to the slightest personal violence that may be done to the operator.

Some ten years since, while the writer was living in Stamford, Conn., Mr. C. P. Price, who lived in an adjoining house, accidentally cut off the end of the index finger of his left hand, while employed in cutting hay for his horse. Mr. P. walked directly to the house. leaving the dissevered portion of his finger in the hay at the barn. One after another, the physicians, to the number of three, were sent for ; but they were all absent. In this emergency the writer was called in—when some twenty minutes had elapsed after the accident—and the separated portion of the finger was quite

---

[1] Dr. Esdaile's Journal, Chap. VII., pp. 189, 190.

cold. But I conceived the idea that if it were properly adjusted to the stump, and the electro-vital action could be restored by magnetic manipulations, it might be possible to restore it. Accordingly, I procured the end of the finger and adjusted it as accurately as possible, with the aid of the needle and several narrow strips of adhesive plaster. When this was properly done, I commenced the magneto-electric action, making the passes from above the third joint to the end of the finger. This was continued until the natural temperature was restored to the dissevered portion, when it was carefully bound up in brown sugar and spirits.

At night, when the doctors returned, they were disposed to amuse themselves at the expense of the writer and his patient. Of course the village authorities in medical science all concurred in the opinion, that it was impossible to save the finger, and that it would inevitably mortify. However, it united completely by the first intention, and *in three weeks it was entirely well*, except that the sensation was not quite as acute as before.[1] If the doctors never put on limbs when amputation has occurred accidently, it must be confessed that they make up for every such deficiency by the cheerful grace with which they cut them off!

" They laugh at scars who never felt a wound.

[1] It is worthy of record, that not long after the occurrence already de-scribed—while I was far from home—a youthful member of the writer's family had the misfortune to lose *two fingers* in the same machine. On this occasion, Dr. Lockwood (one of the physicians just referred to as having witnessed the results of my own experiment on Mr. Price) was immediately called, but he made no effort to save the fingers.

CHAPTER XXII.

THE PHANTOM CREATION.

Illusions of the Senses—How to test the accuracy of our Perceptions—Objects and their Shadows — Descartes' theory—Newton's discovery—The Mirage on the Eastern deserts—The Fata Morgana, seen at the Straits of Messina —M. Monge's Explanation before the Institute at Cairo, in Egypt—The forms of Ideas—The Phantom World—Philosophy of Sensorial Illusions— Illustrations from Dr. Ambercrombie—Sir Isaac Newton on Ocular Spectra —The sense of Hearing deceived—Louis Brabant, the Ventriloquist, and the beautiful Heiress—Personation of the Father's ghost—The Banker of Lyons and his ideal Visitors—Louis obtains a fortune and marries his Mistress—M. St. Gill in a Convent—Remarkable Ventriloquial power— Chanting to a Voice—The Phantom Hosts of Disease and Dissipation

THE organs of sensation do not always convey correct information to the mind. When the coporeal instruments are not imperfect in their structure, or their general integrity otherwise impaired, the functions may still be temporarily deranged by the improper distribution of the medium of vital motion and sensation. The subtile agent that transmits the images of outward objects to the sensorium, may possibly be so disturbed, from causes within and without, as to occasion all sorts of illusions, and

"Strange phantoms, rising as the mists arise "

deceive us with their mysterious semblance of reality. The slightest organic imperfection may change the general appearance, or modify the particular aspects of the whole objective creation. Whenever the nature of the case suggests

the possibility of deception, it is proper to test the revelations of one sense by the exercise of all the others, (so far
as they may be employed in the trial,) and by the aid of
Reason. It is seldom that an illusion of more than one
sense occurs at the same time ; and hence, if we have the
concurrent testimony of two or more of the senses to the
fact of the existence or occurrence of any outward object or
event, the probability of our being deceived by sensorial illusions is greatly diminished ; and the strength of the evidence—of the reality of what appears to have an objective
existence—is increased in proportion to the number of these
witnesses and the general coherence of their testimony.

Wherever substantial things exist we may reasonably expect to find their shadows, more or less clearly defined, and
as widely varied as the nature of the objects themselves, the
degrees of light—state of the atmosphere, and the strength
and clearness of the individual powers of perception. The
irisated arch has its secondary bow, formed by the second
reflection and refraction of the sun's rays, and these are seg-
ments of concentric circles. Descartes doubtless furnished
the true theory of the exterior bow, in his *Dioptrics ;* and
the philosophy of this splendid meteoric phenomenon was
clearly explained—and the disposition of the colors in the
solar spectrum accounted for—by Newton's great discovery
of the unequal refrangibility of the different primal rays.
The shadows or images of natural objects often appear at
great distances from the bodies they represent, as in eclipses
of the sun and moon and the transits of the planets. But
the optical phenomenon known as the *mirage,* offers a more
suggestive illustration. This is sometimes seen by the trav-

eler on the great Eastern deserts, but more frequently by persons at sea. Ships have been perceived and recognized at the distance of thirty miles or more—even before they were visible above the horizon's verge—by their inverted images seen in the upper strata of the atmosphere. This singular illusion—known among the Italians as the *Fata Morgana*— is perhaps nowhere more perfect than along the Straits of Messina, where, if we may credit the testimony of travelers, the various objects on shore are represented with remarkable fidelity in the aërial regions above the sea. M. Monge, who read a philosophical paper on the subject, before the Institute at Cairo—at the time of the invasion of Egypt by the French—referred this singular phenomenon to the difference in the density of the upper and lower strata of the atmosphere. He supposed that the rays coming from the lower portions of the atmospheric heavens are refracted by coming in contact with a stratum of air of different density, and in such a manner as to produce the images of terrestrial objects in the sky.

The laws of light and the philosophy of vision may possibly aid us to suggest the proper explanation of many optical and spectral illusions. It is worthy of observation that *ideas have forms*, which are only imperfectly represented in their material incarnation ; and a mental conception may be sufficiently forcible to leave a distinct image seemingly before the eye as well as the mind. When the electric forces of the brain are deranged, and, especially, when they are greatly intensified in their action, from whatever cause, the ideal images become so vivid that *they may be duplicated by reflection*, and thus be made to assume every appearance of outstanding forms of the objective creation. A whole Phantom World is thus suddenly called into being. The fantastic shapes stand by the midnight watcher in his lonely vigil ; they haunt the untenanted houses; they appear in the dim twilight about graveyards ; they are multitudinous in the deserted halls of old castles ; and they start out from the deep shadows of every venerable ruin ; while the guilty man hears their low wail in the autumn winds, or their footsteps in the rustling of the leaves. The brain and the visual organs become a kind of *phantasmagoria*, the images of what is within being cast up from the cerebral camera, and made to appear like tangible objects. Even in the broad light of day

> " The soul—
> Wrapt in strange visions of the unreal,
> ——paints the illusive form."

That our ideas and emotions do, in some important sense, take forms, and are ultimated or expressed outside of our selves, even at a distance, is made evident from the capacity of thousands to take impressions from other minds, through some silent agent and by an invisible process. Moreover, if ideas or mental conceptions, by their more direct action, occasion a similar electrical excitation at the sensorium, to that which is produced by external objects through the subtile medium that pervades the optic nerve, it must be obvious that our ideas may—when conceived with sufficient energy— *assume visible forms.* In every case where tangible objects are presented to the eye, their images are *subjective.* In other words, *they are all in the brain,* and remain more or less perfectly defined when the material forms have been withdrawn from the outward field of observation. Though the objects themselves are *outstanding*, the pictures presented in the ocular spectrum are *all in the man*, doubtless on the choroid membrane, or the second coat of the eye. When the images are derived from external forms, they are transmitted by means of the electrical excitation at the extremity of the optic nerve, occasioned by the rays of light reflected from the surfaces of such objects. That an intense mental action and cerebral excitement may suffice to produce similar pictures on the same delicate membrane, and that such images would appear to be *objective*—perhaps at a distance from the observer—there can be no occasion for a rational doubt. Thus it appears that highly imaginative persons, whose thoughts and passions are strongly conceived and powerfully exercised, sometimes project images of their ideal conceptions from the brain, and are startled on beholding the forms of their own creation.

Some of the phrenologists profess to have discovered and located a particular organ, whose office is said to be the production of *spectral illusions ;* but this assumption does not so well accord with the facts in the case as the view in which they are regarded as reflex images of ideas, produced by the retroactive powers of the mind, more or less clearly defined according to the distinctness of the primary image. Dr. Abercrombie refers to the experience of Dr. Ferriar, who, after viewing any interesting natural scenery, a military review, or some venerable ruin, could reproduce the whole picture at pleasure—whenever he had occasion to retire to a dark room—and with all the apparent reality and brilliancy of the real scene as actually viewed by daylight. The same author speaks of a man who had been looking steadily, and with intense interest, at a picture of the Virgin, until—on suddenly raising his head—he was startled and amazed at beholding the same figure at the opposite end of the apartment. Sir Isaac Newton appears to have been the first really scientific observer of the phenomena of ocular spectra. Concerning his observations in this direction, I extract the following passage from a popular author, already named in this connection :

" When he produced a spectrum of the sun by looking at it with the right eye, the left being uncovered, upon uncovering the left, and looking upon a white ground, a spectrum of the sun was seen with it also. He likewise acquired the power of recalling the spectra, after they had ceased, when he went into the dark, and directed his mind intensely, ' as when a man looks earnestly to see a thing which is difficult to be seen.' By repeating these experiments frequently, such an effect was produced on his eyes, ' that for some months after,' he says, ' the spectrum of the sun began to return as often as I began to meditate upon the phenomena, even though I lay in bed at midnight with my curtains drawn.' " [1]

If you stop in the street with the attention fixed, and —pointing in a particular direction—you proceed in an earnest manner to describe a balloon which you have just discovered at a great altitude, you will be surprised to learn that about one in three or five of the bystanders—after gazing for a few moments—will be able to see it, though no such thing exists save as an ideal image. Thus the more susceptible and imaginative observers discern the form of a mental image or conception, produced by the cunning device of a trickster, aided by the psycho-dynamic action of their own minds. The psychological hallucinations, of which I

---

[1] " Inquires concerning the Intellectual Powers, etc.," by John Abercrombie, M. D., F.R.S. Harper's Edition. p. 64.

shall treat in another Chapter, are in part illustrations of this class. The sense of hearing is often deceived in a similar manner, by the remarkable ventriloquial powers of certain persons—different voices appearing to proceed from above and beneath, and likewise from various localities remote from the position occupied by the speaker. This entertaining deception altogether depends on a skillful imitation of sounds, assisted by the capacity of the hearer to assign them any specific locality, that may be determined by his preconceived idea.

It is now a century and a half since the English aristocracy and the whole fashionable world, in and about the British Metropolis, attended, night after night, to witness the performances of the celebrated Tom King, the crowning feature of which consisted in killing a calf. The ventriloquist retired behind a screen where the whole performance was enacted. The animal was dragged in, the dog barked, several men conversed respecting the value of the animal, the price paid, and the prospective profits of the investment, all of which was accompanied by the sounds of knife, and steel, and rope, following in immediate succession. At the very instant of the catastrophe the curtain was removed when only King remained—quietly seated in his chair ; the calf, a dog, and three butchers having been kindly supplied by the imaginations of his polite hearers. [1]

An interesting story is related of Louis Brabant, who was valet de chambre to Francis I. The accomplished but mischievous Louis was deeply enamored with a young lady who possessed all the attractions of youth, beauty and wealth ;

---

[1] Blake's Encyclopedia—Art., Ventriloquism. p. 933.

but he had been rejected by her parents on account of his inferiority in rank and fortune. At length the father of the beautiful heiress departed this life, and Brabant soon found an occasion to visit the widow and her daughter. During the interview he was successful in personating the deceased husband and father. The widow was most impressively addressed by a voice so much like that of her husband, that she was forced to believe that he had spoken to her from within the vail. The oracular shade commanded her to give the daughter to their guest—who was worthy of her—and he declared that he was himself suffering the pains of purgatory for having refused his consent to their union. Of course young Brabant was politely complimented as a man of fine accomplishments and an excellent character. It is scarcely necessary to add, that with this emphatic indorsement from on high, the venerable matron decided to accept the unscrupulous valet for her son-in-law.

But the drama was not yet complete. The next scene opened at Lyons in the mansion of a rich banker by the name of Cornu. After cultivating this man's acquaintance and acquiring his confidence in a good degree, he one day interested him in a conversation concerning the Invisible World. During the interview, the banker heard the voices of his father, and other deceased relations, commanding him in the name of God to assist his guest by giving him a large sum of money, for a certain humane and religious object. The cunning valet did not omit to affect the utmost surprise on the occasion, accompanied by expressive signs of awe and apprehension. Cornu took time to deliberate, his avarice, however—more than anything in the nature of the performance—having excited his suspicions. The ghosts were more imperative at a subsequent interview, and the banker could no longer resist the voices which appeared to come from above, and with the authority of Heaven. Cornu yielded to the mysterious oracles, and Louis Brabant returned to Paris with ten thousand crowns, and soon after led the object of his idolatry to the altar.

Mons. St. Gill, the ventriloquist, having on one occasion sought shelter from a storm in a Convent, found the community overshadowed by a great bereavement. The fraternity had just been deprived of one of its most distinguished members. While M. St. Gill was standing by the tomb—in conversation with several persons who accompanied him, and who spoke with much feeling of the virtues and graces of the defunct—the voice of the departed was suddenly heard in tones of deep lamentation and words of stern reproof. The voice seemed to fall from the roof of the choir, and to inspire emotions of the deepest solemnity in the minds of all who were present. The shade complained, as in the former case, that he was in purgatory, and he solicited the performance of special religious services in his own behalf. The whole community was immediately called together, and while they were chanting, a *De Profundis*, in a full choir, the ghost employed the occasion—during the intervals in the performance to express his satisfaction, and to intimate the timely relief derived from their devotional exercises.

The phantoms that haunt the minds of the sick are very numerous and greatly diversified. They often take form and appear to the sense of vision as independent objects, and the patient never suspects that he has had anything to do with their origin or continued existence. A patient when recovering from the measles—so observes Dr. Abercrombie —saw all objects diminished to the smallest discernible proportions. When a patient who had typhoid fever began to convalesce, he all at once discovered that he was ten feet high, and that his bed was about eight feet from the floor ! The same author mentions, on the authority of Baron Larry, the case of a gentleman who—after being partially cured of amaurosis—saw all objects immensely magnified ; and it is also recorded of the man whom Jesus restored, that he saw " *men as trees walking.*" The writer once had a singular experience that may be noticed here. I was suffering from a bilious fever, and for many days could see my own body, and conceive of myself, only as a pile of hickory plank by the road-side. Being greatly worn and attenuated by a long confinement, it was not without an adequate reason that I was constantly troubled by *great pressure on the bottom plank,* which was required to support the superincumbent weight of all the others. Thus the senses are deranged by disease. In inflammatory fevers, especially when there is great electro-nervous excitation in the region of the brain, the shadowy hosts of the Phantom World gather in great numbers about the sick man. When health returns,

> "They strike their cloudy tents, and silently
> Shrink to their own nonentity again."

Ambition and fancy build their airy castles; the living creations of Genius are unvailed in our presence, and Utopian visions, born of the poetic imagination, are cast up from the cerebral camera into the moral heavens. If the phantom throng were all of this pleasant description, they might be very comfortably endured, and many persons, no doubt, would be inclined to say with Pope,

" Ye soft illusions, dear deceits, arise !"

But, alas, the hosts of hell follow in the train ! Those who make a free use of narcotics and stimulants, sooner or later disturb the forces of the nervous system, and many learn at last that their own disordered faculties are the open portals of Pandemonium. The senses of the opium-eater are often strangely deranged, and his faculties sadly impaired. The poor wretch made delirious by alcoholic stimulants, is left to wrestle desperately with foul demons and every nameless monster. Basilisks charm him with their fatal magnetism, and fiery serpents coil about the distracted brain. When the delirium subsides and the fearful tension is succeeded by the reäction, the nervous system resembles an untuned lyre. The nerves are morbidly impressible ; all sounds seem to be harsh, and all scenes are repulsive or terrible. The poor victim starts at a footfall, or turns pale at the rustling of a leaf. The gentlest music of the summer winds is hollow and mournful as the desparing wail of imprisoned spirits. Where once he beheld only graceful forms, warmed with youthful fire, and all glowing with love, now cold, spectral shapes, appear—grim-featured and ghastly—to haunt the long, deep midnight of the soul. It is granted that these are extreme conditions ; yet in delirium tremens and other forms of disease, which follow from excessive dissipation and protracted abuse of the nervous system, they frequently occur. Such cases impressively admonish us that we trifle with our peace, when we defile the temple of the soul.

CHAPTER XXIII.

PSYCHOLOGICAL HALLUCINATIONS.

Nature the multiform expression of the Infinite Thought—The Psychological Power—Conditions of Impressibility—Action of material agents on the Body—Influence of Objects and Ideas on the Mind—Strong Men often the most Susceptible—The power of Speech—The Silent Language —Shadows of Ideas—Philosophy of Thought-reading—Electrical influence of Oratory and Poetry—The mysterious Inward Fire—It kindles in the eye and burns on the lip—Summary of Illustrative Facts—Appeals to the Common Experience—Influence of visitors on Sick Persons—Inferences from the Author's Experimental Investigations.

> "So gaze met gaze,
> And heart saw heart, translucid through the rays.
> One same harmonious, universal law,
> Atom to atom, star to star can draw
> And mind to mind! Swift darts, as from the sun,
> The strong attraction, and the charm is done."

THE idea that ascribes the Universe to Infinite Intelligence, and recognizes its adaptation to beneficent results, accords as well with the reason of the Philosopher as with the reverence of the Christian. If we may not trace the chain of universal relation and dependence, we may still rest assured that no link is wanting to render that chain complete. Everything is related to all things, and all motion, form, life, sensation and thought, are but outward expressions of archetypes existing forever in the Divine consciousness. The concatenation of intermediate agencies may be so complex and infinitesimal as to baffle the most subtile powers of analysis; but could we follow the chain of causation throughout, we should doubtless at last trace all mental and physical phenomena to spiritual causes. Moreover, all material changes and transformations, from the simplest process in the laboratory up to the most stupendous revolutions in the world of Matter, are governed by established laws. The invisible, eternal forces, and their *modus operandi* in Nature, are but the multifarious expression of the Infinite Idea. If all matter is thus subservient to the Supreme volition, the universe of Mind *can not* be left to lawless disobedience ; but, in a certain qualified sense, the Divine Wisdom must be more conspicuously revealed in the realms of mind than in the domain of matter—in so far as the former exhibits a nearer approximation to himself. It can neither be vain nor unwise for the Christian philosopher to pursue his investigations in this department ; for if the truth, concerning the Mind, is more difficult of discovery or elucidation, it certainly cannot be said to be less real in itself or important in its inculcations.

That phase of Psychological Science which comprehends the relations of animal electricity to the vital and mental functions, and the influence of mind over mind, has, within a few years, been signalized by a great number and variety of curious experiments. But men, long accustomed to doubt and dispute, who have always an objection, but seldom a reason, have boldly questioned the reality of the phenomena. The fact that all persons are not alike susceptible of the influence of the same agent, is presumed to furnish the ground of a grave and difficult objection. Yet nothing is more obvious than that certain *conditions*—either comprehended or unknown—are essential to success in every experiment; and this is equally true in its application to all departments of scientific investigation. Among the conditions requisite in the particular case under consideration, one alone will suffice to destroy the influence of this objection. Electrical phenomena are known to depend, in all cases, on the existence of positive and negative states, relations and forces. Vital electricity, being the agent through which the biological or psychological experimenter acts on the nerves and muscular fibers, in the production of the diversified and remarkable physical and mental experiments, it follows that these opposite conditions must meet in the operator and the subject, to develop any striking results. When we reflect that probably no two persons in a thousand will be found to sustain precisely the same relation to the experimenter, it will be perceived that the various degrees of susceptibility, exhibited by different individuals, can only be regarded as natural and inevitable results, and as strong presumptive proofs of the genuineness of the phenomena.

General observation and universal experience establish the fact, that all persons are not influenced in the same degree, nor in a similar manner, by any one of the thousand agents in the world of matter and of mind. Our frequent atmospheric changes induce colds or fevers, in some persons, while others escape unharmed. One walks securely among the unseen agents of infection, while another falls a victim to the invisible shafts of the destroyer. The writer has been vaccinated some twenty times, with as little effect as the same operation would have on the bark of a tree; at the same time the agent has been powerfully operative in others. Nor

are the effects wrought by external agency on the body more
multifarious than those produced by outward forms and mental faculties on the mind. An object, regarded by one man
with profound indifference, kindles in the bosom of another
the fires of consuming passion ; and the great thought that,
in its conception and birth, thrilled the soul of Genius with
its marvelous beauty and significance, is but a meaningless
mystery with the world. That men, corporeally and mentally, are so diversely constituted as to exhibit these conflict-
ing results—when subjected to the action of the same agent
—is quite too manifest to be denied. Neither are the weak
in body nor the imbecile in mind always the first, as many
suppose, to be affected by foreign agents, whether material
or spiritual. The mightiest mind, like the strong oak, has
been smitten and laid low. We have known the giant to
suffer from miasma when the dwarf escaped; and the feebleness of infancy has more than once survived the action of
frost, and the little child has been found alive and nestling
in the frozen and pulseless bosom of its mother.

The mental control over the vital action, as exhibited in
the constitution of man, has already been illustrated, in this
treatise, by a citation of numerous facts and a discussion of
essential principles. But if we are reciprocally affected by
whatever relates to the physical condition of each other, so
that health and disease may be imbibed or communicated,
we are certainly not less susceptible of influences emanating
from *the minds* of those with whom we are in correspondence. Nor is this power of mind wholly dependent on the
ordinary and sensible modes of communication. As the superior faculties are progressively developed, the grosser

vehicles of thought may be gradually laid aside ; the presence of the mind may be felt and its desires made known through a more ethereal medium than the common speech of the world. The pen may be mightier far than sword, and spear, and kingly scepter ; the language of the lips may drive the blood back frozen to the heart, or send it in burning torrents to the brain, kindling into intense combustion the magazine of the passions ; it may nerve the stout heart and arm to deeds of desperate daring ; or, like an all-penetrating, fiery music, fall gently on the charmed senses, entrancing the soul by its mysterious power.

But the human mind in its progress employs media and methods of communication, suited to the several stages of its development. However serviceable these instrumentalities may be—each in its appropriate time and place—they may be inadequate to meet the higher demands of more enlightened periods. We realize the insufficiency of written and oral language to express the highest thoughts and the deepest emotions. There is another—it may possibly become—a more perfect medium of communication. This language, though unwritten and unspoken, may be adequate to a fuller expression of all we feel and know. It is not unfrequently the means—little as it is practiced and understood—of revealing thoughts, and impulses to which a vocal utterance has been denied. We give forms to thoughts, and impress those forms on the receptive mind ; we have power to hold up the ideal images we have created before the transfigured spirit, it may be as higher natures cast the shadows of their thoughts on the inspired mind, and write their higher laws in the willing heart.

It is well known that those who are highly susceptible of electro-nervous disturbances, may be influenced, and often controlled, by the will of another person, even when there is no direct physical contact. If you chance to occupy the same apartment with persons of this description, a vigorous effort of mind will enable you to command their attention without seeming to regard them. Enter a room where a person of this class is in a profound slumber—fix your eyes steadily on the face of the sleeper—exert the will powerfully, and you will produce such a disturbance of the electro-nervous circulation as will cause him to awake. It not unfrequently occurs that persons are singularly anticipated in what they are about to say—some other person giving utterance to the same thought in the same words. Lovers, and all persons of intuitive and impressible natures, especially when united by a strong attachment, readily divine each other's thoughts, and read—in a silent but deeply expressive language—the secret conceptions and impulses of the mind and heart.

This intercommunication of mind with mind, is carried on through an excitation of the electrical medium of the nervous system, which is quite as readily produced by mental forces as by physical forms. When there is no corporeal conjunction of the parties, the impression is obviously transmitted through the intervening electrical medium of the earth and atmosphere. We have had occasion to observe that this power is perceptible in the ability of some men to tame wild beasts, and to subdue their enemies. It is strikingly displayed in the electrical excitement that runs through and pervades a vast multitude, when some inspired orator moves

—as by a single impulse—the hearts of thousands. We have felt its thrilling power—

> " In the song of the poet, when love's bright spells
> O'er the strings of his wild harp sweep ;"

in the responsive utterances of kindred spirits, and the sweet cadence of commingling voices in the vespers. It is felt when we press the warm hand, and heart answers to heart in the rapid measure of intense delight. We are sensible of the mysterious power when the electric fires of congenial souls kindle in the eye and burn on the parted lips of Genius and Love ; and ever do we yield to the intangible and irresistible presence, as impulses wild, joyous, or terrible, come leaping up from the unfathomable depths of Being.

About fifteen years since I commenced an experimental investigation of this subject, which has been continued as opportunity has offered until the present time. The course of experiment has been greatly diversified, and the results have been carefully observed. Curious and startling phenomena have met me at every step in my progress, and these all furnish instructive and impressive illustrations of the amazing power of mind over the functions and the faculties of animals and men. The facts are deeply suggestive, and the whole subject opens an immeasurable field for scientific research. I have met with many persons to whom I could readily, yet silently, communicate the inmost secrets of the mind. When in immediate *rapport* with such persons, it is never difficult to direct the whole current of thought and feeling. In this way a constant succession of images may be rendered distinctly visible, while they have merely an ideal existence in the controlling mind. These effects, and a vari-

ety of sensorial impressions—not demanding a precise specification in this connection—are manifestly produced agreeably to the same general principles which govern ordinary
sensation. Thus thoughts and feelings, corresponding to
our own, are—by a mental-electric process—awakened or
inspired in the passive mind. Indeed, the greatest electro-
nervous excitements result from the emotional and executive
powers of the soul. This electrical excitation is communicated to and through the sensor nerves of the subject, and
corresponding cerebral impressions are produced. These
electrical disturbances at the sensorium occasion all the diversified phenomena of sensation, and their interpretation
by the soul constitutes thought.

The casual illustrations of this power of the mind have
been numerous, and they should be convincing. Ideas are
often transmitted by mental-electrical currents to kindred
minds in the same assembly. By some invisible means we
are frequently reminded of absent persons, and made to feel
and believe that they are approaching some time before the
fact is cognizable by the senses. Many persons experience a
slight spastic action of the nerves whenever they converse
with one who expresses his thoughts with uncommon earnestness. We have experienced something resembling the
chills and fever while witnessing a masterly dramatic performance, and a powerful speaker may even raise the hearer
from his seat, by the mysterious force that elevates the mind
to the highest heaven of imagination. Some people are conscious of a soporific influence, when within the spheres or
magnetic emanations of certain individuals, while other
persons banish sleep from our presence. This susceptibility

is often greatly increased by disease. There are friends who come to the sick room, whose presence is an anodyne ; others greatly aggravate the nervous irritability and wakefulness of the patient. Sleep is often driven from the couch of pain by the anxiety and restlessness of sympathising friends, whose minds are fixed on the sufferer. Thus the mind, acting through the subtile medium of vital motion and sensation, produces both physiological and psychological effects. The sensorial impressions—made by the tangible objects of the terrestrial world—are certainly not more intense and lasting than the electrical excitation and mental emotions produced by thoughts when they are armed with the power of volition.

The instances wherein we are singularly anticipated in what we are about to say, numerous as they are, might be presumed to depend on an association of ideas ; or they might be ascribed to a similarity in the intellectual development and general habits of thought peculiar to the individuals, did they not often occur under such circumstances as must preclude the adoption of either of these hypotheses. The thought conceived and simultaneously expressed very often sustains no relation, however remote, to any subject of previous remark. Nor are we able to discern, always or generally, any marked resemblance of the parties to each other ; either in their cerebral conformation or other physical and mental peculiarities. Nevertheless, the facts are matters of common observation and experience, and the philosophic mind is disposed to seek for some law to which such mental phenomena may be referred.

A fact that is perpetually recurring, proves the existence

of some active principle and regulating law, of which such fact or phenomenon is the appropriate and natural expression. In the course of my investigations it has been clearly demonstrated—by experiments on a great number of persons—that the mind exerts a direct power over the subtile medium of vital motion and sensation, and hence that it may influence both the voluntary and involuntary functions of animals and men. It is further manifest from these experiments that the earth and atmosphere, or more properly their imponderables, may serve to establish this connection, and thus to open the intercommunication of mind with mind. This observation is confirmed by every experiment wherein one person is controlled or influenced—when at a distance —by the unexpressed will or thought of another.* The electro-physiological and psychological changes, produced by mental action, are facts as real and indisputable as any within the whole domain of physical science. The vital aura is so highly sublimated that it is readily disturbed by the slightest causes, producing nervous vibrations and cerebral impressions. Its ebb and flow mark the occurrence of every emotion—the gentle no less than the terrible—while in the flaming intensity of passion, as well as in the mysterious and delicate enginery of thought, we have the stirring revelations of its presence and its power.

---

* The mind that acts with the greatest vigor and method, will be the most likely to excite distinct emotions and clearly defined ideas by this psycho-electric process; at the same time, it will be equally obvious that the absence of the executive power of the mind—or the temporary suspension of its functions—will greatly increase the susceptibility of the subject to impressions by the Mental Telegraph.

CHAPTER XXIV.

MENTAL TELEGRAPHING.

> And thoughts, like sun-fires penetrate the world,
> And go where they are sent : thus mind meets mind
> Though mountains rise and oceans roll between.

THE results of individual experience constitute the accumulated wisdom of the world. It is cheerfully conceded that the experience of other persons may be fraught with a deeper interest than our own ; but those who restrict themselves to the repetition of what others may have felt, and thought, and spoken, add little or nothing to the common stock of ideas. The man who has a serious purpose will find more useful and honorable employment. Moreover, to seek a name in this way is to rob the dead of their immortality. It were far more commendable to die and leave no memorial, than to tax the nerves and employ the brains of other men to build a monument.

Long before undertaking the labor of a systematic inquiry into the philosophy of the vital functions and the laws of mind, I had witnessed and performed some experiments, attended with results so remarkable as to render them worthy of being preserved among the more interesting incidents of my private experience. I have not heretofore omitted to record other facts, occurring without the range of personal observation, whenever they afforded the most suitable illustrations of my subject; nor do I deem it necessary to offer an apology for presenting the experimental results of my own investigations as often as these will best serve my purpose. From an observation of facts incidentally occurring, I was prompted to a succession of voluntary efforts, which were signalized by still more remarkable results. In numerous instances I tried the experiment of thinking intensely of some person, present or absent, with a view to ascertain whether the mind of that person would not revert to me at the same time. This experiment, though many times repeated, with different subjects—frequently with persons at a distance—was eminently successful. The individuals selected were usually, though not always, personal friends and familiar acquaintances of the writer; but the success of the experiments did not appear to depend at all on the previous intimacy of the parties.

The curious facts in this department, whether comprehended under the several heads of " Magnetism," " Mesmerism," " Pathetism," " Electro-Psychology," " Biology," or

any other term—properly or improperly derived and applied
—are all illustrations (when they are real) of the same essential principles and laws. Moreover, the men who, severally, either claim to have made an original discovery, or to
have founded a distinct branch of science, are generally
mere pretenders, who at most have only varied the forms of
experiment, or, perhaps, coined a new and less appropriate
name for the same thing. Many of the professed expound-
ers of the psychological hallucinations, and other similar
phenomena, have illustrated nothing more clearly than their
own ignorance of the philosophy of the whole subject ; while
their public experiments have, for the most part, been of so
gross and repulsive a character as to justly offend the good
taste and the moral sense of the intelligent and refined spectator. More than one poor catch-penny, prompted alike by
coarseness and avarice to pander to a vitiated and vulgar
taste, has compelled an intelligent human being to walk on
all-fours, to bark like a dog, or to bray like a donkey ! The
writer once witnessed such a performance, with a feeling of
almost irrepressible indignation, that a MAN should be thus
degraded—even in imagination, for a moment—to the level
of four-footed beasts. No man who has not already unfortunately defiled his own garments by a groveling and beastly
life, and thus disfigured or obscured the image of God in his
own soul, would so prostitute his mental powers and debase
the common humanity.

Those who utterly disregard the claims of science and
willingly brutalize their own species, are seldom capable of
giving any intelligible idea of the subject on which they
profess to discourse. They are usually very positive in their

assumptions, and extremely negative in their proofs. The public experiments of such professed interpreters of the psychological mysteries, are designed to amuse rather than to instruct, and the pretended results are often transparent frauds. The operators of this class are accustomed to tell the subject, in a most emphatic manner, precisely what they expect him to see, hear, feel, taste, smell or do, so that there is every opportunity for collusion, and—if the subject has fine imitative powers—he may deceive the uninitiated spectator. A biological " doctor," whom the writer once met at Louisville, Ky.—a rough Stone in the temple of humanity— assured his audiences that the experiments *did not require the exercise of the will ;* also that *mind* (meaning the mind of the operator) had nothing to do with the results ; (others thought so in his particular case) but that all the effects on the body and mind of the subject, were to be accounted for " *on the doctrine of impressions.*" This unmeaning assertion —repeated often and with peculiar emphasis—the Doctor appeared to regard as a most lucid exposition of the whole subject ; and, accordingly, he traveled from place to place —by land and sea—

> " Explaining his mysteries to the nations,
> But never explaining his explanations."

The experimental illustrations which follow in this connection are of a widely different character ; at the same time they demonstrate the fact of a silent intercourse of mind with mind through the subtile medium of sensation. They leave no room to doubt that passions, sentiments and thoughts—not less than external forms and physical phenomena—serve to disturb the electric aura of the nervous system, through which their images are conveyed to the corporeal seat of sensation, and thence reflected to the inner consciousness of the spirit. I now propose to illustrate the nature and results of my experiments by the introduction of particular examples.

Miss Wilder, of Leominster, Mass., possessed a melodious voice, and no little skill in musical execution. She was so extremely impressible that any piece of music, of which one might chance to be thinking in her presence, could be communicated to her by the slightest touch. When, occasionally, the impression was indefinite, she would seem to be listening for an instant, and then—starting as though she had heard a voice—would exclaim, "Yes, I hear! I have it!" and immediately commence singing, at the same time furnishing her own accompaniment on the guitar. Mr. Davis, an amateur violinist, and several others, repeated the experiment, at my suggestion, with similar success. This lady was, on numerous occasions, the subject of many curious experiments, in which the electro-mental susceptibility displayed was extremely beautiful in its nature, and truly wonderful in its results.

Some time since, while the writer was in Louisville, Ky., a number of experiments were made with Miss Bulkeley, an interesting young lady who displayed remarkable readiness in receiving communications by the mental telegraph. The subject was eminently free from any tendency to disease, and the experimental results, in her case, were such as to excite the admiration of many intelligent ladies and gentlemen. Being in electro-mental *rapport* with Miss B., the writer received—from strangers and disint rc: ted persons—cards and slips of paper to the number of twelve or fifteen, on each of which the name of some flower had been previously written. The collection embraced the violet, pink, rose, dahlia, sunflower, tulip, honeysuckle, snowball, water-lily, and others of which our recollection is imperfect. Taking these severally in my hand, I formed an ideal image of the particular flower designated on each separate card or slip of paper, and the images were successively conveyed by this silent, psychological process to the mind of the young lady, who—with scarcely a moment's delay in any instance—pronounced the names of the flowers, each in its proper place, as the card bearing the corresponding name was taken up. All the flowers named above were thus designated except the snowball, which, though not named, was otherwise described as *a large white flower.*

A middle-aged Lady, residing in Louisville, whose nervous system was so morbidly impressible that she would start with a violent, involuntary motion, whenever the door of her room was opened or closed suddenly, was also a highly susceptible subject. In her case, the external avenues of sensation could be opened and closed at pleasure. In presence of a large audience she distinguished sugar, salt, pepper, vinegar, and other articles, the instant I tasted of each, notwithstanding I was ten feet from her at the time, and she had not the slightest reason to presume that any one of the articles named was in the room, or could be conveniently obtained under the circumstances. With a glass of magnetic water, and a few manipulations, accompanied by the action of the will, I completely suspended sensation in five minutes or less. With a view of trying the sense of hearing by a severe and demonstrative test, a Kentuckian furnished me with a heavily loaded revolver, three barrels of which I instantly discharged over the back of the Lady's head, without causing the slightest motion of a single muscle.

Mrs. Rice, of Worcester, Mass., was distinguished for a most delicate susceptibility of mental impressions. Having been invited to visit her one afternoon—at her residence, and in company with several friends—I seated myself at her side, at the same time requesting her to take an excursion, and to describe whatever she might observe by the way. Without giving the slightest intimation respecting the direction we were to travel, I proceeded on an ideal journey, by railroad and steamboat, to New York. Madam Rice described with singular fidelity all the important ob'ects on the route of which the writer could form a distinct conception—spoke of persons whom she met by the way, and repeated the very words they were by me supposed to utter. On the same occasion, I imag'ned a letter to be placed before her, when she suddenly exclaimed, "Here is a letter from Mr. ——," mentioning the name of an absent friend of whom I was thinking at that moment; and going through with the appropriate motions, as if she were really breaking a seal and unfolding the sheet, she commenced and read *verbatim*, from my mind, for several minutes. These were the first and only experiments made with Mrs. Rice.

I once attended a social party given by Mrs. Kirkpatrick. at her residence in Albany. In the company was a lady (Mrs. Mills) whom I had been led to infer might be highly susceptible of electro-nervous impressions, though I had never confirmed my opinion by a single experiment. Taking

a seat by a gentleman who was known to be extremely skeptical, I observed that it might be possible to demonstrate the
existence of a mental power he was disposed to deny ; that,
although I had never conversed with Mrs. M. on the subject,
nor made the slightest effort to subject her to psychological
impressions, I had little hesitation in saying, that the voluntary functions of mind and body might be controlled—without physical contact—by the unaided power of volition.

This gentleman having expressed a desire to witness the
experiment, it was agreed that I should cause the lady to
leave her place at the opposite side of the room, and occupy
a vacant chair by his side. In less than one minute she
obeyed the silent action of my will and seated herself in the
unoccupied chair. In like manner she was impelled to
change her position several times, and finally to leave the
room temporarily, with no specific object in view, and without so much as suspecting the origin of an impulse she was
quite unable to resist.

The tea-table was the scene of an interesting experiment.
Mrs. Mills was in the act of removing from the board—
having finished her repast—when several dishes were handed
to her, all of which were refused. Mrs. Kirkpatrick urged
Mrs. M. to accept another dish of tea, which the latter positively declined. Without uttering a word, I succeeded in
changing her inclination, and, obedient to my volition, she
immediately drew her chair again to the table, and called
for a dish of tea. On my passing the several dishes she had
just refused, Mrs. Mills freely partook of each, as if it were
for the first time.

At an early hour she proposed to go home ; but my friend

who had given the entertainment, apprehensive that others might follow the example, and thus the company be broken up, desired me to restrain her. Mrs. Mills instantly obeyed the executive action of the mind, observing that the attractions the occasion presented were so numerous, and withal so powerful, that she could not break away. In this manner her desire to go home was neutralized, and Mrs. M. remained until the company separated.

Several years ago, while spending an afternoon with several ladies and gentlemen—mostly strangers to the writer—some illustrations of mental telegraping were called for by the company. Among the persons present, two or three were more or less influenced. But Miss. A———, a lady of intelligence and refinement, with whom the writer had had no previous acquaintance, was discovered to yield with great readiness and astonishing precision to the action of the will. Though at the time perfectly awake—and until then totally unconscious of possessing any such susceptibility—this lady bestowed several rings and other valuables on different members of the party, following in every instance, and in a most unerring manner, the writer's volition. Without affording the slightest opportunity for the fair subject to learn, by any external indications, the nature of the requests made, a number of difficult trials were suggested by persons composing the company. Several of these experiments— attended with the most satisfactory results—may be thus briefly mentioned : Miss. A. promptly obeyed the silent mandate of my mind, and going to the center-table, selected a particular book, that had been singled out from among a number of others equally conspicuous. Some one required that she might be incited to take up another book, of five hundred pages, and turn to a short poem—somewhere about the middle of the volume—which was accordingly done without the least hesitation. Again, by a similar effort, this lady was influenced to make choice of a particular engraving, from amongst a number contained in an annual. While looking at my watch, she announced the time within a few seconds. On a subsequent occasion, similar efforts were made to impress the mind of this person, but from some defect in the requisite conditions, the results were certainly not satisfactory.

When the mental and moral gravitation has been mutual I have been scarcely less successful in my experiments on persons at a distance. On one occasion, while spending a few days at Waterbury, Conn., I found it necessary to see a young man in the village. The immediate presence of the youth was of considerable importance to me, but not knowing his residence, place of business, or even his name, I could not send for him. In this emergency, I undertook to telegraph him, by concentrating my mind on the young man, with a fixed determination to bring him to me. Some ten minutes had elapsed when he came to the house and inquired for the writer. Meeting a gentleman at the door, he asked, with much apparent interest, whether I wanted to see him. On being interrogated by this individual, he stated that a few moments before, and while actively engaged in his workshop —distant one fourth of a mile—he suddenly felt that he must seek my presence without delay. He declared that he was conscious of the existence and influence of some strange power, acting chiefly on the anterior portion of his brain, and drawing him with irresistible energy. His work being urgent, he resolved at first to resist this unaccountable inclination, but after a determined effort, found himself unequal to the task.

While employed in lecturing at New Canaan, Conn., several years since, I chanced one night to be thinking earnestly of a young man who was living in the adjoining town of Norwalk—at a distance of several miles—and who had been the subject of some experiments on a previous occasion. This youth happened at that precise time, as I subsequently learned, to be in company with several gentlemen who were subjecting him to some similar experiments, when all at once —and in a manner most unaccountable to all present—he escaped from their influence, declaring, with great earnestness, that Mr. Brittan wanted to see him, and that he must go immediately.

The wife of Rev. C. H. Gardner proved to be an excellent telegraphic instrument. I had personally subjected the lady to a single experiment, resulting in the cure of a distressing asthma, from which she had suffered intensely and for a long time. I had not spoken with this person for three months, when one day her arrival, in company with her husband, was unexpectedly announced. After a brief interview, which did not occupy more than five minutes, I withdrew and retired to my study to complete the task I had left unfinished, leaving Mr. and Mrs. G. with my family and several other persons. Not the slightest allusion had been made to any further experiments, and certainly none were then premeditated.

Several hours elapsed—I know not how long—when the

silence of my apartment was broken by sounds of mirth proceeding from the company below. They were engaged in some amusement which excited a spirited conversation and immoderate laughter. The voice of Mrs. Gardner was distinctly heard. At that moment the idea of taking her from the company occurred to me. But the occasion seemed to be in all respects unfavorable. She had no intimation that any such effort would be made ; she was in a remote part of the house, and we were separated by a long flight of stairs and two partitions. Moreover, surrounded by others, and excited by outward circumstances, the soul is not in the most suitable state to be successfully approached and strongly influenced through the subtile, invisible media employed by the mind. Nevertheless, I resolved to make the experiment. Closing my eyes to shut out all external objects, I fixed my mind on Mrs. G., with a determination to bring her to the library. Doubtless the mental effort, in that instance, would have been quite sufficient—had it been applied through the muscles—to overcome the physical resistance of an object equal to the weight of the lady's person. I was, however, not a little astonished on witnessing the result of this experiment. In about two minutes the door opened and Mrs. Gardner entered with her eyes closed, when the following conversation ensued :

" You appeared to be very happy with the friends below." I observed, inquiringly.

" I was."

" Why, then, did you leave the company ?"

" I don't know."

" Why, or for what purpose, did you come here ?"

" I thought you wanted me, and I could not help obeying the summons."

While on a visit at Newtown, Conn., some seven or eight years since, I became acquainted with Miss Grace Goodyear, whose extreme impressibility was evident from her readiness to divine the thoughts and feelings of those around her. In the course of our interview, an experiment was suggested for the purpose of ascertaining whether her exquisite susceptibility would admit of her receiving telegraphic communications from a distance. It was mutually agreed that on the succeeding Tuesday evening, at ten o'clock, she should retire to her private apartment, and write her thoughts for half an hour, during which time I was to telegraph her, if possible, from my house in Bridgeport, the distance being about an hour's ride by railway. The time set apart for the trial found me occupied with a subject of such absorbing interest, that the hour actually passed before I suspected it had arrived. It was precisely thirty minutes after ten, when I was suddenly reminded of my engagement, but it was then too late to make the proposed trial. Under these circumstances I resolved to make an experiment that, if successful, would be still more convincing, because unpremeditated. Accordingly, I waited until eleven o'clock and thirty minutes, when presuming that she must be asleep, I occupied the remaining half hour before midnight in an effort to project certain images before the mind, at a distance of eighteen miles! The ideal picture represented a sylvan scene, enlivened by clear flowing waters, and a variety of such natural objects as are necessary to complete an enchanting landscape ; while beneath the inviting shade—on the flowery margin of the stream—I placed the subject of the experiment, and a tall, graceful youth with a guitar, whose music fixed attention and entranced the soul.

Several days after, I received a letter containing, in substance, the following :—" You either did not make the experiment at the time, and in the manner proposed, or else did not succeed, as I received no impression, during the half hour, that could be traced to any foreign source. But after retiring for the night, and falling into a natural slumber, a beautiful dream-like vision passed before me." Subsequently, at my request, she related the dream—her narrative commencing thus :—" I was standing by a clear stream, whose banks were covered with beautiful groves ;" and the remainder of the recital indicated a striking resemblance of the dream to the images formed in the mind of the writer. Requesting the lady to denote, as nearly as possible, the hour of her singular experience, she stated that she retired at eleven o'clock, and, on awaking from the dream, found the precise time to be *ten minutes past twelve*, which determines the hour with sufficient exactness to warrant the conclusion that there may have been, and doubtless was, actual commerce of thought and feeling, carried on through the intervening distance between Newtown and Bridgeport.

From among the numerous examples of this power, I shall record but one more in this connection. In the month of September, 1847, I was one night on my way from New York city to New London, Conn. In its solemn silence and spiritual beauty, the night was more enchanting than the day. The elements were in a state of profound repose, and the full moon poured a flood of silvery light far over the

distant land and the surrounding waters. Long Island
Sound seemed like a sea of glass, in which the gods might
see their faces, and wherein the sublime and glorious heavens
were faithfully mirrored. It was a time for meditation and
deep communion of soul, when the presence of the absent is
felt, and the portals of the Spirit-home are open to man.
Gazing away into the infinite inane, it seemed that the unre-
vealed glory of the Invisible was only concealed from mortal
eyes by thin nebulous curtains, let down by Angel-hands
over the windows of heaven. Looking away over the peaceful waters, and up through the luminous atmosphere, I
fancied that the spirit, like light, might travel afar over
mountain and plain to the objects for which it has affinity.
And why not? the spirit within involuntarily demanded.
Surely the spirit—the man—the immortal—is as subtile as
light. In the order of Nature, the soul exceeds. in the degree
of its refinement, all that is subject to sensuous observation.
Mind is far more ethereal than electricity ; thought may,
therefore, travel with more than electric speed. With no
battery but the brain, with no clumsy intervention of telegraphic posts and wires, the mind may send out its thoughts,
on invisible electric waves, to the remembered and distant
objects of its devotion.

It was about midnight when I resolved on an effort to
impress the mind of Mrs. Brittan. We were separated by
an intervening distance of about one hundred and fifty miles
in a direct line. Abstracting the mind from the sphere of
outward and visible objects, I labored for some time—I know
not how long—in one intense effort of mind. I sought to
invest my thoughts with forms, and to bear them away to

the hearth and home where the shadows of their forms might fall on the passive spirit, causing it to have dreams and visions of the objects and scenes my fancy had portrayed. Nor was this an abortive effort. On my return, Mrs. B. related a singular dream that occurred in my absence, and on the identical night already described. Improbable as the statement may appear to many persons, the dream corresponded, in its essential particulars, to the imaginary images I had fashioned on the occasion of that midnight abstraction.

It may be objected that a knowledge of such mysterious agents, and the exercise of such faculties, confer a dangerous power. That will depend on the character of those who possess the knowledge and exercise the faculty. All power is dangerous in the hands of bad men. The man who has a large, muscular arm may seize his victim in the public highway—rob him of his purse or of his life—but it is nevertheless desirable to have a strong arm. The voice that thrills us with its divine music may be used to beguile. The syren may float on the stream of its burnished eloquence, only to entrance the unconscious victim with a bewildering and fatal enchantment. The Press, though among the world's greatest blessings, may be so perverted as to become its most withering curse. When wielded by unscrupulous men—men who denounce the noblest gifts of Heaven as satanic emanations— it becomes a scourge. When the innocent and the humble are defamed—the poor defrauded of reputation and the means of usefulness—when Reason and Science are

"Impeached of Godlessness,"

then does the Press become a dangerous power ; and the

fearful responsibility of its prostitution to some of these unholy purposes will be likely to rest on a somewhat numerous class of American journalists.

Delicate nerves are doubtless sometimes temporarily deranged by an inexperienced practitioner. But this furnishes no substantial ground of objection. It does not prove that the agent is necessarily a dangerous one ; but it forcibly illustrates the great danger of that *incorrigible ignorance* which so many affectionately cherish. A clumsy and unpracticed surgeon might sever an artery, and leave his patient to expire from loss of blood ; but we must look elsewhere for a valid objection to surgery, since this only too clearly demonstrates the paramount importance of a thorough knowledge of the subject. There have always been ignorant pretenders in every art and science, as there have been hypocrites in religion for whose ignoble conduct, neither the sacred cause itself, nor its more faithful disciples, should be deemed responsible. Examples are not wanting wherein every great and God-like attribute has been perverted ; and there is no position, how exalted soever, that has not been invaded by the tempter, and from which men have not descended to realms where dwell the children of perdition. The apostleship of " one of the twelve" was the very instrumentality employed in the betrayal and death of the Master ; but Religion is still a sublime reality ; and Jesus—viewed at the coronation of Calvary—is shorn of none of his peculiar glory.

CHAPTER XXV.

THE FACULTY OF ABSTRACTION.

Introversion of the Mind—Ideal and practical Men—Facts universally perceived—Principles seldom comprehended—Analytical and synthetical Powers—Vulgar conceptions of Utility—Fasting and Asceticism—Customs of the Ancient Prophets—Worshiping in Groves and Mountains—The Druids—Consecration of desolate places —Influence of mental Introversion on Sensation—Archimedes of Syracuse—Statesmen, Philosophers and Poets—The mental Foci—State of Entrancement—Perversion of the Faculty—Vital and organic Derangements—Tendency to Fanaticism—Roger Bacon and Simeon Stylites.

THE capacity of the soul to withdraw itself from the physical avenues of sensation, and the mental and corporeal effects known to accompany the exercise of that power, will constitute the subject of the present Chapter. All persons accustomed to reflection are conscious of being able to separate the mind, in some degree at least, from the sphere of outward perception and action. The measure of this power varies as the peculiarities of original constitution are more or less favorable to its exercise ; and is inert or operative according to the temperament, disposition, habits and general pursuits of the individual. Of the nature of this power, and the magnitude of its consequences, very few entertain an adequate conception.

Certain pursuits require great concentration of mind ; but

it is readily granted that others are most successfully prosecuted by those who are capable of a kind *mental diffusion*
The greatest intensity and power are exhibited when the
mental energies concenter. I would not speak disrespect-
fully of any class of minds, nor designedly undervalue the
feeblest effort, if well intended ; but among the so-called
practical men—the men who know how to make money, and
to keep it—there is an unbecoming disposition to ridicule, as
mere dreamers, all who entertain an ideal that transcends
the dusty walks of vulgar life. It is conceded that those who
pursue some miscellaneous business—for example, the man
who sells goods and the writer of short items for the newspaper—would accomplish comparatively little, if given to intense concentration and profound abstraction of mind, since
the successful discharge of their respective duties is made to
depend on the facility with which the mind passes from one
object to another. But however indispensable this transitive
faculty may be to the man of the world, it is seldom associated
with the creative energy of acknowledged genius, or the vast
comprehensiveness of the real philosopher. The class denominated practical men, may be men of great research and
careful observation ; but they are neither distinguished for an
intuitive perception of truth, nor for profourd and independent thought. Their minds are almost wholly employed
in the outer world. They feel the force of facts rather than
of principles, and hence realize the value of the Senses while
they scarcely comprehend the use of Reason. Such persons
seldom attempt to fathom the depths of human nature, while
they as rarely respect the highest demands of the time.
Nevertheless, they have their appropriate place in the scale

19

of being, and, doubtless, well perform their peculiar functions.

It must be conceded that material objects and physical
phenomena still furnish the forms of evidence which appeal
with the greatest power to most minds. This is manifestly
true of the multitudes in whom the reasoning faculties are
but feebly exercised. An essential service may, therefore,
be rendered by recording the facts of daily experience, even
when the individual himself is not qualified to weigh an argument or to feel the force of a logical deduction. It however requires but little intelligence to perceive a fact that
addresses itself to the outward sense ; and yet millions are
prone to restrict the operations of their minds to the low
sphere of sensuous observation. They are often heard to say,
" I will only believe when I can have the evidence of my
senses—I must see, hear, or handle, as the case may require,
for myself." Thus they unconsciously but clearly define
their true position ; and virtually proclaim the fact that
they occupy the animal plane of existence. The dog knows
enough to follow his instincts ; the wild beasts run to their
hiding-places when the tempest approaches ; even the *ass*,
(proverbial for his stupidity,) would inevitably become cog-
nizant of the particular fact, should the roof of the stable
fall on his head, though his ears might never be open to
a discussion of the general laws of attraction. The philosophy of such people—when they have any—is generally
fragmentary and superficial. Seldom or never admitted
into close communion with the hidden principles of Nature,
they are chiefly qualified to notice her outward expressions,
while it is given to other minds to receive her sublime oracles,

Thus it would seem to be the peculiar province of one class to observe and record ; of the other, to reveal and create.

Among the decomposing agents in Nature may be justly comprehended a certain class of minds, gifted with peculiar powers of analysis, and holding a kind of hereditary mas- tery over the great realm of little things. These are often *sharp critics*, but seldom, indeed, has one been a great poet, a profound philosopher, or a comprehensive historian. To this class of minds, the Universe is not ONE, but a disorderly aggregation of separate forms and distinct entities, sustain- ing no very intimate relations. Another, and as we conceive a far higher power is necessary in grouping the disorganized elements, so as to form them into new and living creations. It requires but an ordinary medical student and a scalpel to dissect a body that only God could create.

Many of our practical men appear to be materialists, whatever they may be in fact or in their own estimation. They very properly esteem the cultivation of potatoes and the growth of cotton as matters of universal concern ; but the production of ideas and the culture of the soul are deemed to be interesting chiefly to divines, metaphyscians, and the fraternity of dreamers. These inveterate utilitarians esti- mate all things—not even excepting the grace of God and the ministry of Angels—by their capacity to yield an im- mediate practical result—*a result that may be included in the next inventory.* The genuine fire of Prometheus is worthless, except it will supply the place of *fuel ;* and the Muses, are they not all fools, unless Parnassus be made a corn-field ! Such views, however prevalent, have not the power to enlist those who are greatly distinguished for independent thought and super-sensual attainments. The man of intuitive nature would rather be numbered with dreamers, than lose sight of his immortality.

Not only the noblest thoughts are evolved in seasons of profound mental abstraction, but the mind is made to feel a deeper consciousness of its relations to the invisible, and is rendered more susceptible of the influence of super-terrestrial natures. Fasting and asceticism materially aid in this retirement of the soul from the senses. The ancient Prophets and Seers were accustomed to seek the wilderness, or some lonely mountain, where they would invoke the spiritual presence. Moses withdrew from the idolatrous multitude into the Mount, where, surrounded by the sublimities of Nature, he is supposed to have received the Law. It was when the Prophet bowed his head and covered his face with his mantle —shutting out from his senses the impressive symbols of the tempest and the fire—that the " still small voice" obtained an utterance in his soul. Christ found in the desert solitudes the spiritual strength which earthly companionship could not afford. Protracted fasting, a home in the wilderness, and silent communion with the Spirit-world, served to diminish his susceptibility of mere physical suffering, and to render him strong in spirit, and mighty to endure his trial. The ancients seem to have been deeply conscious of the fact that retirement from the world was necessary to the highest functions of the immortal nature, and to all the noblest triumphs of the mind. Hence the Patriarchs planted groves as places of worship, and preferred to perform their religious rites on the summits of lofty mountains. The Druids, who were held in the greatest veneration by the ancient Britons and Gauls, consecrated the most desolate scenes in nature to the purposes of their religion, and to the education of their youth, who were required to retire into caves and the deepest recesses of the forest, sometimes for a period of twenty years. Manifestly, all these discerned the shadow of the same great law, and sought to quicken and invigorate the soul by withdrawing it from the scenes of its earthly life.

Since the mind may govern the distribution of the forces of vital motion, it is but natural that all the fluids, and more especially that refined aura which pervades the nervous system, and is the agent of its mysterious functions—should recede from the external surfaces of the body, whenever the mind is deeply abstracted. If, in the order of the Universe, mind be superior to matter, we are authorized to presume that the latter is of necessity subject to the former. That mind is an ever active force, and that matter, separately considered, is inert and destitute of the power of motion, is illustrated by the various phenomena which spring from their most intimate relations. In proportion, therefore, as the mind is abstracted, the sensorial medium must be withdrawn from the extremities of the nerves, and the natural susceptibility of the organs be temporarily suspended. But we are not necessarily confined to the argument *a priori* in the illustration of our proposition. Facts, cognizable by the senses, are disclosed to the observation of all, and these lead us to the same general conclusion. It is well known that whenever a state of mental abstraction is induced, it serves to deaden the sensibility to pain, and to diminish the consciousness of outward danger. When all the powers of the soul are engrossed with some one great object or idea, no room is left for the intrusion of thoughts or purposes of inferior moment. Then earth and time, with their gilded treasures and empty honors, are disregarded, and in our transfiguration we forget that we are mortal.

It can not be necessary to cite a great number of facts in this connection. Yet illustrations of the principle are scattered through all history. The martyrs of Liberty and Religion, whose shouts of victory and songs of triumph have risen above the discord of war, or been heard amidst the crackling fagots at the stake, show how regardless mortals are of danger, how almost insensible to pain is man, when the soul is fired by a holy enthusiasm, and all its powers consecrated to a sacred cause. But not in these pursuits and conquests alone do men experience this deadening of the external senses. All persons of *studious habits* are conscious of a similar loss of physical sensibility, whenever the mind is profoundly occupied. Some men possess this power of abstraction in a very remarkable degree ; and persons of this class have often been greatly distinguished for their boldness and originality of thought. A gentleman, known to many of our readers, has, on several occasions, while addressing public assemblies on some important subject, experienced a temporary loss of sensation, accompanied by an abnormal quickening of the mental and moral faculties ; so that while all forms of persons, and other objects within the range of vision, were gradually obliterated, the understanding was mysteriously illuminated. While under the influence of this spell, he loses all consciousness of time and place, and speaks with far more than his accustomed ease and power.

That this abstraction diminishes physical sensibility, and renders the mind indifferent to outward objects, and even regardless of the body, is forcibly illustrated in the case of Archimedes of Syracuse. When his native city was besieged and taken by the Romans, Metellus, their commander, desired to spare the life of this distinguished man ; but, in the midst of the conflict, a soldier entered his apartment and placed a glittering sword at his throat. The great geometrician was engaged in the solution of a problem, and so deeply absorbed that he remained calm and unawed by the certain prospect of death. At length, with great apparent calmness, he said, " Hold, but for one moment, and my demonstration will be finished !" But the soldier seeing a box in which Archimedes kept his instruments, and think ing it contained gold, was unable to resist the temptation, and killed him on the spot.

To be greatly distinguished in any department of thought, it becomes necessary that the theme should engross all the mental energies ; and this demands a separation of the faculties of the mind from other objects, and, in a degree, from the whole sphere of sensuous impressions. We may judge of the extent of the mind's abstraction from the body by the increasing insensibility to outward objects and circumstances. In proportion as the soul is engaged by internal realities, we lose the consciousness of external forms, and become insensible to impressions on the physical organs. The statesman is lost in the midst of his profound design ; when oppressed with the nation's care, he heeds not the beauty that crowds the gilded avenues of fashionable life. The philosopher loses his own individuality in the deeper consciousness of all that is around, beneath and above him. Awed by the sublime presence of Nature ; standing unvailed before her august ministers, and questioning her living oracles, he heeds no more the petty strifes of common men. The poet is charmed in his reveries. Far away from earth and its grossness, he feels the pulses of a life more spiritual and divine. An angelic magnetism separates him from the world, and he is borne away to other spheres, and worlds invisible are disclosed to the mysterious vision of Genius.

It is especially when man is thus separated from the earth-life, that the soul gives birth to its noblest creations, and realizes something of the divine in its ideal. The highest truths are begotten from the Heavens. It is only when the soul retires to the inmost, and receives its impregnation from the forces of angelic life and thought, that its conceptions are truly exalted and spiritual. When the mental energies are divided and dissipated among a variety of outward objects, the mind makes no conquests. Mist and darkness gather around the highest subjects of human thought. Minds thus constituted and exercised cause a divergence of the light that shines through them, while others possess a mighty *focal power*, under which all subjects become luminous ; the light of the mental world finds a point of concentration, and the soul burns up the very grossness and darkness which obstructed its vision. In all things the intensity of action is dependent on the accumulation of forces. The various agents in Nature are rendered potent by the processes necessary to concentrate their essential virtues and their peculiar action. Archimedes, the great geometrician of antiquity, destroyed a Roman fleet, more than two thousand years ago, setting it on fire by the glasses with which he concentrated the sun's rays. When the electric medium is everywhere equally diffused, its power is neutralized and we are insensible of its presence ; but when powerfully concentrated, it rends the darkest cloud, and reveals to us the glory of the heavens beyond. Thus, when the mental forces converge, we become aware of the mind's power ; the clouds that vailed the deepest problems of Nature, break and pass away, and amid the illuminated mysteries we follow the kindling soul by its track of fire !

Those who are profoundly abstracted, are often magnetized by the Angels. Not merely as an agreeable fancy, but rather as a solemn and beautiful reality, do I entertain and express the thought. Some higher intelligence wins the rapt soul away from earth, and it dwells above and blends with the Infinite. In the charmed hours when we are able to retire from the dull sphere of grosser life, we think most deeply and truly. Only when earthly sounds are hushed, when earthly scenes grow dim and then invisible, do we ascend to the highest heaven of thought. Communion with external nature ; the investigation of her interior laws ; the consciousness of the still higher spiritual realities that surround us, and the soul's true worship, are the subjects and exercises best adapted to induce this state of mind. When wholly absorbed with the material objects and events of time, the mind is fettered in its thought. Chained down to earth by a material magnetism, it is difficult to rise above the cramped plane of artificial life. For this reason the mind's noblest monuments have ever been wrought out from invisible worlds, where, vailed forever, are the sources of its highest inspiration.

In conclusion, I must speak briefly of *the dangers* incidental to the exercise of this power. While a just observance of the principle under consideration must serve to quicken and inspire the faculties, history has recorded many melancholy examples of its perversion to the most painful and fatal ends. So great is the power of mind over the body, that portions of the animal economy are sometimes paralyzed by its action. Constant exercise of mind, without the use of the senses, not only tends to withdraw the circulating medium of the nervous system from the external surfaces, but, of necessity, renders the health and life of the body insecure. Intense thought—when long continued—may occasion an undue determination of the vital forces and fluids to the brain, and thus produce congestion or some derangement of the faculties. The conditions of mind and body, which cause a temporary suspension of sensation, may, if greatly protracted, preclude the restoration of the physical functions. I have known several authors who have prematurely lost the sense of hearing, as there is reason to believe, from this cause.

But there are other dangers not less fatal to personal usefulness, and far more destructive to the interests of society. This disposition to withdraw from the world has prompted many to neglect the ordinary duties of life. Not a few have been tempted to fly from all civilized society, and have spent their lives in caves and mountains, away from the ills which they had not the manhood to meet. It is a morbid alienation of reason, with a sickly disgust of life and all temporal interests, that leads to these extremes. Neither Nature nor the spirit of Divine wisdom can be the incentive to action, when men thus disregard their relations to this world, and treat the gifts of God and the blessings of earth with pious scorn. The asceticism that prevailed in the early church, and the coporeal inflictions that men in different ages have voluntarily suffered, witness to us how sadly the noblest powers and privileges may be perverted. Think of old Roger Bacon, the Anchoret. He lived two years in a hole under a church wall, and at last dug his own grave with his finger-nails; and all that he might escape from the world, and show his contempt for physical suffering! And Simeon Stylites, distinguished among the Ascetics as the renowned pillar-saint, what a martyr was he![1] There may be no more like these; but there are, yet in the flesh, many victims of their own melancholy whims; men whose disgust of this laboring world proceeds from a love of indolence and a fondness for dreaming; gifted souls whose mission is not to labor—gifted with visions in arm-chairs—visions of ease projected from their own brains—and who, if only their usefulness is to be considered, might as well follow the example of the English monk.

---

[1] Simeon Stylites was a native of Syria. He lived during a period of thirty-seven years on the top of a pillar, gradually increasing its hight as he became lean in body and sublimated in soul, until he obtained the elevation, coporeal and spiritual, of some sixty feet. Having progressed to this sublime extent, he acquired a great reputation as an oracle, and became the head of a sect, the history of which can be distinctly traced for more than five hundred years.

CHAPTER XXVI.

THE PHILOSOPHY OF SLEEP.

Introductory Observations—Analogy between the Vegetable and Animal Kingdoms—Uninterrupted slumber of the Fœtus—Remarkable tendency to somnolence in Young Children—Reasons why they require more Sleep than Adults—General condition and aspects of the Sleeper—Philosophy of the Physical Phenomena—Boerhaave's brass pan and water Soporific—Universal Action and Reaction—Diurnal ebb and flow of Vital Forces and Fluids—Brief Digest of Physiological Facts and Observations—We sleep and wake under the action of an irresistible Law—Loss of the Vital Equilibrium in Cataleptic and other Trances—Sleep essential to Vital Harmony and the preservation of Life—Its Moral Influence and Spiritual Ministry.

> ———"Sleep hath its own world
> And a wide realm of wild reality,
> And dreams in their development have breath,
> And tears, and tortures, and the touch of joy."

THE remarkable physiological changes invariably developed in Sleep, and the mysterious psychical phenomena that frequently accompany the state, have engaged the attention of ancient and modern philosophers, and given birth to many curious conjectures and speculative theories.[1] Yet so little has been positively determined, in respect to the true philosophy of Sleep, and the immediate or remote causes of

---

[1] Those who desire to become acquainted with the facts and theories observed and entertained by the most distinguished authors who have written on the subject, may peruse the works of Aristotle, Lucretius, Democritus, Locke, Newton, Stewart, Abercrombie, Macnish, and Dr. George Moore.

its corporeal and metaphysical concomitants, that the author of the last physiological treatise commences his chapter on this particular subject, thus : " What is Sleep ? *We do not know.*" After this very modest confession, the author referred to occupies twenty-two pages with a view of imparting instruction to others. That the subject presents many difficult problems, is readily granted ; and the present writer has not the vanity to presume that he will be able to afford such a solution, in every instance, as will wholly satisfy the judgment of the reader. Nevertheless, the discovery and elucidation of certain fundamental principles—overlooked or disregarded by others—may furnish to some future inquirer a key wherewith he shall unlock the Arcana of our unconscious existence, and more fully explore the enchanted avenues that lead to our eternal life.

The state denominated SLEEP occurs with considerable regularity through all the gradations of human and animal existence. Moreover, a condition resembling this—in its essential nature, and phenomenal aspects—is scarcely less perceptible in the economy of vegetable life. The leaves of plants alternately droop or assume an erect position, and the flowers open and close their petals, as they are exposed to the alternations of light and shade, and the vicissitudes of moisture and temperature. In the vegetable as well as in the animal kingdom, the period of repose is not the same with all the species and genera. While the *Acacia* spreads its leaves horizontally to the rising sun, or vertically

" When the sun is high in his meridian tower,"

the night blooming *Cerea* (a species of cactus, indigenous

in the island of Jamaica) only opens the enormous corolla
in darkness, and pours out the wealth of precious aroma on
the midnight air.   Nor does the analogy between these two
great kingdoms in Nature, terminate here.   It is well known
that the process of assimilation, in all organized forms, is
accelerated during the period of Sleep ; and it is no less apparent that the condition of many plants in winter resembles
the hibernating existence of certain animals.

The exceptions to the general law may be few or many ;
still light and darkness doubtless sustain natural relations to
activity and repose.   The world awakes in the morning, not
so much from the force of habit as by the power of an irresistible law.   The god of day opens the palace halls of the
Orient that the earth may rejoice in the light of his smile.
In his presence the majestic mountains are arrayed in soft
robes of living beauty, while the valleys blossom and offer
grateful incense.   Weird strains of sweet and joyful music
echo through Nature's airy halls ; there is prayer in the aspiring tendency of all things ; the Divine presence is everywhere visible in outward forms ; and life itself is a manifold
benediction.   In the morning man goes to his labor with a
light heart and elastic step ; and millions of sentient beings
are made glad by the possession of conscious and delighted
existence.   Labor and rest are alike divine benefactions.
When they succeed each other at proper intervals, they are
equally pleasurable.   After protracted toil and incessant
activity we become weary, and a season of relaxation is required to restore the normal energies of the system.   Then
the discordant sounds of day give place to silence, and vigorous action is succeeded by profound repose.   While the

busy world quietly slumbers through the night watches, the
earth is clothed with fresher verdure and more vivid beauty ;
and with the coming light Man goes forth with all his
powers renewed.

In the opinion of many physiologists Sleep is uninterrupted during the periods of embryotic formation and fœtal
development. This is doubtless true so far as regards consciousness ; the use of the organs of special sensation, and
the exercise of all the voluntary powers of mind and body.
Thus we commence our individual existence in a state of
oblivious repose, and having completed the career on earth,

> " Our life is rounded with a sleep."

Moreover, with the new born child the extraordinary tendency to somnolence continues for some time after the outward conditions of being are entirely changed ; and very
young children—so long as they are neither disturbed by
pain nor the imperative demands for food—pass most of
their time in sleep. At this early period of human life, a
strong inward concentration of the electric forces is doubtless required to develop the vital powers and to stimulate the
functions of the entire nutritive system. The processes of digestion and assimilation are known to be extremely rapid in
infant children. Hence the growth of the body is greatest
during the earliest periods of our existence. But by degrees, as the human economy is unfolded, the chemical action
and organic movement become slower, and the molecular
deposits are proportionately less. The individual is more
wakeful, and the electrical motive power of the organs
exhibits a greater determination to the nerves and muscles

of voluntary motion. This is accompanied with increased vascular action, a higher temperature, and the development of muscular power. Wherever the agent of vital motion and sensation is especially employed, or most powerfully concentrated, there the most decided effects will be produced. Hence the greater activity of the digestive and nutritive powers of young children, and their amazing growth during the first year of their lives. Here, also, we may discover the reason why the subsequent stages of corporeal development become slower in proportion as our years are multiplied, and we are prompted by inclination or necessity to expend a greater portion of vital energy in the active pursuits of life.

I propose to discuss the philosophy of Sleep chiefly in its relations to human nature. The electric agent of all vital and voluntary motion, and of our sensorial impressions, is rapidly expended while we are actively employed. During our waking hours the forces of the nervous system go out in an increased degree to the extremities, and to the entire external surface of the body. The voluntary nerves and muscles are electrically charged, which quickens the vascular functions in all the organs that are directly influenced by the will ; at the same time the temperature at the surface is increased in a correspondent degree. But as the vital motive power—accumulated during the previous season of repose—is gradually dissipated, by the mental efforts and industrial pursuits of the day, the whole body is enfeebled ; a feeling of general lassitude seizes every faculty ; the functions are all performed with greater labor, and are attended by a constantly increasing sensation of fatigue and exhaustion.

At length the electro-nervous forces suddenly *react*, and the whole circulation at once exhibits a similar tendency toward the centers of nervous energy, and the organs of vital motion. Sensorial susceptibility is rapidly diminished; the impressions on the mind are gradually obscured, distorted and, at last, obliterated; there is less action in the sub-cutaneous nerves and in all the superficial ramifications of the arterial and venous systems; the muscles are completely relaxed; every limb is chained and motionless, and the giant is as powerless as the child.

It is worthy of observation that the reaction of the nervous forces—as it occurs in natural sleep—may be induced by various artificial means. Several expedients have been successfully resorted to with a view of producing this state. Indeed, whatever may serve to disengage the mental faculties, or to limit their exercise; in short, any device that will call home the thoughts, and fix the attention on a single idea or object, will materially aid in producing the psycho-physiological condition that results in Sleep. When the mind is withdrawn from the external world, and the forms and elements adapted to excite a variety of sensations—whether of pleasure or pain—are persistently disregarded, the senses, one by one, cease to act, and we approach the mystical realm of forgetfulness. When a single sensation or thought is all that yet remains, it is only necessary to obliterate the last impression from the mind, and total obliviousness must necessarily supervene. Hence those occupations that demand the combined exercise of several faculties, render the actors wakeful, while monotonous employments are quite likely to produce opposite effects on all who are thus en-

20

gaged. Monotonous sounds invariably exert a similar influence on the sensories and the mind. When Boerhaave had
a restless patient who could not sleep, he prescribed the regular dropping of water on a brass pan as a soporific. Looking steadily in one direction, and at the same object, will
produce the same general results. For this reason the psychological experimenters are accustomed to place a small
coin or other object in the hand of the subject, and on which
he is required to fix his attention. A speaker who chiefly
exercises a single faculty, will be sure to make his hearers
drowsy, while one who agreeably diversifies his discourse, by
successful appeals to a number of different faculties, will so
excite the electric forces of the brain as to render the hearer
wakeful and attentive. The orator whose voice is skillfully
managed, whose argument is clothed with poetic imagery,
and whose " eloquence is logic set on fire," will always command attention, and sway a scepter over the whole realm of
thought and feeling.

In every part of the universal economy of being there is
constant action and reaction. A common law — variously
modified by the simple elements and the organic structures
which it governs—runs through the entire creation. Light
and darkness succeed each other in regular alternation ;
the flowers open during the seasons of their waking life, and
close when they sleep ; the ocean tides rise and fall, and the
waters ascend and descend ; all Nature expands and contracts at the approach of the Seasons ; there is perpetual
influx and efflux through all things, animate and inanimate ;
and plants, and animals, and worlds respire. The same law
that directs the atmospheric currents regulates the pulses of

the sea, and governs alike the attractions and repulsions of atoms and orbs, of souls and systems. Action and reaction are thus beautifully illustrated in all the phenomena of life ; especially in respiration, and in the diastaltic and systolic motion of the heart and the arteries. Moreover, the vital tides have their *diurnal* ebb and flow. In the morning, and during the season of our waking existence, the nervous forces and the arterial circulation flow out to the surface, and with evening comes the period of recession, when the tide of life sets back, the outward channels are closed, and the Soul retires in silence to the Inward World.

This alternate ebb and flow of the nerve-aura, and, consequently, of the fluids of living bodies, is clearly illustrated by many of the phenomena of organic and animal life. Moreover, if we may presume that the sun and moon regulate the ocean tides, and otherwise modify the elements and determine the conditions of physical existence on earth, it would be preposterous to affirm that human beings are utterly free from the influence of all foreign agents, and beyond the dominion of super-terrestrial powers. It is not, however, my purpose to consider—at this time—an intricate question that is so remotely related to the subject of the present inquiry. But the philosophy of Sleep, and the writer's theory of the vital functions, may be placed in a clearer light and more forcibly illustrated, by the following summary statement of physiological facts and observations :

1. It is well known that the objects and elements of the external world make no impressions on the organs of sensation during the continuance of perfect sleep. As life, however, remains, and all the faculties of the mind still exist ;

and especially as the organic instruments of sensorial perception are in no degree impaired, we are left to ascribe the
temporary suspension of their appropriate functions to a
withdrawal of the subtile medium of sensation from the extremities of the nerves.

2. The relaxed state of the cutaneous vessels and the voluntary muscles; and, withal, the total absence of the contractile force of the muscular fibers—possessed and exercised in our waking hours—furnishes another proof of the
absence of the principle, that (under the direction of the
will) imparts to them a surprising activity and power.

3. The circulation is less rapid in sleep, and a similar
change occurs in the thoracic movement; at the same time,
the processes of digestion and molecular assimilation are
accelerated. These facts indicate an important change in
the determination of the motive forces of the system, and one
that accords with the writer's theory of electro-vital action
and reäction.

4. In Sleep the circulation through all the organs of volition is materially diminished, while the cerebrum contracts
and is inactive. This is not merely apparent, but the fact
has been demonstrated by Blumenbach, who—in the operation of trepanning a patient—so exposed the brain that he
could make careful observations. There was an obvious
contraction among the congeries and convolutions of that
organ when the patient was sleeping. It seemed to close
like the flowers at night; and like them it opened in the
morning, or whenever the cerebrum resumed its functions.

5. A similar contraction of the whole body occurs in
Sleep, and edematous swellings frequently disappear in the

night, or during the intervals of oblivious repose. These effects doubtless result from the internal tendency of the forces that govern the circulation of the animal fluids, and the consequent activity of the lymphatic or absorbent vessels[1]

6. The diminished action of the ganglionic nerves of common sensation, and the limited circulation through all the superficial channels of the arterial, venous, and capillary systems, is further confirmed by thermometrical observations, showing the influence of Sleep in reducing the temperature of the surface of the body.

7. Diseased persons, who have an unnatural heat and dryness of the skin, are often relieved from these symptoms during the season of rest and unconsciousness. These results are to be attributed in part to the reaction of the electro-vital forces from the surface ; and, in a greater or less degree, to the dissipation of animal electricity from the body, which occurs on the conductive principle. The increased perspiration while we sleep renders the cuticle a better conductor, and the subtile agent—an excess of which

---

[1] Macknish mentions a fact in the experience of Dr. Solander, who accompanied Captain Cook in one or more of his voyages, which will illustrate this point. The Doctor—in company with a friend and two colored servants—was engaged in collecting botanical specimens among the mountains, when he was overcome with cold and an irresistible inclination to sleep. No one member of the party was so well qualified to comprehend the danger of sleeping under such circumstances, as Dr. Solander himself ; but in spite of the earnest efforts of his friend (Mr. Banks) to keep him awake, he resigned his self-control and fell asleep. As soon as Mr. B. could kindle a fire he roused the Doctor ; but during that brief slumber the powerful determination of the electric forces and the fluids toward the nervous centers and vital organs so contracted his limbs that " his shoes fell from his feet."—(*Lewes' "Physiology of Common Life,* pp. 296–7.)

never fails to produce fevers or inflammations—is more readily disengaged or imparted to the surrounding objects and elements of the earth and atmosphere.

8. The vital action and reäction, or the periodical ebb and flow of nervous energy, is still further illustrated by the psycho-electric or magnetic powers of Man. Many practition ers in the department of Animal Magnetism have observed that this power gradually increases during the morning hours—exhibiting the utmost strength and intensity as the sun approaches the meridian—and that it as regularly declines toward the close of the day.

It should be observed that the proportion of time required to restore the vital energies to the normal standard, is varied by the age, health, habits, pursuits and other circumstances of the individual. Hence arbitrary rules and authorities that prescribe the same limits in all cases are manifestly incompatible with the laws of health. Young children require more sleep than adults, and unless this demand of Nature is duly respected, the development of the body will be slow and incomplete. Moreover, invalids and all persons whose vital constitutions are feeble, must have more time for repose than those vigorous persons in whom the recuperative powers are strong and the processes of physical renovation more rapid and uniform. Whenever the vital tide reaches the proper point, the reäction occurs naturally ; the nervous and arterial currents flow toward the surface in an increased measure, and the sleeper awakes in obedience to an essential law of his nature.

But the law here referred to, admits of several important exceptions. These consist of occasional examples of profound mental abstraction or introversion; a predisposition to congestion of the vital organs, and other forms of physical derangement, involving a temporary loss of the vital balance. Such persons are liable to be suddenly deprived of sensation, voluntary motion or consciousness; and they sometimes relapse into cataleptic trances in which the organic functions are entirely suspended for several days together. It should be remembered that a vigorous application of natural agents and artificial means may—in such cases—aid in the recovery of the vital equilibrium. Nevertheless, the organic forces react with remarkable precision, as often as the process of assimilation has repaired the diurnal waste of the system; and with occasional exceptions, (the more important ones are comprehended in our specification,) Nature should be allowed to determine the respective limits of our sleeping and waking existence.

The regular alternation of the periods of conscious and unconscious life constitutes a wise and beneficent arrangement in the Divine economy of human existence. We could not long exist without Sleep. The constant tension would soon destroy the integrity of the nervous system; the continuous action of outward elements and objects on the sensories, and the perpetual exercise of the voluntary faculties—without so much as the possibility of repose, would drive the world to madness; the very tissues would waste away like parchments exposed to the fire; and the brain itself soften and decompose under the ceaseless and intense action of electric forces. But slumber is our savior from these terrible evils; nor does its peaceful ministry terminate here. Viewed in another aspect, Sleep comes to the restless and sorrowing

world with a healing balm and a holy benediction.   The
poor forget their poverty; beggars become princes; and the
exiled, friendless and forgotten are honored with ovations.

Nor is the moral influence of Sleep less conducive to the
highest human interests.   The peace of multitudes is daily
interrupted by unpleasant discords, and the elements of our
own little world are frequently and harshly disturbed.
Many are annoyed, and not a few exasperated, by the experience of every day ; but slumber subdues their resentment,
and they awake at peace with the world.   It is worthy of
remark that capital offences are rarely committed early in
the morning, except when the perpetrators have been awake
through the night.   It is usually after the battle of the day,
when the blood is heated ; after the nerves have been subjected to the daily torture, and while the selfish passions
are excited, that men of discordant natures become reckless
and are driven to deeds of desperation.   To all such Sleep
is a minister of righteousness.   The frequent recurrence of
this state prevents our becoming wholly absorbed with the
ephemeral interests of earth and time.   It disengages the
mind, temporarily, at least, from the scenes of its groveling
and its imprisonment.   By an invisible hand we are led
away to the very confines of mortal being, that we may
stand for a brief season by the veiled portals of the invisible Temple.   Next to DEATH, the supreme pacificator, Sleep
is the chief conqueror of the passions, and the great harmonizer of moral elements.

> " Sleep that knits up the ravelled sleeve of care,
>   The death of each day's life, sore labor's bath ;
>   Balm of hurt minds, great Nature's second course,
>   Chief nourisher in life's feast."

CHAPTER XXVII.

PSYCHOLOGICAL MYSTERIES OF SLEEP.

General Observations on the Nature of Sleep—Relations of Dreams to Physical Objects and Physiological Laws—Dr. Gregory's Dream—Relations of certain Dreams to the Passions—Phreno-Magnetism—Dreams inspired by Whispering in the Ear—Amusing Experiments on a Military Officer—Influence of Established Principles and Ideas in Dreams—Cuvier's Humerous Illustration—Psychometric Dreaming—Remarkable Examples—Dreams Discovering lost Property—Witnessing distant Occurrences in Sleep—A thrilling Instance—Philosophy of Allegorical Dreams—The Author's Examples—Socrates and the Youth with the Flaming Torch—Reference to Professor Draper's Views—Relations of the Soul to Mental and Moral Forces—Nature and Dream-Land.

MAN is susceptible of no condition that is more remarkable for its beautiful mysteries than Sleep. The functions of the eye and the ear are suspended, and all the outward avenues of the senses are closed and sealed. The connection and intercourse with the external world being interrupted, our earthly plans are disregarded and forgotten ; at the same time the scenes and objects presented in dreams and " visions of the night," are discerned through inward vistas and more ethereal media. Having devoted the preceding Chapter to the electro-chemical and physiological forces, functions and aspects of living beings, as the same are illustrated in Sleep, we are now to consider the psychological mysteries of the slumbering world.

It is well known that Sleep ordinarily occurs in conse-

quence of physical exhaustion ; but it may be induced by
several other causes. Extreme cold—by driving the electrical forces and animal fluids from the surface of the body toward the centers of vital energy—invariably occasions
drowsiness, and often an irresistible inclination to sleep.
All persons who experience death from this cause, gradually
lose sensation and consciousness in a profound slumber, from
which they awake no more on earth.   Sleep may also be induced by magnetic manipulations, the administration of certain drugs, and by a variety of other means.

It is worthy of remark that most persons of careless observation and superficial thought readily conclude that the
magnetic sleep must be fundamentally different from a natural slumber, apparently, for the same reason that they conceive of the ordinary phenomena of life as subject to natural
law, whilst such occurrences as are extraordinary—in the
sense of being infrequent—are presumed to be miraculous.
But this is unreasonable and false.   In fact, and in the comprehensive judgment of the philosopher, all objects and
events are subject to law.   Moreover, the specific conditions
of body and mind are never so various as the particular circumstances that operate in their production.   For illustration—the proximate causes of fever are numerous, and require no specification ; consumption is one form of disease,
whether produced by a cold or a scrofulous diathesis ; and
insanity is only modified by the peculiar constitution and
incidental experiences of the individual.   It is equally true
that Sleep is intrinsically *the same state*, whether occurring
from natural causes or as the result of artificial expedients.

If there are satisfactory illustrations of our philosophy in the physiological phenomena of Sleep, we may find others not less convincing in the coïncident operations of the mind. At times the mind travels amongst a multitude of obscure and grotesque images ; its impressions being all indefinite, and its vagaries numerous, wild and improbable. While the mind thus wanders along the dim confines of our conscious existence—surrounded by a phantom creation—the Imagination may be intensely active whilst Reason reposes or becomes unreliable. This is obviously true in respect to the psychical phenomena developed in ordinary sleep ; and the mental processes of the magnetic sleeper are neither more nor less than a kind of *dreaming.* But while dreams are often confused, disjointed and meaningless, they are sometimes orderly, connected, and deeply significant.[1] If in the magnetic slumber the mind occasionally exhibits amazing powers, and important disclosures are made, it is no less apparent that dreams are in some instances prophetic, or are otherwise rendered the vehicles of important information. It may also be observed that the vision of the Somnambulist and the Clairvoyance developed in a state of magnetic coma, are essentially the same, and may be equally clear and reliable.

Moreover, the mind may be constantly active in sleep, though our inward experiences leave no traces in the walking memory. A large proportion of our dreams doubtless consist of the irregular exercises of certain faculties, in a

---

[1] The suggestions made to the mind in sleep were carefully studied by the Ancients. It is stated on the authority of Cicero that a dream of Cecilia, daughter of Barbaricus, elicited a decree of the Senate, and according to Plutarch, a grandson of Aristides made the interpretation of dreams a profession, from which he realized his wealth.

state of incomplete slumber ; at the same time the organic functions of other faculties are temporarily suspended, and the avenues of sensation imperfectly closed. Such dreams may originate in the existing states of the system ; also from the position of the body, or from its relations to the elements, objects and forces of the visible and invisible worlds. Any condition, object or circumstance, that either obstructs respiration, or serves to attract the circulation to a particular part of the body, may—by its influence in the distribution of the animal fluids—develop certain psychological phenomena. Sleeping with a tight cravat might cause a person to dream of hanging himself, or of being strangled in some other way ; and the additional weight of two or three extra quilts might very naturally cause the sleeper to dream of bearing some heavy burden.

Some time since the writer, having retired at a late hour, without opening a window of the apartment occupied, dreamed—in the course of the night—of being partially suffocated in the confined atmosphere of a tomb. In this case it is obvious that the want of proper ventilation and a free respiration, produced the dream ; and—by a law of association—supplied the scene, and the particular images that accompanied the mental proceedure.[1]

When two or more persons are in electro-psychological *rapport*—established by direct physical contact—the circu-

---

[1] The late Dr. Gregory, of Scotland, having one night retired with a bottle of hot water at his feet, dreamed that he was ascending Mount Etna, and that the intense heat of the ground rendered his journey unpleasant and painful. Dreams of the Inquisition have originated in a paroxism of gout and Macnish mentions the case of a person who was inspired by a blister on his head, and dreamed that he was *scalped* by a party of Indians.

lation in both will tend toward the points of conjunction. agreeably to a natural and irresistible law. This will be made apparent by simply holding the hand of another person. If the hand be cold when the connection is established, it soon becomes warm. The positive and negative conditions and relations of bodies thus conjoined, cause an immediate determination of the electrical currents toward the more negative portions of the vital circuit, and such a mutual attraction of the elements of the circulation that the blood vessels become distended, and the color of the skin clearly indicates increased vascular action. Moreover, whatever changes the determination of the nervous currents, or otherwise influences sensation, is liable to produce various psychological effects.

The several processes of secretion, and the predominance of certain faculties, affections and passions, operate as immediate causes in the production of many dreams and visions. Uncover the sleeper in a frosty night and he may dream of being cold, and his sensations will be quite likely to suggest to the mind the desolate scenes of winter. Hydrocephalus may cause one to dream of water, or of drowning ; while inflammation of the brain would as naturally—through a sensation of intense heat—produce the congruous images of fire and its effects. The excessive accumulation of water in the bladder will cause young children to dream, and the reaction of the mind on the organs of the body often produces involuntary relief. During the period of lactation mothers are liable to dream of nursing their children ; and dreams of offspring frequently accompany the later stages of utero-gestation. These, by their vivid semblance of real-

ity, inspire the mind of the fair sleeper with all that tender
solicitude and intense pleasure which naturally belong to
maternity. The mind of the hero—even when he sleeps—
may be peopled with the images of war—of long marches, of
bloody battle-fields and brilliant victories ; whilst the man
of great reverence dreams of consecrated places and solemn
assemblies ; of devotional feelings and religious ceremonies.

The most active faculties and the strongest impulses generally influence and frequently determine the operations of
the mind in sleep. A person in whom the sexual passion
and the imagination are equally active and strong, will be
very likely to dream of Love and its ideal forms and actual
concomitants. In such a case, slight pressure on the procre-
ative organs, by attracting the vital, electric forces, may
produce aphrodisiacal effects, while the physical orgasm inevitably projects analogous images before the mind. The
sleeper finds forbidden pleasures in some enchanted bower ;
or, in his amatory expeditions.

> " He capers nimbly in some lady's chamber,
>   To the lascivious pleasing of a lute."

The virtuous lover as naturally dreams of the altar and the
ceremonial—of the domestic fireside and the bridal couch—
of Love's silent ecstacy and the bliss of sweet repose, where
peaceful

> " Sleep is on velvet eyelids lightly pressed,
>   And dreamy sights upheave the spotless breast."

The relation of the physical to the mental processes, in
the illustrations already cited, must be clearly perceived by
any person of ordinary capacity, and it may be further illustrated by a variety of experiments. The sense of hearing

generally continues in operation some time after the appropriate functions of the other organs of sensation are suspended. The sleeper may hear imperfectly, and even answer if directly addressed, when he no longer possesses his normal consciousness. Whispering in the ear at this stage of mental introversion will often excite the faculties ; and while the sensorial impressions may be wholly forgotten, the operations of the mind may be distinctly remembered. Pressing a finger on or over any particular organ or portion of the brain, will attract the nervous circulation to that part ; and this convergence of the electrical forces will necessarily increase the cerebral action, and the functions of the organs may be involuntarily performed. Such experiments belong to what has been denominated *Phreno-magnetism ;* and though they have—with rare exceptions—been confined to subjects in the magnetic sleep, they may be equally successful at the proper stage of a natural slumber.

An interesting and authentic illustration of this sensorial susceptibility, and its relations to the psychological phenomena of sleep, is furnished by Dr. Gregory. An officer engaged in the expedition to Louisburgh, in 1685, exhibited while asleep, a remarkable degree of mental impressibility through the auditory nerve. He was the unconscious subject of many experiments which greatly amused his companions. They could readily inspire a dream by whispering in his ear. On one occasion they involved him in a quarrel, going through with all the details, including the preliminaries for a hostile meeting. When, at length, his imaginary antagonist was supposed to be present, and ready for the mortal contest, a loaded pistol was placed in the hands of the sleeper, which he promptly discharged, and was awakened by the report.

On another occasion, while he was sleeping on a locker in the cabin, some one of his companions caused him to dream of falling overboard. He was told that a shark was after him, and urged to swim for his life. He instantly obeyed the suggestion, striking out with such vehemence as to throw himself from the locker on to the floor of the cabin.

After the landing of the army at Louisburgh, his friends finding him asleep one day in his tent, amused themselves again at his expense. At first they annoyed the officer by fiercely cannonading his position. When his apprehensions were awakened, he manifested a desire to run. They remonstrated against a precipitate retreat, but still played upon his fears, by representing the shouts of the enemy and the groans of his dying friends. At length he was told that the man at his side had fallen, whereupon he instantly jumped up and rushed out, stumbling over the tent-ropes in his violent effort to escape.

Notwithstanding our dreams are often wholly incompatible with the ideas we are accustomed to entertain when awake, still in many instances they appear to be determined or strongly influenced by our established opinions and habits of thought. Especially those who have firm convictions —in whom the force of education and the normal action of the mind are intense and strong—are liable to be so influenced. We sometimes dream of contending earnestly for our most cherished principles and ideas. If the man of unyielding virtue is exposed to great temptations in his dreams, the expression of his feelings may be governed by a nice sense of propriety, and his ideal acts be in consonance with the sober dictates of reason and conscience. On the contrary, the man of weak resolution and lose habits is not likely to even dream of resisting temptation.[1]

Forms and substances on which others have left the subtile emanations from their bodies, are not unfrequently instrumental in determining the operations of the mind in sleep. In another part of this treatise the reader's attention has been called to several convincing illustrations of the fact, that an impalpable effluence proceeds from the mind and body, and that it pervades all objects that we have handled and every expression of our thoughts. This may be denominated *psychometric dreaming.* The illustrations of this class are very curious and suggestive. Through these emanations persons sleeping in the same bed, especially if they touch each other, are liable to have a commerce of ideas, or similar dreams, and occasionally the operations of two minds, thus related, have been identical both in fact and time. Of this general class of dreams two illustrative examples may be sufficient.

The following singular case of psychometric dreaming is stated on the authority of a respectable physician who resides in Brooklyn, New York. In the winter of 18— a fatal accident occurred on the Schuylkill river, near Philadelphia.

---

[1] The influence of scientific pursuits and established ideas on the mind in sleep, is illustrated by a humorous anecdote that is related of Cuvier. The great naturalist dreamed one night that the devil came to him in form as he is represented in the popular superstition, and threatened to eat him up. Cuvier calmly surveyed the strange cloven-footed beast from head to foot, and then exclaimed, " *You,* eat me ! Horns ! Hoofs !—*Graminivorous !* I am not afraid of you."

To vary the amusements of the multitude that daily went to
the River for exercise and recreation, a post had been set
up through the ice. Attached by a pivot and a socket to
the upper end of the perpendicular post was a horizontal
revolving shaft, to the opposite end of which a large sled
was fastened by a rope. The shaft could be made to rotate
so that the persons on the sled were moved round in a circle,
and with great rapidity. One day, while a negro occupied
the sled, it was made to revolve with such velocity that he
was hurled headlong from his seat by the centrifugal force
against fragments of ice—abruptly piled up by the currents
—and instantly killed !

Among the persons who witnessed the accident was a
physician who, the same evening, had occasion to prepare
some pills for a lady of very delicate organization, and
withal exquisitely susceptible of the magnetic influence.
Several persons were in his office while he was employed in
compounding the medicine, to whom he related all the circumstances of the accident on the river ; at the same time
he was shaping the pills in his fingers. The Doctor sent the
pills to his patient, who took them on retiring for the night.
The lady had no knowledge of the accident, but on falling
asleep, had an unusually vivid dream, which she related on
the following morning. She was on the ice, and in the
midst of a great company of persons, who were amusing
themselves on skates, and otherwise. In the crowd she observed a negro seating himself on the revolving sled ; and
she declared that he was instantly killed by being thrown
with great violence against a cake of ice.

The philosophical mind will not be the first to dispute

this curious fact. It is well known that the processes of vegetable and animal chemistry develop new properties in matter and prepare the simple elements for superior functions and uses. The more frequently they are made to assume organic forms and relations the more sublimated they become, and the higher is the degree of their manifest vitality. It is also to be observed that the triturations and chemical combinations of the laboratory greatly modify the substances employed in our *Materia Medica*. Moreover, it is manifest to the critical observer, that the operation of any remedial agent is liable to be influenced by the manipulations of the person who prepares and administers the same, and that, too, in a degree that far transcends the conception of the ordinary practitioner. A glass of water from the hand of a skillful magnetiser may operate on a sensitive person, either as an emetic, cathartic, tonic or soporific. In a similar manner we are liable to modify—whether consciously or otherwise—the active properties of matter and the conditions of all the forms of sentient existence with which we may chance to sustain intimate relations. If the mercury marks every change in the temperature, and the needle of a delicate electrometer is moved by the slightest galvanic current, why may not the mind feel the action of mental forces, when a suitable connecting medium is placed in direct contact with the most delicate nerves of sensation?

On one occasion, having at a late hour received a written message from a near relative, for whom I cherished a very strong and tender attachment. I retired with the open letter in my hand. I soon fell asleep and had a dream, in which that person was most strikingly portrayed and extremely

active. On waking I felt assured that there was some subtile connecting agent between the letter and the dream. I
was still in physical contact with the paper, and my knowledge of the dynamics of mysterious agents appeared to justify the conclusion, that the impalpable emanations from the
mind of my correspondent—imparted to me through the
medium of his letter—had suggested or inspired the concurrent operations of my own mind. Desiring to render the
experiment as conclusive as the nature of the case would
admit, I placed the open sheet on the pillow, and resting
my head on the same, once more fell asleep and again
dreamed of the author of the communication, who appeared
with such preternatural vividness as to awaken a deep sense
of the reality of his presence.

The mind wanders in sleep, and by a mysterious power
of cognition often perceives distant objects and occurrences, or discovers its lost treasures and absent friends. An
object that we have once possessed—if mislaid, lost or
stolen—is far more likely to be found, by the clairvoyant or
the ordinary dreamer, than one that has never been in our
hands. We establish a kind of magnetic *rapport* with everything we touch, and that serves to connect the mind with
the object. By a kind of instinct the dreamer sometimes
traces the obscure connections between himself and his lost
possessions, or, in obedience to a species of spiritual gravitation, he may find the remote but well-remembered objects
of his love.

A case of truthful dreaming, involving the recovery of a
treasure, was originally published in the Los Angelos *Star*,
in the Spring of 1854. Colonel Reese and his train had,

among other misfortunes, lost a considerable sum of money, but precisely how or where could not be determined by any member of his party. On arriving at San Bernardino, Col. R. had a dream, in which the locality of the money was so vividly impressed on his mind, that he resolved to go back and find it. Some days after, Reese and his company returned to San Bernardino, having visited the spot indicated in the Colonel's dream, where they found the entire sum of money in a buckskin bag.

Some years since the *Highland Eagle* of Westchester County, New York, published the fact that Mr. Dykeman, Deputy Sheriff of Putnam County, had made a singular discovery in a dream. It was stated that George F. Sherman, of Cold Spring, had lost his pocket-book, containing three hundred and seventy-two dollars. On the night following the Deputy Sheriff dreamed that a clerk by the name of McNary had the money. Unable to resist the suspicion excited in his mind, Mr. Dykeman arrested McNary, who thereupon made a confession, and restored over three hundred dollars of the money, which he had concealed in places indicated in the dream.

General Stephen Rowe Bradley, formerly of Westminster, Vermont, a distinguished lawyer, and Senator in Congress from that State, being absent from home at a distance of one hundred miles, dreamed that his son was drowned. The General was a man of firm nerves and rational judgment, and not at all likely to be influenced by superstitious notions; but so intense and profound was the impression made on his mind, that he immediately started for home. On his arrival he found the funeral procession just leaving

the house, bearing to the grave what was mortal of his son.
In this part of my classification I will only offer one additional example. The following account of a remarkable case
of reliable dreaming, comprehending all the particulars of a
tragic scene that was enacted in California, on the 6th of
December, 1854, originally appeared in the editorial columns
of the Cincinnati *Times*. The subject of this singular experience was a young married lady, in that city—wife of a
merchant doing business on Main street—and it should be
observed that her dream and the actual occurrence were
simultaneous :

She dreamed of seeing her brother, who in 1852 left home to brave the
hardships of a life in California, that he might secure a competence for himself and his sister, She saw him rise from a bed, in a small hut-like tenement, and running his hand under the pillow, draw from thence a revolver
and a huge bowie-knife, both of which he placed in a belt that encircled his
body. The time was not far from midnight, for the embers were yet smok-
ing on the rude hearth ; and as they cast their lurid glare over his countenance, she thought that perhaps it was all a dream ; but then she concluded
that no dream could be so real, and became convinced that all was actual.
While she gazed on his countenance, the expression suddenly changed—
It betrayed an intense watchfulness ; all motion seemed suspended, and
every heart throb muffled, while the eye was fixed on a particular spot near
the head of the bed, where—through a small aperture not noticed before—a
human hand was visible, grasping a short, keen instrument, looking terribly
like a dagger. It apparently sought the head of the bed, for as it touched
the pillow it passed slowly down to about the supposed region of the heart,
and poised for a second, as if to make sure its aim. That second was sufficient for the brother to rise noiselessly from his seat, draw his bowie-knife
from his belt, and advance a single step toward the bed. Just as the dagger
descended into the blankets, the knife of the brother came down like a
meat-axe, close to the aperture, completely severing the hand of the would-
be assassin above the wrist, and causing the dagger and limb to fall on the
bed, trophies of his victory. A deep, prolonged yell sounded from without,
and on rushing to the aperture and convincing himself that there was but
one, the brother unbolted the door and stepped out The moon was shining,
and by its light was discovered a man writhing as if in the last agonies.
The miner drew the body to the door, and turning his face to the fire,

beheld the visage of a Mexican who, for some fanc'ed injury, had sworn to
never rest content until he had taken his (the brother's) life. On examining
the man closely, he was discovered to have a wound near the heart, which
a long, sharp, two edged blade in his left hand abundantly accounted for.
Failing in the attempt to assassinate his intended victim. he had, with his
only remaining hand, driven another knife to his own heart. The lady
awoke, and, vividly impressed with the dream, related its substance to her
husband, as it is here recorded. Judge, then, of their surprise when, not
long after, they received a letter from their brother in California (by the
North Star), relating an adventure that occurred on the night of the. sixth
of D cember. corresponding in all its particulars with the scene witnessed
by the lady in her dream.

The foregoing illustrations clearly indicate that the soul
is not necessarily confined by its corporeal restraints to any
specific locality ; but that it is free to traverse the world,
and that distance can oppose no obstacle to its free communion with all kindred natures.   The facts of this class are
very numerous, but it is unnecessary to multiply examples.
In the hours of sleep we often visit distant places, and the
scenes that pass before the inward vision have at once the
semblance and the substance of reality.   Indeed, in some
essential sense, the soul *leaves* the body, and makes excur-
sions into remote regions; and in many cases our dreams,
no less than the mental impressions of our waking life, are
found to be faithful representations of actual circumstances
and events.

Many dreams are doubtless to be attributed to the continued activity of a particular class of faculties, after the
action of others has been temporarily suspended by sleep.
All allegorical dreams and visions may be—perhaps generally—embraced in this category.   If we suppose Ideality
and Comparison to be unusually large, and the moral and
perceptive faculties of the sleeper to be extremely active,

it may not be difficult to account for many allegorical **representations** in dreams. It is well known that the **dominant** faculties are the last to yield to the magnetism of **sleep**. In such an organization as I have supposed, the **imagination**, or creative power of the mind, being still awake, **continues** to form its images in the cerebral camera, and those **images**, by the coöperation of the moral sentiments, are **made to** assume relations to certain ideas, principles, objects **and** events. By a law of nature and our moral constitution, **we** associate particular qualities and characteristics with **certain •forms**, and those forms often become the **universally** recognized symbols of moral and other qualities. By common consent deception is represented by the serpent, **fidelity** by the dog, innocence by the lamb, and peace by the **dove**. We also recognize similar relations of particular ideas **and** individual attributes to inanimate objects and their **uses**. The strong mind that demolishes the theories and **systems** of ages may be likened to a battering ram ; a clumsy **critic**, or a stupid, careless fellow, is called a blunderbus; **whilst** a rapier is the polished and pointed symbol of caustic **wit** and pungent satire. The mind of the sleeper may **continue** to recognize these relations of special qualities and abstract ideas to specific forms and individual characters, and **hence** the development of this class of dreams.

Three illustrative examples will suffice in this connection. A friend, who is a critical and able writer, having **been** vehemently opposed and falsely accused by certain **parties—** who were too ignorant and groveling to either **comprehend** his principles or to appreciate his character—retired **one** evening after reviewing the conduct of his enemies, **and** dreamed that while traveling in a barren and sandy region he suddenly encountered a serpent. The reptile was large, black, and seemingly venomous. The dreamer finding himself armed with a long whip, proceeded to lash the snake about the head, which caused the most violent and painful contortions, while the monster vainly attempted to escape. Occasionally the serpent would bury his head in the sand to protect it from the lash; but the dust blinded him, while his whole form writhed beneath the blows of the assailant.

On another occasion the same gentleman, having completed a just but severe and scathing review of a certain secular journal, folded the paper and laid it on the table. The same evening a lady of remarkable psychological susceptibility—in whose mind ideas were commonly represented by appropriate symbols—called on the reviewer, in company with several other persons. This lady had no knowledge of the particular business that had occupied my friend during the day. In the course of the evening, while reposing in an easy chair, she became somniloquent and declared that she saw a glittering two-edged sword, drawn by a strong hand from its scabbard and placed on the identical table at which the reviewer had performed his task, and whereon he had left his manuscript.

The remaining example is selected from the writer's personal experience. Some time before the commencement of the Italian Revolution under Garibaldi, I was on one occasion seated in my room, and in meditation on the affairs of Europe, when I fell asleep. A brief interval of oblivious repose was succeeded by a state of inward waking and a significant dream or vision. The time was early morning.

I was standing on high ground, commanding an extended view of the surrounding country. On every side objects of classic beauty and impressive emblems of decay were visible in the gray twilight, while over all reigned the silence of death. Moreover, there was a strange glory diffused over the heavens, irradiating the mountain-tops, while darkness yet vailed the plains and valleys and every object beneath.

Suddenly a strong man appeared standing on an eminence before me. His countenance was highly illuminated as if the first rays of a rising sun had fallen like a golden baptism on his head. Majestic in form, and with a bearing more than kingly, he at once inspired me with profound respect and admiration. At first his right hand was on his left breast, and concealed beneath the folds of his mantle. But at length he drew from his bosom a great Lens which was made to revolve at the slightest suggestion of his will, and to assume every conceivable position with respect to the light and the objects to be illuminated. I was informed that the strong man was Garibaldi, and that the great moving Lens in his right hand was REVOLUTION! As the Lens revolved the concentrated rays shot arrow-like through the shades below, discovering in their course the forms of noble men chained and prostrate. But as rapidly as the light was diffused among them, their chains fell asunder like untwisted flax when it is touched by a burning brand. The number of the disenthralled increased every moment until a vast multitude stood erect and rejoicing in their recovered freedom.

Again the Lens revolved, and the burning shaft fell in thick darkness, revealing a form clothed in faded and filthy robes, and surrounded by the shattered symbols of regal authority. The form was wasted ; the tissues seemed to be shriveled, and the fluids dissipated, as if by the action of internal fires. The lips were compressed but tremulous, while the expression of the eye was restless and malignant. The visage revealed no trace of human sympathy. A dingy crown encircled the brow and, the right hand grasped a broken scepter. I was made to know that this figure was the embodied representation of the existing political and spiritual despotisms. At length the scorching rays were brought to a focus on the scepter, which ignited and consumed away, the ashes falling over the palsied hand.

From his elevated situation the Genius of Revolution calmly witnessed the spectacle. Once more the Lens moved in his hand, and as the consuming rays played over the blackened and blasted brow, the crown was fused and ran down the furrowed face like a scalding and bloody sweat. The form was now fearfully convulsed ; the throne crumbled at its base, and a frightful spasm seized the solid ground on which I was standing. The shock was powerful and diverted my attention for an instant. Recovering from my surprise, I looked again, but the smitten form and broken symbols of despotic authority were visible no more. The earth had closed over them !¹

---

¹ Of this class was the significant dream of the great Athenian philosopher. On the night before he took the deleterious hemlock he slept calmly. and in the morning, being attended by his chief disciples, he described his vision in this simple and touching language. Socrates proceeded :

I saw a beautiful youth come in to me. On his countenance were that still composure, and calm sobriety, which belong to the form divine. In his right hand he bore a burning torch, and a reddish glow, like that of evening, was diffused over the darkness of my prison.

The godlike youth gradually let down the torch ; but I seized his arm, as it seemed to me, and exclaimed : What are you going to do ? He re-

A complete classification would include other important psychological phenomena developed in sleep. Dreams that have led to discoveries in the Mechanic Arts, and such as have resulted in contributions to popular literature, will furnish the subject of the succeeding Chapter ; while the writer's suggestions respecting *prophetic dreaming* will be presented in the elucidation of the Law of Prophecy. I am admonished that there are yet other dreams—of deep and peculiar import—that admit of no rational explanation on any principles, either comprehended by the common mind or recognized in the systems of material philosophy.

> "———— Powers there are
> That touch each other to the quick, in modes
> Which the gross world no sense hath to perceive,
> No soul to dream of ————."

The most subtile forces in Nature and the great powers of the moral world are seldom appreciated. While they are irresistible, they operate so silently that they elude the ordinary observer. Indeed, they are frequently quite overlooked by authors of acknowledged erudition. Dr. John William Draper, in his late work, while referring to the sources of cerebral action and mental impressions in sleep, does not appear to recognize the presence of any forces, or

plied : "I am extinguishing the torch !" Oh! I entreat, do it not! It is to me a friendly light in the darkness of my prison.

He smiled and said : It is the torch of the earthly life. Thou hast no further need of it. For as soon as it is extinguished thine earthly eyes close forever, and thou soarest aloft to a higher world, where a pure and heavenly light beams around thee. Of what use to thee any longer is the self-consuming earthly torch ?

The flame was quenched ; and the philosopher, with a serene spirit awoke to find himself overshadowed by the gloom of his prison. Just then the door was opened, and Socrates welcomed the youth who bore the cup which was to extinguish the torch of Life.

the active influence of any agents, except such as belong to the material creation. In the intellectual operations of the sleeper he finds little more than the fantastic creations of the unrestrained or distempered imagination, and the incongruous association of sensorial images, originally derived from the objects of the external world. I extract the following from the author's "History of the Intellectual Development of Europe :"

In the brain of man, impressions of whatever he has seen or heard, of whatever has been made manifest to him by his other senses, nay, even the vestiges of his former thoughts, are stored up. These traces are most vivid at first, but by degrees they decline in force, though they never probably completely die out. During our waking hours, while we are perpetually receiving new impressions from things that surround us, such vestiges are overpowered, and can not attract the attention of the mind. But in the period of sleep, when external influences cease, they present themselves to our regard, and the mind, submitting to the delusion, groups them into the fantastic forms of dreams. By the use of opium and other drugs which can blunt our sensibility to passing events, these phantoms may be made to emerge. They also offer themselves in the delirium of fevers and in the hour of death.

It is immaterial in what manner or by what agency our susceptibility to the impressions of surrounding objects is benumbed, whether by drugs or sleep, or disease, as soon as their force is no greater than that of forms already registered in the brain, these last will emerge before us, and dreams and apparitions are the result. So liable is the mind to practice deception on itself, that with the utmost difficulty it is aware of the delusion. (Pp. 317–18.)

The learned author looks among the phenomena of sleep for some shadowy suggestions of the life to come ; but only finds in dreams and "visions of the night,"

" —— Combinations of disjointed things,
And forms impalpable ——."

Whilst admitting the realities of another world, his distant fellowship for the celestial authorities does not permit of diplomatic relations or the commerce of ideas. The invisible, inspiring agents of the human race, very generally recognized in the past, by Pagans, Jews, Mohammedans and Christians, may have been mere phantoms and hallucinations. If the dæmon of Socrates was not his own "conscience, we must infer that he labored under a mental malady."[1] In the interest of popular materialism it is thus presumed, that the noblest man and the most celebrated philosopher of antiquity, was so diseased in mind that he could not distinguish the promptings of his own moral nature from the foreign influence and distinct personality of another. In consonance with such views it is but natural that Professor Draper should regard many profound religious experiences as idle vagaries or strong delusions.

Medical authors, and all whose investigations are limited to their inquiry into the laws and operations of physical nature, are liable to become faithless. They are prone to lose sight of the obvious fact, that the human mind exists, at all times, in the midst of a vast realm, every part of which is pervaded by mental and moral forces, and peopled by the invisible ministers of the Omnipresent One. These being inseparable from the sphere of the soul's existence, now and hereafter, it follows that they all influence the mind as naturally and inevitably as the body is acted on by mat rial forms and physical forces. Immersed in this mental deep, as in one fathomless and shoreless sea, the mind is never beyond the influence of silent forces and inspiring agents adapted to excite the faculties. Those secret forces touch

---

[1] See History of the Intellectual Development of Europe. (p. 110.)

the hidden springs of our common nature, and gentle beings
move around us,

> "With feet that make no sound upon the floors."

Sleep half unbars the portals of that realm of mystery.
At death the soul enters and leaves the door ajar, when
those who are near catch glimpses of the life that is to be.
The mind brings back some precious tokens of divine ideas
and visitations, and we feel that we are haunted as by some
living presence. Nature inspires the soul through the sense.
The low notes of the forest bird; the faint echoes of distant
water-falls; the voices of children in the vespers; the soft
murmurs of the shells along the strand, and the tremulous
accents of first love—these, indeed, are all sweetly solemn
and strangely pleasing. But Genius and Nature offer no
suggestions that are more significant and beautiful than such
as come to the innocent in Sleep.

> "Such is the country. over whose exi-tence
>   The brooding shades of mortal doubt are cast ;
> Such is the realm that, dim with night and distance,
>   Lies unexplored and vast.
>
> "But when the Morning comes the spell is broken,
>   And like a dream the wondrous record seems ;
> And memory holds the solitary token
>   Of the dim LAND OF DREAMS."

CHAPTER XXVIII.

INSPIRATIONS OF THE NIGHT.

The Mental Faculties in Sleep—Illustrations of their concentrated and orderly action—Curious Discoveries in Dream-Land—Cases of Mary Lyall and Cornelius Broomer—Experiences of De Quincey and Macnish—A rapid Voyage to India—An hour among the Pyramids of the Nile—Mechanical Inventions—Experiences of Dr. Franklin and Professor Gregory—Sermonizing in Sleep—A Legal Opinion by a Dreamer—Production of a Parody on Piron—Schonemann's Improvisations—Fragments from the Temple of the Muses—Tartini and the Devil's Sonata—Philosophical Suggestions and Conclusion.

> "—— Day rules the sensuous mind,
> But Night the fettered spirit doth unbind.
> And through the silver palace-gates of Light,
> In dream and trance, she leads the soul away
> To the wide landscapes of the inner Day."—HARRIS.

MENTAL faculties, not less than physical forces, may be strengthened by concentration. To produce the most decisive results they must be withdrawn from the wide realm of outward observation and thought, and directed in a single channel and to a particular subject. When the mind is occupied with many things at the same time, its forces are of necessity widely diffused; and this dissipation of the mental energies renders their action feeble; at the same time great ideas and living thoughts are conceived, individualized, and illuminated in the foci of the mind. Whatever, therefore, serves to concentrate the faculties and give them a specific direction, also intensifies their action, and thus renders the forms of their outward expression—whether in the parts of speech or the works of art—more forcible and complete.

This mental concentration is very liable to occur in sleep, when only a part of the faculties find repose, and our slumbers are

" But a continuance of enduring thought."

The more active powers of the mind are especially liable to be thus wakeful, while the others may be entirely inactive. Moreover, their operations are frequently direct, forcible and orderly in an eminent degree. This convergence of mental forces has developed some surprising results, and the subject might be illustrated by striking examples derived from the experience of many persons. Men of genius are occasionally inspired in dreams, and original conceptions take form before the inward vision, or they may be embodied in appropriate language and imagery. Several literary compositions; also works belonging to the departments of Mechanical Invention and the Elegant Arts, have surely originated in this way, without any previous thought or conscious effort on the part of the sleeper.

When the external avenues of sensation are closed, and the mind is measurably released from corporeal restraints, it readily associates with the homogeneous elements in all things. If, in the waking condition, it holds direct relations to external objects and physical phenomena, it may, in sleep, be no less intimately associated with their interior principles and essential laws. Thus our dual nature and corresponding two-fold life alternately bring us, in some manner, into correspondence with the visible and invisible realms of

22

being. The periodical introversion of the faculties, which occurs at night—in the seasons of slumber—and the shadowy suggestions of our microcosmical existence, all point to a sphere of inward realities ; and they lead the rational soul to the contemplation of a far more glorious World than the great Macrocosm that stands revealed to our organic perceptions in the clear light of day.

A dream consists of an indefinite succession of thoughts, occurring in immediate connection, and during the hours of sleep ; though we very naturally limit the application of the term to such acts or operations of the mind as occupy a place and preserve their relations in the waking memory. A vision is a dream in which the sense of *sight* is excited by the mind's action, or otherwise by subjective causes ; so that, by its coöperation, it embodies and represents the images of whatever is comprehended in the mental conception and process. In sleep the soul may wander abroad, free from the physical restraints it is accustomed to recognize in the waking life ; and the occurrence of circumstances and events which Reason would regard as utterly impossible, seldom excite the least astonishment in the mind of the dreamer. Time and space are annihilated, and remote periods and distant objects appear to be present. If one could sleep for months or years, without interruption, he would not, on waking, be able to form any proper conception of the lapse of time.

The facts that illustrate the particular theme of this Chapter are curious and diversified. Mary Lyall slept *five weeks*, and on being restored to a state of normal conscious. ness, supposed that her profound slumber had been limited to a single night.[1] The case of Cornelius Broomer, son of a farmer in Genesee County, N. Y., was still more remarkable. He fell into a cataleptic sleep, which continued—with occasional interruptions at irregular intervals—during a period of several years. When his normal consciousness and the voluntary functions of his body were restored, after an uninterrupted slumber of four months, he had no conception of the lapse of time. The fact that we often make long and laborious journeys in one hour, and have a conscious experience, varied by all the thrilling realities of pleasure and pain—apparently requiring several days or weeks for the accomplishment of the whole train of events —is not less significant in its bearing on this point.

In sleep, all our ideas respecting the relations of events and objects to the circumstances of time and space, are utterly disregarded.[2] De Quincey saw objects immensely enlarged and otherwise exaggerated in his dreams. Estimating time by the number of sensorial changes or mental impressions, and the vastness of his experience while under the influence of opium, he occasionally felt that he had lived a century between sunset and dawn. Dr. Abercrombie refers to a friend who, in a dream, crossed the Atlantic and spent *two weeks* in America. On reëmbarking he accidentally fell into the sea, when he awoke and found that he had only been in bed ten minutes! Macnish, in his work on Sleep, assures us that he made a voyage to India, spending several

---

[1] For an authentic statement of this case, the reader is referred to the Eighth Volume of the "Transactions of the Royal Society of Edinburgh."

[2] The involuntary character of our dreams led Mr. Baxter to ascribe them to the immediate presence and direct influence of separate spirits.—*Dugald Stewart's "Philosophy of the Human Mind."—p.* 293.

days in Calcutta ; that he subsequently continued his journey to Egypt, visiting the cataracts and pyramids of the
Nile ; and, moreover, that he had confidential interviews
with Mehemet Ali, Cleopatra and Saladin. The whole of
this remarkable experience — though it appeared to the
dreamer to extend through a period of many months, may
possibly have occupied a single hour. These facts plainly
indicate that the mind, in sleep, sustains no arbitrary or
fixed relations, either to time or space ; and hence, in attempting to solve the problem involved in such dreams, we
must not conceive of the faculties of the mind as being subject to mundane laws and limitations.

A distinguished inventor informed the writer that all his
discoveries—involving the application of mechanical laws to
the construction of machinery—were made *in dreams.* Another mechanic, whose business it was to exercise a constant
supervision over the machinery of a large factory, was at
one time annoyed by the irregular motion of a machine used
in shearing cloth. Several pieces of goods were damaged ;
and yet, after repeated examinations of every part of the
machine—separately and in the relations of each to the
whole—he could discover no cause for the irregularity of
the movement. After spending three or four days in fruitless attempts to detect the cause of the mischief, he one night
retired, discouraged and mortified in view of his seeming inability to discharge the duties of the place assigned him.
In the course of the night he had a dream that disclosed the
whole secret, and on the following morning he was enabled
to obviate the difficulty in fifteen minutes !¹

---

¹ The *Courier de l'Europe* mentions the fact that Cœlius Rhodizinus, when

The facts in the case of a little girl—who displayed remarkable originality and skill in embroidery—were recently communicated to the writer. She obtained all her patterns while asleep. The designs were various, unique and beautiful, and their execution remarkably perfect. Moreover, the mother of the child confirmed the statement that they were drawn from archetypal forms or images presented to the mind and impressed on the memory in dreams.[1]

A correspondent of the United States *Gazette* some time since gave an account of the manner in which the mode of making round shot was originally discovered. It is alleged that the mind of a plumber was long and severely exercised on the subject, but without his accomplishing any valuable practical result. One night he was suddenly awakened by a blow from his wife, who assured him that she " had found out how to make round shot." She dreamed of going into a shop to purchase a hat for her child, and whilst there made the discovery. Hearing a hissing sound, which seemed to proceed from an inner room, she inquired the cause, and was informed that they were making round shot. On looking up she saw a man pouring melted lead through a sieve from the top of the building, which fell into a tub of water

---

laboring to correct the text of Pliny, which he is said to have obscured, was puzzled by a single word. He toiled a whole week in vain to ascertain the meaning. At length, wearied by his exertions, he fell asleep and obtained the solution in a dream.

[1] Addison, in speaking of the inventive powers of the mind in sleep, says : " There is not a more painful action of the mind than invention ; yet in dreams it works with such ease and activity,. that we are not sensible when the faculty is employed. For instance, I believe every one, some time or other, dreams that he is reading papers, books or letters ; in which case the invention prompts so readily, that the mind is imposed on, and mistakes its own suggestions for the composition of another."

on the floor; and on examination she found the tub contained shot that were perfectly round. At an early hour the next morning the plumber commenced his experiments by pouring the melted lead from the top of the stairs. The result satisfied him that the suggestions of his wife's dream were highly important, and that he was about to accomplish his object. He then fused some lead and poured it from the top of the highest tower in the city, with still better results. Finally, he went to a mine in the neighborhood, and pouring the melted metal down a perpendicular shaft, he was delighted to find that he produced round shot.

Grave and profound questions have been mysteriously answered in the mind of the dreamer; and the records of Psychology furnish illustrations of scientific instruction, legal wisdom and literary composition, resulting from the orderly exercises of the mind in sleep. It is alleged that Dr. Franklin obtained a solution of certain political problems in his dreams, and that impending events were foreshadowed in a similar manner. The late Dr. Gregory, Professor of Electricity and Chemistry in the University of Edinburgh, often obtained important ideas, scientific illustrations, and even particular forms of expression in his dreams, which were subsequently used in his lectures, before the classes in the University, and in his published works.[1]

Abercrombie mentions the case of an eminent lawyer who

---

[1] The late Rev. Menzes Rayner—formerly and for many years a respected and able minister in the Episcopal and Universalist Churches—was on one occasion inspired with a complete sermon in a dream. In the morning the entire discourse was vividly impressed on his mind, and without any mental effort the mechanical labor of transcription was speedily performed. Mr. R assured the writer that he had preached that sermon in many places, and that it was everywhere regarded as one of his best efforts.

belonged to a distinguished family in Scotland.   For several days he had been constantly occcupied with a very intricate case of great importance.   One night he left his bed
and seating himself at a desk in his sleeping apartment, he
commenced writing.   His wife, who was a silent spectator
of his movements, observed that he prepared a long paper
which he deposited in the desk, and then returned to bed.
The next morning he related to his wife what he remembered of his nocturnal experience.   He dreamed of preparing
a very lucid and masterly legal opinion in the case which
had so engrossed and perplexed his mind, and lamented that
he could not recover the train of thought. which had only
left obscure images in his memory.   His wife thereupon directed him to the desk, where he found his opinion written
out in fine style and with surpassing accuracy.[1]   The same
author refers to a literary gentleman in Edinburgh, who, in
a dream, composed a facetious parody on an epigram by
Piron, which the latter had perpetrated at the expense of
the French Academy.   Von Hennings also mentions the
improvisations of Schonemann.   He was but a poor poet
when awake, but in a natural sleep often extemporized very
fine verses, on themes furnished by his friends ; the manner
of their utterance being deeply impressive.   Schonemann's
poems never occupied a place in the waking memory of the
ostensible author ; but they were in part preserved by an
amanuensis, and are extant in the German language.[2]

Khubla Khan, by Coleridge, is an exquisite fragment of
a dream.   The poet being in ill health, had retired to a

[1] " Inquiries Concerning the Intellectual Powers," etc.
[2] See " Dreams and Somnambulism," p. 509.

quiet place not far from Devonshire. While under the influence of an anodyne—which the nature of his indisposition had rendered necessary—his waking consciousness was gradually suspended, and in a tranquil siesta his brain gave a graceful form and becoming drapery to the beautiful conception. Macnish, in his " Philosophy of Sleep," also mentions the fact that Tartini, a celebrated violinist, once dreamed that the Devil came to him and challenged him to a trial of skill on his favorite instrument. The inspiration that immediately followed the proposal resulted in the production of his remarkable musical composition, entitled the *Devil's Sonata.*[1]

Christabel is the poetic record of a vision. It is full of startling and beautiful images, while the very soul of music breathes in the masterly modulation of the verse. Retiring from the sphere of outward consciousness, and sinking gently to rest,

" Like a pearl diver through the deep,"

he brought up the treasure to the surface of his waking life.

---

[1] The singular story respecting the origin of the Devil's Sonata rests on the authority of M. de Lande, chapel master to Louis XIV.—" One night, in the year 1713, he dreamed he had made a compact with the devil, and bound him to his service. In order to ascertain the musical abilities of his new associate, he gave him his violin, and desired him, as the first proof of his obedience, to play him a solo ; which, to his great surprise, Satan executed with such surpassing sweetness, and in so masterly a manner, that, awaking in the ecstacy which it produced, he sprang out of bed, and instantly seizing his instrument, endeavored to recall the delicious, fleeting sounds. Although not attended with the desired success, his efforts were yet so far effectual as to give rise to the piece since generally admired under the name of ' The Devil's Sonata.' Still the production was so inferior to that which he had heard in his sleep, as to cause him to declare that, could he have procured subsistence in any other line, he should have broken his violin in despair, and renounced music forever."

It is said that he awoke with the mysterious music of Christabel in his soul, and with what appeared to be its recital
ringing in his ear. Without intellectual effort he immediately transcribed the first part of the poem from memory.
The termination is abrupt, showing that the inspiration was
suddenly suspended, or that only a part of the vision was
recollected. Nor was the poet ever able to complete it in
the style and spirit in which it was commenced. Indeed, he
never completed it at all. In the language of another, " it
would have been almost as difficult to complete the Faëry
Queen, as to continue in the same spirit that witching strain
of supernatural fancy and melodious verse."[1] Christabel
was one of the inspirations of the night—a broken but beautiful fragment from the inner temple of the Muses. It is
worthy of remark that Coleridge comprehended in his faith
and philosophy what appears so beautiful in the light of his
poetic inspiration.

> "The massive gates of Paradise are thrown
> Wide open, and forth come, in fragments wild,
> Sweet echoes of unearthly melody,
> And odors snatched from beds of amaranth."

The faculties that exhibit the greatest activity will be the
last to find repose. Hence the Mechanic dreamed of machinery, and the Professor of the sciences to which he was
chiefly devoted ; at the same time the Lawyer, the Poet and
the Musician, each pursued a train of thought peculiar to
himself, and clearly manifesting the association of ideas in
sleep with the pursuits of our waking existence, and the
continued normal action of the dominant faculties. More-

---

[1] See Chamber's Cyclopædia of English Literature, p. 335.

over, this psycho-physiological condition, like a state of voluntary abstraction, may render the powers that remain wakeful, unusually active and strong. This convergence of mental forces not only presents the particular subject in a strong light before the mental vision of the dreamer, but it may give to his conceptions sharp, bold outlines, and an intense expression.

Whatever may serve to suspend the organic functions of a part of our faculties, is quite likely, by concentrating the mental energies, to augment other powers of the mind, giving them at once a preternatural activity and a more forcible expression. This is one of the peculiarities of genius. Those who startle the world with the boldness and originality of their thoughts, are, with rare exceptions, men in whom some particular class of faculties will be found to predominate, arresting and holding in subordination all the inferior powers of the mind. The dominant faculties thus give a particular direction to the electric forces of the brain, and an intense expression to the imperial idea and the ruling passion. It is this that kindles the fire on the orator's lip, and converts the parts of speech into music. It illuminates the darkest problems in Nature; it imparts the " fine frenzy" to the poet's eye, and makes his language like lightning. As sleep sometimes only suspends the exercise of a part of the faculties, it may, by bringing the mental energies to a focus, intensify the light that thus falls on the particular subjects that occupy the mind.

Without either affirming or denying the interposition of foreign intelligent agents, in the occurrence of the more extraordinary facts cited above, I may observe that the phenomena indicate, that the particular faculties employed in their production were awake and organically active at the time, while the functions of other organs were suspended. Those powers of the mind which are most freely, constantly and vigorously employed, will always be most wakeful, and their orderly exercise will naturally continue some time after Sleep has chained the weaker faculties, and closed up the avenues that connect the mind with the external world.

If the unconscious elements may be God's messengers in the natural world, he is not without suitable agents and ministers in the higher departments of his Empire. Indeed, the Universe—in the most comprehensive sense—is one vast storehouse of means and instruments, all subject to his command. And if the incarnate soul, whereon his seal is set, may possess the key to the penetralia of Nature, other beings, of finer composition and superior endowments, may serve his purpose effectually by informing the common mind. Whoever will condemn the idea, either as a vulgar superstition or as a dangerous heresy, must be prepared to convict —with a multitude of others—the authors of Paradise Lost and the Epistle to the Hebrews. Both believed and taught that spiritual beings are wont to perform a silent but ceaseless ministry among men, being Divinely commissioned to

> " ——walk the earth
> Unseen, both when we wake and when we sleep."

CHAPTER XXIX.

SOMNAMBULISM AND SOMNILOQUISM.

Physiological Aspects of the Sleep-walker—Somnambulism in the Lyric Drama—Dangers incidental to the State—Curious Case of a Dog—Examples from Dr. Gall, Mertinet, Dr. Prichard and Professor Soave—The Author's Facts—Remarkable Case of a Student at Athens—An Amusing Instance—Somniloquism—Influence of our Pursuits—Lady Macbeth, and the Sleep-walker in Bellini's Opera—Case of Rev. J. M. Cook—Personal Experiences—An Audience in the Bed-chamber—Philosophical Suggestions—Association of Ideas and Movements—Testimony of Müller—Examples from Perty's "Mystical Revelations"—Jenny Lind and the Musical Somnambulist—Principles and Revelations of Nature.

> " The souls of men are wanderer's while they sleep,
> And Life's continuous current ever flows,
> Whether to outward bliss the pulses leap,
> Or languid glide in silence and repose."—HARRIS.

THE powers of locomotion and speech are often exercised in sleep, and the faculty of the seer is conjointly exhibited in many curious and startling phenomena. The design of this work would be manifestly incomplete without a brief analysis and exposition of the facts illustrating this department of my subject, and hence the present Chapter may very properly be devoted to an elucidation of the two general classes of facts, developed in the exercise of the faculties already named. The functions of Somnambulation, and Somniloquism, may each be manifested separately, or they may both be performed at one time, and by the same person. As they are liable to occur in this conjunction, it is possible the several facts cited in this connection may equally well illustrate the two phases of the general subject.

Somnambulism, from the Latin *somno* and *ambulare*, is the more familiar term employed to represent the act of walking in sleep, the examples of which—especially among young persons of nervous temperaments and active habits—are far more numerous than careless observers would be led to imagine. The Somnambulist generally walks with his eyes wide open, though this is not always the case; but whether the lids be opened or closed, the pupil is invariably dilated to its utmost capacity. The six muscles that move the eye appear to be motionless, and the expression is fixed, vacant and glassy. In this state the eye is evidently useless as the organic instrument of vision, since the optic nerve no longer conveys images of external objects to the mind. The pupil, though exposed to the solar rays, will never contract in the smallest appreciable degree; nor is the influence of the strongest light perceptible in the action of the *glandulæ lachrymales*. These facts indicate with sufficient clearness, that the appropriate functions of the eye are temporarily suspended by a deathlike paralysis of the optic nerve, which is complete so long as the state continues.

> " You see the eyes are open,
> But their sense is shut."

But while the earthly instruments of vision are inoperative, it often appears that the Sleep-walker discerns present objects and occurrences with the greatest distinctness— by a mysterious power of vision that is equally independent of physical organs, of the natural light, and every artificial *means of* illumination. The functions of the soul may not necessarily depend on the bodily organs. Moreover, the immortal nature is not subject to the same law of gravitation that acts on physical objects; and as sleep serves to obscure its corporeal relations, it is perhaps but natural that it should be indifferent to the dangers that menace the body with destruction. Hence the Somnambulist often walks in darkness, as well as in the light, and he usually shuns the obstacles in his pathway. He will even stand on the very verge of the steepest declivity, or walk on the roof of the house, seemingly without the least apprehension of falling, or so much as the consciousness of imminent danger. [1]

The Somnambulist, though he occasionally ventures into

---

[1] Somnambulism has been effectively employed in the Lyric Drama The chief interest of Bellini's beautiful Opera centers in the character of Amina, an innocent girl who lived in a valley among the mountains of Switzerland. The maid was accustomed to walk when asleep, carrying a flickering light in one hand, and the superstitious people described her as a shade, robed in white,

"With stream'ng hair and glaring eyes."

A room in the village inn was often visited by the fair apparition. One night the beautiful specter entered the haunted chamber, while it was occupied by Count Rodolpho. Just then a deputation from the village came to welcome the Count, and discovered Amina, who was apparently unconscious; but her sleep was presumed to be feigned. She was suspected of being unchaste, and spurned by Elvino, to whom she was betrothed. In the excitement that follows the spell is broken, and Amina, greatly terrified, vaguely imagines she is dreaming. The poor girl becomes the unhappy victim of all the village gossips, till at length the discovery of her somnambulism is made. The village phantom is seen walking on a ruined bridge—long abandoned as impassable—above an impetuous torrent. The people discover that it is Amina, and gaze in mute astonishment, expecting every moment to see her plunged into the foaming flood. But she crosses in safety, thus unconsciously vindicating her virgin innocence before the people. Elvino witnesses the thrilling spectacle; and with the restored confidence and affection of her lover, Amina awakes to find that he has returned the espousal ring to her finger.

most perilous situations, seldom falls or is otherwise injured if left undisturbed. But there is certainly great danger of some personal injury to the Sleep-walker if he is awakened while thus exposed. The sudden return to a state of normal consciousness, and the fears at once excited by the sense of danger, act so powerfully on the subtile medium of voluntary motion as to render his control over the muscles uncertain, and his locomotion, at best, irregular. The accidents that happen to persons who walk in sleep doubtless result —with rare exceptions—from a sudden interruption of the somnambulic trance, which may occur from the influence of outward disturbances on the sensory nerves, or from the operation of inward causes.

It should be observed that our pursuits during the day may be of such a nature as to cause a preternatural tendency of the electric forces to certain voluntary muscles ; and this undue determination of nervous energy toward such portions of the muscular system as have been most exercised, may continue in a degree after the direct action of the will has been suspended by Sleep. The consequent accumulation of vital electricity—in other words, the concentration of the nervous power—may occasion involuntary action. We have witnessed illustrations of this involuntary movement in the dog. When he falls asleep after a long chase, he often barks and moves his legs as if attempting to run. [1]

The physiological and mental phenomena exhibited by the

---

[1] The following curious instance is related by a correspondent of the *Spirit of the Times.* He had returned with his dog from a day's sport in the field, and in the course of the evening witnessed the phenomena he thus describes :

" I was attracted by a very curious sound from the dog, and a strange, fixed look from his ey's, which were set as though glazed in death, and

Somnambulist are greatly diversified, and the employments he seeks are generally such as have occupied his mind or engaged his hands during the day. Dr. Gall gives an account of a miller who was in the habit of rising every night and running his mill. Mertinet mentions the case of a saddler who worked at his trade when sleeping ; and Dr. Prichard that of a farmer who got out of bed, dressed himself, saddled his horse, and rode to market while asleep. Professor Soave reports the case of an Apothecary's clerk who not only walked while asleep, but would kindle his fire ; pursue his studies, examining authorities ; classify botanical specimens ; engage in animated controversies—with his employer or Professor Soave—on Chemistry and other scientific themes ; and, indeed, perform any duty or service that he was accustomed to do in his waking hours. He would carefully compound medicines, according to the prescriptions that were before him, but conscientiously declined filling false prescriptions, or such as would be likely to injure the patient.[1] Mrs. Newton, a relative of the writer, was a skillful seamstress and was accustomed to the unconscious

neither changed nor quivered in the slightest degree, though the blaze of a cheerful wood-fire shone brightly upon them. To my infinite astonishment, after stretching his limbs several times and whining, he gradually arose to his feet and assumed the attitude of pointing, in every particular just as I have seen him do a hundred times in the field, when the aroma from an entire covey was warm on the mild breeze. His lips were set, and quivered with eager but suppressed excitement—which a good pointer ever manifests when near his game—and the chiseled marble could not remain more stanch than this exhibition of his point. When my surprise had a little abated, I spoke to the dog ; but he manifested no consciousness, nor took the slightest notice of my voice, though several times repeated ; and it was only when I touched him that the spell was broken ; when, running several times round the room, he quietly resumed his place before the fire."

[1] Opuscoli Scelti, Vol. III., p. 1780. See, also, Perty's " Mystical Revelations of Human Nature," p. 121.

use of her needle for hours at night, when there was no light in her room. A friend, who was an accomplished horseman, often rode many miles while he was in a profound slumber ; and it is a still more remarkable fact—but well authenticated—that in the disastrous retreat of Sir John Moore, before the battle of Corunna, many of the soldiers fell asleep, yet continued to march with their comrades.

The subjects that most deeply impress the mind are very likely to determine the movements of the Sleep-walker. Sometimes the student is so completely occupied with his studies that the mind's exercise is not suspended in sleep, but it continues to act, as a ponderable body, that has acquired a certain momentum, will still move after the propelling force has been withdrawn. Some years since, while a young lady—a member of the Author's family—was at school, it was observed that she succeeded in her Latin exercises, without apparently devoting much time or attention to the subject. At length the secret of her easy progress was discovered. She was observed to leave her room at night—and taking her class books—she proceeded to a certain place on the bank of a small stream, where she remained but a short time, and then returned to the house. In the morning she was invariably unconscious of what had occurred during the night, but a glance at the lesson for the day usually resulted in the discovery that it was already quite as familiar to her mind as household words.

The facts of a similar case were published in a late number of "Notes and Queries," by D. J. Rhodocanakis, a gentleman from Greece, who now resides in Arthur Terrace, Manchester, England. The material portions of the statement will interest the reader, and accordingly they are submitted in this connection :

"When, in 1856, I was studying in a college at Athens, there was in the same class with me a young student from an island of the Greek Archipelago, who, though extremely stupid and unable to learn any lesson by heart, was yet making the best Latin exercises and solving the most difficult problems of geometry and algebra. . . . The professors, although astonished at the correctness of his themes and problems, for a long time forbore to inquire how they could be the productions of a mind apparently so dull. At last, however, the director of the college, suspecting that some member of a higher class was doing his work for him, locked him—for experiment, one night—in a room adjoining his own, and told him that he should visit him very early next morning, in order to see if he had solved his geometrical problem.

"Next morning, according to his promise, the director went to the room of the unhappy imprisoned scholar, and asked him if he had done his task. He answered, 'Yes ; but how I cannot explain. Last night, after trying many hours to solve it, and not being able, I slept, and when in the morning I awoke, and was sorry beyond expression, thinking of the punishment I should receive, O, wonder! as I approached my writing table, I found it already solved, and in my own handwriting.'

"The director, greatly surprised, immediately communicated the affair to the doctor of the college, who, thinking that the boy might be subject to somnambulism, and that under its influence he was solving the problems and making the exercises, decided to watch his proceedings during the next night. Accordingly, as soon as the young man locked his door, and, after reading for an hour, went to bed, the doctor walked into his room from a secret door, and took his seat. After waiting for nearly three hours, and when he was on the point of leaving the room, the boy awoke, lit his candle, began to write, and after half an hour's labor, extinguished his candle, and again went to bed. The doctor at that retired to his room, and in the morning narrated his discovery to the director and the other professors, who immediately commenced debating how to prevent the same thing occurring again." [1]

---

[1] The writer in "Notes and Queries" assures us that the young man

It appears that the Somnambulist is not very likely to be disturbed by such circumstances as he is led to apprehend ; and the slumber is not liable to be broken except by vital causes, the occurrence of unexpected events, or some arbitrary change in his outward relations which may abruptly disturb the electrical equilibration of the nervous system. Hence, while the regular exercise of locomotion does not interrupt the trance, a false step might cause him to awake. A glass of cold water—dashed in the face—might instantly awaken a Somnambulist, for the obvious reason that this sudden violence would be wholly unexpected ; but when the sleep-walker anticipates what is coming, the nervous system seems to be so braced by the mind's action that the shock is resisted, and the slumber continues unbroken. I have somewhere read an amusing account of the nocturnal movements of a man who occasionally, on waking in the morning, found himself *sans culottes*. The mysterious disappearance of his garments could not be accounted for until some one watched at night in his apartment. and discovered that he left his bed, and with only a portion of his ordinary clothing on, proceeded to the river, which was not far off· On reaching the bank he disrobed himself, and folding up his garments carefully placed them under a fallen tree, and plunged into the stream. The nightly ablution being over the Somnambulist, as usual, returned to his chamber, leaving his clothes where he had placed them, and where all

---

could never be made to believe that he was a somnambulist ; but he insisted that his deputed " moth·r. pitying him, and not wishing him to be punished by his professors, came every night while he was sleeping, and solved his problems and wrote his themes, imitating his handwriting, in order not to be detected by the professors."

the missing articles from his wardrobe were subsequently found. In this case the mind and the sensories were properly fortified, and the shock occasioned by a plunge bath, with the water many degrees below the vital temperature, did not in the least disturb the sleeper.

Somniloquism, from *somnus* and *loquor*, is the practice of talking in sleep ; but when sleep results from sympathy—is induced by the magnetic process—the act of speaking is usually expressed by the term *somniloquy*. The reader has doubtless observed that children of an active temperament are inclined to be constantly on their feet during the day ; they are, moreover, disposed to converse more freely—if not subject to arbitrary restraints—than older people. Nor do they cease to exhibit these proclivities at night, since they are far more inclined to walk and talk in sleep than persons of maturer years. We have already noticed the influence of our waking pursuits on the mind in a state of somnolence. and agreeably to this observation it will be found that persons whose intellectual faculties act with great intensity, and especially the orator, and all such as have large conversational powers, are most likely to be communicative in sleep.

Somniloquism is one of the most interesting of the psycho-physiological phenomena of a natural slumber   The author of *La Sonnambula* makes the beautiful Sleep-walker lisp the name of her lover, and talk of the lost ring, while she wanders by night ; and the great dramatist, who more than any other poet, ancient or modern—comprehended the philosophy of human nature, describes Lady Macbeth in the act of " discharging the secrets of her infected mind to her deaf pillow." It is especially when some subject engages all the faculties, or events of great moment weigh heavily on the mind at the close of the day, that we are most likely to give utterance to what is passing in the mind during the hours of Sleep. While multitudes, under such circumstances, talk incoherently, there are here and there persons who discuss grave questions with admirable method and surprising eloquence. My limits will not admit of the citation of many examples ; nor are they required. Indeed, the proper elucidation of the subject does not so much depend on the number as on the *nature* of the facts presented, and the use that is made of them in the treatment of the general subject.

Among the more conspicuous illustrations, occurring within the sphere of personal observation, I may mention the case of the late Rev. J. M. Cook, a Clergyman of the Universalist denomination, whose somniloquism was extraordinary. He was accustomed to extemporize his discourses, and he was at once a very natural and forcible speaker. This gentleman, while asleep, frequently conducted the entire religious services according to the formula of his Church. On one occasion, when returning from a convention—being a passenger on a boat and asleep in his berth—he gravely commenced the usual form of the public service by reciting a portion of Scripture, which attracted the attention of the other passengers. He then gave out a hymn, and after offering prayer took his text and preached a powerful discourse in illustration and defense of the doctrines of his Church.

Among the conditions essential to successful intercourse with the sleeper, such relations as establish a psycho-electrical *rapport*, and that inward sympathy which results from similar intellectual developments and moral attributes, are, perhaps, the most important. When there is mutual sympathy, a nice adjustment of personal relations, and the circumstances are quite favorable, the Somniloquist may respond with great freedom and in a pertinent manner. Perty, in his "Mystical Revelations," refers to the case of Mrs. Von U——, a natural Somnambulist, who conversed with ease and fluency whenever her husband took hold of her hand. She made exact revelations of the thoughts and designs of persons in her presence, and her communications were occasionally prophetic, foreshadowing the events that were to occur on the succeeding day.

I have a personal experience to relate. In the period of childhood and early youth, Sleep-walking was a common occurrence, and the practice continued until an exciting and somewhat painful experience terminated my nocturnal adventures. Being absent from home, on one occasion, it became necessary for me to sleep in an open garret. In the course of the night I dreamed of traveling, and the body moved off under this action of the mind. Whether the accident that followed was the result of a false step, or of a sudden interruption of the somnambulic trance, from some other cause. it is impossible to determine ; but at length I found myself at the foot of the stairs, and in a horizontal position, having accomplished the descent by the force of gravity, unaided by locomotion.

The rambling utterances that frequently accompanied the phenomenon of sleep-walking were succeeded, at a later period in life, by speeches that exhibited (if I may accept the testimony of many witnesses) an uninterrupted flow of ideas, expressed in coherent and forcible language. It was after adopting the clerical profession—which made it necessary for me to address public assemblies—that this practice of extemporizing in sleep assumed an orderly form, and began to awaken a lively interest in the minds of such persons as chanced to be my auditors. It was frequently remarked by the listeners that the discourses thus given were characterized by unusual boldness and originality of thought; peculiar fitness and freshness in the modes of illustration, combined with logical discrimination and remarkable freedom in the use of language. It was evident that the nature of my profession strongly influenced the operations of the mind in sleep ; nor did the suspension of the clerical functions finally terminate those ministrations that often broke the impressive silence of the night.

On resigning my original profession I did not find it convenient to assume a strictly private relation ; but during a period of ten years I visited no less than twenty-three States of the Union in the capacity of a lecturer on moral and metaphysical philosophy. This constant use of a particular class of faculties, combined with the exercise of the organs of speech, increased the tendency to somniloquism, and the free lectures, to private classes in dark chambers, became more frequent. I am reminded of an instance that occurred some years since at a Hotel in Connecticut. Wearied by the labors of the day, I retired at an early hour and immediately fell asleep. On my return to a state of outward consciousness there were phantom-shapes moving in the room, which were plainly discerned by the light from the street lamp. I was not long in making the discovery that my visitors were incarnate spirits, and that I had uncon-

seriously summoned a very respectable audience (not exactly
in full dress), consisting of the proprietor's family and a
number of his guests.

As the soul doubtless wanders when the sleeper is made
to walk, so when he dreams of addressing public assemblies,
or of conducting a conversation, he is most likely to become
somniloquous. In one case the mind, by its involuntary action, naturally directs the nervous forces to the muscles of
locomotion ; in the other case, to the organs of speech ; and
in both producing the appropriate bodily functions. These
are but the organic expressions of the faculties employed,
and the manner of their exercise. Thus when the mind
travels the body is liable to be moved, and the somniloquist
is but a dreamer whose thoughts are vocally expressed. [1]

The *magnetic sleeper*, with rare exceptions, will converse
with his magnetizer, or any other person with whom he is
in temporary *rapport*. In this state of coma the subject of
somnipathy often discovers amazing powers of perception
and a wide range of ideas entirely above the normal plain
of his mind. In some cases, especially when the mental and
moral atmosphere, and the magnetic influence of the opera-

---

[1] Müller, in his Physiology of the Senses, Voice, Muscular Motion, etc.,
(p. 944), says : " The connection between ideas and movements is sometimes as close as that between different ideas ; thus when an idea and a
movement have frequently occurred in connection with each other, the idea
often excites the involuntary production of the movement. Hence it is
that a threatening movement before the eyes, even the passing of another
person's hand in front of them, causes the eyelids to be involuntarily
closed ; that we are accustomed always to accompany the expression of
certain ideas with certain gestures, and that we involuntarily move our
hands to catch a falling body. It is a general rule that the more frequently
ideas and movements are voluntarily associated together, the more prone
are the movements to be excited by those ideas rather than by the will."

tor are altogether congenial, the subject is acutely susceptible of the slightest influence exerted on the medium of sensation and motion. Every shade of feeling, and the most
delicate operations of the mind, are all impressed on the
sensorium of the sleeper, by a kind of electro-mental photo-
graphy that can not fail to excite profound astonishment in
the mind of the intelligent observer. In such cases the
powers of perception—on the part of the subject—may be
wholly exercised through the brain of the operator, and the
volition of the latter may determine every sensation and
movement of the former. This automatic perception and
action often displays the most exquisite susceptibility of sensorial and mental impressions, and is further characterized
by a functional precision that is unsurpassed by the most
perfect mathematical and mechanical combinations.

The *rapport* between the magnetizer and his subject is
often so intimate, and the commerce of thought and feeling
so real and unlimited, that great prudence and circumspection, on the part of the former, should be constantly observed. In some cases the sleeper feels every inclination of
the operator, and may possibly be quite as ready to follow
the impulse that actuates him. Nor does this automatic action necessarily depend on the immediate presence of the
magnetizer ; but it is liable to occur at a distance, and may
continue until the slumber is broken, or the magnetic *rapport* is otherwise interrupted. An illustration of this kind
was some years since communicated to the writer by the
late Dr. Lockwood, of Stamford, Connecticut. The Doctor,
having at one time a delicate female patient –not likely to
be benefited by medicine – magnetized the lady and left her

asleep while he went to visit another patient. On his return
he found that the sleeper had, during his absence, experienced all the promptings of his own nature, and had followed
them so literally as to occasion unpleasant consequences.

Dr. Spiritus found a good magnetic subject in the case
of a girl whom he was treating professionally. When in
the sleep she only preserved her conscious connection with
the outward world through the Doctor's senses. She readily perceived whatever affected his sensory nerves. While
she could not hear the report of a gun, she had no difficulty
in hearing the ticking of the Doctor's watch whenever he
placed it by his own ear. When he filled his ears with cotton, she complained that he had made her deaf. If he was
hurt, she felt the pain in the corresponding part of her own
body. On one occasion he voluntarily suspended his respiration, when the girl fainted, and on her recovery she declared that she must have suffocated had the Doctor suppressed his breathing a little longer. Dr. Gmelin once
made the experiment of taking an emetic, in the absence of
a susceptible female patient, who found the medicine to act
in her case as effectually as if she had taken it herself. [1]

Dr. Cataneo, of Genoa, found a rare magnetic subject in a
young painter of Turin. The Doctor was at the time much
exercised in mind with reflections on the life and character
of the conqueror Dschingischan. On one occasion, while
the young artist was in the magnetic sleep, and in mental
rapport with the Doctor, he executed a portrait of the great
chief of the Tartars. At the same time a lady in another
apartment—who was likewise in magnetic sympathy with

---

[1] Perty's "Mystical Revelations of Human Nature," p. 174.

the mind of Cataneo—gave a most graphic description of the same person. [1]

Fernel reports the facts respecting a boy who could speak Greek and Latin when in the magnetic sleep. Lorry also mentions the case of a girl of ten years that would make long speeches when her mother placed one hand on her head. When the hand was removed the flow of words and ideas was immediately interrupted. Professor Agardh, of Lund, Sweden, furnishes another interesting example. He met with a magnetic sleeper in the person of a boy who could speak Latin with greater fluency than his native tongue. He could also converse in French. On one occasion, when a person educated in the English language had expressed doubts of his ability to speak languages he had never learned, the boy immediately commenced a conversation in English, and the skeptic was obliged to acknowledge that he spoke the language as freely and correctly as an educated Englishman. At the same time the teacher affirmed that his pupil had never learned—by the ordinary process of scholastic training—a word that he had uttered. [2]

I find a most striking and perfect example of somnipathetic, sensorial perception and simultaneous muscular motion in the remarkable experiments made by the Swedish Nightingale, some years since, on a magnetic subject in England. Jenny Lind had been invited with several friends to attend a *séance* at the residence of Mr. Braid, under whose direc-

---

[1] Perty's "Mystical Revelations of Human Nature," p. 418.

[2] Macnish met with a girl that spoke Galish, and Prof. La Mothe le Vayer with a citizen of La Ferre, near Rouen, who could answer questions in all languages, ancient and modern.

tion the experiments were made. The account of the magnetic and musical novelties, witnessed on that occasion, originally appeared in the Manchester *Courier*, and the material portions of the same have been extensively re-published by the American press. The following extract will suffice to indicate the surprising nature of the performance, while it furnishes a curious and convincing illustration of my subject.

" Jenny Lind played and sang a slow air, with Swedish words, in which the Somnambulist accompanied her in the most perfect manner, both as regarded words and music. Jenny now seemed resolved to test the powers of the Somnambulist to the utmost by a continued strain of the most difficult roulades and cadenzas, including some of her extraordinary sostinuto notes, with all their inflections from pianissimo to forte crescendo, and again diminished to thread-like pianissimo ; but in all these fantastic tricks and displays of genius, even to the shake, she was so closely and accurately tracked by the Somnambulist that several in the room occasionally could not have told, merely by hearing, that there were two individuals singing- so instantaneously did she catch the notes, and so perfectly did their voices blend and accord.

" Next, Jenny having been told by Mr. Braid that the subject might be tested by some other language, commenced ' Casta Diva,' in which the fidelity of the Somnambulist's performance, both in words and music, fully justified all that Mr. Braid had alleged regarding her powers. The girl has naturally a good voice, and has had a little musical instruction in some of the ' Music for the Million,' but is quite incompetent of performing any such feat in the waking condition, either as regards singing the notes or speaking the words with the accuracy she did when in the somnambulic state She was also tested by Mad'lle Lind in merely imitating language, when she gave most exact imitations ; and Mr. Schwabe also tried her by some difficult combinations of sound, which he said no one was capable of imitating correctly without much practice ; but the Somnambulist imitated them correctly at once, and that whether spoken slowly or quickly."

Whenever two individuals are in personal contact, a blending—more or less perfect—of the electrical forces of their bodies is sure to result from the connection ; and this occurs in the greatest degree when the conjunction is effected at the most sensitive points in the nervous system. This coalescence of the forces—rendered inevitable by the homogeniousness of the vital principle—is measured and determined by the operation of a natural law. If the persons thus united sustain positive and negative relations, respectively to each other, they become as ONE for the time being, and so long as the connection—whether by actual contact or through the electro-magnetic atmospheres that surround them—remains unbroken. In such a case the negative party virtually becomes an additional member of the other, and may even feel through the same sensorium, and be moved by the agency of the same will.

Among the most important magnetic revelations, apparently derived from communion with the subtile powers of the natural world, I may mention the book entitled, "The Principles of Nature, her Divine Revelations, and a Voice to Mankind." It can hardly be necessary to remind the intelligent American reader that this large octavo volume was wholly dictated by, or through, Mr. A. J. Davis, while he was in a state of magnetic entrancement, induced by the manipulations of Dr. S. S. Lyon. The truth of this statement is supported by the concurrent testimony of many witnesses, the author of the present treatise being one of the number. Nature's Revelations were made and published while Mr. Davis was but a youth, destitute of all scholastic attainments and undisciplined in mind ; and yet the work exhibits a peculiar method, great independence of thought, and mysterious powers of insight and comprehension. It is, however, no part of my design to undertake a critical analysis of the contents of this work, for the purpose of showing its intrinsic merits and defects. It is only as a psychological phenomenon that it now claims attention. Viewed in this light, it is a stupendous fact ; and we shall examine the records of psychological science and search all history in vain for one of this class that more forcibly suggests the amazing grandeur of Nature and the sublime possibilities of the Human Mind.

There are few persons susceptible of the magnetic sleep who do not readily converse while in that state, though the inexperienced magnetizer is quite likely to produce a temporary paralysis of the organs of speech, as he is also liable to suspend—for the time being—other voluntary functions. In some instances the sleeper is limited in his ideas and forms of expression to his own range of thought and use of language ; in other cases, his sphere is enlarged by whatever belongs to the mental powers and acquirements of the magnetizer, or the person with whom the subject is in immediate sympathy ; while occasionally he rises, as on eagles' wings, and with unclouded vision, above the normal plane of the human mind ; enters into sympathy with the invisible forces and the great laws of the Universe ; or, it may be, into sublime association and intimate fellowship with the higher sources of Intelligence.

CHAPTER XXX.

THE CLAIRVOYANT VISION.

Preliminary Observations—Relations of Clairvoyance to the Pagan Mysteries
—Illustrations from the Scriptures—Crœsus and the Emperor Trajan con-
sult the Oracles—The Seer of Samos—Revelations of Apollonius—Tes-
timony of St. Augustine—Examples from the Life of Swedenborg—The
Seeress of Prevorst—Illustrative Facts from Dr. de Benneville, Jacob
Böhme, Stilling and Zschokke—Remarkable Cases from Perty's Mystical
Revelations—A Provost Marshall of France among the Seers—Discovery
of Capt. Austin and Sir John Franklin—Clairvoyance of Alexis—A Seeress
in Hartford reads an Epitaph in Bermuda—She Discovers a Remedy for
Yellow Fever—A Doctor mistakes Solids for Fluids - Seeing a Cambric
Needle twenty-four miles off, and a penny at a distance of one thousand
miles !—Surprising Developments — A Fair Infidel and her Inamorato
Exposed—Second Sight of the Highlanders—Application of the Argument to Science—Concluding Observations.

> " The stranger at my fireside can not see
> The forms I see nor hear the sounds I hear ;
> He but perceives what is ; while unto me
> All that has been is visible and clear "—LONGFELLOW

CLAIRVOYANCE, derived from the French, literally sig-
nifies *clear sight;* but the term is especially employed to
represent that mysterious power of perception whereby certain persons discern distant objects and occurrences without
the aid of light or the use of the organic instruments of
vision. This power is more or less perfectly displayed by
many persons and under a variety of conditions. In certain
cases it appears to be a normal faculty ; in others its exercise occurs spontaneously at irregular intervals; while in
many it is induced by the magnetic sleep. It should be observed that the faculty itself is essentially the same in all

cases, whatever may be the immediate incentives to its action, and irrespective of the circumstances that accompany its development. But it is also to be observed, that this faculty varies in *degree*, and in respect to the objects comprehended within the field of vision. Its compass may be limited to material objects and occurrences already past, or actually transpiring at the time ; or it may assume a wider range and embrace coming events and the realities of our spiritual and immortal life.

When the *rapport magnetique* is properly established with a susceptible person, it often happens that the latter perceives the physiological, pathological, mental and moral states and exercises of the former, by a kind of sympathetic feeling or psychometric sensation, which is frequently mistaken by the ordinary observer for Clairvoyance. Sensitive persons are also liable to receive similar impressions—more or less reliable—from such other objects as may be submitted to them for inspection, and about which they may chance to feel a passing interest. This power of perception often discovers the most subtile properties of matter, at the same time it detects personal qualities of the most delicate nature, and private experiences which require concealment, though they may not escape detection. In this state, the sensibility of the subject may be so acute that he will almost instantly perceive the medicinal properties of a drug, as soon as a small portion of the same (which may be inclosed in a wrapper and invisible) is placed in the hand. Give him either a cravat or a finger-ring, that a thief has worn, and he will find the culprit without other warrant or the aid of a policeman. An old shoe will enable him to track the fugitive from justice ; from an autograph he will delineate the character of a stranger, and a lock of hair from the head of a sick person—of whose existence he had no previous knowledge—may be all that he requires, and he will put the doctor to shame by the superior accuracy of his diagnosis.

But in the occurrence of such phenomena there may be no positive evidence of the development of the Clairvoyant Vision. This exquisite and semi-spiritual sensation usually corresponds to *feeling* rather than *sight*. But if one of the senses may be instrumental in this mysterious power of cognition, it is a fair inference that the others may be capable of a similar use, and this conclusion will be supported by the introduction of such facts as clearly demonstrate the existence of that sublime faculty, in the exercise of which the SEER stands alone within the veil of the Temple.

Illustrations of my subject may be found among all the races of men, and every period of human history has furnished examples. Neither the forms of government nor the systems of religion have power to change the essential constitution of the Soul. On the contrary, all human institutions are but outward expressions and organic revelations of whatever belongs to the nature of Man. The Egyptians had their sacred mysteries ; the Roman Senate consulted the Sibylline Oracles ; the Greeks found inspiration in the waters of the Castalian Spring ; the Priestess of Delphi gave clairvoyant responses ; and the Jewish high priest derived his mystical revelations from the Urim and Thummim, which bore a striking likeness to the Pagan Oracles.

A Christian Apostle says that, " God is no respecter of persons," and Nature also inculcates the same doctrine ; but

24

agreeably to the common notion of the **Christian world, he**
has a peculiar respect for the Jews, who are especially associated—at least in the popular conception—with all the
most sacred realities of time and eternity. Even the man of
varied scientific attainments is often led, by the force of his
early theological education, to accredit the ancient Hebrews
with the possession of the most remarkable gifts and divine
graces, while he may be slow in recognizing the existence of
such powers and accomplishments elsewhere among men.
Even when the identical faculties are manifested, by similar
methods, and in our immediate presence, the results are often
regarded as the tricks of the juggler.　Indeed, we often meet
with persons of easy faith, little learning and less reflection,
who are quite disposed to give the Jews a monopoly of all
spiritual faculties and divine endowments.　I can not entertain this unphilosophical view of the subject,　The faculties
and susceptibilities of the Soul are fundamentally the same
in all ages and countries, and therefore Man's relation to
the invisible sources of all inspired thoughts and ideas can
neither be determined by geographical lines, nor otherwise
limited by national distinctions.

The early Apostles, and many of the Christian **Fathers**
and disciples in the Church, for more than three hundred
years, were gifted with the mysterious vision that comprehends foreign persons and objects, while it often detects the
shadows of coming events.　This interior sight appeared to
coexist with the natural vision of Jesus, and it was often
either the source or the medium of important information.
When he was about to make his triumphal entry into Jerusalem, he sent two of his disciples to a neighboring hamlet,

assuring them as soon as they entered the village they would find a colt tied. He anticipated the objection that would be made on their attempting to take the animal away ; he instructed them what to say, and affirmed that the objector would acquiesce. The disciples went their way, and the result confirmed the statement of their Master. On another occasion he directed certain fishermen when and where to cast their nets in the Lake. Following his suggestions, it is said that they filled two ships, so that they were in danger of sinking. (Luke, chap. v. 6–9.) Again, he saw Nathaniel under a fig-tree when the latter was far beyond the limit of natural vision. (John, chap. i : 48–50.) In his interesting interview with the woman at the well, this power was displayed in reading her thoughts, and in such specific references to the incidents of her personal history that, in her report, the woman said, " Come, see a man which told me all things that ever I did." (John, chap. iv.) Once more, when his friend Lazarus fell into a deathlike slumber, he was not personally present *in loco ;* but he at once perceived what had occurred, and said to the disciples that accompanied him, " Our friend Lazarus sleepeth : but I go that I may awake him out of sleep." (John, chap. xi.) The same faculty was exercised by St. Peter in discovering the deception and falsehood of Ananias and his wife, in respect to the price of some property which they had sold. (Acts, chap. v.)

We have the history of some grand exhibitions of this power in the lives of the old Prophets. When the King of Syria made war against Israel, he soon learned that by some means the latter was familiar with all his plans, and was accordingly prepared to check every hostile movement. Following the natural tendencies of his mind, the Syrian king inferred that there must be some traitor in his camp, and, calling his servants together, he demanded to know who was for the King of Israel ? One of the number thereupon answered, "None, my lord, O king ; but Elisha, the prophet that is in Israel, telleth the King of Israel the words that thou speakest in thy bed-chamber." (II. Kings, chap. vi. : 12.) Here was a clairvoyance that was neither obstructed by intervening obstacles nor otherwise limited by darkness or distance ; a clairaudience that detected the whispered words and silent thoughts of the King of Syria. By the same supernal vision he discovered the celestial combatants assembled for his protection, when the Syrians, under cover of darkness, had encamped about the city. The Syrian armies presented a formidable array that alarmed the servant of Elisha ; but the Prophet, and subsequently the servant, beheld a far more numerous host, moving in fiery chariots over the mountains and filling all the air. These illustrations of the spiritual power of cognition comprehend alike the perception of remote and invisible objects; distant events and circumstances ; and the interior forces and immortal entities of the unseen world. ·

But the faculty which distinguished the ancient Prophets and Apostles of Judaism and Christianity was neither confined to them nor limited to their nation. The Pagan world was favored with a similar illumination. The Greeks, especially, furnished distinguished examples. If we may credit the records of authentic history, this power was constantly exercised by the Oracles. On one occasion, Crœsus, desiring to test the capabilities of the Pythoness, dispatched suitable persons to Delphi with instructions to consult the Oracle, *on a particular day*, and, if possible, to ascertain what he (the King of Lydia) was doing. Having obtained an interview, the messengers submitted the question as directed, which at once elicited the following—the oracular response being uttered in hexametric verse :

" I know the number of the sands, and the measure of the sea ; I know what the dumb would say ; I hear him who speaks not. There comes to me the odor of tortoise and lamb's flesh, seething together in a brass vessel ; beneath the flesh is brass ; there is also brass above."

When the representatives of the king returned, Crœsus read the message and was satisfied. " For," according to Herodotus, " after the messenger had been sent to consult the Oracle, *on the appointed day*, he hit upon the following to be done, as something which he supposed might be difficult to detect and describe :—Cutting up a tortoise and a lamb, he boiled them together in a brazen vessel, which also had a cover of brass."

The Emperor Trajan, being about to invade Parthia, and wishing to know the probable result of his expedition, took the precaution to first test the powers of a celebrated Oracle in Syria, before accepting its authority in a matter of so much importance. For this purpose he sent sealed letters, to which he solicited replies in writing. The Oracle directed that blank papers should be sealed and sent. This occasioned no little surprise among the priests, who were unacquainted with the character of the Emperor's letters. Trajan at once comprehended the answer, because *he had sent blank tablets to the god*. This inspired his confidence, and he then forwarded letters inquiring whether he should return to Rome at the close of the contest. Thereupon the Oracle commanded that a vine should be cut in pieces, wrapt in linen, and carried to him. This symbolic answer was signally verified when the bones of the Emperor were at length carried back to Rome. [1]

Pythagoras, the beautiful Seer of Samos, who was regarded with deep and tender reverence, even by the philosophers who succeeded him, spent more than thirty years of his life with the Magi of Egypt and Babylon. He returned to Samos, skilled in all the learning of his time, and there founded a school. The purity of his principles and his life, not less than the beauty of his person and the simplicity of his manners, inspired in others the highest admiration and the purest love. His birth was predicted by the Oracle of Apollo, as his name implies ; and a Samian poet sings :

> " Pythais, fairest of the Samian race,
> Bore, from the embraces of the god of day,
> Renowned Pythagoras. the friend of Jove."

It was prophesied that he would "surpass in beauty and wisdom all that ever lived," and his biographer asserts that " when he exerted all the powers of his intellect, *he easily beheld every thing, as far as ten or twenty ages of the human race.*" The authentic record of his life contains some significant facts that illustrate his powers as a seer. On one occasion he gave an accurate description of a shipwreck, concerning which he had no information through any ordinary or external channel. Again, when drinking from a well, he announced the speedy occurrence of an earthquake, and his statement was immediately confirmed by the fact.

---

[1] " The Apocatastasis," p. 61. See also Macrobius Saturnal. L. i. c. 23.

When certain persons in his presence expressed a wish to possess the treasures which they supposed a certain ship to contain, that was just then coming into port, Pythagoras assured them that they would only have a dead body; and in this he was strictly correct, a corpse being the entire freight of the vessel. With all his knowledge of the occult powers of Nature and the mysteries of the Magi, he was accomplished in Music, and "invented an instrument to measure musical intervals and the lyre." He was, moreover, a profound mathematician and the great astronomer of his age and country. It is alleged, on eminent historical authority, that he announced the Copernican theory, so that the sphericity of the earth, its rotary motion, and revolution round the center of our solar system may have been clairvoyant discoveries five hundred years before the Christian Era.

Apollonius discovered his own clairvoyant powers while in India, through the agency of a distinguished Brahmin, who was both a philosopher and a Seer. Having perfected his education in the Sanscrit language, and in the sacred mysteries of that country, Apollonius returned to be a popular teacher. In his public discourses his remarkable psychical powers were often displayed in a striking manner. On one occasion, while in the Island of Crete, he suddenly exclaimed, "The sea is bringing forth land!" It was subsequently ascertained that, precisely at that hour, an island appeared in the Ægean Sea, not far off, it having been thrown up by an earthquake. Another interesting illustration of his powers occurred while he was addressing a crowd in a grove near Ephesus. The attention of his auditors was attracted by a flock of birds on a tree. At length a solitary bird alighted near them for a moment, whose peculiar note appeared to be the signal which caused the whole flock to fly away. This occasioned an interruption of the discourse, and Apollonius remarked that a boy, near one of the gates of the city—the name and direction of which were given— had spilled a quantity of grain, and that this solitary bird observing this came to inform his companions of the feast. Apollonius continued his discourse, while a number of his hearers hastened to ascertain if he had spoken the truth. The Seer had not finished his address when they returned with enthusiastic expressions of admiration, having verified the correctness of his statement.[1]

At a later period, while discoursing at Ephesus one day, he paused abruptly, as if the train of thought had been suddenly interrupted, or as when one is at a loss for a word. After a moment's hesitation, he exclaimed, "Strike! strike the tyrant!" This eccentric conduct surprised the people, and excited no little curiosity, whereupon Apollonius explained by saying, in substance, " Courage, my friends, for this very day—nay, at the very moment I stopped speaking the tyrant was slain." As soon as intelligence could be received from Rome this statement was confirmed, Domitian, the reigning tyrant, having been assassinated at that hour. (Idem, L. VIII., C. 26.)

St. Augustine, who maintained that demons have power to read men's thoughts, gives circumstantial accounts of cases of clairvoyance that came under his personal observation. Among others, he refers to a presbyter who was *en rapport* with a sick person at the distance of twelve miles. The

[1] Philostratus Vita Apollonii Tyanensis, L. iv. 3.

patient was clairvoyant, and would indicate the precise time
that the presbyter left his house, and accurately mark his progress and near approach. At length he would say, " He is
entering the farm—he has reached the house—he is at the
door ;" and at that moment he was sure to find the visitor
standing in his presence. St. Augustine took an interest in
such phenomena, but entreated that the learned would not
ridicule him for his credulity, at the same time he does not
ask the unlearned to accept what he is pleased to offer on
his individual authority. [1]

The ancient Day was characterized by its own peculiar
glory ; but the light was obscured, and deep, cold shadows
fell on the world when the great Philosophers of Antiquity
and the Apostles of Christianity retired from human observation. Serene in spirit, and calm in their divine repose ;
invested with more than mortal powers and regal honors,
they went up to their great Immortality. Then came a long
—long Night. After the beginning of the fourth century
the human soul seemed to be destitute of any true spiritual
illumination. The mind slept ; while darkness was on the
face of the deep. And many a doubting mortal watched his
brief hour, and thought that Night would never end. And
when the hour—the sad, short hour—of earthly being had
passed, with no light but the faint glimmering of the silent
stars, the watcher went to his repose ; and another—silent,
lonely and desolate—sat in his place. Thus wore the long
Night away, until the Era of Universal Light, Liberty, and
Progress dawned on the World.

Since the revival of letters, the amazing developments of

---

[1] See " Notes and Queries," for June, 1854.

modern science, art and civilization have served to quicken
and strengthen the intellectual and moral faculties among
all enlightened nations. To these developments we are
chiefly indebted for the gradual dissipation of many absurd
superstitions and pernicious errors, all generated in ignorance and nursed in the bosom of the Medieval Ages. But
with the well-grounded hope of true human advancement,
which this change in the state and tendencies of the human
mind naturally inspired, it soon became painfully apparent,
that the more vital and essential principles of the popular
faith were fast losing their place in the minds and their
hold on the affections of the people. A growing skepticism was everywhere visible, especially among the more enlightened classes. A material philosophy, that boldly threatened to overthrow our hopes of immortality, occupied the
places of honor and responsibility, and even stood within
the pale of the Church. But the elements of the Inward
Life were soon moved by the mental and moral forces of the
New Era, and outwardly manifested in many striking examples. The frequent and orderly development of the psychical
faculties, at that period, was only a natural consequence of
the general awakening of the human mind. Indeed, such
illustrations are old as history ; diversified as the characteristics of races and nations, and as widely distributed as the
human inhabitants of the earth.   `

One of the greatest Seers of modern times was Emanuel
Swedenborg, of Stockholm. The Swedish Baron was born
as early as 1688, but his mysterious illumination did not occur until 1743. He was then fifty-five years old ; and his
high character, not less than his profound attainments in

every department of learning, had given him a most honorable position in his own country, and a commanding influence abroad, that was felt and acknowledged in every part of Europe. Among the recorded instances of his clairvoyance are many striking illustrations of my subject, but in this connection I can only make a brief *resume* of some of the more remarkable examples.

It is alleged by M. Dieudonnè Thiebault, Professor of Belles Letters in the Royal Academy of Berlin, that the Count de Montville, Ambassador from Holland to Stockholm, having died suddenly, a shopkeeper demanded of his widow the payment of a bill, which she remembered had been paid in her husband's lifetime. Not being able to find the shopkeeper's receipt, she was induced to consult the distinguished Seer, though she did so less from credulity than curiosity. Swedenborg informed her that her deceased husband had taken the shopkeeper's receipt on a certain day (also naming the hour), while he was reading such an article in Bayle's Dictionary, in his cabinet; and that his attention being called immediately to some other concern, he put the receipt into the book to mark the place at which he left off; where, in fact, it was found at the page described!

The Queen Dowager of Sweden, Louisa Ulrica, desiring to test the powers of Swedenborg, demanded a repetition of the words spoken by her deceased brother, the Prince Royal of Prussia, at the moment of her taking leave of him for the Court of Stockholm. The Seer requested a private audience, whereupon they retired to another apartment, when Swedenborg replied to her interrogatory by saying, in substance, that she took leave of her august brother at Charlottenburg

—naming the day and the hour—that, while passing through
the long gallery of the Castle, they met again, when the
Prince, taking her hand, led her to a retired situation by a
particular window which he described, where the last words
were spoken. The Queen did not disclose the words, but
protested with great solemnity, that they were the precise
words pronounced by her brother at the termination of their
parting interview !

When Swedenborg was in Gottenburg, three hundred
miles from Stockholm, he announced the occurrence of a
great fire in his native city, giving the facts respecting the
time, place, and circumstances of its origin, and accurately
describing its progress and termination. It was on Saturday
night that this conflagration was described as occurring at
that time. The Seer repeated the substance of his statement to the Governor on Sunday morning. This was substantially confirmed by a dispatch, received from Gottenburg on Monday evening, and on Tuesday morning the arrival of the royal courier furnished an unqualified attestation of the truth of all the particulars of the clairvoyant
revelation. These facts rest on no doubtful authority. Their
authenticity is sanctioned by Kant, the great German metaphysician, in whose judgment—to use his own words—they
" set the assertion of the extraordinary gift of Swedenborg
out of all possibility of doubt."

The state of inward waking and the same remarkable
powers of perception, were soon illustrated by examples occurring in Germany and elsewhere. In the little village of
Prevorst—situated far up among the mountains, near the
town of Löwenstein—Frederica Hauffé was born in 1801.

Secluded from the great world among the rugged summits of Würtemburg, her young life was characterized by great simplicity. She was an uncorrupted child of Nature, endowed with remarkable powers of perception, and with a mind that was all unclouded by the superficial arts and pernicious customs of fashionable society. At an early age she had prophetic dreams and presentiments; and it is said by her conscientious biographer, that she discovered hidden springs and mineral deposits by some occult power.

The singular powers of Frederica increased as she advanced in years. Her extreme susceptibility of impressions, even from remote objects and events, enabled her to perceive absent persons and distant occurrences, often with great distinctness.[1] Though her early mental culture was extremely limited, she displayed unusual knowledge of many profound subjects, and her clairvoyant revelations were curious and instructive. Moreover, her whole experience contributed to give her an unusual moral elevation, to inspire constant devotional feeling, and to fashion a truly religious character. Her gifts continued, and her vision was unclouded until the fifth of August, 1829, when suddenly—at the tenth hour of

---

[1] Leibnitz and Von Helmont said: "The soul is a mirror of the Universe;" and the Seeress of Prevorst, in the elucidation of her Sun-circle, says: The life-circle, which is the soul, lies under the sun-circle, and thus becomes a mirror to it. So long as the soul continues in the center, she sees all round her—into the past, the future, and the infinite. She sees the world in all its laws, relations and properties, which are implanted in it through time and space. She sees all this without veil or partition-wall interposing. But in proportion as the soul is drawn from the center, by the attractions of the outer world, she advances into darkness, and loses this all-embracing vision and knowledge of the nature and properties of all that surrounds her. This insight is now given to us in the magnetic sleep, when we are withdrawn from the senses!—*History of the Supernatural*, p. 79.

the day—she experienced a new illumination, and, in an ecstacy of joy and with a cry of triumph, her enfranchised soul left the earthly temple its presence had glorified.

During the War of Independence, Dr. George de Benneville exhibited remarkable prescience and unerring knowledge of certain events occurring at a distance, and beyond the utmost stretch of the ordinary powers of perception. While in Reading, Pa.—where he lived during the Revolutionary period—he informed his friends and neighbors of the precise time that the British forces evacuated Philadelphia. Jacob Böhme and the good Jung Stilling experienced a similar illumination in their time; and Heinrich Zschokke, a popular German author, became a waking Seer of extraordinary powers. He read the unwritten histories of strangers as they approached him, including the most secret transactions of their lives. This mysterious illumination disclosed the dresses and movements of the actors; also the rooms, furniture, and other accessories. For a long time he was prone to regard such visions as delusions of the fancy, or a kind of mental jugglery, and he felt an involuntary shudder as often as his auditors confirmed his statements. I subjoin (somewhat condensed) Zschokke's description of a single illustration of his powers :

"In company with two young student foresters, I entered the Vine Inn, at Waldshut. We supped with a numerous company at the *table d'hôte*, where the guests were making merry with the peculiarities of the Swiss, with Mesmer's magnetism. Lavater's physiognomy, etc. One of my companions, whose national pride was wounded, begged me to make some reply, particularly to a handsome young man opposite to me, and who allowed himself extraordinary license. This man's life was at that moment presented to my mind. I asked him whether he would answer me candidly if I related to him some of the most secret passages of his life, I knowing as little of him personally as he did of me? That would be going a little further than Lavater did with his physiognomy He promised, if I were correct, to admit it frankly. I then related what my vision had shown, and the whole company were made acquainted with the private history of the young merchant; his school-years, his youthful errors, and lastly, with a fault committed in reference to the strong-box of his principal. I described to him the uninhabited room with whitened walls, where, to the right of the brown door, on a table, stood a black money-box, etc. A dead silence prevailed during the narrative, which I alone occasionally interrupted by inquiring whether I spoke the truth? The young man confirmed every particular. Touched by his candor, I shook hands with him, and said no more."

The Provost Marshal of Pithiviers, while playing cards with some friends, suddenly paused in the game, at 4 o'clock P. M.; he appeared to be abstracted for a moment, and then exclaimed, "The King is just murdered!" On the same afternoon—in the village of Patay, near Orleans—a young girl, of some fourteen years, named Simonne, inquired of her father who the King was? On being answered that he was the chief person in France, whom the people were all bound to obey, the child exclaimed, "Good gracious! that man has just been slain!" Pithiviers and Orleans are at a distance of several hundred miles from the scene of the tragic occurrence.[1] D'Aubigné (Memoirs Collection de Panthéon, p. 513) speaks of a man, in his service, who exhibited the same faculty in an eminent degree. He could communicate, respecting any stranger, the particulars of his birth-place, family connections, situation in life, and his thoughts at the time. He reported what Henry IV. of France was doing

---

[1] Richelieu Memoirs Collection Michaud Ponjoulat, Second Series, Vol. VII., p. 22. Perty's Mystical Revelations of Human Nature.

on a particular day and hour ; named the persons in his suite and company ; and he also announced the time and manner of the King's death before it occurred.[1]

Dr. Garcia had a patient, by the name of Michael, who could induce the magnetic sleep *ad libitum*. As often as some absent person was named, Michael would give a very accurate description of both the person and character. His vision extended to foreign countries, and embraced persons and their actions, together with other objects and their relations. On one occasion he was directed to visit a certain Castle, and to report his discoveries. The hour was ten o'clock, P. M., when he saw four persons playing cards, and he gave a full description of their persons and vestments. In like manner he also witnessed the storming of Constantine, in Algiers, and announced the death of General Damremont, who fell in the first breach. In the year 1833, he gave a full and graphic account of the loss of the ship Lilloise, and so real was the scene that at the moment he appeared to suffer from intense cold, and to experience all the hardships to which the crew were subjected, and as they were subsequently reported by the actual sufferers.[2] (Idem, p. 583.) Debay, in his " Mysteries of the Magnetic Sleep,"

---

[1] See Perty's Mystical Revelations of Human Nature, p. 583.

[2] A similar case occurred some years since in presence of the writer, Mrs. Harriet Porter, witnessing in a vision the destruction of a steamboat on the Hudson river. While seated in her room at Bridgeport, Connecticut, she declared that the steamer Henry Clay was on fire ; and that, with the other objects presented, she could distinctly see the village of Yonkers. The sad catastrophe was described at length as if it were occurring in the immediate presence of the Seeress. The next morning the New York papers contained the particulars of that disaster, from which it appeared that her description of the thrilling scene and the actual occurrence were— in respect to the essential facts and the precise time—in strict coincidence.

page 61, mentions the clairvoyant vision of Mrs. De Saulce. The lady was in the midst of a great assembly of the fashionable world, in the city of Paris, when she suddenly fell back in her chair, with the exclamation, " My God, Mr. De Saulce [her husband] is dead!" The terrible reality of her vision was soon confirmed by information through the ordinary channels, Mr. De Saulce having been killed at that time by the negroes in Saint Domingo. (Idem, p. 584.)

An interesting clairvoyant revelation was made in Scotland on the 17th day of February, 1851. Letters written by Captain Austin and Sir John Franklin were placed in the hands of a Lady, who was at the time magnetically entranced. On being questioned concerning the respective positions and circumstances of those Arctic explorers, she stated that Captain Austin was at that hour in longitude 95° 45′ west; that Sir John Franklin was, at the same time, in longitude 101° 45′, or about four hundred miles from the former, in a westerly direction; that the latter had been previously relieved, and that the relief ship and his two vessels were fast in the ice. These statements were noticed at the time in several foreign journals, and they also appeared in a work by the late Dr. Gregory, of the University of Edinburg, where they will be found on page 306 of the American edition. The book was published long before the return of Captain Austin's Expedition. The revelations of this Scotch Seeress were at length confirmed by the most positive evidence. In the London *Times*, of the date of September 12th, Captain Austin's report will be found *in extenso*, from which it appears, that from the 14th of February, 1851, until after the 18th of that month, he was confined in the ice between Cape

25

Martyr and Griffith Island. By referring to Johnson's Map of the Arctic Zones, it will be perceived that the place named in the Captain's report is in longitude 95° 45' west from Greenwich.[1]

Alexis claims attention as, perhaps, the most distinguished magnetic sleeper and Seer in Europe. For several years he has entertained the curious and astonished the savans by the illustrations of his Clairvoyance. With thick masses of cotton bound over his eyes, so as to preclude the possibility of his seeing in the ordinary way, he plays various games with experts, and usually wins. The Paris correspondent of our *Daily Times*, in 1853, had an interview with Alexis, at an American saloon in Paris. In this particular case the proofs of a clear and independent sight were so numerous and convincing that the skepticism of several gentlemen gave way to rational convictions. A brief extract will suffice to indicate the nature of the phenomena on that occasion :

"Alexis played a game of *ecarte* with a gentleman from Orleans, and won it. He picked up the tricks with a rapidity that showed how clearly he knew the position of the cards upon the table. Keeping those dealt to him in his left hand, he held the card he meant to play in his right, and never once changed it upon the play of his partner. He knew his adversary's hand as well as he knew his own. I may add, that the cards used were bought at a grocer's half an hour before, by myself, and that any suspicion of prepared cards would be completely idle and absurd. . . . Mr. Goodrich, who was an unbeliever, had brought from his office a letter, hidden in the corner of half a dozen envelopes, and the nature of whose contents no one knew but himself. He was willing to believe, if Alexis read the signature. After slight hesitation, and one error, in the first letter, *he did read it.* He

---

[1] The New York *Evening Post* noticed and published the clairvoyant statement, at the time it appeared. with the sanction of Dr. Gregory, and likewise its confirmation by Captain Austin's report, as published in the *Times.*

took a pencil and paper and wrote—*Victor D g--*. He then exclaimed, without finishing the word, 'C'est Victor Hugo!' The envelopes were then opened, the letter was unfolded, and the signature, Victor Hugo, was certainly at the bottom of it. The H much resembled a D, and Alexis had taken it for one, until the sight of the remaining letters caused him to look back and correct the error."

The *Times'* correspondent gave several other illustrative examples of the clairvoyance of Alexis. When a daguerreotype of Hudson's bust of WASHINGTON—inclosed in a morocco case—was placed before him, he commenced to write the name; but, without finishing it, he seized a book on America, which he had been reading, and—turning over the leaves rapidly—pointed to an engraved portrait of WASHINGTON, and said, with emphasis, " *That's it ; the engraving and daguerreotype are one and the same.*" When requested to point out the best pianist in the room, several gentlemen present extended their hands to him, but each in turn was rejected. When left to make his choice, he seized the hand of M. JULES COHEN, a young man not eighteen years of age, who had won four first prizes at the Conservatoire, and was really the best pianist of his age in Europe.

Mrs. Semantha Mettler, of Hartford, Conn., has long exercised her clairvoyant powers in discovering the immediate and remote causes of disease, its organic relations—noting, at any distance, its essential character and its phenomenal aspects –and in selecting from the great pharmacopœia of Nature the appropriate remedies for her patients. During a period of fifteen years she has been constantly before the public, in a professional capacity, and her diagnoses – made in the course of her daily transfigurations – amount to more than 40,000 in number. In numerous instances the repre-

sentatives of accredited science have been put to shame by
Mrs. Mettler's disclosures respecting the original cause, the
particular seat, the precise nature, and the ultimate result of
a disease, when these were previously all unknown by the
afflicted parties, and not to be detected by ordinary professional sagacity. But of her labors let those speak to whom
she has been a minister of hope, and health and life.

Dr. T. Lea Smith, of Hamilton, Bermuda, in his account
of an interview with Mrs. M., which occurred in Hartford,
in the year 1853, declares that she gave accurate, general,
and precise descriptions of objects in and around his Island
home. Among other things, she discovered a plant that
grows in great abundance in that Island—which the Doctor
had previously regarded as a useless weed—and assured him
that it would cure the yellow fever. In a letter written at
Hamilton, under date of Oct. 29th, 1856, Dr. Smith says:
" During the last three months the fever has been making
sad havoc in Bermuda, and we know not where it will stop;
it is very bad among the troops ; but I am happy to say
that, *out of two hundred cases, treated by Mrs. Mettler's prescription, only four have died !"* The Doctor mentions—
as occuring at a previous interview—another singular illustration of the powers of the Seeress. While in the magnetic
trance, at Hartford, she visited the Island, went to the Ceme-
tery at Hamilton, and *read an inscription on a tombstone!*

The writer could easily fill a volume of facts illustrative
of the Clairvoyance of Mrs. Mettler, but a brief digest of a •
few well-authenticated facts must suffice in this connection.
Mrs. William B. Hodget, of Springfield, Mass., had extreme
pain and inflammation in one of her limbs. Mrs. M. made

an examination at the distance of twenty-four miles, and discovered a fine cambric needle concealed in the flesh. This
staggered the faith of Mr. Hodget, and the family Physician
was equally skeptical on the point of the needle ; but, to
remove all doubts, he applied his lancet, when the needle
was discovered and removed. Mrs. K. H. Smith, of Ravens-
wood, L. I., was treated by her physician for dropsy. The
symptoms did not subside under professional treatment, and
the attention of the Seeress was called to the case. Mrs.
Mettler at once discovered that she was *enceinte*, and that
the difficulty which her physician had regarded as incurable
would—in the natural course of things—be entirely removed
in about three months. The family Physician treated the
revelations of the Clairvoyant with unmeasured derision and
contempt. As often as his professional visits were repeated,
he made himself merry at the expense of the Seeress and her
dupes. However, at the expiration of three months, the doctor was one day startled and amazed at witnessing the unexpected recovery of his patient, whose sudden restoration
added another " little responsibility to the Smith family!

In the autumn of 1855, Mr. Charles Barker, of Jackson,
Michigan, while out on a hunting excursion with a neighboring youth, was accidentally shot by his companion. The
charge passed through the pocket of his pantaloons, shiver-
ing his knife, trunk key, etc., and together with a portion
of the contents of his pocket, was deeply buried in the fleshy
part of his thigh. This unfortunate occurrence occasioned
extreme suffering and close confinement for several months.
At the time of the writer's visit to Jackson, in the succeeding January, his continued pain, extreme debility, and in-

creasing emaciation, awakened in the minds of his friends intense anxiety for his safety. On my return from the West I took an early opportunity to submit this distressing case to the clairvoyant inspection of Mrs. Mettler, merely telling her that she was requested to examine a young man who had been shot. There was no intimation respecting the circumstances attending the accident, the seat, or the extent of the injury ; nor was the existing condition of the young man in any way implied or referred to. In the course of the investigation and diagnosis—conducted at Hartford, while the patient was in Central Michigan—Mrs. M. discovered *a piece of copper* in the limb, and observed that the wound would not heal until it was removed. But young Barker was sure that he had no copper in his pocket at the time of the accident ; and, inasmuch as the medical attendant had made no such discovery, it was presumed that the Seeress was mistaken. But some time after the foreign substance described became visible, when Mr. Barker's mother—with a pair of embroidery scissors—removed *a penny* from the wound ! In such a case science is a stupid, sightless guide, and must stand out of the way. The doctors in Michigan could not see that penny when it was within their reach, and their eyes were wide open ; but this Seeress discovered it at a distance of nearly 1,000 miles with her eyes closed !

I will here introduce but two additional illustrations of Mrs. Mettler's clear sight. The names of the parties in both cases are withheld for reasons which the mind of the reader will readily suggest An Editor of a widely circulated journal, published in New York city, one day called on Mrs. M. at her residence. In the course of a brief *séance*, the clairvoyant—without so much as a suggestion from the gentleman—went to visit his wife, who was then in Bridgeport, over fifty miles from the scene of this interview. The general physical condition of the lady was accurately described; but one particular statement occasioned no little surprise, and at the time it was supposed to be incorrect. The clairvoyant alleged that Mrs. —— was *enceinte*, and that the case involved something abnormal. It appeared to her that there was *a malformation;* but it was observed that at that early period of utero-gestation she could not discern clearly the nature of the difficulty. Our editorial friend did not disclose this singular piece of information. Seven months after, having occasion to visit Hartford, he again called on the Seeress, who (being in the trance) informed him that she could then perceive the precise nature of the case, which had been but obscurely foreshadowed in the former diagnosis. She then proceeded to make some very definite statements, the following points being distinctly affirmed, namely, ' There was a plural conception ;' ' the vital forces have been insufficient to develop the two forms ;' ' the organic structure of one is altogether incomplete, though its weight may be some five pounds ;' ' the other is perfect in organization and beautifully developed ;' ' it is a boy, and will weigh about nine pounds.' Four weeks after the date of this interview, the accoucheur was sent for, when, strange to say, *the foregoing statement of the clairvoyant was, in every particular, verified by the facts.* The writer's authorities in this case are, the gentleman himself and the attendant physician.[1]

---

[1] In the Life of General Charles James Napier is the record of a singular incident in the experience of General Fox, who accompanied the Duke of

In the year 185–, a gentleman, whose home is in "the land of steady habits," had an interview with Mrs. Mettler —while she was entranced—which resulted in singular and important disclosures. He was told that his young wife— who was distinguished for remarkable personal beauty—was engaged in an intrigue with another man. The clairvoyant described a certain letter just received, and which the husband might find by going to her trunk ; and it was further observed that the letter would probably be answered in the afternoon of that day. On leaving the rooms of Mrs. M., the gentleman went immediately home and to his wife's trunk ; and finding the identical letter, he at once resolved to intercept the reply. At 3 o'clock, P. M., the answer was deposited in the Post-office, and by a previous arrangement with one of the clerks, it fell into the hands of the injured husband. The clairvoyant subsequently disclosed the intentions of the false fair one, pointed out the places where she would meet her inamorato, and likewise mentioned the fact that the wife was purchasing goods on her husband's account preparatory to leaving him forever. All these statements were fully confirmed by persons employed to observe her movements. Very soon the husband had in his possession abundant evidence of the infidelity of his wife to her mar-

York to Flanders. Soon after the General's departure his wife was confined. He was absent more than two years ; and, during that period, Mrs. Fox changed her residence and the child died. The father never saw the little one in the flesh ; but, becoming clairvoyant one night, he had a distinct vision in which the room occupied, the furniture and the child, were all clearly revealed. He also mentioned the day and hour of the child's death. On his return he was introduced into a room in which he had never been before, whereupon he immediately identified all the objects in the apartment, including a picture of his child.

riage vows, including several letters written by the beautiful amorette herself, and containing unmistakable proofs of her amours. Founding his claim on the evidence thus elicited, he applied for and readily obtained a bill of divorce without the trouble of going to Indiana.

The world is perpetually changing in its more superficial aspects, but the inherent principles of matter and the essential laws of mind operate with unvarying precision. Nature, like a vast kaleidoscope, shows new forms and combinations with every movement of the elements, but the superstructure remains, matter is indestructible, and life immortal. The fundamental principles of Nature and the laws that regulate the economy of human existence, are the same in all ages and countries; but certain periods and particular localities may be especially favorable to their high and orderly development. The ancient Prophets found the pure air and the solemn silence of the most elevated regions conducive to the highest moral states and spiritual attainments. Accordingly, they erected altars on the summits of mountains, and Jesus of Nazareth consecrated the hills that overlooked Jerusalem, alike by his frequent visits and his most impressive teachings.

There is something in the atmosphere of certain mountainous districts that is favorable to inward growth and a peculiar mental illumination. This is true in respect to portions of Germany, Denmark and Switzerland,[1] and the gift of second sight, or clairvoyance, has long distinguished the

---

[1] The Swiss have a tradition that the patriot William Tell and the founders of the Helvetic Confederation sleep together in a cave, near Lake Lucerne; and that when their country is imperiled, they will awake to assert the rights and defend the liberties of the people.

Scotch Highlanders. Even the superstitions of the ignorant; the wild legends of the country, and all the incongruous elements and supernatural powers of a fanciful Spiritualism, absurd as they may appear in the light of a rational philosophy, nevertheless clearly indicate the tendency of the common mind to a recognition of the psychical faculties and relations of human nature. If in the polytheistic features and ordinary details of the manifestation of this spiritual element in the Highland life and character, there is much that is imaginary and false, there is also much that is deeply suggestive and essentially true. Those who dwell among the mountains, not only possess vital and muscular strength but often that clearness of perception which enables them to interpret the mysteries of Nature by the light of the Soul. The lake region of Scotland is full of the elements of poetic imagery and devout suggestion. The green banks of

" Wooded Windermere, the river-lake,"

and that enchanting spot known as Belle Isle, with its sweet home in the midst, appearing to the distant observer like

"A Grecian temple rising from the deep;"

the lofty peaks that point heavenward to the hight of two thousand feet; the ruins of old castles and Druidical temples, with historic associations that stir the blood or solemnize the mind; the strange legends of the wood and the flood; the habitations of great poets and the sacred memorials of their genius—these all contribute to exalt the mind and to spiritualize the faculties. There is enchantment in every scene and inspiration in the very atmosphere. Mrs.

Hemans must have felt the subtile magnetism of Nature, and realized the presence of the invisible " powers of the air," when she sung thus of the sweet Vale of Grasmere :

" O vale and lake, within your mountain urn,
  Smiling so tranquilly, and set so deep !
Oft doth your dreamy loveliness return,
  Coloring the tender shadows of my sleep
  With light Elysian ; for the hues that steep
Your shores in melting luster, seem to float
On golden clouds from Spirit-lands, remote
Isles of the blest ; and in our memory keep
Their place with holiest harmonics. Fair scene,
Most loved by evening and her dewy star !
Oh ! ne'er may man, with touch unhallow'd, jar
The perfect music of the charm serene !
Still, still unchanged, may *one* sweet region wear
Smiles that subdue the soul to love, and tears and prayer !'

The examples presented in illustration of this part of my subject are altogether sufficient to place the cardinal fact of Clairvoyance among the demonstrated realties of human experience. Hereafter we may as well doubt the existence of the sense of vision itself as to dispute the proofs of this super-exalted power of perception. The facts are profoundly suggestive. Their relation to man's spiritual nature and the great question of our immortality, will be considered hereafter. While they demonstrate the development—in many persons—of this amazing power of vision, they also as clearly prove that the physical organs are, at the same time, utterly useless. The strongest light does not produce the slightest effect on the optic nerve, while the objects inspected are as clearly discovered through solid walls and in midnight darkness, as if they were surrounded on all sides by the impalpable ether, made transparent by the complete illumination and unclouded glory of noonday.

But it is often objected that the results of this extraordinary exercise or function of the sense of sight, can not be depended upon ; that if such a power really exists, it is wholly unreliable. This assumption indicates but a superficial investigation of the subject, and a disposition to form very hasty conclusions. Clairvoyance means *clear vision*, and clear sight *is* reliable ; for a distinct perception of any object, event or circumstance, must qualify the party, who perceives its existence or occurrence, to speak with confidence. Common observers are deceived, not because Clairvoyance is a lying oracle ; but the truth is, *their own imperfect acquaintance with the subject does not enable them to determine infallibly when and where this power exists, and the precise limits of the sphere in which it is operative.*

The field of vision, though more or less extended in different persons, and otherwise limited or enlarged by individual idiosyncrasies, may possibly comprehend, in the totality of its exercise, all persons, objects, events and circumstances, whether within the range of ordinary perception and investigation, or beyond the utmost reach of the senses in their normal exercise. Among the things revealed by the Clairvoyant are the subtile powers and the supra-mortal personalities of the invisible life and world. The old Prophet and his servant beheld the shadowy hosts that peopled the ethereal regions—whose presence was as an impenetrable shield or wall of fire between them and their enemies ; the Woman of Endor saw and described Samuel ; Moses and Elias were visible to the disciples who witnessed the transfiguration; Jesus, by this power of interior perception, 'knew what was in man'; heaven was opened to Peter, and Paul saw things of which it was not lawful for him to speak.

Now it is worthy of remark that the Seers of other countries and other times have asserted their claims to the possession and exercise of the same faculty. This is true in respect to several of the clairvoyants named in the preceding classification. Swedenborg was one day walking along Cheapside with a friend, when he suddenly bowed very low. On being interrogated, he affirmed that 'he saw Moses pass by.' Moreover, he claimed to have been intromitted to the heavens, and that he perceived the states of men after death. The pious Frederica Hauffé professed to see the inhabitants of the other world. The Rev. William Tennent, of New Jersey—a Presbyterian divine, who for ten days was in a trance resembling the *post mortem* state—seems, like Paul, to have been 'caught up into heaven.' Like the Apostle, he was little disposed to converse respecting his vision of the eternal world; but it is certain that the influence of that experience on the mind and character of the man continued until the close of his life on earth. In fact most of the persons who really have possessed the inward vision, have asserted the same claims with the utmost confidence and apparently with great sincerity.[1]

---

[1] So generally do the Magnetic Seers of the present time set up this claim, that in the "Secrets of the Life to Come, Revealed through Magnetism," the author, L. ALPH. CAHAGNET, affirms that "the existence, the form, and the occupations, of the Soul after its separation from the body, are proved by many years' experiments, by the means of Eight Ecstatic Somnambulists, who had eighty perceptions of thirty-six deceased persons of various conditions;" and whose aspects, characters, and conversations are described and recorded in his curious book.

Now what is the rational presumption in view of these
extraordinary facts and claims? The author is neither
inclined to blind credulity nor an unreasoning skepticism.
The philosophical inquirer will scarcely be disposed to dogmatize on a point of this nature, and he certainly will not
dispute the testimony of so many conscientious witnesses.
If, when a witness testifies to several facts, we can and do
readily demonstrate the reliability of his perception, and
his fidelity to truth, in all of the facts but one, it will not
be denied that the logical inference is in favor of the acceptance of his testimony in respect to the remaining fact, which
does not admit of such demonstration. Such is the state of
facts and the nature of the evidence in the case under review. When the Seer describes unknown persons, foreign
countries, invisible objects and remote events; reads sealed
letters, perceives the properties of different substances, discovers the thoughts of men, unveils the forgotten past and
penetrates into the unkown future of this world, we are able
to verify his statements. In respect to all these, we have
found Clairvoyance to be a strictly reliable witness; and it
now remains for us to either accept or reject such testimony
—respecting the higher realities of the Inward Life—as the
spirit of a rational faith and the dicta of a scientific philosophy may determine.

In the selection of facts I have been confined to no particular nation or period in human history. Moreover, the
examples are sufficiently diversified to illustrate the several
degrees and phases of Clairvoyance; and they certainly
warrant the conclusion that this power is essentially the
same in all ages and countries. Now, if we are to credit

the ancient Hebrew Seers, when they profess to look into the invisible world, every principle of justice and rule of logic demand that we should respect the legitimate claims of the Seers of other nations and of modern times. Natural sight was the same in the Madonna and the Magdalen, in the chief Apostle and the vilest apostate. In like manner, Clairvoyance, or the vision of the Seer, is one and the same, whether exercised by an ancient Jew or a modern Gentile; by a canonized saint or a common sinner; by a Pagan, Mohammedan or Christian. Will it be said that this superior power of perception is a divine faculty when displayed by an Apostle and that it becomes a profane endowment, or at best a worthless gift when in the possession of a heretic or an infidel? Such arbitrary distinctions are not founded on any fundamental difference in the nature of the facts, and they can only be supported by the arrogant assumptions of pretended philosophers and theological dogmatists.

It is not strange that scientific investigation so often leads to skepticism, since the *savans* confine themselves to their material methods, and insist on using only such tests as are applicable in the department of physics. Everything must be weighed and measured, dissected or put in a crucible. The presence of the Soul can not be determined by such means. Perhaps it will not turn the balance; it can not be mutilated by the scalpel, confined in a retort, or fused in the fire; hence our modern masters are skeptical respecting the existence of the Soul. Indeed, nothing can more clearly illustrate the materialism of the age, than the prevalent disposition to ascribe all psychical phenomena to a disordered action of the bodily organs. This is especially true in respect to the schools ; and so great is the ignorance on this subject that our *soi disant* philosophers, and even some accredited authorities in modern science, are unable to distinguish between a vision of heaven and an attack of nightmare! The somnambulist is generally presumed to be a sick man ; the illuminated Seer is treated as *a patient ;* and all those powers that indicate, in their development, the supremacy of the spirit over the flesh, are regarded as evidences of vital or mental derangement—except such as are comprehended in the experience of the ancient Jews and early Christians. This is virtually presuming that the perfection of the individual, and his accord with Nature, are best realized when his powers of perception are blunted by the influence of a material philosophy and a sensuous life ; and he is unconscious of the slightest possible illumination from super-terrestial sources.

" Angels and ministers of grace, defend us"

from the titled empiricism that would lead the world to such gross and infidel issues! Truly, the depths of apostacy are sounded, and Reason is immolated by those learned men (?) who thus include the highest developments of the soul and the physical maladies of the body in the same category !

The schools are prone to be delving among the fossil remains of dead and forgotten things ; but when we invite them to investigate the most significant phenomena that spring from the relations of the soul and the body, they seem inclined to regard the whole subject as beyond the proper domain of science. True, the remarkable experiences of the Jews are ostensibly accepted as intrinsically probable ; but modern facts of analogous character, and obviously depending on the same general laws, are ungraciously rejected. But no candid man will profess to pursue the scientific method in his investigations, while he thus makes an arbitrary distinction in favor of one particular nation, over all the men of every age and country who have witnessed the occurrence of similar facts. This course is utterly hostile to the true spirit of scientific investigation. Science knows no such distinctions; and the philosopher has no right to recognize any, except such as grow out of, and necessarily depend on, existing natural differences.

If there is anything sacred in the Scriptural illustrations of my subject, it surely is not in the languages that served to record the experiences of Prophets, and Apostles, and Seers. Verily the divine benefaction is not to be sought and found in Hebrew and Greek manuscripts—neither in chemical elements nor chirographical characters. But it was, and it is, in the great mental and moral illumination that renders an existence of poverty glorious, and life a sublime achievement, even when its termination is the death of the cross. If the same faculty still exists and is exercised among men, has it no longer a claim to our respectful consideration? If the power to penetrate the unseen and to discern what is in man, was once a divine gift, who shall say that it has become a profane juggle? Yet such is the inconsistency of poor human nature, that multitudes—who cherish the simple history of Elisha's clairvoyance, as a Divine communication and a priceless inheritance—would not so much as cross the street to witness the most impressive revelations of the same power. They speak of the old Prophets with voices modulated by the deepest reverence,

while they may regard the living Seer, either as a fool or a
knave, a lunatic, or at best as the victim of some strange
hallucination.

But I must respect the Seer as an interpreter of Nature,
commissioned to stand in the inner courts of the temple,
and to unfold the Divine mysteries. Through the forms of
things, he yet discerns their hidden properties; he uncovers
the minds of men, and looks into the vital precincts of all
living things ; he reverently removes the shroud from the
buried nations, and speaks for such as have no voice. The
distance of time is not required to invest his office with an
air of enchantment. I shall not wait for his apotheosis ; I
will not consider the remote probabilities of his being canonized ; it is sufficient that I have examined his credentials.
Others may suspend judgment, if they will, until the dust of
centuries has silently settled over his forgotten grave ; but
I will recognize the divinity of his mission now. He stands
beneath the Sun-circle of the Universe ; and his function is
solemn and sublime as when the heavens opened to his
enraptured vision above the mountains of Judea. He still
holds the golden key to the penetralia of the Future ; and
while men sleep he lifts the great veil from off the face
of the World, that " the invisible things of God" may be
clearly seen in the light of his recognized presence.

> " O, thought ineffable ! O, vision blest ;
>   Though worthless our conceptions all of Thee,
>   Yet shall thy shadowed image fill each breast,
>   And waft its homage to thy Deity.
> God : thus above my lonely thoughts can soar ;
>   Thus seek thy presence. Being wise and good !
> 'Midst thy vast works admire, obey, adore !
> And when the tongue is eloquent no more.
>   The soul shall speak in songs of gratitude.''

CHAPTER XXXI.

THE LAW OF PROPHECY.

Material tendencies of Science—Influence of Literature and the Elegant Arts—Premonitions, a phase of Prophetic Inspiration—Reference to Sir Walter Scott—The prophetic element in Poetry—Wordsworth and Campbell - Death of Governor Marcy—His Daughter's Premonition—Hon. N. P. Tallmadge, and the accident on the U. S. War Steamer Princeton— Miss M— and the Officer in the Peninsular Campaign—Loss of the Arctic —Prophetic Intimations to Five Persons—Life saved by a Premonition at the Norwalk Railroad Disaster—Prophecy of the Burning of the Henry Clay—Mrs. Swisshelm's Report of Dr Wilson's Prophecies—Death of the Emperor Nicholas predicted three months before it occurred—Jaspers, the Westphalian Shepherd—Letter to President Taylor concerning ancient Peruvian Prophecies—Goethe's Experience—Prophecy of Cardiere, from the Life of Michael Angelo—Remarkable Prophecies by Roger Bacon— Inspiration, Heroic Achievements, and Martyrdom of the Shepherdess of Lorraine—Exposition of the Law of Prophecy.

> " There is no doubt that there exist such voices,
> Yet I will not call them
> Voices of warning that announce to us
> Only the inevitable.   As the sun,
> Ere it be risen, sometimes paints its image
> In the atmosphere ; so often do the spirits
> Of great events stride on before the events ;
> And in to-day already walks to-morrow."—COLERIDGE.

SCIENCE has enabled us to determine the superficial dimensions of the earth ; to read its history in its several strata ; to analyze its rocks and earths ; to estimate its solid contents, and to ascertain the direction and velocity of its movements ; to weigh its atmosphere and measure its waters ; to classify the vegetables and animals on its surface, and to divide men into distinct races. But what has accredited science done to unveil the subtile agents employed by the

Creator as the proximate causes of these elemental changes and organic formations? Which of the material philosophers has traced the mysterious forces of gravitation, chemical affinity, and molecular attraction to their invisible sources? What man has followed the occult powers to their ultimate hiding-places, and wrung from great Nature the secret whereby she conducts her stupendous operations? How far has science disclosed the laws that individualize life and regulate the functions of organized existence? Has any physiologist been fully conscious of the intimate relations of mental to vital motion as exhibited in Man? Where shall we find the man—in all the crowds that frequent the halls of science—who has solved the problem of animal sensation and instinct, and of human consciousness and reason? Who has fully explained the philosophy of thought and the divine mystery of love? It must be confessed that the most distinguished votaries of science have shed no ray of light on the inmost nature and relations of Man. The soul has never ceased to press certain grave questions concerning the indestructibility of its constitution, its undeveloped powers, and its immortal destiny; but in respect to all these, Science has been dumb as a Pagan idol, and the dead are not so voiceless as those who wear her insignia to-day.

The materialism of science was scarcely more apparent in the earliest stages of its development. We know something of the properties and uses of the simple elements, and of the results of their various combinations; but comparatively little respecting the nature and capabilities of the imponderable agents. The schools have accomplished little more than a classification of mere physical forms and phenomena, and the elaboration of their technical disquisitions on whatever is least vital and significant. Thus human science and human minds have been materialized together, and it is now quite frequently acknowledged that great scientific attainments are unfavorable to religion ; that philosophy and faith are incompatible ; and that the study of Nature leads the soul away from God. But this results from the superficial nature of our knowledge. Lord Bacon observed that a shallow philosophy, comprehending only the surface of things and the operation of second causes, led men into Atheism ; but that a profound philosophy must lead the wandering soul back to repose on the bosom of the Infinite. The man who confines his observations to what is merely external and apparent can not rationally expect to comprehend the essential constitution and internal reality of being. He may survey the surface of things and look at the outside of the world forever, and not satisfy his mind respecting the vital principles of existence, just as a hungry man might examine the shell of an oyster with the utmost care, and yet derive neither knowledge nor nourishment from what it contains. If then the influence of modern science has not made men more devout, in a rational and true sense, it is because our science has been essentially external and material. But those who have ventured to break away from the arbitrary restraints of the schools, regardless of the limits prescribed by the accepted authorities—who have dared to explore the Unseen and to question the Infinite—have been rendered reverent by study.

In proposing to accompany my classification of facts with philosophical suggestions on the subject of Prophecy, I may be regarded as a profane adventurer by those who view the whole field as forbidden ground. So long have men been taught that the exercise of reason, on subjects of this nature, is hostile to Religion and dangerous to the soul, that few have felt authorized to pursue their inquiries on rational grounds. Hence doubt and irresolution have characterized the attempts to unveil the ethereal mysteries, and each step toward the Invisible has been taken with fear and trembling. Whatever is beyond the limits already defined by the acknowledged masters in Philosophy, Morals and Religion, is treated with as much caution and reserve as if it were a magazine of thunderbolts, or a Pandora's box charged with the elements of the soul's destruction.

But we can not sympathize with those craven souls, whose fears have been their counsellors ; nor can we abandon the investigation because the subject is presumed to be far beyond the reach of our finite powers. They are feeble or indolent beings who will not reverently scan the Creator's works and read the record of his word in all things. The subject is neither above human comprehension nor beyond the proper domain of science. If we fail, it is not because success is impossible, but rather for the reason that we question the ultimate designs of Providence, and have formed no just estimate of the sublime possibilities of human nature. The man of large faith and strong determination seldom fails, while the weak and irresolute rarely succeed. Thus we discover that

> " Our doubts are traitors,
> And make us lose the good we oft might win,
> By fearing to attempt."

The assumption that science must be forever confined to

physics, is too preposterous to merit a formal refutation. We are willing to indulge the instincts that prompt so many to dive and delve; but if others are impelled to rise—by virtue of a divine attraction, and the supreme law of their own affinities—into the higher departments of the Universe, there is no reason to question the wisdom of their choice. There are new and untrodden fields that must be explored; and the minds of this class—by their superior power of cognition—must discern our relations to those grand realities that open inward and upward from the plain of our common life. Surely the realm of divine principles and silent forces is subject to law, and characterized by a beautiful method and a sublime order. Those principles may be investigated; the laws of the inner life are disclosed to our spiritual consciousness, and the modes of the Divine procedure are revealed in Nature and in history. If then the faculties and susceptibilities of the human mind—in the higher sphere of its action—are regulated by fixed principles, it follows that psychical phenomena may be observed and classified, and the laws that govern them may be discovered and explained. Such a classification of actual facts and expositions of essential laws, constitute science. And thus, step by step—by the unerring line of a far-reaching induction—Science may ascend from the smallest particulars on earth to the grandest realities of Heaven; and at last—shaking the dust from her garments—be baptized in " the River of Life."

But while our scientific authorities have done but little to foster the religious sentiment, and much to encourage popular materialism, Literature, on the contrary, has, to a great

extent, conserved these elements in human nature and its
institutions. All nations have had their spiritual books;
and the spiritual idea-

" Like crystal streams that murmur through the meads"—

runs noislessly through a large portion of the best literature
of all countries, marking its silent progress, along every
walk of life, with perennial freshness and beauty, and. causing the moral wildernesses to bloom like Paradise.

The Elegant Arts have all been eloquent exponents of
divine ideas. They are beautiful ministers that wait in the
temples, and whose purest offerings have been laid on the
altars of Religion. Painting, Sculpture, Poetry, Music,
Oratory and Architecture, have all contributed to restrain
and refine the passions, and to furnish the most exalted
ideals for human contemplation. They have spiritualized
the popular thought and the common life of the world.
Painting presents impressive illustrations on the walls of
the Farnesian Palace and the Sistine Chapel, where Raphael
and Michael Angelo left their immortal creations in the
Banquet of the Gods and the Last Judgment. The hand of
the latter is never to be mistaken, and is visible in Riccia-
relli's Christ and the Women, in the.Descent from the Cross.
The feminine delicacy, exquisite pathos, and dramatic effect
combined in the Frescos and other works of Raphael; the
epic grandeur and profound solemnity of Angelo's vast conceptions; and the faultless harmony and mysterious spells
by which Correggio enchains the refined sense and enlightened soul, until it is entranced with " the soft emotions of a
delicious dream"—all, *all* attest the spiritual ministry of Art.

But Painting is not the only form of Art that is morally

influential. Greece gave the world marble revelations, in
the beautiful forms of her gods and goddesses ; the " frozen
music" of Architecture, performed in innumerable temples,
whose spires point upward to heaven ; ·the stately mauso-
læums of kings, and saints, and martyrs, and the enduring
memorials of all the illustrious dead, suggest the supreme
authority of our religious impressions and spiritual aspirations.   Making no particular references to the ordinary
poetry and music, employed in the private devotions and
public services of the church, we can only hint at the importance of the grandest illustrations of poetic and musical
inspiration.   In Poetry, we have the *Divina Commedia* of
Dante ; Milton's Paradise Lost and Regained, and the Golden
Age of Harris.   In Music, the *Laudi Spirituali* of the Flor-
entines ; the Ascension, by Bach, and the Death of Jesus, by
Graun ; Haydn's Creation, Handel's Messiah, and the Requiems of Mozart, Jomelli and Cherubine, are all significant
recognitions of the religious nature of man, or the dominion
of spiritual ideas in the developments of Genius and Art.

Before attempting to explain or even to suggest the Law
of Prophecy, it will be proper to examine such facts as may
best serve to illustrate the subject.   To discover the law we
must necessarily go to the theater of its operations.   Like
the perception of the seer, the gift of prophetic inspiration
is neither confined to a single nation nor restricted to particular periods in human history ; at the same time personal
habits and national conditions may either accelerate or restrain its development.   This surprising gift is exhibited in
several degrees, and in greater or less perfection in the same
individual, agreeably to the ever-varying states of mind, and

other circumstances that may influence the functions of his moral nature. The lowest degree of prophetic inspiration is widely manifested. It consists of a sudden and unaccountable impulse or feeling, often of apprehension, apparently causeless and generally undefinable. It is a vague shadow on the mind, and an imperfect consciousness that some event, of more than ordinary consequence, is about to transpire. The person thus impressed may neither have a distinct conception of the specific character of that event, nor be able to determine the precise time when it will occur. However, when the impression is strong, the inference that the impending event is near is inevitable, and its essential nature may be apprehended from the effects produced on the mind.

The phenomena referred to—as embracing the lowest phase of prophetic communication—are usually denominated *Premonitions;* and the psychology of common life is often illustrated by such impressive admonitions. The ambitious attempts of certain metaphysicians to dispose of the facts of this class, in a satisfactory manner, have been melancholy failures. The examples are very numerous and deeply suggestive. While the ignorant are generally prone to regard them as supernatural in their origin, the learned—with rare exceptions—have been disposed to set them aside as sensorial illusions, remarkable coincidences, or as the offspring of a prolific but distempered fancy. Sir Walter Scott could neither dispute the existence of such facts nor account for them on philosophical principles. He found the evidence of their reality in all history, and especially in the legends of his country and the fireside memories of his own people. The facts were more potent than any spell of popular skepticism, and hence the exorcisms of genius and learning were as powerless to conceal them as to prevent their occurrence. Indeed, if Scott's volumes on "Demonology and Witchcraft," illustrate one thing more clearly than another, it is the obvious truth, that many facts in human experience are of such a nature that material philosophers can neither comprehend nor explain them.

Wordsworth evidently believed that the spirit of prophecy was, and is, given to men in every age and country ; and that the inner avenues of perception may be opened, either by a process of natural development or by superterrestrial influence. In the preface to the "Excursion" he thus invokes the presence of the spirit :

> "Descend, prophetic spirit! that inspirest
> The human soul of universal earth,
> Dreaming of things to come ; and dost possess
> A metropolitan temple in the hearts
> Of mighty poets ; upon me bestow
> A gift of genuine *insight*."

This mysterious perception of coming events has been otherwise used as an element in poetry, of which we have an example in the interview between the Seer and the warlike Chief of the Camerons. The latter is on his way to join the standard of Charles Stuart, when he is met by the Seer who predicts his overthrow. Lochiel denounces him as a vile wizzard ; but the prophet is made to say—in the language of the Poet—that he can not hide the terrible vision of impending disaster :

> "For, dark and despairing, my sight I may seal,
> But man can not cover what God would reveal ;
> 'Tis the sunset of life gives me mystical lore,
> And coming events cast their shadows before."

The Seer proceeds, and the catastrophe is described. The

field and the conflict are before him, and as the Pretender and his legions fly in vision from the bloody scenes of Culloden. the Prophet invokes the 'wild tempests to rise and cover his flight,' as if the elements themselves were intelligent agents, or subject to the influence of "the prince of the power of the air."

It has already been observed that the phase of prophetic impression or inspiration, exhibited in premonitions, is not always such as distinctly reveals the precise nature of the coming event, though the general character and influence of the same may be clearly indicated. The facts of this class are innumerable, but for the purpose of the present elucidation, the subjoined examples are sufficient.

The daughter of the late Governor Marcy, of New York, spent the fourth of July, 18—, at the residence of a friend in Troy, a party of ladies and gentlemen being present. The company appeared to be in excellent spirits, Miss Marcy excepted, who early in the day exhibited unusual depression. Her apparent unhappiness was the subject of remark, and occasional inquiries respecting the cause of her dejection. In reply to the interrogatories of her friends, she expressed the apprehension that an extraordinary calamity had overtaken some member of the family. Early in the afternoon the news of the death of her father reached the city, and was communicated to some of the gentlemen who had been in the same company with Miss Marcy in the morning. While these gentlemen were in a room by themselves, deliberating on the proper manner of communicating the painful intelligence to the daughter, and before she could have received the least intimation of her bereavement through any ordinary channel, her grief became ungovernable, and covering her face with her handkerchief she retired from the apartment.

In 1844, Hon. N. P. Tallmadge was •one of a company, invited by Commodore Stockton to make an excursion down the Potomac on the United States War Steamer Princeton. The party included the President and members of the Cabinet, together with many other distinguished gentlemen and ladies. The Commodore proposed to signalize the occasion by firing his "Peace-maker"—a wrought-iron gun of large caliber. Accordingly, a portion of the company assembled upon the forward deck, Governor Tallmadge occupying a position at the breech of the gun. He felt no apprehension of danger ; and the first, second and third discharges were unaccompanied by any unpleasant results. The party then went below for refreshments. After dinner the Governor returned to the deck, when he observed that the great gun was about to be discharged for the fourth and last time. He at once assumed his former position. But the Commodore, President, and heads of the Executive Departments, were still below, and the firing was delayed for a few moments on their account. It was then that a mysterious feeling of apprehension and dread suddenly seized the Governor, and under an irresistible impulse he turned away and followed the ladies into the cabin. Immediately the report was heard, and the next moment came the startling and terrible intelligence that five distinguished gentlemen, including two members of the Cabinet, had been instantly killed by the last discharge. In his description of that frightful accident, Governor Tallmadge says: "I rushed on deck, saw the lifeless and mangled bodies, and found that the gun had burst at the very spot where I had stood at the three former fires, and where—if I had remained at the fourth fire—I should have been perfectly demolished.[1]"

Miss M—— had a pure and deep affection for a young officer who accompanied Sir John Moore in the Peninsular Campaign. Her knowledge of the fact that her lover was constantly exposed to danger visibly disturbed her mind and impaired her health. By degrees the color faded from her cheek, and gradually she resigned herself to the dominion of a settled melancholy. She felt a positive conviction when she parted from her lover that they would meet no more on earth. Her friends tried to comfort her, but were pained to witness the failure of every scheme to dissipate the shadows from her mind. One fearful thought haunted her night and day. Opulence was powerless to command relief. Music had lost its enchantment; and in the midst of the gay crowd she was solitary. The tide of impetuous life ; the glittering phantoms of the fashionable world ; the heraldry of beauty and bravery ; inspiring mirth and sparkling wit ; the voices of revelry and the words of prayer—all were powerless to recall her from her abstraction.

This young lady possessed the vision that is neither limited by distance nor obscured by darkness ; and one night—so she affirmed—her lover, wounded, pale and gory, entered her apartment ; and with the utmost gentleness informed her that he had fallen in battle. Others said that the phantom was the offspring of the anxious heart and the disordered imagination. But there was too much of reality in the vision

---

[1] Introduction to " The Healing of the Nations " by Hon. N. P. Tallmadge, formerly United States Senator from New York and Governor of Wisconsin.

and its consequences : for, under the pressure of the sorrowful conviction, the maiden died in a few days. It was not long after that her friends received intelligence that the officer had lost his life at the battle of Corunna, and but a few hours before the occurrence of the mysterious visitation.

The following instances of prophetic intimations of the same event all occurred, and were published in the New York papers, about the time of the loss of the Arctic. A lady who had intended to secure her passage on that steamer dreamed, two nights in succession, that the vessel had foundered at sea. Such was the impression on her mind that she persuaded several friends to change their purpose, and to take passage with her on the Baltic. Her dream, and the strange conviction it produced, were the subject of familiar conversation among the passengers, before anything had transpired to verify its painful suggestions.

A gentleman who had a relative on board the Arctic, went to the wharf, on the Sunday when she was due, and was surprised on finding Mr. E. K. Collins there. Mr. C. said he scarcely expected to find the steamer in, and explained the occasion of his presence by saying, that he had been made a little uneasy by dreaming that she was wrecked.

Three or four days before the news of the loss of the Arctic reached New York, a man entered the office of Mr. Collins, exhibiting great excitement. He declared that the Arctic was wrecked — that only thirty of her passengers were saved, and that among the lost was his brother.

Mr. George Smith, of the commercial house of Messrs. Leupp and Company, was one of the passengers who perished in the Arctic. On the third of October, six days after the disaster, and before the steamer could be considered over-due, a son of Mr. Smith died in New York. Some time before his dissolution the youth assured his relatives that his father had lost his life at sea, and that they would soon be convinced of the truth of his statement.

A gentleman, whose wife and daughter were in England, and designing to return in the Arctic, were warned by him in a letter not to take passage in that steamer, as he was apprehensive some accident would occur. But the ladies, having several friends who had secured state-rooms in that vessel, concluded to embark with them. The fact that the request of the husband and father had been disregarded weighed heavily on the wife's mind. She immediately began to experience the most painful forebodings, and was mysteriously impressed with the tolling of the alarm-bell, on Bell Buoy, in the Irish Channel. Both ladies were lost!

The writer was present to witness the melancholy wreck of human life that resulted from the great railroad accident at Norwalk, Connecticut. In that case the life of one person, at least, was saved by a timely premonition. A gentleman, who was occupying a seat at the forward end of one of the cars, was suddenly disturbed by an unaccountable apprehension of danger. So strong was the impression that he left his seat and walked back and seated himself at the other end of the car, after which he felt at ease. Immediately another man, on entering the car, took the seat he had resigned. In ten minutes the terrible catastrophe occurred, the locomotive and several of the cars being precipitated through the draw into the river. Strange to say, the train was so far arrested that only one half of the car, containing the persons referred to, projected over the draw. This car broke in two in the middle, the forward part going into the river, and the other portion remaining on the bridge. The gentleman who had been mysteriously admonished, escaped unharmed ; but when the mangled bodies were removed from the wreck, it was discovered that the man who occupied the abandoned seat was dead, a large splint from the side of the car having been driven directly through his brain.

But. there are other cases wherein the shadows of coming events assume more definite proportions, and instead of a blind impulse or feeling, unaccompanied by a mental conception, a distinct impression is made on the mind, which may admit of a precise description. In other words, the impending events—in their proper order, and in their relations to time, space, persons, institutions and circumstances—produce corresponding mental images, and these may be otherwise intelligibly expressed in language. The succeeding examples illustrate the superior phases of this prophetic inspiration.

The writer and several other persons were witnesses of a prophetic announcement of the destruction of the steamer Henry Clay, on the Hudson River, made by Mrs. Harriet Porter, at Bridgeport, Connecticut, on the 27th day of July, 1852—the day before that boat was actually burned. On the 28th, at about the hour of three o'clock, P. M., Mrs. Porter—being entranced in presence of several persons—again referred to the subject, and proceeded to describe the terrible catastrophe, which was then, as she affirmed, being enacted before her. She declared with great emphasis that a steamboat was burning on the Hudson; that she could see the name—HENRY CLAY; and that the village of Yonkers

27

was also distinctly visible. She appeared to be thrilled and terrified at the spectacle, and expressed the deepest anguish on account of the loss of so many lives. On the following morning the public journals contained the verification of all she had said, in the details of the mournful disaster, so mysteriously foreshadowed and so graphically portrayed at the very hour of the fatal occurrence.

Mrs. Swisshelm, in her public correspondence, records certain prophecies made by Rev. Dr. Wilson, who, in 1855, was settled in Alleghany City. Among the events predicted were the great fire of 1845 in Pittsburg; the Mexican war and its results: the war between Russia and the Western Powers, and the speedy limitation of the political power of the Pope. It may be very improper to recognize a prophet in Alleghany City, but it is worthy of remark that the events foretold have become history. Had this Professor of Theology lived two or three thousand years ago, and on the right side of the Ægean and Mediterranean seas, he would, doubtless, have enjoyed a fair reputation by this time. But Mr. Wilson is probably alive yet, and it is decreed by an ancient proverb, that a prophet may not hope to have honor " in his own country."

Mr. John F. Coles published in the New York *Daily Times*, of the date of December 3d, 1854, and more fully in the *Sunday Dispatch*, of December 10th, a prophecy of the death of the Emperor Nicholas. Having declared, on the night of the 29th of November, that in three months more — reckoning from that hour—the sudden death of a crowned head would astonish and bewilder the magnates of the Old World ; and having also compared the monarchies of Europe to a stupendous pyramid, which could be demolished by removing one stone at a time, the prophetic utterance—having reference to the Emperor—was thus continued :—" There is trouble brewing between Nicholas and Menschikoff. *Nicholas is the top stone of the European pyramid.* For thirty years he has lain quietly in his bed. The earth around the base is loosened—the top stone is already in motion." It is a fact that in just three months from the date of this prophecy —making the proper allowance for the difference of time between St. Petersburgh and New York—the late Emperor of Russia died, suddenly ; and the last public act of his life was the removal of Menschikoff from his command at Sebastopol, and the appointment of another General in his place. It will be perceived that these facts were published by the American press, three months before they were made known at St. Petersburg; and the principal fact the death of the Czar—ninety days before the event occurred.[1]

Among the German peasantry are many persons who have

---

[1] " There is something so pointed and direct of KOSSUTH as a prophet, that we cannot pass it by. I allude to the prophecy uttered in his speech at Glasgow. His spirit. yearning over prostrate, sorrowing nations broke forth in that speech. and he prophesied to England and the world. that the proud alliance armed against Russia could not triumph while its goal was but the propping of old despotisms, and not the freedom of enslaved peoples. He prophesied that the great fleets and armies would fail ; that the steppes of the Crimea would become the sepulchers of Briton and Frank ere victory should crown the lioned and eagled flags ; that of all the brave souls sent, up to that hour. from Albion's shore, to war to a false end not one in five would ever return. Many believed his words. and even the heart of throned power trembled at the prophecy ; but the alliance kept on its way. A few months have elapsed and every line of the prophecy is fulfilled The alliance is baffled — four out of five of · England's braves' have fallen ; eleven thousand widows, brooding over their semi-orphaned children and desolate homes, wail aloud in confirmation of the Prophet."—CARLOS D. STUART.

remarkable prescience, and the power to foresee events is
often possessed by those simple-hearted people. In 1850 a
collection of their prophecies was published in *Blackwood's
Magazine*. I can only cite a single example in this connection:

"A Westphalian shepherd, by the name of Jaspers, a sincere and devout
man, predicted in 1830—before the construction of the first English railway
—that just before his death 'a great road would be carried through the
country, from west to east, which will pass through the forest of Bodel-
schwing. On this road carriages will run without horses, and cause a
dreadful noise. At the commencement of this work, great scarcity will
prevail. . . Before this road is quite completed, a frightful war will
break out, in which a small Northern Power will be conqueror."

Jaspers has gone to dwell with the elder prophets in the
fold of the Good Shepherd; but his predictions have been
literally verified. The line of railway from Cologne to
Minden is through the district mentioned in the prophecy.
Before the road was finished the partial famine occurred,
and also the war, in which "a small Northern Power (Denmark) was conqueror."

Dr. Justo Sahaurauria, of the ancient Peruvian city of
Cuzco, who claimed—on what appeared to be convincing
evidence—to be a lineal descendant from Huaynaccapac, the
last reigning Inca, addressed a letter to President Taylor,
containing some curious facts illustrative of the prophetic
inspiration of the aboriginal Peruvians. A son of the venerable Doctor was burned alive in the plaza of Caxamorca,
by the Spanish conquerors of the country. I extract the
following from the letter to General Taylor, from which it
will appear that the royal and sacerdotal classes of that
peculiar people enjoyed the light of the prophetic spirit:

"When the Spaniards entered the Peruvian empire, they found in the principal temple of Cuzco various prophecies, and among them one which foretold the destruction of the empire, together with its rites and ceremonies ; and that this was to take place in the reign of the twelfth Emperor. When the Emperor Huaynaccapac was told by his vassals in Tumpis, that there had appeared on the coast certain canoe-like houses, the crews of which were composed of bearded men, he said that a tradition existed among the members of the royal family to the effect, that there should come from beyond the sea an unknown people who would destroy the empire its religion, rights and ceremonies, and that this was to take place in the reign of the twelfth Emperor ; and as he was the twelfth, the prediction was doubtless about to be fulfilled."

The prophetic impulse may be experienced long before the occurrence of the event, and it may also be accompanied by impressions made through the nerves of special sensation. I extract the following illustration of this kind from the Memoirs of the German poet, Gœthe :

" Notwithstanding the anxiety and extreme affliction I felt, I could not withstand the desire of seeing Frederica once more ; it was a cruel day to us, and its circumstances will never be effaced from my memory. When I had mounted my horse and offered my hand for the last time, I saw tears swimming in her eyes, and my heart suffered as much as hers. I proceeded along a path that leads to Drusenheim, when a strange vision, which must have been a presentiment, suddenly disturbed my mind I thought I saw my own image advancing toward me on horseback, in the same road. The figure wore a grey coat with gold lace, such as I had never worn. This singular illusion diverted my thoughts, for the time, from the grief of parting ; I felt my regret at quitting this fine country, and all that was lovely and beloved in it, gradually softened ; I roused myself at length from the extreme affliction in which this farewell day had plunged me, and I pursued my journey with greater serenity. It is singular enough that eight years after, as I was going to see Frederica once more, I found myself in the same road, dressed as I had dreamed—and wearing such a coat, accidentally, and without having chosen it "

The material philosophers would hastily dispose of this

case by saying that the figure resembling Gœthe was only an optical or spectral illusion, and that his subsequent return in the costume of the phantom was merely a circumstantial coincidence. This assertion is easily made, but it involves no explanation. Why the Poet's brain should, at that particular time, project an image of himself—in a dress he had never worn, and was not therefore likely to conceive of—is a question that finds no proper solution in a flippant and shallow assumption. Moreover, why such a vision should afford immediate relief from mental suffering, and restore a serene state of mind, does not appear from any suggestion derived from the illusion hypothesis. But if it be admitted that invisible, intelligent beings may have an interest in mundane affairs, and that they may establish psychological relations with the human mind on earth, so as to influence sensation, awaken emotions, and inspire thoughts, all similar mysteries may be readily and philosophically explained.

Cardiere, an improvisatore of remarkable ability, and a personal friend of Michael Angelo, was employed in the house of Piero, where he exercised his singular powers of improvisation by singing on festive and other occasions, with a lyre accompaniment. This man, while in the presence of Angelo, predicted that Piero would be driven from his house to return no more. The great painter attached so much importance to this statement that he urged his friend to communicate his conviction to Piero, but Cardiere hesitated from an apprehension of unpleasant consequences. Subsequently Michael Angelo, meeting Cardiere in the cortile of the palace, observed that the latter was terrified and sorrowful. The prophetic impression rested with increased

weight on his mind. Angelo reproved him for neglecting
to disclose his apprehensions to the party whom they most
deeply concerned. At length Cardiere resolved to hazard
the consequences of the proposed disclosures, and accordingly started on foot for the villa belonging to the Medici
family, which was situated about three miles from Florence.
While on the way he met Piero and his suit, who laughed at
the revelation and ridiculed the fears of the prophet, one of
the number—afterward Cardinal de Bibbiena—telling him
that he was out of his mind.

The result of this interview was the humiliation of Cardiere, who deplored the consequences; but Michael Angelo,
becoming persuaded that the prediction was likely to be fulfilled, left Florence, with two of his companions, and went to
Bologna. The biographer of Michael Angelo adds :—"To
whatever cause this prediction may be attributed, it so happened that it was verified ; for the family de Medici, with
all their suit, were driven from Florence and arrived at Bologna while Michael Angelo was there, and lodged in the
house de Rossi ; Piero himself never returned to Florence,
but after suffering a succession of mortifications came to an
untimely death."[1]

Among the persons especially gifted with the power to
discern future events, Friar Bacon deserves particular notice
as one whose remarkable prophecies have been most literally fulfilled. Six hundred years ago some of the greatest
modern inventions were thus foreshadowed by his prophetic
inspiration :

"Bridges, unsupported by arches, will be made to span the foaming

---

[1] The authority for this statement is Duppa's Life of Michael Angelo.

current. Man shall descend to the bottom of the ocean, safely breathing, and treading with firm step on the golden sands, never brightened by the light of day. Call but the sacred powers of Sol and Luna into action, and behold a single steersman sitting at the helm, guiding the vessel, which divides the waves with greater rapidity than if she had been filled with a crew of mariners toiling at the oars; and the loaded chariot no longer encumbered by the panting steeds, shall dart on its course with resistless force and rapidity. Let the simple elements do the labor; bind the eternal forces and yoke them to the same plow "

When the foregoing predictions were made the author must have been regarded as a poet, or an early speculator in fancy stocks, rather than as a rational philosopher or a reliable seer. It will be perceived that he embraces the Suspension Bridge, the Diving Bell, Steam Navigation, the Railroad and the Steam Plow, in the same chain of prophecies, and all of which are among the accomplished realities of to-day.[1] The seclusion of the cloister, and the rigid discipline of his monastic life, did not prevent the soul of the monk from asserting its relations to the great practical interests of time. By the exercise of a sublime power the veil of the temple of his spirit was rent, that he might look out from the dim religious light of the monastery, far over the cloudy summits of the intervening ages, and behold the splendid achievements of modern Science and Art.

Jeanne d'Arc, the spotless shepherd girl, came from the solitudes of the forest that environed her native village of Domremy, to be the grave counsellor of kings and the defender of her country. The shepherds of Bethlehem were

---

[1] Friar Bacon was doubtless the original inventor of the telescope; and it is evident that he had a correct idea of the composition of gunpowder, for he affirms that by the use of charcoal. sulphur and saltpeter, the phenomena of thunder and lightning may be successfully imitated.

honored by an Angel's visit, and the proclamation of 'glad
tidings to all people ;' and this fair shepherdess—at once so
comely in person, elevated in spirit, and divinely beautiful
in her life, with the freshness and bloom of the hills and
valleys on her cheek, and the fire of genius in her eye—likewise professed to commune with departed saints and heroes ;
to have visions of immortal realities, and to hear the voices
of angelic ministers. And why may they not have spoken to
her ? If they addressed those who watched their flocks on
the plains of Judea, surely this pure-hearted and divinely-
gifted shepherdess of Domremy was not beneath their regard.
She also was called by Providence, being inspired with a
divine life and prophetic spirit. Such was the virgin Evangelist, whose foot prints are yet " beautiful on the mountains"
of Lorraine.

The spirit of prophecy taught the Maid of Orleans that
she was to be instrumental in restoring the nationality of·
France. She believed ; and suddenly emerging from the
quiet seclusion of her pastoral life, she went forth to battle
against the enemies of her king and country. Rising thus
from an obscure position, in the humbler walks of life, she
at once assumed the direction of public affairs, and became
the chief inspiring agent of the French people. The King
of England was ready to lay his hand on the scepter of
France ; Orleans was closely besieged ; Charles VII.—the
heir of the throne—was irresolute in the assertion of his
claim, and the people were divided. The shadow of a great
cross was in the path of the fair chieftain, but she was too
heroic either to falter or turn aside. Never regarding her
personal safety, she cheerfully obeyed the summons, but with

the calm consciousness that she must uphold the throne and deliver her people by the sacrifice of herself.

It was at this critical juncture that Joan of Arc sought the presence of Charles, who, with a view of testing her peculiar powers, protested that he was not the King. But disregarding his words and passing by his courtiers, she fell at his feet, and proposed to raise the siege and conduct him to his coronation at Rheims. She demanded a particular sword in the Church of St. Catherine. The King acquiesced, and the consecrated weapon was placed in her hands. With courage equal to the most trying situation ; with an unwavering faith in the accomplishment of her purpose, and the sublime enthusiasm of a Christian Apostle, she led the armies of France to victory and her King to his throne. Having placed the crown on the head of its rightful possessor, she felt that the chief object of her mission was accomplished ; but she continued in the same perilous service until she was taken prisoner and delivered into the hands of the English.

Jeanne d'Arc was but nineteen years of age when she was brought to trial for sorcery. The noblest virtues and graces which have ever adorned the human character, had been beautifully exemplified in her life. Not a single deed of cruelty, a word of irreverence, or so much as a feeling of selfishness could be justly charged to her account. Nevertheless she was reviled as an apostate, and condemned by her heartless inquisitors to be burnt alive. She accepted the crown of martyrdom with cheerful grace and religious resignation—apparently with as much cordiality as she had placed the crown of France on the head of her king. On the character of the duke of Bedford—third son of Henry IV. of

England—rests the foul stain of causing her execution in the public market-place at Rouen. When the torch was applied to the faggots, she betrayed no weakness. Those who crucified her looked in vain for some sign of irresolution and feeling of displeasure; but her solemn purpose to meet death with composure was unshaken, and the serenity of her mind undisturbed. Thus ran the pure current of her life toward the shoreless ocean,

> " Like a clear streamlet o'er its jagged bed,
> That by no torture can be hushed asleep."

She did not die ; but, robed with flaming fire, went up to her great immortality ! Her last words were spent in prayer, and the name of Jesus was on her lip when the remorseless flames stifled her utterance. A purer spirit never ascended to the Father. The scene was impressive beyond description. An English soldier who had avowed his readiness to add fuel to the burning pile was smitten and overwhelmed by the moral grandeur of this last conquest—THE VICTORY OVER DEATH !— and turning from the thrilling spectacle, in deep contrition, he declared that from the ashes of the martyr a dove with white pinions went up to heaven.

Among the problems that have puzzled the brains of the metaphysicians, the frequent cases of *Prevision* are among the last in their judgment to admit of a satisfactory solution. The foregoing examples will suffice to show that many persons are susceptible of such impressions. With a certain class of minds they are day-light experiences ; but they happen to a much larger number during the hours of sleep. It may not be the peculiar province of the writer to trace out the more obscure and intricate lines in the complex web of our mental operations. We may not always determine in what manner natural (physical) principles and moral laws coälesce in the economy of human life. It may often be difficult to discern precisely where they meet, and how they coöperate in the dynamics of universal existence and progress ; nevertheless, the results of their united action are constantly subject to our inspection.

Without presuming to dogmatize on so intricate a subject, I will here suggest my idea of the law of prophecy. In the most essential sense all things have a permanent existence, extending backward through the long chain of causation and forward through the unlimited succession of immediate effects and remote consequences; and as all events really exist in the causes that produce them, before they actually transpire in the outward world of effects, it naturally follows that whenever the mind—by whatever means—is uplifted to the proper moral and spiritual altitude, it perceives the event before it occurs in the sphere of outward manifestation. The man gifted with prevision foresees what will happen, *because he is able to discover the operative causes which already exist, and must inevitably develop the apprehended results.* Thus our premonitions ; the visions of future occurrences ; and every prophetic impulse, may be subject to law and susceptible of a rational explanation.

When an event depends on the secret designs of individuals, or the general state of public feeling, its future occurrence may be readily apprehended, for the reason that the prescient mind may be *en rapport* with the person or people actuated by such purposes and passions as must inevitably find their ultimate expression in the predicted events. For example, should an incendiary either conceive the idea or entertain the design, of firing his neighbor's dwelling, or a band of conspirators plot the overthrow of the government, the mind gifted with this subtile power of cognition might— agreeably to psychological laws—perceive the existence of such criminal designs as soon as they were formed, and thus be enabled to predict their consummation.

Many cases of prophecy are doubtless to be referred to this perception—by the prescient mind—of existing principles and laws which are yet to find an ultimate expression in cosmical changes and human affairs. The forces and faculties of simple elements and organized beings, are superior to the mere material processes and functions which result from their action. In like manner all causes precede their effects in the order of time. If we can perceive existing causes, we may anticipate future events, with a degree of precision—in respect to time, place, and other circumstances —only equal to the clearness of our perception, and the accuracy of the judgment employed in estimating the operation of inward principles in the production of external developments. The intervention of human acts and motives, in any supposed case, may serve to complicate the instrumentalities employed without obscuring the event which they combine to produce. We may predict that the tree will decay if we can perceive the omniverous worm at its root. Political prophets see the decline and fall of empires, in and through the existing causes of national weakness and degeneracy. If the measure of life on earth be determined by the strength of the life principle in the individual, and otherwise by the operation of undeviating laws, it may be possible for an illuminated mind to perceive the measure of the vital force, and to comprehend those laws which determine the limits of physical endurance. But in order to accurately number our days, the prescient mind must correctly estimate the vital capacity, and accurately weigh all the circumstances likely to modify the conditions of being. When the rare gifts and comprehensive powers of the prophetic seer and the true philosopher are thus united in the same individual, he may be able to foretell events with surprising accuracy. Occasionally, a physician—whose profound insight qualifies him to comprehend the influence of certain forms of disease on the vital principle and organic action—is enabled to predict the day, and possibly the very hour when the death of his patient will occur ; and the prognosis sometimes embraces the more important symptoms that precede and accompany the final suspension of vital motion.[1]

It may be objected that our limited observation and imperfect knowledge of the subject do not warrant the supposition that prophetic communications result from the slow process of deliberate reflection and logical deduction. On the contrary, they appear to be spontaneous utterances of unexpected revelations. It is not difficult to suggest the proper answer to this objection. We have had occasion to intimate already that the mind, in its most exalted moods,

[1] Thomas Devin Reilly. who figured in an editorial capacity in the Irish journals in 1848, and subsequently as a writer for the *Democratic Review*, died at Washington, on the 7th of March, 1854. At the age of fifteen he had an attack of apoplexy, and was successfully treated by a celebrated surgeon of Dublin. who expressed the conviction that he would have another attack at the age of thirty, which would either destroy his life or shatter his constitution. The second attack occurred as predicted and was fatal.

acts with preternatural force and precision. In the department of mathematical science, several modern prodigies have
appeared, who could solve the most difficult problems in an
instant, and with infallible certainty. In those physical and
psychological conditions which involve the greatest intellectual freedom and moral elevation the intuitive mind instantly
comprehends many particulars, and arrives at final results
with amazing rapidity; as the eye, at a glance, takes in the
intervening space and objects. between the observer and the
utmost limit of his vision.

Doubtless the common and the extraordinary events of the
world, and all visible phenomena result from invisible physical, mental and moral forces and laws, and hence they must
virtually exist, in the most essential sense, some time before
they occur in the external world, where alone they are cognizable by the powers of sensation. The truth of this proposition is rendered so obvious, by the very nature of the case,
that it will hardly be questioned by any rational mind. But
the facts, in this particular department, that suggest the greatest possible difficulties are those that appear to be fortuitous.
The destruction of property and life is often *casual*, and many
other circumstances and occurrences appear to be *accidental*.
The chief difficulty here consists in the apparent absence of
any natural law in such cases. In the common mind an accident is an occurrence that does not depend on any natural
principle or established law. The popular definition is doubtless a false one, that serves to magnify the difficulties in the
way of a philosophical explanation of such mysteries. Nevertheless, these casualties are not so easily disposed of as many
other facts in human experience. When our dwellings decay,

by slow degrees, from the natural action of the elements;
when the tree withers in consequence of the gradual loss of
its vitality ; and when human bodies are dissolved because
they are rendered unserviceable by time—or some disaster
has made them unsuitable tenements for the developed spirit
—we can readily apprehend the existence, and to some extent
the nature of the laws that govern these results.   But when
the tree is either uprooted by a tornado or blasted by a thunderbolt ; when our house is fired by lightning or the carelessness of a domestic ; when steam-boilers explode and men
lose their lives in consequence; when ships collide at sea and
multitudes sink beneath the wave, because the night-watch
for a moment slept at his post ; it may be far more difficult
to perceive how the event can be foretold with certainty by
any mundane intelligence.

But the utmost limits of the finite capacity are not to be
determined by the standard of our individual powers and attainments ; nor does the inability to perceive a law disprove
its existence.   Only a shallow mind, intoxicated with self-
conceit and blinded by an infidel skepticism, will presume
to measure all natural laws and divine prerogatives by its
own want of perception and lack of knowledge.   Moreover,
if there are intelligent beings, of a superior order, existing
either here or elsewhere, they may be capable of entering
into psychological relations with the human mind on earth;
and it is consistent with our highest reason to infer, that they
may have some interest in human affairs.   From the high
plain of their divine life and thought the past and future of
this world may be clearly revealed, and the events of centuries, in their relations to the universal chain of causation,

may be present to the angelic perception and consciousness. If such beings exist and are attracted to us, either by the memory of former natural relations; the laws of spiritual affinity, or by a disinterested desire for our elevation, they may inspire the human mind with their own superior wisdom. The possibility of such intervention will certainly be admitted in any enlightened view of the philosophy of prophecy.[1]

To the mind of the prophetic Seer not only the past is present, but the great FUTURE may be comprehended within the field of his mysterious vision, long before Time unrolls the panorama of events. Wide as the sphere of intelligent existence, and the arena of our spiritual activities; deep as the springs of life, and high as the latent capabilities of the aspiring mind, is this faith in these sublime possibilities of human nature. There are illuminated souls who stand within the veil, while they break the seals of the book of fate and unfold our destiny. We have physiological Seers who measure the vital forces and determine the limits of organic action; political Seers who anticipate the rise, progress, fall and desolation of empires; spiritual Seers who unveil the arcana of the Invisible World; and the effigies of many prophets occupy the common Pantheon of all Religions

Many terrible events have cast their shadows on the world, obscuring its hopes and darkening the pages of its history, and sensitive natures have struggled long and fearfully with a cruel destiny. The heavy cross, the crown of thorns, and the wormwood and gall, are expressive symbols of the com-

[1] "It is a sublime and beautiful doc'rine, inculcated by the fathers, that there are guardian angels appointed to watch over cities and nations, to take care of good men, and to guard and guide the footsteps of helpless infancy."— IRVING.

mon crucifixion. But it is a fact of profound significance that the inspired minds of different ages and countries, in their most exalted moods, have anticipated the ultimate triumph of good over evil and a peaceful future for the earth and its inhabitants. That period may be far away ; but it is comprehended in the faith of the world. Oppression and War may triumph for a season, but the universal hope, and the Christian's prayer for the coming of a divine kingdom on earth, must have some basis in reality. In the sublime vision of Isaiah the liberating Eras rise in their majesty, and the songs of great poets ring out like sphere-music along the path of the departed Ages. They all sing of the time when the Divine harmonies shall be translated into the practical language of human actions and institutions. The faint and distant images of that day, dazzled the sight of the ancient Bards, and the slumbering strings of many harps were swept to their highest notes of inspiration.

CHAPTER XXXII.

APPARITIONS OF THE LIVING.

Preliminary Observations—Extraordinary Experience of a Lady—Facts from "The Night Side of Nature"—Professor Becker meets his own Shade—An Apparition appeals to Linnæus—A Man goes to Europe without his Body—Mysterious Interview in a London Coffee-house—Mr. Wilson is visible in Hamilton while he is dreaming in Toronto—An Actor in New York when he is in Washington—A Lunatic in and out of the Asylum at the same time—Apparition of the late Joseph T. Bailey—Midnight Visit to a Boudoir in Lafayette Place—The Author's Shadow in Louisville when his Substance is Five Hundred Miles off—Exciting Scene in a Ball-room—Refutation of Sir David Brewster's Theory—Assumptions of the Sadducean Philosophers—Explanation of the Phenomena.

THE relations and laws of the human mind are such, that whenever two individuals are in sympathetic association, the one may very naturally feel the presence or influence of the other. In this case the mind that is gifted with the greater degree of activity and power at once becomes an inspiring agent to the other. The psycho-magnetic *rapport* may be established by corporeal contact, or otherwise, through those subtile media which pervade the Universe and serve as the airy vehicles of intelligent intercourse. In like manner, from sources superior to ourselves, the very elements of thought flow into our minds; and thus the intellect is quickened, the moral sentiments inspired, and the nobler passions of the soul awakened. Even every living thing, according to its peculiar nature and discrete degree, derives a kind of inspiration from higher elements and forms of life.

The psychological powers and susceptibilities of the mind are illustrated by the occasional appearance of living men at a distance from their bodies. There are many facts of this class that may be clearly authenticated, and their profound significance entitles them to special consideration in the present treatise. The reader's attention has already been called to various phenomena that suggest at least the possibility of Apparitions of the Living. Every example of the transmission of thought, from one mind to another, by mental telegraph—without the use of language or any recognized medium of communication—involves such a suggestion. If an absent friend may be made to *feel* the action of the faculties and passions of our minds, this fact may neither determine the limits of our mental powers, nor discover in our friend the last degree of psychological impressibility. Indeed, many persons who receive impressions in this way have, at the same time, a vague, mysterious sense of the *essential presence* of the individual from whom the same are derived. When a mind of strong executive powers properly concentrates and directs all its forces, not only is it possible to infuse thoughts and ideas into the mind, but distinct impressions may be made, (apparently) on the organs of special sensation. In this manner susceptible persons are sometimes informed of distant occurrences, especially such as great public calamities and the loss of their friends.[1]

---

[1] A fact that occurred during the war with Mexico, will illustrate this class of impressions on the sensories. My authority for the statement is Mr. Bogardus, a man of undoubted veracity, who lives near Albany. A lady, with whom Mr. B. was personally acquainted, had a son—a soldier, who lost his life in the expedition against Mexico. One morning when the soldier's mother (who lived near Mr. B. on the West bank of the Hudson,)

I may now offer the illustrative examples of the extraordinary psychical phenomena indicated by the title of this Chapter. Mrs. Crowe's "Night Side of Nature," contains several striking facts of this class. Among the number she relates the experience of Mr. H——, an artist, and a gentleman of scientific attainments. It occurred " on the evening of the 12th of March, 1792." H——= had spent the evening in reading the Philosophical Transactions, and was about to retire for the night. His mind was engrossed by a mathematical problem, when his uncle, Mr. R...., suddenly appeared to him in a straight-jacket. Some time after he learned that at the precise time when his reflections were disturbed by the apparition, his uncle had attempted suicide, and that a straight-jacket had actually been put on him.

Professor Becker, of Rostock, while engaged in a theological controversy with some friends, had occasion to go to his library to obtain a book, with a view of settling some controverted point. On entering the library, he saw himself seated at the table, in the chair he was accustomed to occupy. The mysterious figure appeared to be reading in a book, and, on approaching, he perceived that it was pointing with one finger of the right hand to these words: "Make

came to the breakfast table, it was observed by the family that she was weeping. On being interrogated respecting the cause of her depression. she said, 'John is dead!'" She was told that she had been dreaming and had better dismiss the thought. But it was quite impossible to shake her conviction. She declared that John had just been shot; described the scene. the actors, and the attendant circumstances, and affirmed that she distinctly heard the report of the gun. saw her son fall, and that he would return to them no more. On the same morning. at sunrise. in Mexico—far from the presence of his mother—John lost his life in the manner described, and indeed the whole statement of his mother was literally verified by the actual facts.

ready thy house, for thou must die!" It is further stated, that having taken leave of his friends, he expired at six o'clock on the evening of the following day.

I believe it is Stilling who relates a similar fact, on the authority of a gentleman who was, at that time, Sheriff of Frankfort. Mr. T——, had just sent his secretary away on some business, but the latter soon after returned to the apartment and seized a volume of Linnæus. His master, surprised at his unexpected reäppearance, demanded the cause of his speedy return, whereupon the book fell to the floor and the figure vanished. When the secretary returned at evening, he stated that he had been engaged in a warm discussion of some botanical question, with a friend whom he met on the way, and that he had much desired to refer to his Linnæus.

Jung Stilling also gives an interesting account of a man of singular and retired habits, who, about the year 1740, lived in the vicinity of Philadelphia. This man was reputed to possess a knowledge of the most mysterious things, and to be capable of discovering the profoundest secrets. Among the more remarkable illustrations of his powers, the following appears to have been fully credited by Stilling :

The wife of a ship-captain, whose husband was on a visit to Europe and Africa, and from whom she had been long without tidings, overwhelmed with anxiety for his safety, was induced to address herself to this person. Having listened to her story, he begged her to excuse him for a while, when he would bring her the intelligence she required. He then passed into an inner room, and she sat herself down to wait ; but his absence continuing longer than she expected, she became impatient, thinking he had forgotten her ; and so, softly approaching the door, she peeped through some aperture, and beheld him lying on a sofa, motionless as if dead. She waited his return, when he told her that her husband had not been able to write to

her, for such and such reasons; but that he was then in a coffee-house in
London, and would very shortly be home again. Accordingly he arrived,
and as the lady learned from him, that the causes of his unusual silence had
been precisely those alleged by the man, she felt extremely desirous of
ascertaining the truth of the rest of the information; and in this she was
gratified; for he no sooner set his eyes on the magician than he said that he
had seen him before, on a certain day, in a coffee-house in London; and
that he had told him that his wife was extremely uneasy about him; and
that he, the captain, had thereupon mentioned how he had been prevented
from writing, adding that he was on the eve of embarking for America. He
had then lost sight of the stranger among the throng, and knew nothing
more about him.

A remarkable fact of this general class was several years
since communicated to the author in a letter from Mr. E. V.
Wilson. My correspondent resided at the time in Toronto.
On the nineteenth day of May, 1854, while he was employed
in writing at his desk, Mr. Wilson fell asleep, and dreamed
that he was in the city of Hamilton, some forty miles west
of Toronto. After attending to some business, he proceeded
in his dream to make a friendly call on Mrs. D——s. On
arriving at the house he rang the bell, and a servant came
to the door, who informed him that her mistress had gone
out and would not return for an hour. The dreamer thereupon left his name and compliments for Mrs. D., and started
for home. At length, awaking from his slumber, Mr. Wilson
found himself precisely where he had lost himself, half an
hour before, queitly seated at his writing desk in Toronto.

Some days after the occurrence of this incident, a lady in
the family of Mr. Wilson received a letter from Mrs. D——,
of Hamilton, in which she incidentally mentioned that Mr.
W. had called at her house, a few days before, while she was
out. She complained that he did not await her return, and

said that, on learning that he had been there, she had visited all the hotels in Hamilton in the hope of finding him.

On perusing this letter Mr. Wilson suggested that his fair friend must be crazy, since he had not been in Hamilton for a month ; and that on the particular day and hour mentioned, he was at his place of business and in a deep sleep. His curiosity was, however, excited, and inviting several friends to join him, the party went to Hamilton and called at the house of Mrs. D. The lady herself met them at the door, and they were invited into the parlor. While the party remained, Mrs. D., on some plausible pretext, directed her servants to go into the room, and suggested that they should notice the gentlemen present and tell her if there were any familiar faces among them. *Two of the servants instantly identified Mr. Wilson as the person who called ten days before, and, in the absence of their mistress, left his name, which they remembered and repeated.* [1]

An extraordinary instance of the apparition of a living man, at a distance from his corporeal form, occurred in Indiana, in the year 1855. A full and authentic account of the facts and circumstances of this peculiar case appeared at the time, in the Indianapolis *Sentinel*, with the Editor's unqualified indorsement, alike of the veracity of the witnesses

---

[1] It is alleged respecting a popular Actor, that he has repeatedly appeared to his friends in the city of New York, when it was well known that he was either in Philadelphia, Baltimore or Washington. It is said that on one occasion he spent an evening at a certain place in New York when he was advertised to p rsonate a character at the Theater in Washington. Several gentlemen assert that they were in his company in New York on that night; and yet, strange to say, the Washington papers of the following morning announced that he had actually made his appearance in that city, and his performance was also made the subject of dramatic criticism.

and the reality of the facts.   The details would occupy too
much space in this connection where only a brief statement
is required.

It was in the early part of fifty-five, and during the session of the Legislature of Indiana, that two members of that
body—representing a portion of the South-western part of
the State, more than one hundred and fifty miles from the
Capitol—called on Dr. Anthon, Superintendent of the Insane Hospital at Indianapolis, and asked for the reasons
that prompted him to discharge one Alexander F., a patient
from Perry County.   "They stated that they had received
letters from different persons, mentioning the fact that Mr.
Alexander F. was wandering at large in neighborhoods near
his old home ; that the citizens were afraid of him, and were
anxious that he should be returned to the institution without
delay."   Dr. Anthon informed the parties that Alexander
was still in the Asylum, that he had not been home, and that
his early discharge need not be anticipated.

On the following day Dr. Anthon received a letter from
the guardian of the insane man, making similar inquiries,
and desiring to know when, and in what condition of mind,
he left the Hospital.   In his reply, Dr. A. assured his correspondent that " the veritable Alexander" was still in his keeping, and that " the people need not be alarmed at his elon-
gated shadow."   This called forth another letter containing
a circumstantial account of Alexander's mysterious visit to
his old home, on or about the 27th of February, 1855.   The
writer named the places where he was seen, the persons with
whom he conversed, and the strange things that were said
and done by the lunatic.   The reappearance of Alexander

naturally occasioned great surprise among his friends and former neighbors, and his movements were closely observed by several persons who had been familiar with him for years. The witnesses concurred in saying that he did not look well; that he was pale, and that he was indisposed to converse; but not one entertained the slightest doubt of his identity.

Alexander was questioned respecting the time when he was in Perry County last, and he replied that it was three weeks since he made a flying visit home. On being informed that he had not been absent from the Hospital since his admission on the 19th of June, 1854, he indignantly disputed the statement, saying : " I tell you that I did go. My spirit flew down there quick, and left this pair of clothes, and the rest of me that you see here in the ward to take care of Antichrist, and keep the Devil out of the bath-room." Alexander mentioned the fact that he visited a distillery, where he obtained some whiskey, named the persons he met there, and gave circumstantial accounts of his sayings and doings, all of which—at least in the essential particulars of the statement—were in correspondence with the facts, as detailed by his guardian in the letter to Dr. Anthon. Alexander thus describes his return from Perry County to Indianapolis :

"I did not see anybody on the road—I was so high up; came with the pigeons; they were a-cheering me—ha! ha! ha!—and didn't make no time at all; I got home first; I'm going back to-morrow. The whisky .... made my head swim—run against the lightning, which singed my whiskers—colored 'em red. The truth is, Doc, they are all crazy."

The author of the communication in the *Sentinel* observes in conclusion, that " We have the positive assurance of ten or more reliable men, who had known him for years, that

Alexander was in Perry County on or about the 27th of February, and the slightly unconnected, but corroborating narrative of Alexander himself. On the other hand, the officers of the Hospital, and at least twenty others connected with the institution, will solemnly affirm that they have seen and conversed with Alexander two or three times every day for nine months.

I am not without some personal experiences of this nature, the first of which occurred in 1850. I had been spending several days in the valley of the Naugatuck, and at the time was in Ansonia, at the residence of W. G. Creamer, some fifteen miles from Bridgeport, Connecticut. This strange phenomenon of the apparition of a living man occurred early in the morning. The sun had risen, and I was about leaving my sleeping apartment, when (after having my attention directed for a moment to the opposite side of the room) I suddenly turned toward the door, which was closed, and— to my great surprise—saw the late JOSEPH T. BAILEY, of Philadelphia. He was standing about three feet from the door, and looking earnestly in my face, he addressed me, when a brief colloquy ensued.

In his first audible words Mr. Bailey declared that he would call on me the next day; whereupon I inquired what was to be done on the occasion of his next visit. With an expression of peculiar interest, and speaking with increased emphasis, Mr. Bailey said, " *Remember ! I shall call on you to-morrow.*" I asked him to explain the object of his unexpected appearance, and to tell me what was to occur on the succeeding day. He gave me no answer; but the figure moved slowly as if it were about to disappear by the door.

"Stay, friend!" I exclaimed, "Will you not explain the purpose of this mysterious visitation?" My friend made no direct reply, but commenced speaking in a low tone. I listened, and discovered that he was talking of a mutual friend, Mr. F——. Much that he said was inaudible, but I distinctly heard his last words, which were these: "A dark cloud has settled down over the earthly destiny of that man."

The figure vanished as the last words were uttered, and I was left to muse alone on this strange experience. By a most singular train of circumstances, the author met Mr. Bailey the next day, in a car on the New York and New Haven Railroad. He had been in Boston the preceding day or two, and was there at the time his apparition entered my chamber in Ansonia. In the course of the interview that succeeded our actual meeting, Mr. Bailey spoke with much feeling concerning the misfortunes of our mutual friend, Mr. F——; and, strange as it may appear, when about to take leave of the writer, he uttered the precise words of the apparition:—"*A dark cloud has settled down over the earthly destiny of that man.*"

My second experience occurred some years since, after spending an evening at the residence and in the company of Mr. M—— and his wife, of Lafayette Place, New York. The latter manifested a high degree of mental susceptibility, and in the course of our interview exhibited some interesting psychological phenomena. At a late hour I left Lafayette Place and went to my lodgings, in a remote part of the city. Finding that the elder members of the family had not retired, but were awaiting my return, I gave them a description of Madam M., and the details of our interview. The

hour was midnight. The personal appearance of the lady,
her conversation, manners, and all the incidents of the evening, were still vividly impressed on the mind ; and they were
communicated without a thought that the distant subject of
the recital could thus be consciously influenced.

On the following morning, when Madame M. presented
herself at the breakfast table she referred to the writer, and
affirmed that some time after Mr. B. left, on the previous
night, he had returned, and that at twelve o'clock he mysteriously appeared in her private apartment, entering and
retiring without opening the door. As the evidence in this
case was quite sufficient to establish an *alibi*, the gravity of
the personal charge was materially modified, and the accused
party gracefully excused for his unconscious intrusion.

In the early part of 1858, the writer was at a social party
one evening, given at the house of Madam ——, in Louisville, Kentucky, when the particular class of phenomena embraced in this Chapter became the subject of conversation.
Several persons having expressed their interest in psychological investigations, Madam ——, at length requested—in
behalf of herself and a friend—that a trial might be made,
as she had no fear of apparitions either of the living or the
dead. Accordingly, the hour between eleven and twelve
o'clock on the succeeding Tuesday evening, was set apart
for the experiment. As had been anticipated, the writer
was traveling on Tuesday night, and at a distance of some
five hundred miles from Louisville. Madam and her friend
were prompt in meeting the engagement. At the appointed
hour they were seated in the parlor, with closed doors,
awaiting the result of the trial with a lively curiosity.

The hour had nearly expired, and the conditions had all been faithfully observed ; but still there was no visible presence. Less than five minutes of the hour yet remained, when Madam ——, concluding that success was impossible, and half reproaching herself for the foolish credulity that prompted the trial—left the room for the purpose of securing the doors in the back part of the house. At the same time her companion approached the door leading into the front hall with the intention of retiring for the night. As she opened the parlor door the image of the author's personality stood before her (so the lady affirms) in all its natural proportions, and with every aspect of actual life. A sudden exclamation of surprise brought her friend into the room, who also affirms that she saw and recognized the figure as it moved, with a gliding locomotion, from its position by the door and disappeared.

The reader will permit the introduction of a single additional example of this class from the records of my private experience. One stormy night, in the winter of 1858-9, I was seated alone in my room, at a hotel in Coldwater, Michigan. But I was there only *in propria persona*, being absent in spirit. On the table before me was the autograph of a friend, whose name and image are associated with pleasant memories. The student of human nature is privileged to subject the characters of others to a just analysis, so long as his work is done in silence. I felt at liberty on that occasion ; and it never occurred to me that my voiceless meditation might disturb the mental and vital equilibrium of the person who occupied my thoughts. At the very hour my mind was thus employed my friend—who was presumed to be at home—was absent in a neighboring town, and surrounded by a gay company. While standing at ease in a quadrille, engaged in a spirited conversation, a sudden attack of syncope interrupted the dance, and my friend was borne insensible from the room. The cause of this sudden loss of the vital balance was soon explained. My friend, on recovering the use of the faculties, declared that the present writer mysteriously appeared—a silent spectator in the midst of the assembly. It was absolutely known that I was at the time, in a distant city, and hence the apparition at once suggested the possible termination of the life on earth.

There are few more difficult questions in this department of mental science than the one that relates to the proper solution of these mysteries. Speculative minds may be able to invent various hypotheses, but I shall only notice such as are either sustained by distinguished authority or are perceived to be consistent with the laws and relations of the human mind. Sir David Brewster presumed that all such appearances were projected from the brain on the retina, and hence that they were wholly *subjective*. If it were so, the images would inevitably bear some resemblance to the thoughts occupying the mind, and thus exercising the brain at the precise time of their occurrence. But unfortunately for Sir David Brewster, and all the illusion philosophers, the facts are at war with their material speculations. These apparitions take shapes that are obviously independent of the ideas entertained by those who are forced to recognize their presence. The phantoms come uncalled; they demean themselves as they will, and without the slightest regard to our sense of propriety. Moreover, they depart at pleasure, and will not stay a moment to oblige us. There is, therefore, no sufficient reason to conclude that they are the abnormal creations of the minds that perceive them, and the rational metaphysician will be little disposed to accept the subjective theory.

The illustrations employed in this Chapter are manifestly not mere illusions, but *actual facts*. Indeed, the supposition that they are all phantoms, born of the excited mind and disordered brain, is so utterly preposterous that it is difficult to account for its acceptance by any man of ordinary intelligence and discrimination. In a normal condition different persons may perceive the same things, and substantially agree in their testimony respecting the objects and events which they are led to observe ; and it must be remembered that this concurrence characterizes the testimony of the witnesses who saw Alexander F—— at the distance of one hundred and fifty miles from his physical body. The servants of Mrs. D., of Hamilton, both recognized Mr. Wilson; and the two ladies in Louisville corroborated the testimony of each other. On the contrary, men of diseased brains, and those whose faculties are otherwise deranged, exhibit no similar correspondence. They are never haunted by the same phantoms. Every disordered intellect has its peculiar crotchet, while the illusions of the senses and the hallucinations of the mind are strangely incongruous and infinitely diversified.

If we submit Sir David Brewster's hypothesis to trial by the facts already cited in this connection, the thoughtful reader will perceive that it is little better than a mere hallucination. The hypothesis under review presupposes the

existence of an idea or mental conception, previously formed ; and that intense cerebral action may produce a shadow,
image, or picture of the same, which is perceived by the
sense of vision, and appears to be *objective*. But the form
of one's uncle in a straight-jacket surely sustains no possible
relation to a mathematical problem. When Becker, in the
heat of a theological discussion, went to his library for a
book, he evidently did not think of meeting himself; much
less did he expect to be admonished of his approaching dissolution. When the Sheriff of Frankfort was sitting quietly
in his room, with the impression on his mind that his secretary would be absent till evening, the action of his brain
certainly could not have produced the sensorial impression
of the secretary's presence. The sea-captain, in the coffee-
house in London, had no reason to expect that he would see
an unknown man who was at that time in the United States.
Admitting this hypothesis, the friends of the actor referred to
could never see him in New York so long as they felt assured that he was in Washington; nor could Mrs. D——s'
servants, in Hamilton, who probably never heard of Mr.
Wilson, evolve his image from their brains, rendering his
form, features, expression and voice with such surprising
fidelity that the real man was instantly recognized, when—
ten days thereafter—they were brought into his presence.
The writer had no thought of Mr. Bailey until it was suggested by his apparition. Madam M—— could not entertain the thought that a gentleman—whose personal knowledge of herself was derived from a single interview—would
invade the sanctity of her *boudoir* at midnight. The two
friends in Louisville saw nothing while they were waiting

and watching—when alone the anxious expectation could, by a possibility, have created an optical illusion, corresponding to the conception by the mind—but it was when they had ceased to entertain any such expectation—had even relinquished their feeble faith in the possibility of the occurrence—that the shadow of the absent friend stood at the door like a living presence. Moreover, the person in the ball-room, with the faculties otherwise employed—the senses being entranced by the magnetism of music, the forms of beauty, and "the poetry of motion"—could not be expected to see a man who—at that particular time—was known to be elsewhere and far away.

It will be perceived that the foregoing facts involve a complete refutation of Sir David Brewster's theory. And this is about all that the accepted philosophies have done toward a solution of these mysteries. Abercrombie, in his interesting treatise on the intellectual faculties, entertains a similar notion ; and all material philosophers, who have written on the phenomena of mind, have adopted—with slight modifications—the theory of spectral illusions. Such men are eminently Sadducean in their bold and unqualified denial of the existence and powers of the mind when separated from the body.

In many cases it is obvious that the persons who thus mysteriously appear at a distance from their bodies, and those who recognize their presence, are mentally *en rapport*. In the present classification are several illustrative facts that may be appropriately referred to this magnetic or psychological conjunction ; and the laws that regulate this blending of subtile forces and association of faculties and ideas, also suggest the proper explanation of many similar phenomena. When this relation is fairly established, and two minds are intimately conjoined by the force of a natural attraction, the functions of the one may be determined by the more positive faculties of the other ; and even the nerves of special sensation—in the impressible party—*may thus be acted upon from within*, or through the mind, in such a manner as to reflect the same images at the sensorium that external scenes and objects naturally produce when surveyed through the organic instruments of perception.

But the psychological theory, as thus explained, is insufficient to cover all the facts. The person who really appears to be essentially present in one place while he is known to be (corporeally) in another and a distant place, does not always have his mind so fixed on those who behold his apparition, as to influence either their mental or physical functions in any possible degree ; nor does it appear that those who perceive and recognize the images of absent persons are especially distinguished for their psychological susceptibility. We have no evidence that the man who desired to refer to his Linnæus to settle a controverted point, was thinking of the person in the library who saw his apparition grasp the volume ; nor is it at all likely that Mrs. D——s' domestics were characterized by the most delicate psychological susceptibilities. It should also be observed that, whenever impressions are made and received in the manner already described, the subject usually perceives only such images as are before the dominant mind, the form of the man being seldom visible. On the contrary, in the examples under discussion, the images of the persons were rendered visible rather than the shadows of ideas and the forms of objects which occupied their minds at the time. From these considerations we may justly conclude that the psychological theory—as commonly defined and apprehended—will not enable us to account for all the phenomena in this connection, in a satisfactory manner, and hence some further explanation is required.

It is a significant fact that in many cases the individuals who appear to be invested with this double personality are not, at the time, completely conscious of their relations to the external world. The phenomena are quite likely to occur when the mind is, either partially or entirely, withdrawn from the physical organs of sensation and the outward field of observation. There may be numerous exceptions, and among them some of the examples I have selected; but many persons, whose magneto-spiritual effigies appear at a distance from all corporeal restraints, will be found to have been at the time in some other than a normal, waking state. In profound mental abstraction, or introversion of the faculties —when the soul looks within; when present objects disappear and temporal interests are forgotten; when the mind is centered on things remote—on absent friends, the events of the past and the realities of the future; "in visions of the night when deep sleep falleth on men;" in the palsy of catalepsis; in magnetic coma and other trances; in periods of protracted sickness, which jar and weaken the soul's material connections; when disaster and death are impending and the shadows of the immortal world fall on the soul—in all these imperfectly defined physical and psychical conditions, it would seem that the spirit, in some potential sense, *leaves the body* while it wanders in distant places, or is possibly intromitted to other worlds.[1]

In the mental and corporeal conditions, included in the foregoing specification, the spirit withdraws in a greater or less degree from the sphere of its earthly relations. In profound trances the organs of sensation and motion are useless because the spirit is not present to employ them; insanity may result from the minds' imperfect possession of its organic instrument; and sleep finds its most appropriate and impressive analogy in death. So long as these conditions continue, the subject appears to occupy a kind of intermediate state between the realms of mortal and immortal existence; and it is but natural that Man—thus partially liberated from earthly restraints—should perform (imperfectly, to be sure) some of the functions of his spiritual and eternal life.

The popular conception of the soul is vague, and its higher life apparently shadowy and unreal, whilst the flesh is so tangible that the body is quite likely to be mistaken for the real man. Material skepticism and chronic ignorance still

---

[1] Saint Paul, (speaking of himself, according to the Biblical Expositors) says that he was acquainted with a man who was " caught up to the third heaven," where he "heard unspeakable words ;" and whether he was " in the body or out of the body," at the time, he could not determine. (2 Cor., chapter XII.) If this is insufficient to establish the fact, it may at least commend our idea to the favorable consideration of those who are accustomed to appeal to Apostolic authority. Paul's language certainly implies that the soul may be temporarily released from its corporeal relations, in a degree that enables a man to ascend even to " the third heaven" and yet return on the same day. When the innermost avenues of perception are opened into the more interior degrees of the mind and the Universe, the man is necessarily brought into correspondence with the heavenly state. In other words, he is at once, either transported to heaven, or that world descends to him, so that its sublime realities are present to his consciousness.

insist on limiting all human intelligences by such conditions
and laws as are only or chiefly applicable to the elements
and forms of matter.   They will have the soul conditioned
in time and space, and they boldly assert the necessary and
absolute dependence of all its faculties on the continued existence of the body and the integrity of its organic relations.
On the contrary, I recognize the divinity and God given
freedom of its inmost nature, and affirm its high prerogative
to govern the world.   In the immortal faculties and deathless affections of the mind I find the individuality of MAN.
It is vain to look for it elsewhere.   "The outward man
perishes, day by day ;" but "the inward man is renewed,"
and the identity is never lost.

Now it is a self-evident proposition, that *a man must inevitably be precisely where the faculties are which constitute
his real manhood.*   Hence, if all the powers of his mind concenter on the opposite side of the globe, and he is thus conjoined to some companion of his soul, and to scenes and
objects that live and bloom in his affections, he must of necessity *be there*, in all the essential elements and attributes
of his intellectual, social and moral being.   Moreover, by a
power of self-identification with all kindred natures they are
made to realize his absolute presence.

CHAPTER XXXIII.

STATES RESEMBLING DEATH.

Preliminary Considerations—Hybernation—Life and Death defined—M. Jobert de Lamballe's Experiments—The Vital Functions restored by Electricity—Institutions for the resuscitation of drowned Persons—A Surprising Story—An Indian Fakir entombed alive—He is restored after ten Months—Dr. George Watterson on Premature Burials—Case of D. C. Mitchell—Reanimation of Mrs. Columbia Lancaster—A Presbyterian Divine leaves the body and returns—A Man resuscitated at Memphis—Remarkable Case before the French Academy - Irresistible power of Love—Case of Rev. William Tennent—Examples from the Scriptures—Resurrection of Lazarus—Reference to M. Renan's Life of Jesus—Concluding Observations.

THE philosophical observer may not always comprehend the relations of recognized facts to natural laws, for the obvious reason that the system of Nature includes many mysteries, and no human sagacity is likely to discover all her secret springs of action. Indeed, we may never hope to solve all the great problems that meet us on every hand, if, in our definition of Nature, we embrace only the mere outward and tangible forms and phases of being. But if, on the other hand, we include the Soul; the internal laws which govern the formation and development of physical forms; and the invisible forces that control all sensible phenomena, it is plain that we can only fail to furnish rational explanations, because our knowledge of Nature and our capacity to reason are too limited.

In certain electro-vital conditions, a partial or total suspension of the phenomena of animation is liable to occur in both animals and men. In the hybernation of some of the insect tribes, the cold-blooded reptilia, and certain superior forms of animated Nature, we find numerous examples and abundant opportunities for observation. This torpid, senseless, and asphyxiated state is usually superinduced by cold, though it is well known that this suspension of vital and voluntary activity often occurs among the insects and reptiles of tropical climates. In this state the organic action and the vital temperature are gradually diminished until sensation and voluntary motion cease altogether. At length respiration is wholly suspended, and with it the capillary circulation and all the processes of vital chemistry, on which the generation of animal heat is made to depend. The waste of the body being thus arrested, the necessity for food no longer exists; and this condition may continue for an indefinite period without involving the total extinction of the vital principle.

The cases of suspended animation among men have been frequent in all periods and countries. When the electric forces—on which the organic action constantly depends—are imperfectly balanced, the functions are especially liable to be suddenly interrupted. Strong mental excitements, sudden shocks, unusual exhaustion of the nervous energies, and a variety of incidental conditions and circumstances, may operate in producing this state. Persons so imperfectly organized as to render the vital equipoise uncertain, often experience a temporary loss of sensation in certain portions of the system; or a difficulty in waking from a sleep that is otherwise natural. Moreover, they are quite sure to suffer from an unequal distribution of the animal fluids, from syncope, catalepsis and paralysis.

Thus we are furnished with constant illustrations of the fact, that not only the functions of voluntary motion and sensation may be temporarily arrested, but even respiration and the heart's action may be wholly suspended—for hours and days together—without the sacrifice of life. These conditions are not unlike the state of suspended animation observed in the lower departments of the animal world. Moreover, it is found that the use of violent friction, sudden shocks, and the application of heat and electrical currents, are among the most effectual agents and methods employed in restoring the functions of both animals and men.

In the appropriate illustrations of my subject Life and Death are brought into intimate relations, and a brief analysis of these opposite states will prepare the mind to more clearly comprehend the facts which follow in this connection. Life, as a phenomenon, is the result of that condition, or perhaps I may say that *it is* the condition, of an organized body, in which all its essential parts coëxist in a sound state and a true relation, and wherein the appropriate functions of the several organs are performed. Now, as all organized bodies have their periods of formation, growth and decay, it follows that life, as it exists in these outward forms, is subject to the same general law. There is a time when we begin to live. At that period the vital principle is but feebly manifested, and may be destroyed by the slightest accident. The light of life burns dimly, and may be extinguished by a breath. But as the body is unfolded, life increases in intensity and power, and the vital action becomes stronger and surer, until Humanity has attained its highest physical perfection. *But there is, also, a time when we begin to die ;* and no sooner has the tide of life reached its highest attainable point than the vital flood begins to recede. The fluids still circulate through the great arteries of life ; outward objects make their impressions on the delicate nerves of sense, while along the mystical avenues, and through the secret chambers of thought, the images yet come and go. By degrees, however, they grew dim and shadowy,

"And look like heralds of Eternity."

The vital momentum is diminished, and the fluids move in lessening currents, until at last the organic action is suspended, and all is silent and motionless! The flame that was kindled at the consecration of the earthly temple, when life was new, almost imperceptibly expires on the altar, and the presiding divinity gradually withdraws its presence, and at last leaves the shrine deserted. Thus it is manifest that as we live by degrees, so also do we die. If we are conscious of increasing vitality and power during the period of Life's flood, we are no less sensible of a corresponding decline when life begins to ebb.

The idea that death is a gradual transformation is clearly illustrated and confirmed by the facts of human experience. When the change occurs naturally it may occupy one-half the entire period of the present organic existence, beginning with the maturity of the body and terminating with its final decomposition. In other words, the formation and complete development of the organic structure require one-half of the period of our corporeal existence, and the natural process of its decay, or death, occupies the remaining part of what men call human life. Death is commonly defined to be a total suspension of the arterial circulation, and a cessation of all the animal functions. But a person may be said to be dying some time before vital motion is suspended, just as truly as the statement can be predicated of what is occurring at *that* precise moment. Men whose judgments are governed by external, visible signs, may fancy that death occurs at the instant which marks the termination of outward consciousness and organic activity. But those who make this mistake are superficial observers. Whoever looks *within*—at the invisible forces and essential laws of life—will inevitably conclude that death is not an instantaneous change, but a gradual transformation ; and that, when it occurs agreeably to the Divine natural order, it must necessarily require a period of many years for its accomplishment.

The transition being thus gradual, it follows that vitality may remain—the spirit may preserve its connection with the body—for hours, and possibly for several days, after voluntary motion, respiration and sensation have ceased, and all outward signs of life are extinct. During this period—the intervening time between the termination of vital motion and decomposition—the application of some powerful agent may reproduce the organic action, and thus restore life. Numerous instances of this kind might be cited from history and the medical journals. Many persons, reduced by disease or subjected to some mysterious influence, have relapsed into profound trances, resembling the *post-mortem* state, and after many days of suspended animation all the functions of life have been restored. The Divine forces in Nature have not been exhausted by excessive use, or paralyzed by time, and we may therefore presume that the grand results of their operations are fundamentally the same in all ages and countries. From what we know of the powers of Electricity and Magnetism, and the relations of these agents to the vital functions, we have reason to believe, that if they could be understandingly applied, many a palsied form, through which the parting soul can make no sign, might be reanimated and clothed with new beauty. If a breath can extinguish the flame, it is not less apparent that a breath may rekindle the fires on Life's crumbling altar, and light up the courts of its earthly temple.[1]

A knowledge of the fact that the functions of life are often restored to those who were apparently dead, has led to the adoption of various natural agents and scientific methods for the accomplishment of this object. During the last and the present centuries several civilized nations have founded societies, having for their chief object the resuscitation of *drowned* persons. The people of Holland, who are more exposed to accidents by water than the inhabitants of most other countries, (owing to the greater number of canals, and of persons employed on their inland waters) were induced to organize the first society of this kind, which was instituted at Amsterdam, in 1767. Through the agency of this association, not

---

[1] In 1853, M. Jobert de Lamballe read a paper before the French Academy of Sciences, on the effects of Electricity in restoring animation in cases where life was apparently extinct. In the course of his observations, he administered chloroform to many animals producing apparent death; and then — by properly graduated shocks from his galvanic pile—he restored animation. In some cases the time that elapsed between the suspension and restoration of the functions, was so great that there seemed to be little chance of success, but by perseverance the desired result was obtained.

less than one hundred and fifty persons were, in a very brief period, restored to life; in other words, raised from the dead. Many of these manifested no sign of returning animation for more than an hour after they were taken from the water. It is reasonable to infer that, in all these cases, *death would have been complete and inevitable*, but for the natural means and humane measures of the Society. Thus the dead may be raised, and by similar modes the medical faculty and others *do* raise the dead almost daily. In 1768, the authorities of Milan and Venice, formed societies of this kind, and in 1771, the Magistracy of Hamburg followed their example. Subsequently, the Royal Humane Society of London was instituted, and similar ones at Paris and Glasgow, and several other places on the continent of Europe.

From among the cases of suspended animation, the selection of a few striking examples will suffice to illustrate my subject. In the year 1838, an East Indian Faqueer, or Fakir, attracted general attention in his own country by demonstrating his capacity to live for months deprived of both air and nourishment. The evidence, by which the facts and circumstances are supported, is so strong that it is difficult to regard this as a case of Indian jugglery. Hon. W. G. Osborne, Military Secretary to the Mission sent to the Court of Runjeet Sing, was present and an eye-witness. I extract the following from Mr. Osborne's account, from which it appears that other distinguished persons certify to the marvelous exploits of the Fakir in successfuly counterfeiting the *post-mortem* state.

" The monotony of our camp life was broken this morning by the arrival of a very celebrated character in the Punjaub.

He is held in extraordinary respect by the Sikhs, from his alleged capacity of being able to bury himself alive for any period of time. Captain Wade (now Sir Claudie Wade), political agent at Loodhianna, told me that he was present at his exhumation, after an interment of some months; General Ventura having buried him, in the presence of the Maharajah and many of his principal Sirdars ; and, as far as I can recollect, these were the particulars, as witnessed by General Ventura.' After going through a regular course of preparation ...... the Faqueer reported himself ready for the interment in a vault which had been prepared for the purpose by order of the Maharajah.

"On the appearance of Runjeet and his Court, he (the Fakir) proceeded to the final preparations that were necessary, in their presence. and after stopping with wax his ears and every other orifice through which it was possible for air to enter his body, except his mouth, he was stripped and placed in a linen bag. The last preparation consisted in turning his tongue back, and thus closing the gullet. whereupon he immediately died away into a sort of lethargy. The bag was then closed and sealed with the Runjeet's own seal, and afterwards placed in a small deal box, which was also locked and sealed. The box was then placed in a vault, the earth, thrown in and trodden down, a crop of barley sown over the spot, and sentries placed round it. The Maharajah was however, very skeptical on the subject, and twice, in the course of the ten months he remained under ground, sent people to dig him up, when he was found to be exactly in the same position, and still in a state of suspended animation."

On the same authority it is affirmed that, at the expiration of ten months, the Fakir was exhumed in the presence of Captain Wade; also the Maharajah and others. The Captain witnessed the breaking of the seals and the opening of the box and bag. He also examined the inanimate body minutely. It was at first motionless and pulseless, though its appearance was otherwise natural. In two hours the process of restoring the faculties and functions was fully accomplished, and the Fakir was apparently as well as ever.

Many persons have been restored to life by various incidental circumstances or accidents, occurring at or about the time of burial. Dr. George Watterson, in an Essay on "Premature Interments, and the Uncertain Signs of Death," published some time since in *Sartain's Magazine*, gives an interesting and graphic account of a number of cases, derived from the historical records of different countries. Several of the more remarkable examples are circumstantially narrated, and many others are referred to in general terms. Referring exclusively to premature burials in France, the writer says :

" In the course of twelve years, it is asserted, that ninety four cases were prevented by fortuitous circumstances. Of these, thirty-four persons came back to life the moment the funeral ceremonies were about to commence ; thirteen recovered by the tender care and attention of their families ; seven from the fall of the coffins ; nine from injuries inflicted by the needle ; five from sensations of suffocation ; nineteen from accidental delays ; and six from doubts entertained of their death."

Some years ago, Mr. D. C. Mitchell, while on his way from Scotland to this country, was suddenly attacked with brain fever. The disease did not yield to professional treatment; but very soon assumed an alarming aspect. Two weeks after—with the impression on his mind that he was leaving the earth—he died, or seemed to die. The bystanders said he was dead ; and the physician confirmed the statement. A friend claimed from the Captain the earthly possessions of the departed, and it was decided to commit the remains to the sea on the following morning. Before three o'clock all things were in readiness, and under the direction of the chief mate, and a committee appointed for that purpose, the body was about to be lowered into the water. A burial at sea, and by night, presents a scene of unusual solemnity. But who can imagine the emotions of the living subject of such obsequies, who, though incapable of the slightest motion, is still conscious of all that is passing. Such was Mr. Mitchell's case ; but the intense agony of the moment was the means of his deliverance. The terrible thought that he was doomed to sleep on the cold floor of the ocean, smote his spirit like a thunderbolt, and swept the palsied nerves like the blast of a tempest! There was a fearful struggle, and he awoke from his trance. The Captain and mate of the vessel that brought Mr. Mitchell to this country, together with the friend who claimed his temporal possessions, are in the world of souls ; but the subject of this painful experience was, but a few years since, still living in the body and in the enjoyment of perfect health. Mr. Mitchell communicated these facts to the writer in an autographic statement, made in August, 1853.[1]

Some time since the writer received from E. G. Fuller, Esq., a gentleman of unquestionable intelligence and veracity

---

[1] For Mr. Mitchell's complete statement of his remarkable experience, see the Author's Telegraph Papers, Vol. I., p 427.

—whose residence is in Coldwater, Michigan—the main facts of a case of peculiar interest, and which will afford a striking illustration of my subject. Columbia Lancaster, a lawyer, who formerly lived in Centerville, St. Joseph's County, Michigan, removed in the autumn of 1840 to Missouri, with a view of going to Oregon in the spring of '41. He accordingly started and pursued his course to the distance of several days' journey beyond Fort Laramie, when his wife, who accompanied him, became seriously ill. He waited a day or two, in the hope that Mrs. L. would speedily recover. But her illness continued, and he directed the rest of the company—except one man, who remained to assist him in the care of his wife—to proceed on their way, himself designing to follow them as soon as the patient was sufficiently recovered, or to return should she be unable to continue the journey.

But Mrs. Lancaster grew worse, and the man who remained with Mr. L. and his lady was sent back to Fort Laramie for medicines. He had been gone but a short time when the patient expired. Mr. L. remained there with the form of his fair companion until the man came back from the Fort. On his return he was accompanied by two Indians, who were strongly attached to Mrs. Lancaster, on account of her previous kindness to them. The Indians formed a litter, by placing blankets and other suitable articles on poles. On this rude carriage the body was placed, and the Indians conveyed it some 300 miles through the wilderness, fording streams and surmounting whatever obstacles were in the way. On arriving at Fort Laramie, preparations were made for the funeral ; but before the remains were finally disposed of,

30

and *eight days after Mrs. Lancaster was supposed to have died, the body exhibited signs of returning life, and by degrees she was fully restored!* When Mrs. L. had so far recovered as to be able to converse, she assured her friends that she was all the while perfectly conscious of every thing that occurred, and she even related the conversation and the several incidents that transpired during the journey. [1]

A few months since, an eminent Presbyterian divine in New York was borne by disease to the very portals of the invisible world. He had a distinct consciousness of his condition. Vailed in light, his spirit rose and hovered over the body. He could distinctly see the wasted form, stretched on the couch beneath him, pale, pulseless and cold, but his immortal self was thrilled with inexpressible peace and joy. Just then his wife, to whom he was tenderly but strongly attached, called to him with the deep earnestness of that undying love which can endure all things but separation from the object of its devotion. The potent magnetism of that loving heart counterpoised the combined attractions of the spheres, and even recalled the unshackled spirit from the Heavens just opening to receive it. He returned to the body. The next moment a gentle voice—calling his name in tones of mingled tenderness and grief—vibrated on the outward ear, reminding him that he was still a dweller in the earth.

There is a power in human love that can repel disease and death, and stay the parting soul. When, for example, a liv-

---

[1] Mr. Lancaster is not unknown as a public man. If the author is not in error, he was the first Delegate elect to Congress from Washington Territory. In 1850 his wife was living, and enjoying her accustomed health.

ing person with strong sympathies and an intense devotion, has for some time been in close contact with the mortal remains of some dear friend, it has occasionally happened that the departed spirit, being *en rapport* with this living and loving medium, has reëntered its deserted dwelling, and perhaps remained for years. Such a resurrection of the dead, so-called, is in strict accordance with the relations of mind and matter, and the laws of natural and spiritual dynamics. I propose to illustrate this point by citing additional examples.

Some time since, the Memphis *Whig* published the facts of an interesting case. A married couple were on their way from New Orleans up the river, when the husband sickened and died. The bereaved widow landed at Memphis with the remains, where she made arrangements for the funeral. The form of her bosom friend was about to be conveyed to the scene of its final repose. But fond affection demanded the privilege of one last, lingering look, and accordingly the lid was removed from the coffin. Bending over the cold and apparently lifeless form, she bathed the brow with her scalding tears, and fervently kissed the frigid lips. In this great struggle, love triumphed over death. *There* was one who had "*slept*" as long, and doubtless as profoundly, as Lazarus; but the Divine Spirit that animates all things—acting through the mediumship of a frail woman—dissolved death's icy chains, and set the captive free. That man recovered, and with his wife soon left Memphis, inspired with the new energy of returning health and emotions of grateful reverence toward the Being in whose hand are the issues of life.

The following illustration of the power of love, and the efficacy of vital magnetism in reänimating the dead, is derived from a paper, read some time since before the French Academy of Science. The subject had exhibited no signs of life for *ten days*, and all the medical attendants declared that she was dead. The bell of the village church was tolling for the funeral, when an old, familiar friend and school-mate came to take a last farewell. She stooped and pressed her lips to those of her departed friend. She remained in this position for some time, until the bystanders, fearing that she might be injured by uncontrollable emotion, attempted to remove her. She silently waved her hand for them to retire, but preserved her connection with the inanimate form of her youthful companion. At length she started with intense surprise, and exclaimed, "She lives!" The signs of life proved to be unequivocal. The spirit, already enfranchised, came back to the scenes of its mortal imprisonment, and it came in answer to love's silent prayer. This subtile power of attraction is so strong that no distance can separate us from kindred souls.

> "Far off their home may be,
> Beneath the glory of an Eastern sky,
> Or where bright isles amid blue waters lie
> And thou mayest no more see
> The forms which were their spirit's earthly shrine,
> But oh! if thou canst love them, *they are thine.*"

In this case, it is evident that the lungs were first moved by the warm life-breath of the friend. Moreover, by direct physical contact, at a point intimately connected with the brain and vital organs, a current of vital electro-magnetism was transmitted from the living, positive organism to the inanimate body, the nerves of which served as conductors in the transfusion of the subtile principle. And thus the dead of *ten days* was raised, by means simple and natural as a sister's kiss. Oh, if you are animated by a love that fears no death and knows no change; love that is stronger than all temptation, and wrong, and cruelty; that gathers strength from life's rudest conflicts, and even amid scenes of decay blooms over lonely sepulchers; then, indeed, you may grapple with Death, and perhaps conquer him on the field of his conquests, and almost take from the remorseless grave the pale and ghastly trophies of his victory!

The case of Rev. William Tennent, of New Jersey, a clergyman of the Presbyterian branch of the Church, is one of the most remarkable on record. While conversing with his brother in Latin, respecting the state of his soul, and his prospects in the life to come, he expressed doubts concerning his future happiness. Just at that moment he suddenly lost the power of speech and voluntary motion; he was apparently insensible, and his friends believed that the spirit had vacated its earthly tabernacle. Arrangements were accordingly made for the appropriate solemnities; but his physician, who was also a warm, personal friend, was not satisfied, and at his request the funeral rites were delayed. Three days had passed: the eyes were rayless, the lips discolored, and the body cold and stiff. The brother insisted that the remains should be entombed. The critical hour at length arrived; the people had assembled, and the occasion was about to be solemnized by appropriate ceremonies, when the whole company was startled by a fearful groan! The eyes were opened for a moment, but closed again, and the form remained silent and motionless for an hour. Again a heavy groan proceeded from the body, and the eyes were opened;

but in an instant all signs of returning animation had vanished.

After another interval of an hour, life and consciousness, with the power of voluntary motion, were measurably restored. After his restoration it was found that Mr. Tennent had lost all recollection of his former life, and the results of his education and experience were wholly obliterated from his mind. He was obliged to learn the alphabet of his vernacular. His memory at length returned, and with it his former mental possessions; but his doubts respecting the future life were all dissipated forever. During his absence from the body he was intromitted to the Heavens, and like Paul, heard and saw things unutterable. The trances and visions of the ancient Prophets and Apostles were intrinsically no more remarkable than this experience of Mr. Tennent.[1]

Among the ancient miracles, so-called, the alleged resurrection of certain dead persons is perhaps regarded as the most mysterious and questionable. If, however, the reänimation of corporeal forms from which life had departed, was and is *a fact*, we shall do nothing to discredit the same by attempting to naturalize this seeming miracle. I shall not undertake to prove that *the dead* may be raised, either by electricity, magnetism, or any other natural agent; or, indeed that any organized body was ever restored to life after decomposition had commenced. It is rather my object to show that in cases of suspended animation, the involuntary action of the organs has often been restored by accident, and by a wise use of natural means. Some of the cases recorded in the Scriptures were obviously examples of this

---

[1] See Christian Family Annual, for an account of his experience.

kind. That the alleged facts were actual occurrences, the writer has no doubt; but it is not so clear that dissolution was complete in any given example. If only the visible indications of life were suspended, we may be authorized to conclude that the appropriate use of natural means might have sufficed to arrest the process of dissolution, and to delay the spirit's final departure. Let us bring the Biblical examples to trial by this principle of interpretation. In the second Book of Kings, it is alleged that Elisha raised a child from the dead ; but the experiment was made only a few hours after the suspension of the vital functions. We may therefore suppose, that the transition was not complete when the prophet arrived, and that he intuitively, or by a clairvoyant vision, perceived that certain natural means would restore life. In the text it is stated, in substance, that he stretched himself on the inanimate body, taking the hands in his own, and putting his mouth to the mouth of the child ; that the flesh waxed warm, the child sneezed and opened its eyes.

I have no disposition to dispute the possibility of a divine or supra-mortal agency in similar occurrences ; but the Scriptural narrative, in this case, rather indicates that the result may have been accomplished by merely natural and human means. The body was cold, and heat was essential to the restoration of life. Accordingly the prophet stretched himself on the body. A current of vital magnetism was thus communicated to the form of the child, and the flesh became warm, because heat is naturally and necessarily diffused or radiated. Respiration had ceased, and to restore it again it was necessary to expand the lungs and to produce an artificial respiration. For this purpose it is said, that Elisha put his mouth to the mouth of the child—he breathed into him and the child sneezed, which was an infallible sign of returning animation. By the introduction of air into the lungs the blood began to be oxygenized, and the whole vital economy was moved again by the mysterious principle of LIFE. Now those who maintain that this was a supernatural occurrence, *in the popular sense of that term*, should answer the following interrogatories : Why was it necessary to warm the body ? For what purpose did the prophet put his mouth to the mouth of the child ? If the body was made warm by contact with another and a living body, and the lungs were inflated with atmospheric air, in order to restore life, were not these *natural means?* Finally, if the agents and methods employed in the process were all natural, can the result be properly regarded as *super*-natural ?

The most notable instances in the New Testament lead the rational inquirer to the same general conclusion. They were obviously cases of suspended animation, and the restoration of the vital functions was doubtless accomplished by the proper application of mental and material forces—not in violation of natural law, but agreeably to the eternal principles of mind and matter. This will appear from an examination of particular examples.

It happended when Paul was preaching a very long sermon at Troas, that a young man fell asleep, while seated in a third story window, and losing his equilibrium fell to the ground. The shock produced an instantaneous paralysis of the whole system ; and it is alleged that he "was taken up [for] dead. And Paul went down and fell on him ;" and

whilst thus embracing the body he addressed the excited
multitude, saying, "Trouble not yourselves, *for his life is in
him.*" It appears that while the Apostle was in this electro-
vital connection with the young man, the latter very naturally recovered from his temporary asphyxia. (Acts, xx.
9—12.)

On one occasion Jesus was called to the house of a certain
ruler whose daughter was supposed to be dead. But perceiving what the crowd could not know, namely, that the
soul had not departed, he said, "Give place, for *the maid is
not dead but sleepeth;* and they laughed him to scorn." But
when Jesus took the girl by the hand she was at once restored to a state of complete animation. (Matt., ix., 23—25.)

The foregoing examples are commonly regarded as miracles, in the theological sense of the term. It is very generally presumed, that the persons whose cases are thus incidentally mentioned in the evangelical narratives, were *really
dead*, in the full sense that imports a complete and final
separation of the soul from the body. But this assumption
can neither be reconciled with the letter nor the spirit of the
evangelical account. Paul declared that the young man was
still alive ; and Jesus affirmed that the ruler's daughter was
not dead. The language is unequivocal ; and in regarding
these as mere examples of suspended animation, we maintain
a rational view of the subject, at the same time we stand by
the record. Those who entertain and defend an opposite
opinion—by insisting that the individuals were actually re-
surrected from a state of absolute death—virtually *dispute
the record*, and are left to conduct their controversy with the
authorities they profess to revere.

Let us select a single additional example from the New
Testament. With a view to test, by the most searching
ordeal, the strength of the rule of interpretation I have
adopted, as compared with the prevailing theological idea,
it shall be the case of LAZARUS. The account of his resurrection may be found in the XIth chapter of John. When
Jesus heard that Lazarus was ill, he said, " *This sickness is
not unto death ;*" "after that he saith unto them, our friend
Lazarus sleepeth ;" and again, " Jesus said plainly Lazarus
is dead." From the terms here employed, as well as from
the nature of the case itself, it is made to appear that Lazarus had fallen into a state of physical insensibility, in which
his external consciousness was wholly destroyed for the time
being, and that the spirit would not have returned again to
the sphere of its mundane relations, had no sufficient effort
been employed to restore the organic action.

This view of the subject will enable us to harmonize the
several statements which the Evangelist has attributed to
Jesus, and in this way alone can they ever be reconciled.
Lazarus was sick, but *not unto death ;* when there were no
longer any perceptible signs of life, he told the disciples that
his friend *slept ;* but perceiving that they were subject to a
misapprehension, in thinking that he had merely "spoken
of taking rest in [natural] sleep, he said plainly, [obviously
for no other purpose but to correct their mistake] *Lazarus
is dead.*" But we discover in the latter expression nothing
inconsistent with the essential features of our explanation.
Death, as has been observed, is a progressive transformation. If the term were only used to denote the *completion*
of such transformation, it could not, with a strict regard to

philosophic precision, have been applied in any case where putrefaction did not exist, this being the only infallible sign that the life on earth is ended. But a person may be said to be *dead* before decomposition begins—even before respiration has ceased, *provided the transformation is surely going on, and the result inevitable ;* as we sometimes say, a man is ruined, undone, lost, or that he is a dead man, when we see that his physical condition, his course of life, or his exposure to some impending disaster must inevitably result in destruction. Many persons in whom the organic action has been suspended for whole days together, still hold their lives by a better tenure than others who have experienced no such interruption of the vital functions. Lazarus was dead—in a qualified sense—during the period of suspended animation, and had not Jesus interposed, the dissolution would have been complete and permanent.

The remains of Lazarus had been deposited in a cave; and, from the record of the circumstances, it may be inferred that the form had remained in an inanimate state for *four days.* But this conclusion is not warranted. It is well known—and no theological student will dispute the fact— that the Jews, in numbering days with reference to any occurrence, not only included the one on which the event transpired, but also the day whereon the same was made a subject of remark. It will be perceived, therefore, that the precise period might have been much less than would otherwise appear from the face of the record. Had the event actually occurred during the last hour of the first day, and been made the subject of reference at the beginning of the fourth, both days, by the Hebrew method, would have been

included, while the precise time might have been little more
than *forty-eight hours.* But allowing the longest possible
time warranted by the phraseology as now commonly understood, the case is not more extraordinary than some of our
modern instances. There are many well authenticated examples of persons having been dead, at least to all human
appearance, for an equal or longer period, who have subsequently been restored, seemingly without the intervention
of any supernatural means.

Those who are determined to have Religion unnatural
and Nature irreligious, make a strong point here, if allowed
to assume what they have never been able to prove, viz.:
that the body of Lazarus was in a partially decomposed state
at the time of its resurrection. The words of Martha (39th
verse) furnish the only conceivable ground for this unwar-
rantable assumption. But Martha did not pretend to speak
from any interior knowledge or perception of the real or
alleged fact. We have no evidence that she was inspired;
the Evangelist does not say so, and it is fair to presume, that
she merely expressed a conviction founded on general observation in similar cases. Of course, no enlightened and well-
balanced mind will attempt to support, by such frail props,
a system that boldly denies our right to reason on religious
subjects, and vainly attempts to bend the essential laws of
Nature to its arbitrary *dicta.*

M. Ernest Renan in his late work reflects no light on this
question.[1] It was not, indeed, anticipated that an author
with so large a basilar development, and with strong consti-

---

[1] See Wilbour's translation of Renan's Life of Jesus, pp. 304-5.

tutional proclivities to a material and sensuous philosophy, would be able to furnish a solution of the profound psychological problems involved in the life of Jesus. A theological education and a persuasive style are not all that is required to qualify one for so difficult a task. On the contrary, the man who would perform this work, with honor to himself, must intuitively recognize the supra-mortal powers and invisible forces that surround him in the Universe, and clearly perceive their relations to the phenomena of the visible world. With an organization and culture adapted to the external plain of observation and thought, one can only survey the *surface* of such a character, while he has no power to discover the hidden springs of that most natural and spiritual life.

But the religious public have a right to demand of the author, who ventures to seriously meddle with the evidences that support the common faith of the Christian world, some measure of consistency and candor in his treatment of so grave a subject. Yet M. Renan presumes, that the friends of Lazarus were so anxious to establish the claims of Jesus to supernatural power, that they were not only capable of great exaggeration, in their statement of the essential facts of the case, but to accomplish their object, they did not hesitate to resort to a pious fraud. It is seriously suggested that, even Lazarus himself, prostrated by extreme illness—which naturally leads the subject to solemn thought and self-examination—"*caused himself to be swathed in grave clothes, as one dead, and shut up in his family tomb!*" In other words, with the termination of his mortal career in view, and the great realities of the eternal world impending, he is supposed to have engaged in this grotesque and solemn farce. With no other purpose but to further the designs of his enthusiastic and unscrupulous relatives, and to establish a false reputation for their common Master, he thus allows himself (in the opinion of this author) to be used as a mere *puppet* in this senseless mockery of death and the grave!

The musical speech and graceful manners of M. Renan but half conceal the destructive tendencies of his book, and the defenders of the faith will scarcely mistake him for a disciple. Had he disproved the cardinal fact; had he demolished the legitimate claims of the Christian religion, or in any manner impaired the foundations. of a rational faith; surely, his eloquent attestation of the superiority of Jesus to other men; his esthetic appreciation of the harmony of his character; of the humane spirit of his teachings; the child-like simplicity of his life, and the transcendent purity of his worship—would *all* have been powerless to repair the mischief. Indeed, the fortress that an enemy has once breached, by the use of his masked batteries, is not to be restored by a thin coat of transparent varnish. though it be applied to the ruins by the most skillful hand.

I have little inclination to dogmatize on a subject of this nature, and how far the examples from the Scriptures resemble the other facts cited in this connection, the reader will judge. Their outward aspects sufficiently indicate that they depend on the same internal principles, and hence they must inevitably be classed together. Indeed, they admit of no other disposition, especially when they serve to elucidate one distinct phase of the operation of the same law. It is of no great importance whether the facts occur in Asia or America. Moreover, they are of no more consequence to science because they are two thousand years old ; nor will the philosophical inquirer prefer the testimony of a foreigner, and a dead man, to that of the living witness who stands in his presence.

The case of Lazarus appears the more remarkable, because it can not be inferred, from the Evangelical narrative, that any visible means were employed ; or, indeed, that the result depended on any direct physical contact. But God, Nature, and the human mind have invisible means and modes of operation. God is unseen, and Nature vails the ministers of his will. Only *effects* are perceptible on the natural plain ; *causes* belong to that world which no mortal eye hath seen. The events that men call miracles, are usually far less wonderful than the familiar operations of Nature. Shall we say that a notable miracle is performed when an inanimate body receives a new quickening, and yet discover no greater miracle *in the very existence of all living things?* Every where I see that the Divine power is working after a uniform and natural order, organizing and animating the most beautiful creations with a portion of his Spirit. This is the greatest of all miracles. It must require a superior divine energy, if possible, to make *a new body*, and to create a deathless soul to dwell in it, than to reanimate an organization which, but yesterday, was inspired with all the powers of life, and sense, and thought.

The human mind is a psycho-electrical magnet and medium, connecting the earth with the heavens, since MAN contains the elements and attributes of both worlds in his two-fold nature. Mind acts on mind without corporeal conjunction. This is demonstrated by every successful attempt to magnetize, or otherwise influence a person without speech or sensible contact. The form of Lazarus was in a perfectly negative state ; and a great physical, spiritual, and divine Magnet, in the person and power of Jesus, stood at the door of the sepulcher. The powers of the Heavens, acting through the concentrated energies of his mind, and the subtile agents of the natural world, established the necessary connection. Virtue descended and went out from Jesus to quicken the lifeless form. The vital fluids began to circulate ; the life-giving energy was transfused through all the veins and arteries ; a subtile, all-communicating spirit ran along the avenues of sensation, and the nerves moved like the strings of an untuned lyre, when they are swept by a mighty wind. A loud voice reëchoed through the cavern, and the sleeper awoke to walk again with the living.

A state of complete physical insensibility, and a total suspension of the power of voluntary motion, may result from a variety of causes. Cataleptic and epileptic diseases, powerful electric shocks, violent concussions, strangulation, drugs that stupify the patient, the inspiration of noxious gases, and total immersion in water, are among the diversified causes and means whereby the functions of animated nature are daily suspended. The action of these agents on the physical and mental states of men, require at our hands a deliberate and patient investigation. Here is a work for the philosopher to perform. The interests of science call for close observation and severe analysis ; and the interests of humanity demand the utmost perseverance in the investigation of the essential faculties, functions and conditions of human nature. Where such momentous issues are involved, indifference is something worse than justifiable homicide. When the question comprehends life and death, it is unsafe to depend on superficial evidence, and carelessness is crime. Experience long since demonstrated that, *decomposition is the only positive sign of dissolution.* All others are frequently deceptive; and at this time, when so many are subject to *trances,* and, consequently, to intervals of suspended animation—in their more external aspects analogous to physical death—great caution is necessary lest we unbar the sepulchre to the living. The prudent man will wait and watch to see the lineaments of beauty obliterated—wait until the images which thought traced on the yielding clay, ere the soul departed, have gradually disappeared

" Before Decay's effacing fingers."

But, in the light of the author's philosophy, death is at most but a circumstance in an endless existence. It destroys nothing. In the progressive scale of the Universe, every death or transformation involves—by an inevitable necessity —a more exalted and enlarged life. The darkest images that fall athwart our mortal pathway, are but the distant shadows of a life that is sublime and immortal. All things that are of Divine origin are imperishable. True, forms dissolve and pass away,

" —— but the changes
Are constant renovation, and not death."

This is likewise true of all the creations of Nature and Art. The despotic institutions of other countries and other times must perish ; old systems and dynasties crumble and fall, and their ruins cover the great globe; while ancient nationalities are obliterated and scarcely live in history.   It is well.

> " 'Tis but the ruin of the bad—
>   The wasting of the wrong and ill ;
> Whate'er of good the Old Time had
>   Is living still."

Whatever is essentially good and fundamentally true, is in trinsically immortal, and must endure forever.   The living and graceful forms which we delight to gaze upon, and to press to our bosoms, may perish and be swept away like autumn leaves ; but the souls that warmed them with vital fire, shall live on in fairer worlds !

> " Let earth dissolve—yon ponderous orbs descend,
>   And grind us into dust—the soul is safe !
>   The MAN emerges—mounts above the wreck
>   As towering flame from Nature's funeral pyre !"

CHAPTER XXXIV.

PHILOSOPHY OF INSPIRATION.

The grand Harmony of the Universe—Nature the Divine Improvisation—
Definition of Inspiration—Men of Genius and their Works—The Poets
and Musicians—Mozart and his Requiem—Remarkable Improvisatores —
Illustrations in the Curiosities of Literature—Harris and the Golden Age
—Sources of Inspired Ideas—Language an imperfect Medium—The Spirit
and the Letter—Inspiration, a Vital Reality rather than a Fact of His-
tory—Imperfect Reports of the Teachings of Jesus and his Apostles—
The Bible and its Authors Cerebral Influence on Revelation—Analysis
of Biblical Examples—The question of Plenary Inspiration—Theological
form of Popular Materialism—Man the great Fact—Sacred Books and
Religious Systems, Phenomena of Human Existence—God speaks to the
World now.

> " There's not the smallest orb which thou beholdest
> But in his motions like an angel sings "

THE Universe may be regarded as a grand musical instrument, on which the Divine oratorio of the Creation—
revealed in the endless scale of ascending forms and faculties—is improvised. Nature is a many-toned Lyre, whose
chords are moved by Deity. To our limited comprehension,
outward objects and events appear to be discordant, only
because their relations to each other, and to the ultimate
designs of the Creator, are either unknown or but imperfectly distinguished. It requires a man of strong faith, of
generous feeling and liberal sentiment, and of vast intellectual comprehensiveness, to reconcile the world's apparent
discords, or to perceive the grand harmony that runs through
all human experience and universal history. But Divine

Wisdom can regulate the scale and dispose of all events.
From the beginning the world has been full of beauty and
melody. Successive periods and unnumbered generations of
men—a stately throng, moving to the great

" Harmony not understood—"

lived, died and were forgotten, before our hearts beat in
unison with the music of the spheres. Innumerable suns
and systems felt the Infinite impulsion, and the shades of
uncreated worlds, clothed in white nebulæ, still repose in
the Supreme presence.   There was order in Heaven, and on
earth an uninterrupted succession of Divine manifestations.
The sun shone on many forms of life and beauty ; the skies
were bright and the waters were clear ; flowers bloomed on
the hills and in the valleys ; the birds carrolled in all the
sylvan arcades ; sweet perfumes and melodious sounds
danced together in the cerebral halls of the soul ; the winds
played with the fair maiden's tresses, whilst Love played
with her heart-strings ; and heroes who were brave in battle
went to dwell in the courts of Valhalla.   From the threshold of time the illuminated seer explored the mysteries of
Eternity ; the philosopher, in his profound abstraction, was
led away to other worlds, and the poet sang his inspired
song in Paradise.

There is sublime harmony in all the works and ways of
the Infinite. A loving purpose and an omnipotent hand
are revealed in the endless *variations* of Being. We were
not present when the performance commenced ; we have not
witnessed its termination, and who will venture to say that
the Divine plan is imperfect?   There were " Sons of God"

who listened to the sublime overture of the singing stars.[1]
Millions of intelligences appeared on the stage before us,
and having performed their respective parts retired behind
the *scenes*. The world did not miss them. In like manner
the great musical drama will proceed without stop or pause,
when our voices are heard by the natural ear no more. But
to the Infinite Understanding, the harmony is unbroken. It
is true that dense clouds, like frowning battle-ships, ride in
the midst of the etherial ocean, and black banners are unfurled against the sky. Suns and systems are obscured, and
the light of immortality shut out from the soul. To the benighted mind, even divine ideas look like frightful monsters ;
inspiration may pass for a species of delirium, and angelic
voices be mistaken for ordinary thunder. (John, chap. xii.,
28, 29.) The world has its mournful scenes and sounds, and
in the music of life there is many a wild refrain. Here are
desolate homes, noisome dungeons, and bloody battle-fields.
Men build sepulchers and compose requiems ; plaintive songs
are heard in the wilderness and notes of terror on the sea.
These all have their place in time and their use in the progress of the race. But there are graceful interludes and
delicate symphonies between the prominent scenes and

---

[1] The author of the most ancient poem that has come down to us, in speaking of the creation, says. "The morning stars sang together, and all the
sons of God shouted for joy." (Job, xxxviii., 7.) Plato entertained the
poetic idea that the Muses constituted the soul of the planetary system ;
while the Pythagorians insisted that the movement of the spheres in their
respective orbits produced music. Sir Isaac Newton not only recognized
the principles of harmory as universal, but from his experiments with
light and the prism, he discovered that the primary colors and their intervening shades occupied spaces, corresponding with the division of the dia-
tonic scale into tones and semi-tones.

solemn acts of life ; and at last, all who have been divinely
great join with the choral angels in the triumphal *finale.*

If the story of Prometheus was once a fable, we may be
sure that—in some important sense—it is fabulous no longer.
The immortal fire is rekindled on our own altars. Through
all the inherent forces and essential laws of the celestial,
spiritual and natural worlds, a Divine energy is interfused,
and Powers unseen speak in the inspired thoughts of living
men who sit hard by the golden gates. In all eras and dis-
pensations the natural and human have sustained intimate
and unbroken relations to the spiritual and divine. The relations of great thoughts and illustrious deeds to the realms
of spiritual causation, are daily becoming more perceptible.
Indeed, this connection is indispensable to the existence of
Nature and Man. Hitherto Literature, Art, Science and
Religion, have left their monuments along the Ages to mark
the world's development. They are diversified and glorious forms of thought! But such forms are often but the
tombs of ideas that once possessed a vital existence. Stones
and parchments have no life-sustaining elements. Men gaze
at the Pyramids, but are not made strong ; courage does not
proceed from the ruins of the Colosseum, nor wisdom from
the Parthenon ; deserted banqueting halls are places where
men hunger and thirst, and thousands die in spirit beneath
the shadow of St. Peters. Men who live in the past, " seek
the livin among the dead ;" but it is our privilege to recog
nize the divine significance in the events of To-day. GOD
IS IN THE PRESENT ; and in the most vital and essential
sense Inspiration· belongs to the LIVING AGE.

Inspiration is from the Latin *inspiro,* and in the physiological sense of the term represents the act of *breathing;* in other words, the admission of the vital air into the lungs by inhalation.   In the spiritual sense, inspiration implies the impregnation of the germs of thought in the mind, and the silent infusion of ideas from some invisible source of intelligence.   In the light of this definition it will be perceived that *all inspiration, whether physiological or psychological, must be confined to the existing age.*   It can not belong to the past, in any vital sense, for the reason that men only live and breathe in the present.   If the process be suspended, there is an end of inspiration ; and all that remains to us are the lifeless records it may have left behind ; and the sweet, solemn memory of a life departed, but whose distant shadow yet haunts the soul, like

> "A lyric voice from the Paradise afar.
> Or harp-notes trembling from some gracious star."

The great realm of the INVISIBLE opens around and within us, and we become truly inspired, in proportion as our natures become refined and exalted.   The thoughts that startle the world with their vastness, power and beauty, are not born of corporeal elements.   On this point we must respect the actual experience of inspired minds rather than the skepticism of those who are incapable of any similar experience.   The latter class should be reminded that it is as truly the privilege of the eagle to *soar* as it is the peculiar province of meaner things to *crawl.*   The dusty speculations of material philosophers, on a question of this nature, are entitled to no credence, since they are obviously as destitute of truth as they are devoid of all incentives to honorable aspirations and a divine life.   If such men have no inspiration, the fact shows clearly enough that they themselves are earthly and sensual ; but it does nothing to prove that others are like them, much less that the common faith of the world is an illusion.

The remarkable powers of the human mind, as developed in men of genius, or displayed by the seers and prophets of all ages, may be rationally referred to a kind of natural inspiration, of which the mind may be, and, indeed, *must be*, receptive in the higher plans of its thought and development. We necessarily derive our impressions from the principles and objects with which we sustain intimate relations. When, therefore, the mind is profoundly engrossed with interior realities, it is proportionably withdrawn from all the objects which appeal to the faculties through the external avenues of sensation; and it receives influxes from the realms of the Invisible, as naturally as at other times it perceives the presence and distinguishes the forms and qualities of more material creations. Not only may this idea of inspiration be entertained, consistently with the laws and relations of the human mind, but it can only be rejected at the sacrifice of our better judgment. All original thoughts and every creation of divine beauty and use, may be supposed to emanate from that ideal realm—from the World of subtile forces and invisible Powers. Else why are they born in moments of profound abstraction, when, by intense mental concentration, the senses are deadened and the soul is quickened? Will the materialist tell us why the spiritual element enters so largely into the writings of all men of genius, if it is not that they are inspired ? Why does it predominate in the works of Dante, Shakespeare, Milton, and all true poets, if it be not for the obvious reason that, in the hours of their greatest elevation they are essentially removed from the sphere of grosser life, and sublimated in thought and feeling by association with the hidden principles of Nature and the intelligences of the immortal world ?

These views entirely accord with the actual experience and personal claims of the most exalted minds. Scarcely a great poet, painter, sculptor, or musician, has ever lived who was not conscious of drawing his inspiration from the clear springs of the immortal life. Not a few men of genius have recognized the presence and acknowledged their dependence on some foreign intelligence. Many of the characters and much of the imagery of Milton's great poem were derived from spheres that mortal eye hath not seen ; and his faith in the perpetual intercourse between the visible and invisible worlds, is thus clearly expressed :

> "God will deign
> To visit oft the dwellings of just men,
> Delighted ; and with frequent intercourse
> Thither will send his wingèd messengers
> On errands of supernal grace."

Shakespeare makes the shades of departed men to appear in Hamlet and in Macbeth ; Wordsworth believed that the spirit of prophecy was given to men in all ages ; Coleridge ascribed his inspiration to the overshadowing presence and influence of celestial visitors ; and Raphael painted the visions of ethereal beauty which his immortalized Mother presented to his vision.

The late CARLOS D. STUART—widely known as an eloquent and forcible writer in prose and verse—assured the author that all his poems, to which he attached any real value, were composed under the influence of a kind of *spell*, which came over him at irregular intervals, and subsided when the work in hand was finished.   Concerning the origin of this influence he possessed no certain knowledge ; but all the mental effort, of which he was conscious, was made at the commencement of the process.   To use his own significant language, " As soon as the poem is fairly started, the whole flows out, seemingly without effort, and winds itself up."   I find the evidence of a similar experience in the brief testimony of another poet, who says — respecting the method and the origin of his poems—

" They are written by my hand, but with little or no mental effort on my part.   The whole of a poem is before my mind at once, and if any person speaks to me while I am writing, it vanishes, and is present again on a subsequent occasion.   That this is a spiritual gift, I have no doubt ; for I have no control over it "

The following account which Mozart gives of his inspired moments, appears to warrant the inference that his grand musical compositions emanated from the inward sphere of the Divine Harmonies :

" When all goes well with me—when I am in a carriage, or walking, or when I cannot sleep at night, the thoughts come streaming in upon me most fluently ; whence, or how, is more than I can tell.   Then follow the counterpoint—and the clang of the different instruments ; and, if I am not disturbed, my soul is fixed, and the thing grows greater, and broader, and clearer ; and I have it all in my head, even when the piece is a long one ; and I *see it*—like a beautiful picture—not hearing the different parts in succession, as they must be played, but *the whole at once*.   That is the delight !   The composing and making is like a beautiful and vivid dream ; but this *hearing* of it is the best of all."

The inspiration of Mozart is further illustrated by the singular admonition he received of his approaching dissolution. It is alleged that a mysterious stranger visited Mozart and requested him to compose a grand Requiem. The latter signified his willingness to comply with the request; terms were proposed and accepted, when the stranger abruptly disappeared. Mozart very soon became deeply interested and absorbed. *He felt that he was preparing the work for himself.* At length the Requiem—which had occupied more time than was at first anticipated—was finished. Fatigued and exhausted by his protracted effort, the great composer fell asleep, but was soon aroused by the light footsteps of his daughter. He called the gentle girl to his side and said : " My Emilie – my task is done—*my* Requiem is finished." Handing her the last notes, into which the parting soul had just breathed the deathless spirit of song, Mozart admonished his child that he was about to leave her, and that he would hear her sing to those notes the hymn of her sainted mother. With a voice tender and tremulous with emotion the gentle girl commenced :

> "Spirit! thy labor is o'er!
> Thy term of probation is run,
> Thy steps are now bound for the untrodden shore,
> And the race of immortals begun."

Having concluded the fourth stanza, Emilie yet lingered a moment on the low, melancholy notes of the piece, when, turning from the instrument to look for her father's approval, she perceived that he was motionless. His face was illuminated by the still, passionless smile that the wrapt and glorified spirit had left on the consecrated clay. In due time the mysterious stranger reappeared, but Mozart was not there.

He had completed his beautiful work as an interpreter of the Divine Harmonies on earth, and ascended to the source of his inspirations.

The inspiration of men of genius is illustrated by those rapid improvisations of poets and musicians which appear to transcend the limits of the normal capacity. As to the Italians, it is on no good authority claimed that they have ever risen in their impromptu utterances, above such brief rhapsodies as are confined to local and momentary topics. Chivalry and Love were the principal themes of the Troubadours ; but to none of these can we find credited any effort worth remembering. Improvising of this kind has generally been a play upon the names and peculiarities of persons, or on the incidental circumstances of the occasion. We have heard maudlin specimens at political and other assemblages, but they have been, without a single remembered exception, as ephemeral as the incidents which prompted their utterance.

D'Israeli, in his " Curiosities of Literature," cites numerous instances of the rapid composition of brief pieces by different poets ; but none of the utterance of a complete work of any moment. Fenelon wrote his " Telemarque," (prose history of the wandering of the son of Ulysses in search of his lost father,) in three months—one of the most rapid performances on record. D'Israeli also alludes to a class of visions or revelations, current in the Middle Ages—represented to have been uttered by superior powers, through studious monks and recluses—and adds that Dante's " Inferno" has been suspected of indebtedness to a poem known as " The Vision of Alberico." The " Culprit Fay." by J.

Rodman Drake, a deceased American poet, a production of singular beauty—but more remarkable because, notwithstanding its length, no human character enters into it—was a very rapid composition. But the poems of THOMAS L. HARRIS are far more remarkable for the rapidity of their creation, beside being immensely superior in purpose and character. Among popular authors there is, perhaps, no one that writes more rapidly than Alexander Dumas; but it appears that Harris—by the special aid of his inspiring agents—far transcends the utmost limit of Dumas' powers of construction and expression.

It would be vain to search the annals of literature for a more striking example of poetic inspiration than is presented in the case of Mr. HARRIS, whose rapid and brilliant improvisations have astonished and delighted many intelligent witnesses, while they have arrested the attention of metaphysical philosophers on account of their profound psychological import. From his youth, Harris has been accustomed to write verse; and many of his earlier Lyrics—already widely circulated through the religious and secular press— have been universally admired. His earlier poems were never mechanically composed - were rarely, if ever, the result of previous thought. On the contrary, they were apparently almost as involuntary as respiration. Whenever he is in active sympathy with the minds of other poets, whether living or dead, he seems to be temporarily endowed with the characteristics of their genius, respectively, and his thoughts find expression in the peculiar style of each. It must be observed, however, that this is no studied attempt to imitate others. On the contrary, it is a spontaneous influx and efflux, which is neither induced nor interrupted by his own volition. The current of inspired thought not only comes unexpectedly, but it flows rapidly and terminates abruptly. As an illustration, a single example will be far more suggestive than the most elaborate description.

On the thirtieth of November, 1854, during a personal interview with Harris, the writer chanced to speak of EDGAR ALLAN POE. In a moment H. appeared to be completely withdrawn from the sphere of his outward relations, and, during his profound abstraction, he improvised two poems. The second one—a bold and graceful utterance, containing over sixty lines—was spoken in *fifteen minutes*. It purports to be a description of the strange and thrilling experience of the Author of the Raven, on his introduction to the realities of the Invisible World. The abrupt and frightful termination of his mortal career; the birth of the soul, surrounded by unearthly and imaginary terrors, and the opening of the inner senses amidst the glories of Paradise, are thus described in the first part of the poem:

> " A lurid mantle wrapped my spirit form,
> Cradled in lightnings and in whirlwinds born,
> Torn from the body, terribly downcast,   .
> Plunged headlong through red furnaces in blast ;
> Those seething torrents maddened me ; I fell.
> But woke in Paradise instead of Hell ;
> Like song waves circling in a golden bell,
> Like fragrant odors in a woodbine dell,
> Like glowing pistiles in a rose unblown,
> Like all sweet dreams to saints in slumber shown,
> Like Heaven itself, like joy incarnate given ;
> And as a ship through wintry whirlwinds driven   .
> Finds land-locked port in Araby the blest,
> So, I, through terror, entered into rest "

A lovely maiden, whose angelic beauty is revealed in the

transcendent light that emanates "from her full bosom," comes to the Poet, who is filled with rapture while she sings:

> "I have waited, I have waited,
> As the Evening Star belated,
> When it lingers pale and lonely by the purple sunset door.
> I have found thee, I have found thee,
> And with heart-spells fast have bound thee ;
> So from out the glowing halo sang the Angel-maid LENORE."

The Poet, "in a fine frenzy," then rehearses the dark scenes of his Earth-life—the poverty, despair, desolation and madness, which broke his heart and veiled his spirit in the gloom of a tempestuous night. The feeling of utter desperation which possessed all his faculties, and burned in his brain like an unquenchable fire, and the blissful repose of the liberated spirit in the Angelic abodes, are thus vividly contrasted in the closing stanzas :

> "And I fled Life's outer portal,
> Deeming anguish was immortal,
> Crying, 'Launch thy heavy thunders, tell me never to adore.
> Hate for hate, and curse for curses,
> Through abyssmal universes.
> Plunge me down as lost Archangels fell despairingly of yore.
>
> So the whirlwind bore my spirit,
> But to lands the Saints inherit,
> And it seems my heart forever like a ruby cup runs o'er.
> I am blest beyond all blessing,
> And an Angel's pure carressing,
> Flows around my soul forever like a stream around its shore."

The gestures that accompanied the utterance of this poem were highly dramatic ; at the same time the features and intonations of the speaker were expressive of all the tender and terrible emotions which the lines so impressively indicate.

The poetic inspiration of Harris is more fully illustrated in several books which were published in 1854 and 1856.

The " Epic of the Starry Heaven," a poem of Four Thousand
Lines—characterized by bold thoughts, and splendid imagery—was improvised in the course of fourteen consecutive
days, the actual time employed in the performance being only
twenty-six hours and sixteen minutes. The " Lyric of the
Morning Land," containing nearly Five Thousand Lines,
was dictated in about *thirty-two hours.* It is every way remarkable, and not less so for its exquisite delicacy and
beauty than for the circumstances of its origin and the
rapidity of its creation. The critics were reminded of
" Queen Mab," and more than one of them was led to infer
that " the mantle of the immortal SHELLEY had truly fallen
on the author's shoulders." " The Golden Age"—a production of much wider scope, extending to Ten Thousand Lines,
and purporting to be the composite utterance of several
eminent English bards—was communicated to the present
writer and other witnesses, in LESS THAN ONE HUNDRED
HOURS. Whoever will regard the intrinsic merits of these
poems, and consider the amazing rapidity of their composition, must inevitably conclude that they are unequalled by
any similar productions in the whole range of literature.

The " Golden Age," especially, is a splendid triumph of
the Ideal. There is a startling reach and boldness in many
of the flights, and the ideas look like revolutions in their
elementary development. The elements of essential beauty
and grandeur here mingle in sublime concord, while the
spirit that pervades the whole is serene, lofty and divinely
just. Error, dissipation and crime; every species of tyranny
and slavery, and all the forms of evil are condemned and
spurned ; Truth and Love are crowned with divine honors,

while personal virtue, practical justice, and universal holiness are hymned as the appropriate graces and accomplishments of purified and perfected humanity.

In all these particulars, and in whatever else is most essential to true poetic excellence, the " Golden Age" will not suffer by a comparison with any similar production of either ancient or modern times. The principal Poets speak with world-awakening voices. Pollock rises far above the standard of his earthly efforts ; the words of Shelley, of Byron, and Rousseau, sound like shrill clarion-notes that summon nations to battle against kings, and priests and tyrannies ; whilst Coleridge lifts his Orphic Lyre and sings as only the " English Plato" was wont to sing. The descriptive portions of this poem are extraordinary, as illustrations of the compass of our language. Indeed, it would severely tax the capabilities of the most gifted mind to coin its phraseology alone ; which, however, is neither strained nor unnatural, but flowing and melodious as a valley brook.

The thoughts of great poets are like silver bells that ring out on the world's ear ; their eloquent words captivate the sense like the tones of some mellow horn and their pure sentiments steal into and thrill the soul like the sweet echoes of a shell. Some souls are so full of love and religion that life is all music, tender and touching. There are also voices that resemble the notes of a clarion, when it is heard from the distant summits in the gray light of the morning, calling peoples to battle and to victory. Then there are Æolion harps that sigh responsively to the gentlest whisper of a zephyr ; and delicate *attachments*, that soften and spiritualize the music of ruder natures. Some speak with trumpet-

voices before the sepulchers of slumbering nations, and they
wake and rise from the dead ; while here and there a deep,
solemn and musical inspiration flows into some lofty soul,
whose great thoughts and illustrious deeds cause the frame-
work of our being to tremble, as the measured tones of a
grand organ shake the consecrated pile.

The man who has no inspiration depends on the outward
channels and the common sources of information—on his
investigation of the outward forms and phenomena of Nature ; on books, and the ordinary intercourse with the world
through the medium of language. The inward avenues of
perception being closed, Nature is mainly a sealed book, and
he is left to inspect its covering only, and to interpret its
profound mysteries in the dim light of his superficial observation.   But the relations of the inspired mind to Nature
are far more intimate. The great Volume is opened and
illuminated to the man whose inward perceptions are quickened by a living inspiration.   When all the interior avenues
of the soul are unobstructed, the powers of sensation blend
and become as ONE ; thus, the eye being single, the whole
being is full of light.

While the inspired mind derives impressions from the inward principles of the natural world, with which its faculties are in correspondence, it is also susceptible of an infusion of ideas from the superior spheres of intelligence.   But
whatever may be the immediate agents and remote sources
of our inspiration, it is true that all inspired ideas are subject to such limitations as necessarily characterize the finite
capacity.   We may admit that infallibility belongs to the
celestial springs of inspired ideas ; but it certainly does not

characterize their terrestrial incarnation. The immortal thought may be precise and unerring in its archetypal form, but infallibility can neither distinguish the mundane instruments nor the earthly forms of its expression. "We have this treasure in earthen vessels," and it is but natural that the treasure itself should be more or less corrupted by its mortal channels and receptacles.

Moreover, language is but a feeble and inflexible medium, which the most intense emotion cannot render sufficiently plastic and powerful to subserve the highest desires of the mind. For the present, however, Thought, with its etherial form and soul of fire, must employ this clumsy vehicle and ride slowly for the world's accommodation. Men of exalted genius and profound learning have exhausted the sources of language in their attempts to incarnate the noblest creations of the mind. Many gifted souls—ascending toward the highest heaven of imagination—have seen and heard what mortal tongues can never express. They are dull, inactive beings, who have never felt that all language is cold, formal, and forever inadequate to express their highest thoughts and deepest emotions. The most subtile and condensed forms of speech appear tame and spiritless to the mind in the light of its transfigurations. Whenever the inspired man has been for a moment elevated to the highest plain of perception, and permitted to view the unnumbered worlds that encircle the Infinite Presence, he has descended with the soul quickened and purified by the inspiration of the Heavens, but only to testify with an Apostle, that he was "Caught up into Paradise and heard unspeakable words."

Most Christians are indebted to the Jews for all the in-

spired or revealed truth they either possess or desire to receive. It is insisted that in the absence of the Bible man
can possess no certain knowledge of the immortal life and
world, and that he is incapable of forming any proper conception of the relations of the human and the Divine. Infallible authority is claimed for the ancient Hebrew records,
at the same time all other claims to genuine inspiration are
positively rejected. It is virtually assumed that there is nothing essentially Divine in Nature ; and hence that a man
may violate the laws of his being and not endanger the safety
of his soul, so long as there is no departure from the letter
of the Jewish oracles. The sectarian Christian has no great
affinity for the soul of the Jew ; his small charity will not
pardon his unbelief ; but he has a devout and unquestioning
reverence for the sacred books, and preserves with the same
fidelity the most beautiful and spiritual revelations, and the
darkest details of idolatry and blood that disfigure the Hebrew history. It is a strange infatuation that despises the
sons of Abraham and stifles the living spirit of Inspiration,
while it persistently clings to old parchments and reverences
the forms of inspired ideas. Blind adoration, that thus worships the stereotyped record of an ancient Revelation, whilst
it virtually denies the immediate presence and inspiring influence of God in the soul !

We neither deny the inspiration of the Scriptures nor reject the imperfect records that have been preserved. A
qualified acceptance of both is as consistent with a rational
philosophy as the demand for still further revelations. Even
the expression of a desire for new forms of inspired and revealed truth may lead some persons to the hasty conclusion

that the author lightly esteems those we already possess. The inference is illogical.   We naturally desire to perpetuate only such things as are of real interest and permanent utility.   This is prominent among the reasons that prompt the demand for further knowledge of the solemn mysteries of life and immortality.   Why should the current of inspired truth be arbitrarily interrupted ?   Has the ultimate Source been exhausted, or has man lost the capacity to receive divine instruction ?   The common view of the subject not only disregards our daily experience, but it is at once unnatural and utterly inconsistent with the laws and relations of the human mind.

But it is said that we do not need any further revelations —that we have enough, and all that can reasonably be desired.   The Jewish and Christian Scriptures are regarded as sufficient for all nations,.and equally suited to every possible degree of human development.   A careful analysis of the contents of the Bible would probably surprise many pious believers who are prone to regard it as a full and complete revelation of all the truth that essentially concerns our common nature, our moral relations and our final destiny. Yet every careful reader of the New Testament may discover, if he will, that we have only some small fragments of what Jesus taught, and a few scraps from the discourses of the Apostles.   The Founder of the Christian religion was employed some three years in his public ministry, and yet all the words that are ascribed to him by his biographers would doubtless occupy much less space than an annual message by the President of the United States.   The chief apostles, Paul, Peter, and John, continued their ministry twenty, thirty,

and fifty years, respectively ; and yet we have not a complete report of a single apostolic sermon. We would like
to read even a brief synopsis of one discourse from each of
the consecrated Twelve ; but the Book does not contain so
much. There were no phonographic writers then ;—no lightning telegraphs, nor steam power-presses, to seize, dissemi-
nate, and embalm the inspired thoughts and words that fell
from their lips like a rain of fire. If, indeed, the little that
has come down to us is *enough* for all men, in all ages of the
world, then, agreeably to this notion, we must infer that
nearly all that Christ and his early ministers did say, might
very properly have been left unspoken ; and hence, the protracted ministry of the Apostles may be regarded as a work
of supererogation.

The authors of the Scriptures were not the only inspired
writers. Several others have experienced the divine afflatus.
The word of God and tongues of fire were given to them.
They may not be generally recognized ; but those who draw
their inspiration from Nature and the Heavens, can afford
to dispense with the favor of kings and the votes of councils. Should one write an eloquent preamble and then resolve that the stars shine, he would be laughed at, chiefly
because the fact is self-evident. Moreover, a great soul need
not stop to write its resolutions and adopt them *viva voce*.
The man who is truly inspired neither requires a diploma nor
a letter of recommendation, and the sealed credentials are
of no use to such men. You feel the power of their inspiration at a distance, and do not pause to debate the question
which the potent magnetism of their presence at once decides.

But we accept the Bible not merely as a work of unusual

interest and value ; it is doubtless worthy to be regarded as
the most remarkable collection of spiritual experiences ever
given to the world.   With a mass of historical information
of great importance, and examples of the finest poetic inspiration, it contains much that evinces a profound insight into
human nature, and numerous convincing illustrations of a
divine agency in the affairs of men.   But the Scripture
writers possessed the ordinary characteristics of other authors.   They were influenced by human passions, and were
liable to err in their judgment respecting the source and the
value of their impressions.   Indeed, no degree of wisdom
short of Omniscience can be exempt from this liability.   They
were, moreover, diversely constituted, and lived under a
great variety of circumstances, extending through a period
of many centuries.   The Scriptures are, for these reasons,
of a mixed character ; and nothing can be more absurd than
to claim the same exalted and Divine inspiration for every
portion of their contents.

The writer cannot esteem it to be profane or irreverent
to question the inspired origin of certain portions of the
Bible.   The truly rational man must doubt either the reverence or the intelligence of those who do not.   Is not that
man strangely irreverent or incorrigibly stupid who will admit
of no just discrimination—who claims for the confessions of
a penitent adulterer the same inspiration that gave the world
the prophecy of Isaiah ?   No reverence in the least allied to
reason will, for a moment, insist that Solomon's Song of his
beloved, and the wonderful Sermon on the Mount, are equally
inspired.   The former is an oriental love song, the imagery
of which determines that, whatever may have been the

source of the reputed author's inspiration, it came through the basilar region of his brain. Nor will any man, whose nature is not sadly perverted, even pretend that the penalties of the Mosaic code and the thunders of Sinai are of equal authority, as revelations of the Divine, with the healing of the sick and the prayer of the Cross.

It will be perceived, I doubt not, that every attempt to command the same degree of respect for all the Scripture writers, and an equal degree of confidence in their reliability can only stupify the rational faculties, while it must inevitably deaden the finer preceptions and more religious sensibilities of men. And this, to a fearful extent, has been the tendency and the result of the dogmatic theology. Freedom of thought has been visited with unsparing condemnation, and the right to reason boldly denied ; Nature has been adjudged to be a profane teacher : human experience ; the revelations of science ; and the soul's aspirations after a divine Ideal, have been distrusted and smothered, that ancient customs and chronicles might be revered, and the world follow its old ways. The *strict letter of a book* has been the final authority among men, and the institution, in its most ancient form, the embodiment of all attainable wisdom. Thus, under the pressure of a terrible necessity, the soul has struggled to quench the fires of its own free thought ; to shackle Reason, and to confine all the energies of immortal expansion within the charmed circle of ecclesiastical indulgence.

The sensuous man seeks support in external things. He looks for security from political and social evils in the outward conditions of his individual and associate life. Temporal alliances are resorted to as the surest means of personal safety and prosperity., Thus millions place their confidence in wealth and fame, the pomp of material power, and the splendor of worldly circumstances. An ostentatious ceremonial worship, gorgeous temples, written creeds and oracular decrees, are made to assume the place of intimate communion with the sources of divine impulsion. Life, and thought, and freedom are robbed of their profound significance, that ancient names, customs, and books may be deified. The words on a dead parchment become more sacred, in the judgment of their possessor, than the instincts of an immortal spirit. In this state man is an idolater; not, indeed, in the most repulsive sense; but still he worships "the creature more than the Creator." He does not aspire to a present direct communion, but is wont to search diligently after sacred relics and antique lore. It is not so much the DIVINE WORD, as it is some *specific record* of a portion of that word, that commands his reverence. Not for a personal, living, and perpetual inspiration does he utter his orisons in faith; but his prayer is rather for a critical understanding of the inspired sayings of other men. Such is the religion and the life of men in the flesh while yet their souls wait to be quickened.

We are accustomed to contemplate other natures through the medium of our own; and our impressions of external forms are determined, not less by the perfection of the organic structure through which they are perceived, than by the nature of the objects themselves. Our thoughts, whether depending on sensorial impressions, a power of mental generation, or an inward communion with more exalted beings, are moulded into a likeness of the mind in which they are cast. Thus, we think as we are; in other words, "As a man thinketh so is he." From whatever source we derive our ideas, it can not be denied that the structure of the brain, the condition of the nervous system, and a variety of spiritual, temperamental, and outward conditions, greatly modify all the forms of thought. A thousand images steal from the vast Unknown, and dance before us like pale shadows in dimly-lighted halls, and then glide noiselessly away, we know not whither, and these, in the variety of their form and aspect, as much depend on the organic medium through which they are discerned, as on the objective reality. We disclose our own internal qualities rather than the specific attributes of things we attempt to describe or unfold. We may fail to make a revelation of the truth, as it relates to the objects which impress either the physical or spiritual sense; their shadows may be imperfectly defined before the vision, or otherwise fall obscurely on the soul; but, in our effort to transfer them, we necessarily, though perhaps unconsciously, reveal ourselves.

In all ages, revelations from the Invisible World have been essentially modified by the physical and mental characteristics of the persons through whom they have been given to mankind. When ideas are received by influx from some other intelligence, there must necessarily be a blending of the operations of two minds, and the revelation to others must be the result of their mingled action. Some times this infusion is labored and difficult, and the foreign influence is only perceptible in a slight abnormal quickening of the human faculties. Again, the *thought* is directly inspired, but is left to be invested by the mind of the medium, from which it takes not only its coloring and clothing, but its specific form. Rarely does the invisible intelligence exercise such unlimited psychological control over the subject as to admit of imbodying the thought in language of its own selection. As, therefore, the language of Revelation is, mainly, of earthly origin, or human dictation—only the spirit, or *truth*, it contains being inspired—it follows that a rigid adherence to *the letter* is not only unwise, but subversive, in a high degree, of its legitimate claims, while it is most emphatically condemned in the New Testament.

The inspired idea may be heavenly in its nature and origin, but, to reach the dull ears of sensual men, it must be moulded into the forms of human thought, and find utterance in the imperfect speech of mortals. The divine light may be ineffably glorious, but even the rays from the Spiritual Sun are often obscured, or intercepted by dark clouds, and grotesque shapes come near and mirror themselves in the soul. The living waters, issuing from beneath the Eternal Throne, are clear as crystal, but they flow down to us through earthly channels, and this contact with gross elements may render the streams impure. Thus, however infallible the immortal thought may be, in itself considered, it loses that exalted character when an erring mortal is left to interpret the divine idea, and to translate it into the imperfect languages of this world.

In the intercourse of human society, all thought is expressed " after the manner of men." Hence, though Angels inspire us, our thoughts are born in the earth, and bear the images of beings like ourselves That the human mind, while in the body, does influence, and, in a measure, determine the

external form or verbal imbodiment of the revelations from
the other life, is confirmed by numerous examples. Whenever the imagination predominates, the communications are
couched in metaphorical language, and the subject is invested
with poetic imagery. When the Rational faculties have the
ascendency, the inspired thought is ultimated in a corresponding form, and is clothed in words that have a logical
fitness and propriety. In some instances the foreign influence conjoins itself to the faculty of Self-love, and finds expression in the most extravagant pretentions and offensive
egotism ; while those in whom the religious element is most
conspicuous, are constantly moved to acts of devotion.

This blending of the elements of human feeling and thought
with the soul's divinely inspired impressions, is forcibly illustrated in all the revelations of the olden time. Not only
were the ancient Hebrews subject to an arbitrary form of
government, but their leaders were warlike and revengeful.
This spirit characterized the revelations of that period, and
hence the *lex talionis*, according to Moses, was the law of
God. In the government of an ignorant and idolatrous
people, the Jewish lawgiver was called to act chiefly in a
legislative and executive capacity. Accordingly the inspiration of Moses assumed a *legal* form. He found it necessary
to awe a superstitious people into submission, and Sinai was
overshadowed by thick clouds, and smitten with thunder-
blasts. With these awful symbols of Jehovah's presence
came the Law !

David was gifted above all the Hebrews as a poet and
musician. He was a lover of Nature, and possessed a lively
appreciation of beauty and harmony. The silence of the

mountain and grove; the sublimity of the visible heavens, and the glory of Zion, inspired his soul with devout meditation and solemn praise. Through him the spirit of Inspiration found expression in Orphic Hymns, which, to this day, constitute a part of the devotional exercises in Jewish and Christian temples, and are read by millions in all the languages of the civilized world.

Isaiah was a remarkable seer or spiritual clairvoyant. He was actuated by pure desires; and existence, in his mind, was rendered supremely grand and beautiful, by the brilliant hopes and lofty aspirations which peopled the Future with images of glory. These attributes seem to have determined the character of his revelations, which were eloquent prophecies of the great Spiritual Era. Above and beyond the summits of the distant Ages, dawned the light of the new Day. The far off reign of righteousness was present to the vision of the Prophet, and earth was transformed into a scene of beauty and a "highway of holiness."

Jeremiah was amiable in his disposition, but he had not the cheerful and hopeful spirit of Isaiah. He seems to have been given to meditation, and inclined to melancholy. Being highly sympathetic in his nature, he was disposed to mourn over the misfortunes of his countrymen, and on this account he has been called "the weeping prophet." His case illustrates the influence of cerebral conditions on Revelation. The inspiration of Jeremiah resulted in the *Lamentations*.

Jesus of Nazareth, whose humble life and death were more glorious to humanity than the conquests of a thousand heroes, was preëminent over all in devotion to his ideal of the celestial life. Amid the noise of passion, and the jarring discords of the world, his soul was at peace. A spirit quickened by divine fire; love that consumes the deepest resentment, and forgiveness which coëxists with all human wrong, were conspicuous in the life of Jesus. When the world was faithless and disobedient, he stood alone—sublimely great—in his solemn trust and his immortal fidelity. That halcyon peace of the soul; that deathless love of Humanity, and Godlike forgiveness of offenders, were incarnate in the revelations of Jesus. The Divine law, as disclosed by the great Spiritual Teacher, was the law of LOVE. Revelation thus takes the form of Law, Poetry and Ethics; and the verbal expression of the inspired thought is made to depend, in a greater or less degree, on various idiosyncratic peculiarities, and the general perfection of earthly media.

The internal evidence of the Scriptures does not support the assumption of their plenary inspiration and infallible authority; nor is the doctrine compatible with the dicta of a rational philosophy. A poor mortal may not hope to reveal divine ideas in all their force and fullness. Not only are all earthly languages imperfect vehicles of thought, but the finite capacity is far too limited to either comprehend or transmit the boundless conception.

> " God writes his thoughts
> In facts, in solid orbs. in living souls ;
> His revelation is the concrete world."

Should one propose to pour the waters of the Mississippi through an inch pipe; or undertake to exhaust the great atmospheric sea with an ordinary air-pump, we might not stop to discuss the very distant probabilities of his success. In fact all this would be sane and sensible compared with the vain attempt to measure and define the Infinite Under-standing by the small rules of grammar and the narrow limits of our phrenological development.

It will be perceived that popular materialism may clothe itself in saintly habiliments and claim the chief seats in the synagogues. It has been known to put on the robes of the priesthood, and to declare from the altar that men are no longer inspired, as if the relations of the Soul to Truth and to God had been fundamentally and eternally changed. The era of revelation and miracle is supposed to have closed forever sometime before the ancient glory was obscured by the Dark Ages. Thus it is virtually assumed that Divine inspiration ceased to exist—died long since and was buried —that it has not yet risen from the dead. Devout men still praise the fashion of its ancient wardrobe and labor to gar-nish its sepulcher, while its deathless spirit stands unrecog-nized in their midst. This theological materialism contends for the supreme authority of the letter (" the letter killeth,") while it is prone to set up a Book against the present actual experience of mankind. If it be proved to the satisfaction of half the world that some men are truly inspired *now*, we must not believe it so long as we can find a single Hebrew or Greek manuscript—made supremely sacred by traditional authority and the votes of ecclesiastical councils—which even vaguely implies that Inspiration is not a living and perpetual reality.

But to the Christian philosopher it is a fact of some con-sequence that God made the eye, the ear, and the understand-ing, and that all the faculties are still instruments of Divine Wisdom and use, whereby we receive knowledge of the sur-

rounding creation. The rational man cannot regard these
as instruments of deception, or cunning devices to lead the
soul astray. Through these powers he may yet be able to
discover that the Divine Life outflows through all the kingdoms of Nature and inflows through all the avenues of the
Soul. Nevertheless, it is said to be irreligious and profane
to attempt to walk in the dim, uncertain light of Nature,
Reason and Intuition, as though Nature were a diabolical
institution : Reason an unholy thing to be despised and ex-
ecrated, and Intuition a dream of insanity. And are we to
regard the highest conceptions and the deepest convictions—
founded on the soul-experiences of Humanity during a period
of nearly two thousand years— as idle phantasies or distempered dreams, while we are not at liberty to so much as
question the mere *record* of the inspiration of other men
and other times ? Those who only worship the God of history are as irreverent as they are unwise. Indeed, they are
positively *atheistical*, their recognition of the Divine Presence being rather in form than in fact. There are pious
enthusiasts who do not think it very wrong to violate such
of God's laws as are not literally comprehended in the Ten
Commandments. It is thus plainly implied that Deity is
not immanent in those laws and the forms they govern—in
Nature, the orderly succession of events, and in Man. This
is the theological form of practical Atheism. Men who virtually assume that the Divine Spirit—in the most essential
sense—is withdrawn from the present sphere of human
thought and action, manifestly do not recognize the Omnipresent One. Such a faith is little better than the scientific
materialism that is trying to find God in galvanism, and all

the powers of thought and feeling in the phosphorescence of the human brain.

We have no fellowship with the materialism that overlooks a grand reality in its impetuous pursuit of its earthly forms and shadows. Sacred books, creeds and rituals, are but aids to our moral culture and spiritual development. They may prove to be great lights, but should never be accepted as absolute authorities. Reason, conscience, and every noble faculty must be free. The writer is neither disposed to undervalue books, nor willing to dispense with any of the instrumentalities whereby the thoughts of inspired minds are embalmed. It is a pious care that preserves them all. But we must not permit the Church to be mistaken for a fossil museum, nor for the grave-yard of our natural faculties and rational hopes, while it should be a garden of fresh flowers; a nursery of living ideas, and the common residence of all the graces. In proportion as we become divinely strong in spirit and beautiful in life, we reverently listen to the sublime disclosures of a living Inspiration. Moreover, we are made to comprehend the fact that we have no inspiration at all unless we ourselves are inspired. All verbal authorities and stereotyped instructions gradually give place to the realization of a more exalted communion. This appears to be a law of general application. The student of Nature leaves his class-books and abandons his mortal guides when he is able to go alone to her sublime oracles. In like manner Paul left his old "schoolmaster," "the law," when he went to Christ, whose superior inspiration rendered measurably obsolete the ancient authority of Moses. In like manner, as other minds, in the course of their development—

whether in this life or that which is to come—are enabled
to draw spiritual instruction from fountains that were opened
to the early Seers, Prophets, and Apostles, the mere records
of their experience will cease to be of vital interest, save as
integral portions of man's religious history.

In this world MAN is the great essential fact, whilst all
ideal conceptions of the Infinite, all revelations of the Beautiful, all systems of theology, every form of worship, all
phases of thought and modes of action, are but phenomena
of his existence. In all ages some men have been inspired ;
but inspiration is the special possession of those periods
which are characterized by outward simplicity and inward
growth. In the natural degree of our being it is essential
to life. As the individual must necessarily *breathe* for himself, so, also, the higher form of inspiration—the silent infusion of the elements of thought into the passive mind—must
be a personal experience or it has no vital existence. Moreover, the thirsty soul can not be satisfied with mere descriptions of living waters ; it must go to the river whose banks
are clothed with immortal verdure. The new disciple—in
the fervor of his first love—will not be dismissed with a free
ticket to Jacob's well ; much less will he be satisfied with a
few bottles of water that have been standing since the days
of the Pharaohs. The Hebrew label and Mosaic indorsement will be insufficient to commend the same to his acceptance, so long as the living fountain is open before him. A
common theological reservoir is useless to the man who finds
the "River of Life" at his own door. It is his privilege
to realize the truth of the promise :—"*It shall be* IN YOU *a
well of water springing up into everlasting life.*"

The soul redeemed from ignorance and the dominion of fleshly lusts, is above all books, and owes no allegiance to mortal masters. It heeds the injunction to "call no man Rabbi." God is immanent and manifest in such a man, as he does not exist in ancient parchments and human institutions. For this reason, the instincts of the Soul are not to be held in subordination to the letter of Revelation. To presume that Man is a mere circumstance, as compared with the Scriptures, the Church and the Sabbath, is a very grave mistake. On the contrary, " the Sabbath was made for man ;" so, also, were the Church, the Bible and all other books. All teachers, whether of Science, Art, or Religion, together with all the means and modes of instruction, including the ritual and the priesthood, are only important to the individual and the Race so far as they develop the spirit in man and thus promote the chief interests of human society. Since Inspiration belongs to the living, we may conclude that GOD SPEAKS TO THE WORLD NOW. His word is freely expressed in the existing life of all things ; in the ways of his universal providence ; in the examples of moral heroism ; in great thoughts that move the Ages ; in the mortal paralysis of old despotisms and the broken symbols of arbitrary power ; in the emancipation of serfs and slaves ; in science, art, and history ; in the ministrations of Angels ; in the solemn reverence and silent aspirations of devout men ; in the pure sympathies and gentle affections of woman ; in the spontaneous happiness of childhood ; and everywhere in the sweet repose and spiritual beauty of the humblest life.

CHAPTER XXXV.

RATIONALE OF WORSHIP.

Natural Religion—Universality of the Sentiment—Illustrations from the inferior Kingdoms of Nature—Perversions of the Religious Principle—Historical Examples—True Religion and a Spiritual Worship defined—Pagan Ideas among Christians—Incompatibility of the Outward Form and Inward Communion—The uses of Religious Symbols—How they assume the place of Essential Principles—Substituting the Shadow for the Substance—Religious influence of Natural Scenes and Objects—Inconsistencies of the Religious World—Grace and Trinity Churches—The Church of the Future—The true Christian Idea of Devotion—The Temple of Toil and the Worshipers.

IT is neither the office of Revelation nor the proper object of the Church to make man a religious being. The essential element whereby he is brought into conscious fellowship with divine realities belongs to his constitution. His religious faculties and capacities are integral in his nature, and do not necessarily depend on a system or institution for their manifestations. There is a principle *in Man* that prompts him to reverence some Higher Power. Wherever man is found are also found the symbols of his faith and the altars of his worship. However limited his mental vision and his moral growth, he has some idea of a Supreme Intelligence. The rude and uncivilized worshiper will not, of course, entertain elevated and comprehensive views of the Divine existence and perfections. His ideas and the rites of his religion will be material and repulsive to more refined beings in proportion as the Divine attributes are latent in man, and the plain of his outward life is low and sensuous. Still Revelation, Inspiration and Worship are not confined to Christendom. The Divine Law is written in the heart. Even the light of Nature, if faithfully improved, would be sufficient to prevent those flagrant abuses of the religious principle which mark the footsteps and disfigure the history of Man in almost every age. The creature is never left in total darkness. Some rays of divine light penetrate the vail that is spread over the most benighted nations. The Pagan sees around and above him glimmerings of the universal Spirit; the oracles of Nature are the voices of the Infinite; and the poor savage

"Sees God in clouds, and hears him in the wind."

But while the spring of all devout emotions and religious ideas is in Man, and flows out from him as naturally as runs the current of his life, it is not less apparent that foreign agents and external circumstances often determine the direction of the stream. Nor is this all. The exercise of the faculty and the right direction of the religious sentiment, diffuse beauty and fertility along every walk of life, and make the summer of our being glorious, and the autumn of existence fruitful in great thoughts and illustrious deeds. On the other hand, its perversions have spread ruin, like a mantle, over the fairest scenes on earth, making homes desolate, and turning splendid temples into prisons and sepulchers, where noble minds are kept in chains of darkness, trembling hearts crushed into dishonored graves, and where the highest hopes and purest joys are buried and forgotten.

Worship, considered as an essential law of a divinely constituted system, or regarded as an integral principle and a natural function of that constitution, exists universally and may be everywhere recognized. The law is plainly discernible in the lower kingdoms of Nature. The gross elements of the material world, by the refining processes of organic chemistry, and the natural modes of etherealization, *seek after God*. The more subtile portions of all physical forms, from the smallest atom to the largest orb, are exhaled; the sublimated elements rise from their organic restraints like the incense of flowers; like the waters that answer the invitations of the sun, and ascend into the atmospheric heavens; and like the aspirations of living souls. All Nature is a perfumed censer, swayed by the Divine hand in the midst of his sun-lighted temple. The smallest plant seeks the light as naturally and perseveringly as the most devoted saint reaches heavenward in his seasons of devout aspiration. The numberless germs that are buried in the earth never grow downward to the center; but they all sprout upward to the surface — toward the ethereal regions. It is a well known fact that when plants are kept in dark rooms, and light is admitted at a single point, they all grow in that precise direction. Thus, even the meanest shrub, if surrounded by darkness, prays—according to the organic law of its nature—for " light, more light !" In like manner, if a vessel of water be placed near a vine in a dry season, the general tendency and particular direction of the vine will be changed : or, if it be planted on the bank of a stream, it will pursue a direct route to the water. Thus the organized forms of the vegetable kingdom seek such natural elements as are indispensable to their growth and life.[1] The vine goes to the water as naturally as the 'hart panteth after the running brooks,' and as truly as the rational soul thirsts for the elements of Truth, of which water is an appropriate and expressive symbol. Thus all material elements and the lowest organic forms perpetually aspire to the higher plains and superior functions of being. By their subserviency to beneficient uses, and their subordination to the principles of natural harmony, they utter constant praise.

The present analysis and definition of Worship involve no such metaphysical subtilties as require sharp lines and delicate distinctions. It may suffice that the most essential constituents of Worship—so far as the subject relates to Man—are love, gratitude, reverence and aspiration. Whether we regard these as elemental principles in the nature of true worship; or as the soul's spiritual exercises, and indispensable to our own inward growth, they should be regulated in their modes of expression, by intelligence and the orderly exercise of reason. Without such illumination and direction, they are liable to lead the mind astray; at the same time they darken the sphere of our outward life and relations, and otherwise degrade the worshiper. Ignorance and superstition have fashioned innumerable gods out of the subjective darkness, and then left their blinded devotees to

---

[1] Hoare, in his treatise on the vine, mentions a striking illustration of something in plants resembling the instinct of animals. A bone was placed in the strong but dry clay of a vine border. The vine sent out a leading or tap root, directly through the clay to the bone. In its passage the principle root put out no fibres in the clay; but on reaching the object of pursuit it put forth its minute tendrils in such numbers as entirely to cover the bone with its delicate tracery, in the net-work of which every thread penetrated some pore of the bone.

stupidly worship those idols instead of the Universal Father.
Wherever the religious sentiment has been perverted in the
mind and heart, or misdirected in its modes of manifestation,
it has fostered the vilest passions, peopled the imagination
with horrid phantoms, shut out the light of reason and obscured the moral vision. Viewed in this aspect, Religion is
made to assume the character and office of a destroying
angel. It lights the consumers' brand in the bottomless pit,
and kindles unholy fires on innumerable altars. Aggressive
War tempers his sword in that flame, and with his merciless
arm hews out a way for Religion to advance ; whilst hell—
the hell whose atmosphere is gross darkness, and whose
ministers are foul superstitions and perverted passions—
follows the bloody trail, and with its fearful lights, deep
shadows and startling colors, completes the mournful picture
of misdirection and depravity.

If one has room but for a single idea, and that is to be
allowed to engross all his faculties and his whole time, he can
scarcely adopt one that is fraught with greater sacrifice to
society than the religious idea. The world has already witnessed many melancholy illustrations of this truth. Think
of the austere manners, the unnatural restraints, the severe
modes of discipline, painful rites and gloomy abstractions,
which have formed the religion of so many men. The notion that the body must be literally crucified, and the intellect dwarfed for all time, that the religious element in human
nature may have unlimited power, is absurd and dangerous
to the last degree. It impairs all the functions of the body,
and renders health and life insecure. It dissipates and deranges the vital forces, producing physical debility, paralysis,

congestion, melancholy, insanity, and death ; and these evils
are transmitted to succeeding generations. The vital elements, the prevailing philosophies, and the practical life of
the world, have all been poisoned by pious madmen. Not
a few have withdrawn from civilized society, and spent their
lives in caves and mountains, away from the responsibilities
and the evils they had not the manhood to meet. The asceticism that prevailed in the early church, and the corporeal
inflictions that men in different ages have voluntarily suffered,
witness to us how sadly the noblest powers and privileges
may be perverted. Thousands shut themselves up in lonely
cells and gloomy caverns, away from the clear light and
pure air. Old Roger Bacon lived two years in a hole under
a church wall, and at last dug his own grave with his finger-
nails ; and all that he might escape from the world and
show his supreme contempt of physical suffering. Others
have been wild enthusiasts, who made religion to consist in
an unhealthy and feverish excitement. But we may as well
expect organic perfection and physical vigor from an occasional fit of the ague, as to depend on a periodical spasm of
the emotional nature to translate the world, or to bring the
New Jerusalem down to us. Heaven is not found in the
fever and frenzy that burn in the brain and madden the
soul ; nor is salvation made secure to those who are only

"Chilled by a cold abnormal piety."

There is no end to the follies and cruelties which ignorant
men have perpetrated in the name of Religion. Not only
have they violated the most essential laws of health and life,
in themselves, but they have everywhere resisted Science,

step by step ; they have anathematized the greatest teachers and benefactors of mankind ; they have fostered the foulest superstitions and upheld the despotisms of the world ; they have spurned all Nature as' an unholy thing, and made merchandize of our hopes of Heaven. With such men faith sustains no relation to science, but it is very closely allied to superstition ; and the zeal that exhausts the worshiper with its extreme fervor is "not according to knowledge." These things have all been done under the pretense of serving the Lord and saving the people. They indicate that among the constituents of our nature the *Religious Element* is, perhaps, the most dangerous when not wisely directed ; and that it is alike destructive of physical health, temporal prosperity, and true morality.   It is a morbid alienation of Reason, with a sickly disgust of life and all temporal interests, that leads to these extremes.   Neither Nature nor the Divine Wisdom can furnish the incentives to action when men thus disregard their relations to this world, and treat the gifts of God with pious scorn.

The spirit of the opposition to Nature and Science, which characterized the blind religionists of past ages, finds an amusing illustration in the conduct of Pope Callextus. About the middle of the sixteenth century, when the Turkish arms had just reduced the great empire, the comet of 1456 made its appearance, and by its long train spread consternation through all Europe.   It was supposed that it might have some mysterious connection with the Turks ; and the idea widely prevailed that comets were ominous of war, pestilence, famine and other great disasters.   The occasion seemed to call on the Pope for some signal demonstration of his power and devotion Accordingly, a special religious service was decreed, in which he formally unathematized the Turks and the comet. Since that event we have repeatedly heard of the Turks, but the comet is supposed to keep at a prudent distance from the seat of papal authority.

That we can not safely depend on this principle alone— the religious element in human nature—to regulate the conduct of men, must be obvious to all persons who have looked into the religious history of the world. Wherever the reasoning faculties have not been developed by suitable mental culture and discipline, the religious sentiment has usually coöperated with the baser passions and become the scourge of mankind. The practice of sacrificing human beings to propitiate the favor of the gods, originated in this union of the religious principle with the baser propensities. The history of many nations is deeply stained with the evidence on this point. It was the custom of the Romans, for a long time, to sacrifice many of their prisoners of war. Cæsar offered three hundred men on the Ides of March. The Gauls also reared their altars for human sacrifices, and amid the gloom of the old forests the Druidical priesthood performed the bloody rite. To turn the tide of victory in their favor the Carthagenians, after being defeated in battle, seized two hundred children of the wealthiest families and put them to death. At the consecration of the great temple of Mexico, it is recorded that the reigning king sacrificed more than sixty thousand prisoners, and the royal Montezuma, though surrounded by many of the arts of refined life, was accustomed to make an annual offering of twenty thousand men to the sun. Nor are these cruelties all distant in respect to time. The wail of expiring Humanity comes up from the islands of the South Sea and Pacific Ocean; it rises from the burning sands of Central Africa, from the temple of India's great idol, and from beneath the wheels of his ponderous car. We might summon a cloud of witnesses that no man could number, whose experience illustrates the dangerous tendencies of the Religious Sentiment, when not directed by Reason. We might invoke the shades of thirty thousand widows, who annually expired on the funeral pyre; call up the infant spirits from the Ganges, and the tender babes that perished in the burning arms of the Phœnician Moloch. The witnesses come by thousands—bloody and mutilated—from the dungeons and racks of the Inquisition; from the tragic scenes of St. Bartholomew's Day; and from all the battle-fields of the Crusaders, to admonish us that mental culture and the exercise of an enlightened reason, as well as a fervent spirit of devotion, are necessary to save the world.

But the human soul is the chosen temple in which the Great Spirit has left the image of a divine personality. It is by no means the proper office of Religion to pollute the sanctuary thus consecrated by the indwelling presence of Deity. If every human being combines—in a miniature form and finite degree—the elements of the Natural World and the attributes of the Divine Mind—is a representative of the universe without and the universe within—it will appear that every man with disordered faculties, inverted affections and perverted passions—is, in a qualified sense, a world in a state of chaos or ruin. Moreover, this disorderly empire requires the calm and orderly exercise of

Reason and every godlike faculty to harmonize its elements. In this work the religious sentiment, when properly illuminated and directed, exerts a beneficient influence and a redeeming power. Crowned with its superior glory Humanity presents such a spectacle as Angels may contemplate with admiration and delight. The harmonic play of divine affections fills this dwelling-place of the Infinite with "psalms and hymns, and spiritual songs," all silent and voiceless, I know, to the mere sensuous worshiper, yet to the awakened spirit distinctly audible. When the soul is thus quickened by a living inspiration, and is qualified to worship in spirit, the solemn and joyful harmonies of the higher life naturally flow down into it, and echo through the mystical aisles and beneath the illuminated dome of this temple. Angelic ministers frequent its courts ; they kindle sacred fires on its altars ; they look from heaven into its windows ; or descend to unbar its portals that new hopes, living ideas, immortal joys, and divine ecstacies may enter in and dwell there.

If men worship an omniscient Being who discerns the inmost secrets of the mind and heart, the outward exhibition of their spiritual moods and modes can never be essential to true worship. These do not establish the soul's conscious connection with the Divine. That must preëxist, or the outward service is a false pretense, rendered the more hollow and hypocritical by the feigned solemnity that is made to characterize the performance. The spiritual idea of worship is supremely beautiful and immeasurably exalted above all others in the intrinsic purity and dignity of the conception. To be in sympathy with the heavens, is virtually to enter the angelic abodes ; to be in conscious communion with the divine, is to realize the Infinite Presence. In this state, prayer and praise are something more than rhetorical exercises. Moreover, they are unceasing ; the aspirations of the worshiper and the incense of gratitude perpetually ascend from the altar of the mind and heart. Thus, true religion, viewed subjectively, may be briefly defined to be the harmonic action of all the human faculties and affections ; and Worship may be regarded as the soul's natural gravitation toward God and the sphere of divine activities.

It can not be said in truth that the author undervalues Religion, or that he is opposed to true worship. Indeed, the practice of any form—not attended with barbarous rites —that the individual worshiper may deem to be most conducive to his growth, in all the faculties and graces of a perfect manhood, should be approved. So far as religious symbols and ceremonies are aids to a clearer perception of truth, and incentives to a life of practical goodness, the use of them deserves to be encouraged. At best, however, they are but the shadows of substantial things. If any one is qualified to appropriate and enjoy the divine substance, he, surely, need not keep on grasping at the earthly shadow, like one who clutches the air and embraces nothing. At least it is our privilege to contemplate the better time,

> ' All mirrored in the far off future years,
> When men will cast their idol creeds to dust,
> And know the Evangel in its very heart,
> Regardless of the form !"

The poet may not worship according to the ritual, and the philosopher may question the propriety of advertising his prayers, by a formal proclamation, either in the papers or the synagogues. But the vulgar inference that such men are irreligious is a grave mistake. They may be devout in a degree that transcends all familiar modes of expression. The philosopher has a clearer perception and a broader charity, and he will observe a decent respect for every sincere worshiper. The man who is morally upright and religiously conscientious in his observance of the prevailing forms of faith and worship—however unenlightened and erroneous those forms may be—is entitled to more confidence and respect than those who hold the most enlightened views in adulterous fellowship with a life of practical infidelity. Even the Pagan, who has acquired no knowledge of the Law, when by nature he performs the things which the law requires, is accounted a better subject of the Divine administration, than the man who has a clear, intellectual comprehension of its moral claims and bearings, while he disregards its chief requirements and crucifies its essential spirit.

But while we respect the sincere formal worshiper for his fidelity to his convictions, we are at liberty to remember that the thoughts of some men are larger than the parts of speech, and that the deepest emotions may transcend the compass of language. We have heard great souls defamed because they rejected the stereotyped form and only worshiped in spirit. And yet the prevailing formalism can not be essential to true worship, if we may give the term a Christian definition. The common exercise of prayer seems to have originated from two causes : first, a consciousness in the mind of the petitioner of some unsatisfied demand of his nature ; and, secondly, from faith in the existence of a higher Power which was presumed to be able to supply that demand. The fancied necessity for praying aloud doubtless had its origin in the heathen notion that the being addressed is organized like a man ; and that the worshiper must reach his understanding through the sense of hearing. The whole conception is altogether external and 'extremely sensuous. Yet nevertheless, some professed Christian worshipers pray with as much vehemence as did the four hundred and fifty prophets of Baal ; and, possibly, for the same reason—because they imagine that their Lord may be at a distance, or otherwise occupied, and that an unusual effort may be required to secure his attention.[1] If they do not entertain Pagan ideas, why do they imitate the example of the heathen, who "think that they shall be heard for their much speaking." Incessant importunities are surely not always nor generally the strongest indications of profound reverence for the power we recognize. This becomes the more apparent in the light of a Christian philosophy, and the observation derives additional emphasis from the explicit testimony of Jesus—"The Father knoweth what things ye have need of before ye ask him."

Moreover, as all mundane languages belong to the external plain of the human intellect, it follows that the soul is naturally and necessarily withdrawn from the interior state of communion, in and by the very act of giving oral expression to its devout conceptions. It must leave "the closet"—the inward sanctuary—where the Divine presence is most clearly perceived and truly worshiped. Instead of remaining in the spiritual temple, the worshiper must go out and explore

---

[1] See the description of an ancient prayer me ting, I. Kings. chap. xviii.

the dim halls of his earthly memory, and search the wardrobe of the imagination in clothing his ideas ; and thus prayer becomes a philological exercise. In traversing the material and sensuous avenues that lead outwardly to the natural world—which it must do in order to conduct the process of external communication—the spirit itself is externalized, in respect to the direction and exercise of its powers. The internal process of communion with the Divine is thus suspended by a law of the mental constitution—a law which prevents the free and successful exercise of its internal and external faculties at the same time.

It may be possible to conduct two distinct mental processes at the same moment ; but this is rendered extremely difficult if not absolutely impossible, whenever the separate operations of the mind necessarily involve different psychological conditions. It neither requires a subtile metaphysician nor a profound psychologist to comprehend this view of the subject. In the degree that the mind retires to the internal realm of perception and action, we become oblivious in respect to the objects and occurrences of the external world. This is illustrated in states of profound mental abstraction, and especially by the phenomena of the magnetic sleep, and the ordinary incapacity of the mind to carry the impressions received in one state to the other, without a special effort and the assistance of the magnetic operator. Thus, in order to enter into intimate conscious relations with the realities of the interior life and world, it is necessary to lose our outward consciousness in a degree that is incompatible with orderly intercourse through external channels. It is said that in our devotions we should forget all earthly things,

34

and that all the faculties should be concentrated on the object of worship. But in proportion as the powers of thought and affection concenter, and are thus exercised in one direction and on a single object, we are rendered incapable of performing any function that depends on a division or dissipation of the mental forces. We realize this in the influence of certain outward scenes and objects on the mind. We indulge in familiar gossip, on the flowery bank of some babbling stream, but we are speechless before Niagara. When the tempest is on the sea—when a vision of disaster haunts the startled soul, an unbroken seal is set on the mariner's lip—he is silent, because one thought engages all his powers. Let the man who converses with the greatest volubility gaze for five minutes at the starry heavens, and he will be silent. In like manner, whoever would enter into most intimate relations with the Invisible and enjoy the closest communion, must disconnect the mind from all other objects and exercises. ONE, alone, and a single purpose of the mind, must absorb all feeling, all thought, and all action. After this manner do men worship when they worship in spirit. This exercise of the religious faculties is too profound to be noisy. Reverence is too deep, aspiration too high, and joy too intense for utterance. Religion, in a great inspired soul, is infinitely larger than all its fashionable clothing, and the first successful effort to reveal it would shiver its mortal symbols. Empty minds babble, but when the soul is full, the tongue is chained and the lips are sealed.

Worship too often consists in mere forms, which at best present only distorted pictures of living realities; or automatic expressions of a dying spirituality, that gasps for

breath beneath the weight of its gilded covering. Thus the
temples of Religion become its sepulchers. I am not insensible of the great beauty and significance of that eloquent
symbolism wherewith the ancient nations clothed their ideas.
But all that was most vital in their religious systems was
beyond and within them. Their symbols were only serviceable so far as they contributed to inform and impress the
mind with the knowledge of the facts and duties they were
designed to represent and inculcate. So long as visible
images were suggestive of essential principles, they were
instructive and useful; but wherever the semblance has
been mistaken for the substance—whenever the reality is
not before the mind and in the heart—the image alone is
worshiped, and the whole system is rendered corrupt and
idolatrous.

It will be perceived that the religious idea often suffers a
base incarceration in its outward forms. Too often, indeed,
is it left to languish in darkness and in chains. Daylight
is excluded from the fane, and the waning fires on its deserted altars, like dim tapers burning in the thick atmosphere
of tombs, throws a sickly glare over the scene of moral and
spiritual death. But the religious sentiment can never die.
Its ancient temples may fall; unclean birds may inhabit the
ruins; the infidel may revel where the altar stood; the ox
draw the ploughshare over consecrated ground, and wild
beasts dwell by its haunted streams and in its sacred mountains; but Religion—deathless as the soul itself—hears the
trumpet of the resurrection in the very shock that hurls its
material symbols and deserted temples to the dust.

Grand and imposing as are the outward revelations of

inward principles; widely extended and diversified as are the visible illustrations of the religious thought; they are only dim shadows that haunt the early morning of our immortality--images that dance in the soul's twilight—fleeting forms of everlasting realities which the coming daylight will disclose. In a profound and enduring sense, that which is visible, *is not ;* whilst that which is not seen, was from the beginning and shall remain forever. In other words, all outward forms and visible phenomena are but *appearances*—fleeting shadows of invisible realities. This is true of the natural world and of human institutions. Indeed, all sensuous manifestations of the religious idea ; all stereotyped creeds, prayers and confessions of faith ; the peculiar claims of sacred manuscripts, and the supreme authority of carved stones; all temples and altars that human hands have reared from the beginning ; all sacred places and solemn sounds, are less—less by a degree that admits of no comparison —than the religious sentiment itself, as it dwells apart and alone in the charmed silence of the conscious soul.

Words are not worship. True devotion does not consist in gilded periods ; and men may not adore in solemn looks and tones. Nor yet by folding the limbs together do they rise from the base elements and cold formalism of this dull sphere into those supernal realms where all worship is spiritual and real. To worship truly, the human faculties and affections must be harmonized. The spirit must retire in silence from the earthly orbit of its being, toward that central world where indestructible principles assume the place of temporal objects ; where thoughts are things more palpable than marble walls, and essential qualities are more tan-

gible than material forms. It is from this world within
that the soul derives the elements of its strength. Here it
finds true liberty and divine light. This intercourse of the
spirit with the great souls and sublime realities of the invisible empire, is—with occasional exceptions—most perfect
when we have least to do with earthly interests and pursuits.
We have enjoyed the clearest perceptions of spiritual things,
and felt the deepest sense of the importance of true worship,
when far from the haunts of men. Not in the cathedral
service, when the measured tones of the organ shake the
consecrated pile, have we formed our highest conception of
universal harmonies ; it was not there that we felt the deepest sense of the Divine presence. These, in our personal
experience, have been realized—if they have been realized
at all—in the great temple of Nature. Standing on some
lonely mountain, or by the restless ocean, with the winds
and waves as divine ministers to teach lessons of freedom,
we have felt the presence and inspiration of thoughts which
have no voice and no language on the earth. Here, in this
temple of the Infinite, the elements are all assembled to im-
provise the Creator's praise. Through crystal caverns of
the deep, and from the air-chambers, where thunders tune
their awful voices, rolls out the solemn bass in Nature's harmony ; and all things, above, beneath, and around move on
forever—move

> " To that great anthem calm and slow
> Which God repeats."

No special service is required to consecrate the place. The
Divine presence pervades the whole sanctuary. On the

mountain, in the wilderness, and by the sea, the elements
come to us as divine messengers ; they wake the world in the
morning ; and with voices musical as chiming rills, and clear
as the tones of silver bells, on the still evening air, they call
us to vespers in His own great Temple. Even here, in this
house of God, whose pillars uphold the solid earth on which
we stand, and whose vast dome is lighted by unnumbered
suns, the reverent and thoughtful man *must* worship, because
worship is alike the law of the place and of his being.

Rational religion never immolates the natural affections.
It sets up no cruel creed as the cross whereon the conscience
must be crucified. It denounces no man for an honest opinion, but appeals to the mind and heart with irresistible power.
It has the intelligence to perceive that thousands can no
more recognize a moral distinction than a blind man can
distinguish colors. While it is the custom of our religious
society to turn over all the former to the police and the
penitentiary, it makes liberal donations to the blind asylum.
But true religion does not propose to cure our moral infirmities by torturing either the body or the soul. It would no
more consign a man to hell for an inherited moral weakness
than it would damn him for general debility. If one man
inherits the scrofula as his portion, and another is born with
a propensity to steal, it must regard both with compassion.
How unlike the conduct of the institution that consigns one
to the care of the doctor and sends the other to the devil !

Many men have mistaken cruelty for justice and delirium
for devotion ; but the world will yet discover its errors and
correct them. Vital religion will be found at last to consist in the orderly development and harmonic exercise of

the human faculties and affections, exhibited in all the relations of a beautiful and divine existence ; and worship will
be the spontaneous but silent gravitation of the soul toward
the central Life. The forms of worship may change and
pass away ; but the indwelling spirit of Religion can never
die. We find something like demonstration of this in the
individual consciousness and the universal history of man.
From innumerable altars in many lands ; from the sacred
urns wherein the ashes of moral heroes and spiritual re-
formers are garnered up, come the invitations to worship ;
and Nature, with countless voices echoing through

> "—— that Fane most Catholic and solemn,
> Which God hath planned —"

speaks to command our reverence and to inspire our praise.

We are prone to mistake theology for religion ; whilst
learned disquisitions and imposing ceremonies are substi-
tuted for the means of grace. For this reason, salvation, as
a present, personal and practical thing, is about as rare as
summer flowers in December. The people are not saved yet.
The rich are not redeemed from their avarice nor the poor
from their poverty. The modern articles of faith and popular
forms of worship have neither healed the sick, opened the
eyes of the spiritually blind, quickened the morally dead,
nor cast out the foul demons of pride and oppression from
the human heart. These evils yet remain, and, in the judgment of the Christian world, still operate with undiminished
power. The church—as an outward institution—is disposed
to reject any new revelations that—in the progress of the
world—may come through channels which itself has not

opened and consecrated. Other avenues it hedges up, and
bars the windows against the light of the Present. We are
not wanting in a significant illustration. Grace Church, in
the City of New York, (most conspicuous amongst similar
institutions for all the *graces* of fashionable life,) some time
since, erected a solid wall against the side of Dodworth's
Academy, in which children dance through the week and
heretics worship on Sunday. Without the least apparent '
compunction it darkened the windows in that particular
direction, forgetting that the common Father "maketh his
sun to shine alike on the evil and on the good." This is
not precisely the dispensation of grace that the world needs.
Nevertheless, in a moral and spiritual sense the example is
so extensively followed that innumerable partition walls and
other barriers are erected by the Church, and through which
millions may never discern the great light of To-day.

The Church, as a human institution, values ancient authorities rather than living ideas ; at the same time it performs
many ceremonies to the neglect of divine charities. Imposing establishments are supported at vast expense ; and
these foster the pride of the priesthood, while the worshiper
pays homage to the dim shadows and gilded images of invisible realities. The splendid temple, the eloquent minister, the ceremonial worship, as well as sacred relics, solemn
memories, and the effigies of the Saints and Apostles, are
only serviceable if they attract the soul to the Infinite. But
when the mind is diverted ; or is led astray, and left to bow
before unworthy objects ; when the religious thought can
not live in its consecrated symbols, but is buried beneath
them ; then, indeed, has Religion lost its spirituality ; the

common faith of the Church is materialized, and its worship becomes a superior phase of idolatry.

Have we not a right to demand a more liberal, spiritual, and practical religion? The strength and prosperity of the Church are too often determined by the value of its temporal possessions and the number of its members. Where the figures are large, the cause is said to be prosperous. The present power and prospective triumph of the Redeemer's kingdom are not presumed to have any special relation to a positive growth in the graces of a divine life; much less do we look to the modern disciple for the exhibition of any genuine "spiritual gifts." Such gifts are readily attributed to many characters in sacred history; but they are as freely denied to all the living. Such a system is hollow as it is fashionable. How long shall these things be, and when may we look to the visible Church for a practical illustration of the simple faith and all-embracing charity of the crucified Reformer? When will the institution, established in his name, be baptized into the spirit that works by love, and with the fire that shall consume its corruptions? The theological gladiators may be left to finish their contest; but the Christian should begin to live " in the spirit." Shall we not at last test the efficacy of praying *in deed?* A present divine revelation to the soul, and especially in the life, is what the age demands. A long sermon is not worth a dime to a hungry man. He wants a new dispensation of bread; the prisoner calls for pure air and more light; and many slaves yet wait to hear the proclamation of the gospel of their individual freedom. Moreover, the image of God— covered with rags and filth, and otherwise fearfully dese-

crated—may be seen every day in the year on the front steps
of Trinity—the wealthiest church establishment on the continent. The saints are liable to stumble over it when they
go to worship. As they pass, the image looks on them re-
proachfully ; but they heed it not. No one sees the divine
likeness in the poor wretch on the stone steps. They have
not time to make a discovery ; they go there to worship the
Holy Trinity, and then go away to profane the same Trinity
through the week, by using it to distinguish a proud monied
aristocracy, that recognizes no proper distinction between
godliness and gain. We have hope for the world, but Oh,
when shall such institutions be redeemed from this golden
idolatry, and this bitter mockery of the penury of Jesus ?
Gothic architecture and the finest rhetoric are worthless as
an atonement ; the grand incantations, on the first day of
the week, are powerless to disenthrall the sordid mind ; and
a single ablution of the body may do nothing to purify the
perverted affections. To accomplish this work we need,
and we must have, a new infusion of the spiritual element
and the baptism of fire.

There are great moral forces in the world, whose action
is rapidly decomposing the ancient systems. Institutions,
founded on the prostrate rights of man, whether originating
in the social relations, political and international policy, or
in the religious faith and worship of nations and races, must
inevitably yield to the progress of the Age. It is time that
the theories and institutions which have invested the spirit
of Love with immortal hate, should pass away, that they
may shackle the mind and encumber the earth no more.
Such distorted and unnatural forms of the religious thought

can never more be animated by the indwelling divinity, whose abiding place is not in the sepulchers among " dead men's bones." It must and will go out to quicken new and more beautiful creations. Some dismal souls may still linger behind to weep over the old body, but the true disciple will rejoice ; and, 'leaving the dead to bury their dead,' follow the deathless spirit to the consecration of other temples, and to the altars of a purer worship.

There is not an instance of Christian forgiveness ; not an attempt to equalize labor and the gifts of Providence, that does not present an argument against those exclusive and sectarian institutions that divide and distract the people. Every effort to promote peace and good will among men ; every earnest word spoken against cruel laws and vindictive punishments, is a blow aimed at the foundation on which they stand. Every instance of affection to an ungrateful child ; every tear the mother sheds in secret for her way-ward boy ; the love of Jesus for his enemies, and the strug-gles and sacrifices of every sincere Reformer, proclaim, in eloquent and powerful language, the soul's protest against every system of wrong, and its significant prophecy of the Church that is to be. The people whose faith is in creeds ; whose reverence of books and human masters becomes a base idolatry, and whose religion is chiefly comprehended in their theological opinions and Sunday ceremonies, may well tremble at " the signs of the times." But to the great soul whose common law is progress ; whose actual life is a succession of great thoughts and illustrious deeds ; whose religion is constant growth and increasing illumination, and whose prayers are the daily efforts and aspirations of the ready hand and the aspiring mind—the Present is full of encouragement and hope.

The Church of the FUTURE will have no arbitrary rules, regarding the speculative opinions of the believer; no articles of faith that are more sacred and inviolable than the soul—neither compulsive forces, nor unnatural restraints, either within or without. On the contrary, the harmony of its elements, and the union of its members, will be preserved by a moral and spiritual cohesion, and the laws of a divine order. Its sacred books will comprehend the discovered principles and accumulated wisdom of all ages and countries; and its ministers be employed to illustrate the science of religion, and the philosophy of all human relations. In that Church the spirit and life will be paramount over the letter and the form. Its sacraments shall be feasts of charity given to the poor; its constant prayer, one mighty and unceasing effort to do good, and its perpetual and eloquent sermon, a spotless life.

It may be said that these views of religion and worship are not Christain. On this point—without intending any disrespect to modern disciples—I may be allowed to respect the paramount authority of the Master. Jesus of Nazareth recognized as the only true worship that which is spiritual and practical. To the woman whom he met at Jacob's well he said: "The hour cometh and now is when the true worshipers shall worship the Father in spirit and in truth . . . GOD IS A SPIRIT; and they that worship him *must worship him in spirit.*" He held the service of the lips in the lowest possible estimation, but everywhere inculcated the truth, that an earnest labor of the heart and *the hands* might open the doors of the kingdom of heaven. It was not the prayer of words that was most effectual ; but he thus recognized earnest deeds as fervent supplications : " Not every one that saith unto me, Lord, Lord, shall enter into the kingdom of heaven ; but *he that doeth the will* of my Father which is in heaven." These significant words form a part of the memorable " Sermon on the Mount," the delivery of which was not preceded by a formal prayer, or any external act of devotion. The Founder of the Christian's religion was not accustomed to pray in public, save in the silent exercises of his spirit The Apostles never introduced their sermons by oral prayer, or any other religious ceremonies. Moreover, Jesus bade his disciples not to pray thus, on public occasions, in these emphatic words : " *Thou shalt not be as the hypocrites ; for they love to pray standing in the synagogues.*" Those who insist that such external acts of devotion necessarily constitute an essential part of true worship, are at liberty to reconcile their views and the modern custom with the teachings and example of Jesus and his Apostles.

I have intimated that in the beautiful conception of the Nazarine, worship was not only spiritual, but it was also *practical*. It was at once an exercise of the soul and a work of the hands. Hence it has been truly and beautifully said that " LABOR IS PRAYER." A word-petition is only one mode whereby men express their desires. We are not necessarily restricted to this form of expression. It is a false assumption that all prayer must come through the glottis. We are not authorized to regard that particular channel as more sacred than any other. A man may pray quite as reverently through the muscles of his right arm. The exten-

sors are instruments of divine ordination, and their use is
no less consecrated. Indeed, the truth that "actions speak
louder than words," has become a proverb ; and that man
prays most fervently and effectually who *prays in deed.*

An interesting incident, said to have occurred in the life
of Frederick Douglass, will illustrate the superior efficacy of
this kind of prayer. Some time before his escape from
bondage he was accustomed to go daily to a particular place
where he prayed earnestly for deliverance. One day the
form of his prayer was interrupted by a mysterious voice
which recommended the adoption of the practical method,
saying—with a peculiar emphasis—"Frederick! pray with
your legs!" Frederick was very naturally astonished, and,
for a moment, bewildered ; but at length, concluding to act
on the suggestion, he achieved his freedom. I am also informed that the Congregation at Plymouth Church, one
Sunday morning, gave an impressive illustration of practical
prayer. They prayed for a helpless woman, on whose neck
the oppressor (he was, nominally, a Christian oppressor,)
had set his practically infidel foot. The people were united
in spirit, and they prayed earnestly and *in deed*, each putting
his hand in his own pocket, and together contributing the
price of freedom. And it came to pass, in the same hour,
that the arm of the oppressor was paralyzed, and the chains
of the poor slave fell asunder like untwisted flax when it
is touched with a burning brand.

Surely the workers are the worshipers. It is at once
highly honorable and truly religious to labor. The imprisoned victims of disease and ignorance ; multitudes, down-
trodden beneath the heel of despotism, and the virtuous

poor throughout the world, present earnest and solemn invitations to the practical form of worship.   And with what
steady faith and irresistible power do the laboring millions
pray, early and late—the poor seamstress by the dim light
in her cheerless room ; the husbandman in his field ; the
smith at his forge, and the mariner on the sea—*all* who work
faithfully, pray through each quivering nerve, and every
smitten and trembling fiber of a muscle—"pray without
ceasing !"   Verily, there is no petition, in which human
necessities and desires are expressed, that at once displays
so much unity of spirit and continuity of purpose ; such intensity of feeling and grandeur of expression, as the fervent,
sublime and effectual prayer that comes up from the great
temple of TOIL, and is thus literally translated :

"GIVE US THIS DAY OUR DAILY BREAD."

CHAPTER XXXVI.

NATURAL EVIDENCES OF IMORTALITY.

Question of Immortality—Indestructibility of Matter—The Life-Principle in all Substance—Visible and Invisible Elements—Law of Organization—Unseen Realms of Organized Life—The Brain but the Instrument of the Mind—The ultimate seat of Sensation in the Soul—Exercise of the Faculties without the Corporeal Organs—The Body periodically Changed—Testimony of M. Favre before the French Academy—Elimination of Mineral Poisons—M. Orfila's demonstrative Experiments—The Materialist's Objections—The Identity preserved through all Physical Changes—Argument from Memory—Sensation and Consciousness neither suspended nor circumscribed by the Amputation of Limbs—A popular Objection disposed of—The imperishable Body—Reasons for the apparent decay of the Faculties—Conclusion.

If a man die, shall he live again?—*Job.*

There is a natural body, and there is a spiritual body.—*Paul*

OUR interest in Man and his Relations does not terminate here; but it reaches forward and upward far beyond the limited sphere of his existence on earth. Indeed, the great question, compared with which all others are of momentary concern, is that which relates to the life hereafter; and for this reason a brief discussion of the Natural Evidences of Immortality will form an appropriate conclusion of the present treatise. If the relations of human nature to the essential laws, the organized forms, and material elements of the natural world, are eminently worthy to engage the attention of the scientific philosopher, with what profound and solemn interest must the rational mind approach the present inquiry! We are daily reminded that the individual life of man is soon concealed from all mortal observers. If the vital flame is forever extinguished, what significance has human nature; and what permanent interest does the world possess, if this brief existence is all of life? If the light of the soul were obscured at death, in an endless and total eclipse, we should be constrained to regard the crowning work of the Creator as a melancholy failure. But Man is not to be compared to the ephemera—he is not the creature of a day. On the contrary, those who so suddenly elude our imperfect observation are neither annihilated nor lost in impenetrable darkness; they only step within the vail, and assume new relations, in which they become invisible to mortals amidst the superior splendors of another world.

Every living body in its turn is disorganized; material combinations are perpetually changing; and even the solid rocks perish by the gradual process of disintegration. But amidst this scene of constant mutation the material philosopher recognizes the fact that there is nothing lost. Neither the laws of Nature, the methods of Science, nor the instrumentalities of Art, enable us to destroy anything. At most we are only capable of changing the organized forms and specific combinations of the physical world. For this reason the materialist may naturally assume the indestructibility of matter. If we admit the assumption, he, especially, is bound to accept any conclusion that may be fairly drawn from his premises. Matter has its inherent forces, and wherever the one exists the others are necessarily manifested. It is not possible for matter to exist unaccompanied by its own essen-

35

tial qualities and fundamental laws. Indeed the invisible principles that govern the physical elements are inseparable from those elements themselves. In conceiving of the existence of matter, therefore, the rational mind readily apprehends the presence of its vital principles, not as a possible contingency, but as an absolute necessity. Atoms and orbs move, and motion must be perpetual ; the organizing law exists, and the work must proceed forever ; the Life-principle is universally diffused, and wherever there is substance that principle may be revealed in its organic forms. Our microscopic observations and the experiments of certain philosophers, suggest that all Nature moves and is instinct with Life. The essential principle and organic law pervade and govern all matter ; and hence it must follow—matter being indestructible—that life is immortal.

The idea of an invisible creation, peopled by beings, far more ethereal than the inhabitants of the earth, is supported by strong presumptive reasons. In the absence of such a realm and of such natures, it appears to the author that the Universe would be incomplete. We find that matter exists in various degrees of density and tenuity. The rocks and metals, the earths and the waters, are all tangible ; but the atmosphere, the impalpable gases, the electric medium of the earth and air, and other subtile forms of matter, escape the present observation of the senses on account of their extreme rarity. For the present we are left to determine their existence and recognize their presence only by their effects. It is admitted that matter exists in these rarified and supersensible states ; and it is quite likely that the gradations of matter, without and above the sphere of sensuous perception, are quite as numerous as those that are embraced within the present limits of our observation. If matter or substance, when unorganized, may be so sublimated as to elude the senses, on the physical plain of their exercise, (and this is never disputed,) it may be rationally inferred that they so exist in organized bodies. The objection based on the fact that such forms cannot be discerned by the natural eye, has no weight, since the constituents of which the same are presumed to be composed are also invisible. The combination of oxygen and nitrogen, with other gases, in less proportions—forming the elastic medium that surrounds the earth —are all invisible. Nevertheless, this rarefied medium is as essentially material, and exists as absolutely, as the denser substances that make up the solid globe itself. Though the weight of the atmosphere is about fifteen pounds to every square inch of the earth's surface, yet the elements are so rare and attenuate that they are rendered invisible. But we never question the existence of the subtile elements because they are not cognizable by the ordinary powers of sensation. If, then, there is a wide realm wherein unorganized matter escapes our sensuous observation, there must also—to complete the Creation—be an organized world, peopled by beings who are invisible on account of the extreme tenuity of the elements that enter into the composition and structure of their bodies.

There is but one way to avoid this conclusion. It must be rendered apparent that matter, in its more sublimated states, is never subject to the laws of organization. But while the evidence from Nature does nothing to support such a conclusion, it certainly goes far to establish an opposite conviction. We discover that matter in its grossest or densest forms can not be readily organized. There is not sufficient freedom and rapidity in the molecular changes to admit of such an organic arrangement of ultimate atoms. A tree will not take root on the bare surface of a granite rock, and the seed that is deposited in a marble vase, without either earth or water, will never germinate, for the obvious reason that the forms of matter with which it sustains immediate relations are not properly prepared by the natural processes of sublimation to admit of their assimilation, even by the lowest forms of the organized world. It is certain that the organizations of the vegetable kingdom derive their chief support from the invisible elements of the atmosphere. To demonstrate this it is only necessary to place some plant, that grows rapidly and to a large size, in a vessel containing a given quantity of earth. If, in its complete development, the cubic contents of the plant should be equal to the entire mass of earth, it will still be found that the actual quantity of the latter is but little less than before. The facts appear to warrant the conclusion, that the tendency of matter to assume organic forms and relations increases in proportion as the elements become rarified. If I am right, it must follow that the highest states of material attenuation are extremely favorable to the processes of organic chemistry ; and hence the most ethereal essences may be organized. Thus, in admitting the indestructibility of matter, we discover something like a material basis and natural foundation for faith in the existence of an invisible, Spiritual World.

We have no right to assume that the utmost limits of the realm of organized existence are to be determined by the capacity of the natural senses. Such an assumption is at once opposed to reason and science. · The microscope has already opened a new world to our perceptions, and revealed the existence of a vast realm, swarming with innumerable hosts of organized creatures endowed with vital and voluntary motion and sensation. Before the naked eye all these are invisible. Thus we have been forced, by the progress in science and art, to acknowledge the reality of an organic creation, invisible on account of the minuteness of its structures ; and it surely is not unreasonable to infer the existence of other and diviner natures, whose refined substance and superior organs are adapted to perform the appropriate functions of intelligent beings.

But it may be objected, that while the intrinsic forces and laws of matter are as lasting as matter itself, still its specific combinations are constantly changing, and its particular forms are all subject to decay. Hence, a demonstration of the universality and indestructibility of the life-principle, may afford no evidence of our individual immortality. The force of this objection is readily acknowledged, but only in its application to the preceding argument. Happily we are not restricted to such evidence as may only serve to establish a probability. Our claim to a conscious existence after the death of the body may be supported by a different course of reasoning, and more direct evidence derived from the constitution of Man.

The indestructibility of the human mind is impressively indicated by the peculiar nature and unlimited scope of the faculties. If it were only fitted to perceive material forms, and to note the simple facts and circumstances of outward life, there might be some occasion to doubt the perpetuity of being. But the mind has a wider range and a higher sphere, to which it exhibits a direct tendency and specific adaptation. So general is the desire to live, that self-preservation is denominated " the first law of nature ;" and the aspiration for a state of being superior to the present imperfect life, in all its relations and appointments, is scarcely less universal. It is manifestly impossible for any being to occupy a place, to desire a life, or even to conceive of a condition, that is above the plain of its nature—or that condition which it may realize in the subsequent development of its faculties. Can the beast conceive of the relations that exist among men? Evidently not, for the obvious reason that such relations form no part of the destiny that awaits him. The highest development of which his nature is susceptible, must necessarily leave him far beneath the dignity of man's estate.

If the nature of man were altogether earthly, and the destruction of the body were in fact the annihilation of being, from what source could we derive the power to grasp the first principle of spiritual science? And who, in this view of the case, will explain the philosophy of that mysterious and delightful fascination that leads the willing soul far away into an ideal realm? If what we call death has power to disorganize the mind, to destroy its elements, and swallow up the identity to which we so fondly cling, why should man have the least conception of an invisible world and an immortal life? The simplest form of the conception is above all that distinguishes the sphere of mere material and brute existence ; and yet the idea lives in the common mind, and

the hope of Immortality is incorporated with the very elements of our mental constitution. Nor is it always vague
and unsatisfactory. With a serene joy we anticipate the
time when, with a clear vision, we shall perceive the Past
and the Future; when our highest thoughts will no more be
distorted by inflexible and unmeaning forms of speech, and
no arbitrary custom will be left to subvert the great law of
affinity, by which congenial natures meet and mingle together.
The idea of such a life, is the revelation of its existence,
whilst the desire it awakens in the soul is the significant
prophecy of its realization.

Ordinary observers are accustomed to attribute the diversified phenomena of sensation—all the thrilling revelations
of pleasure and pain—to the brain and the nervous system.
And yet the ultimate seat of sensation must be sought elsewhere. The nerves do not feel; it is neither the eye that
sees nor the ear that hears; much less may the brain be
supposed to be the *source* of our intelligence. It is but the
instrument of the mind; and we examine its structure and
its substance in vain, in our search for the soul. Neither a
skillful dissection, a chemical analysis, nor a microscopic
inspection will suffice to discover the human faculties and
affections. The physiologists, who adopt the material philosophy of human nature, have been puzzled to determine
the portion of the brain in which consciousness resides;
and while uncertain where to locate the chief seat of sensation, in the visual organ, they have at length ascertained that the base of the optic nerve has no sensibility.
Thus we discover that our powers of perception are not
necessarily to be found in the organs of general and special

sensation. Even those convolutions of the brain, through which all the noblest faculties are exercised, may be pared off, and the whole cerebral structure removed down to the *corpus callosum,* and still the subject experienced no pain under the operation. Moreover, digestion and all the functions necessary to life still continue.[1]

Now if sensation originates in the brain, as the material philosophers imagine, why is the brain itself insensible? This mystery must be forever inexplicable unless we admit the two-fold nature of Man. On the contrary, if all the senses have their primary seat in the spirit, the question will certainly admit of a rational solution. In fact, if the brain be regarded as the mere instrument of sensorial impressions, it can not be difficult to account for the remarkable fact which Dr. Wigan and several physiologists have observed. Cutting the brain may, therefore, occasion no suffering, for the sufficient reason that sensation does not essentially belong to that organ, but to the soul.

But there are other and still more convincing reasons for entertaining this view of the subject, some of which follow in this connection. The senses are often exercised when their corporeal instruments are not employed, as must be evident from the illustrations presented in another portion of this treatise.[2] If the somnambulist and the magnetic sleeper have the power to see in the absence of light, and without the use of the organic instrument, it is obvious that sight—in the most essential sense—does not belong to the

---

[1] See Dr. Wigan's Treatise on the " Duality of the Mind.

[2] In this connection the reader may find it profitable to refer to the chapter on the Clairvoyant Vision.

eye. Hence the power of vision may not always or necessarily depend on the integrity of the physical organ ; nor,
indeed, on the preservation of the body.

The phenomena developed in the psychological states referred to, suggest the propriety of the same course of reasoning in its application to all the senses and their organs.
But for the purposes of our illustration, the single faculty
of vision and its organic instrument, will suffice. The eye
of the sleep-walker is generally open, and whilst his movements demonstrate that his sight is preternaturally clear, it
is no less manifest that the visual organ is utterly useless
during the continuance of the trance. This is confirmed by
our observation of the following facts. First—The vision
of the natural somnambulist and the magnetic seer is not
subject to the conditions of natural sight, inasmuch as they
are able to see clearly in total darkness. Second—They
also see through the most opaque substances, and all the
solid bodies of the terrestrial world become transparent.
Moreover, as the naked eye of a person in this state may be
exposed to the strongest light, without the slightest contraction of the pupil, we have here another apparent demonstration of the fact that there is no sensibility in the optic nerve.
These observations seem to warrant the inference, that since
the senses are capable of an independent exercise even now,
and whilst we continue in the body, the physical organs are
not absolutely indispensable. If one may have this perfect
use of his senses for an hour—whilst the organs of sense
are rendered temporarily useless—who will affirm that the
same power may not continue forever? These facts, and
this course of reasoning, inevitably lead to the conclusion,

that all the faculties of the mind will remain when the body shall have been finally disorganized.

It is a fact well known to the student of vital chemistry, and clearly enough illustrated in the vegetable and animal physiology, that all the forms of the organic creation are subject to constant mutation. Upon the reciprocal interchange of elementary particles, between the vegetable and animal kingdoms, the life of both essentially depends. That a similar process is constantly going on, in respect to all the constituents of the human body, can scarcely be doubted by any one who has kept pace with the progress of scientific investigation and discovery. Thus, by a gradual process. the effete substances are thrown off from the system, and the places previously occupied by the eliminated particles are supplied by others, deposited and assimilated by the processes of organic chemistry. This truth is well understood and generally admitted. It may be expedient, however, to briefly hint at some of the accredited facts and scientific proofs of the atomic changes which thus proceed without interruption in the living body.

It may be objected that the vital processes do not result in the progressive elimination of *all* the particles; in other words, that the body is not changed in its entirety. But this objection will not, of course, be urged in reference to the fluid portions of the body. It is only in respect to *the solids* that it has so much as a seeming plausibility when—in the full light of modern science—it is submitted to careful inspection. If, then, in its application to the fluid portions of the system, the objection has no validity, it follows that comparatively a very small portion of its substance may be supposed to remain unchanged, since the solids in a full-grown i.uman body seldom exceed ten pounds.   By this simple process of evaporation, the body that weighed one hundred and fifty pounds may be reduced to *twelve ;* and the embalmed bodies exhumed from the Egyptian tombs—from which all the fluids have been completely dissipated—are sometimes found to weigh only *seven or eight pounds.*   Now, if all fluid substances may be exhaled, or otherwise expelled from the system, by the vital forces and processes, it will be perceived that but little remains, and that little is easily disposed of.   It is well known that the very elements of which the muscles and the bones are composed may exist in a fluid state.   Indeed, they did so exist at first ; for the solid tissues are woven from elements held in solution, and constantly circulating through the body.

That the denser substances, in solution, are expelled from the system through the cuticle, is abundantly confirmed by the uniform testimony of physiologists, and demonstrated by the results of scientific experiments.   According to Lovoisier and others, not less than six pounds of matter are often removed from the body, through the perspiratory ducts, in the course of twenty-four hours.[1]   This is not all water. By a skillful analysis of perspiration, M. Favre—as appears from a paper submitted to the French Academy—detected the presence of certain metallic salts ; and from the quantity employed in his experiments, he obtained no less than six grammes of lactate of zinc—*that is, a quarter of an ounce.*[2]

---

[1] See Brand's Encyclopedia.—Article, Perspiration.
[2] The reader is referred to the Annual of Scientific Discovery, for 1853, for an account of Favre's Experiments.

If we may credit the class-books in physiology—now in common use in our schools—"about one per cent." of the perspiration from the human body "consists of solid substances which are the products of the decomposition constantly taking place in the tissues."[1]

That even the substance of the osseous-system is perpetually changing, is demonstrated by the fact that the bones of swine, after they have been eating madder—a plant of the genus Rubia—are found to be colored. If matter is thus readily introduced into the composition and structure of the bones, it must be as readily and as rapidly removed from them or otherwise they would continue to increase in size after the animal had reached the last degree in its normal development. A further illustration may be found in the fact of the admission of mineral poisons into the circulation and the tissues, and their subsequent elimination. On this point we cite the demonstrative experiments of M. Orfila, also of the French Academy :

"In eighteen months I was able to experiment on only four poisonous substances—bichloride of mercury, acetate of lead, sulphate of copper and nitrate of silver. These experiments have taught me that when the above poisonous substances are administered to animals, that mercury disappears in general from the organs in eight or ten days. Lead and copper are found in the intestinal parietes and in the bones eight months after they have c-ased to be introduced into the stomach. Silver, whose presence in the liver may, in some cases, be demonstrated after six months, is not found in any organ of other animals, seven months after the administration of nitrate of silver. * * *

"Should a man survive a poisoning by corrosive sublimate for fifteen days, it is very possible that the chemists, consulted in the case, would find no

---

[1] Appendix to Appleton's Second Edition of Coming's Physiology, p. 255.

mercury in the org ms   They would. however, commit a great error should
they conclude that ther: had been no attempt to poison."

From the foregoing facts and observations, it will be perceived that the molecular changes occur through all the solid
portions of the body, and that the same chemical elements
may assume a fluid and solid form.   The vital action, as observed in the processes of organic chemistry, is essentially
one with combustion ; and while from day to day the vital
fires consume the body, they also prepare the foreign elements wherewith Nature rebuilds the temple of the Soul.

The rational inquirer will neither be the first to dispute
the natural evidences of his own immortality, nor can he
willingly believe in the loss of his identity, and

> " A positive diffusion of the soul
> Among the elements that make the world."

Nevertheless, there are mortals whose chronic skepticism,
prompts them to make every possible effort to subvert the
claims of manhood to an imperishable life.   In such minds
certain objections to the preceding argument very naturally
arise, and as these may diminish the faith and obscure the
prospects of several honest minds, it may be well to expose
the fallacy of the objections.

A distinguished materialist maintains that the corporeal
system can not be changed in its entirety, once in seven
years, more or less ; that if it were so, warts and other
abnormal developments, on the surfaces of animal and human
bodies, would inevitably be removed, whereas they frequently
remain during a much longer period ; and he cites an example of thirty-five years' standing.   But the fact that such

an excrescence has so long continued, precisely where it now is, and still presents the same general appearance, illustrates nothing but the blindness of persons who, finding that their earthly and soulless theories are unsupported by the present normal developments of the human mind, vainly attempt to hang something worse than "a forlorn hope" on the preternatural and superfluous parts of the perishable body. With equal propriety it may be assumed that—since the individual so far resembles himself (as he existed thirty-five years ago) that his friends are still able to identify his person—we are authorized to conclude that the same matter formed his body at the commencement of that period that constitutes it to-day. This is begging the whole question, in a manner that does not comport with the high logical pretentions of men who make such objections. The nails on the writer's fingers present the same specific form and general appearance that distinguished them thirty-five years ago ; but it would be extremely difficult to sustain an argument designed to prove the identity of the ultimate atoms in their composition, after each one of them has been gradually pared off to the extent of two or three feet in all.

The second objection maintains that if the whole composition and structure of the body be thus subject to a gradual decomposition and re-formation—the ultimate particles being thrown off by a natural process, and their places supplied by new molecular deposits—all the old flesh-marks and scars, produced by accident or otherwise, would be completely obliterated. This objection, so well calculated to confound the superficial observer, has really not the slightest weight in the judgment of more enlightened physiologists.

When the injury does not penetrate beneath the epidermis it leaves no scar; but when the instrument that inflicts a wound severs, or otherwise obstructs the channels of the circulation, a scar may remain after the healing process is complete, for the obvious reason that the anastomosis of the vessels through which the fluids circulate is never as perfect as before. The re-formation of the parts must, thereafter, proceed without a complete inosculation, and the subsequent molecular deposits are consequently rendered irregular in time and unequal in measure, as a quantitative analysis, aided by a microscopic inspection, would clearly demonstrate.

Again, it is insisted that human physiology clearly proves that the "mind and body never exist separately or independently of each other." Had the objector merely assumed that the mind never exists except *in a body*, or organic form through which its faculties may be manifested, there would be little occasion for controversy; but since the objection has specific reference to the present organic instrument of the mind—*the corporeal body*—we are authorized to dispute the proposition, and affirm that it is not possible for physiology to prove any such dependence of the mind on the body. Physiological science furnishes abundant evidence to prove that the mind and body are capable of existing together under proper conditions—nothing more. But our imperfect knowledge of what the human intelligence *can do*, under certain specific conditions, does not authorize us to fix arbitrary limits to the exercise of its faculties, under other conditions and circumstances, which have neither occurred in our private experience nor chanced to come within the limited range of our casual observation.

The same material philosopher has another objection to our immortality, which is thus expressed : " The mind is always affected by the conditions of the body, which would hardly be the case if they were distinct." This objection is unsound in fact and infelicitous in the form of the statement. The author evinces a lack of proper discrimination. It is not asserted that the mind and body now exist separately. The real question relates to the innate capacity of the soul to exist in a state of separation from the physical form. It is conceded that the mental functions are influenced by the conditions of the material body, so long as they coëxist ; but this concession can not be used to support the negative proposition that the mind is, and must remain, forever incapable of an independent existence. Different individuals influence each other in the social relation. The writer has often directed the mental faculties, and governed the bodily functions of other people ; but this neither proves that the separate individualities among them were annihilated, nor that their continued existence must depend on the preservation and constant presence of the source of that influence. Agreeably to the peculiar logic exhibited in the objection, if one child in school has the mumps, and communicates the inflammation to the parotid glands of one hundred children, we must conclude that they can no more live if separated from each other. For, if so many are affected by one body, how can we recognize any individual distinctions among them, and what possible claim has any child to an independent existence !

An incorrigible unbeliever—who seemed to hold on to the cold dogma of annihilation with as much tenacity and affection as most men cling to life and a rational hope of immortality—once came to the author, and exposing his right arm, which was pictured over with India ink, said, with an air of triumph, "It is a quarter of a century since these pictures were made on this arm, and in view of this fact, what becomes of your seven years' theory?"   The answer was— India ink is *a foreign substance* that was never naturalized in the human system by the process of assimilation.   Hence, it is no more a portion of the matter belonging to the body, and subject to the processes of organic chemistry, than either a lady's ear-rings; the gold filling of a tooth, or a pistol ball which a duellist may—for half his life time— chance to carry in his body.   The seven years' philosophy is apparently secure enough, but pray what becomes of the objections?

"It is better to reason than to cavil."

Now if it be conceded that the elements, which enter into the chemical composition and organic structure of the body, are completely changed—by the natural processes already described—it will be impossible for the materialist, consistently with his theory, to account for the significant fact that the identity is never lost. If the essential individuality belonged to the flesh, we might rationally infer that it would inevitably be annihilated as often as the body is changed. But the corporeal changes leave all the lines of our individuality unbroken. Whilst it is obvious that the man of half a century must have had a number of bodies, we find that deeply engraven in his consciousness is the history of each and all. The materialist's only reason for presuming that our identity is lost, and that conscious existence terminates at death, is predicated of the simple fact that the physical body is disorganized. The conclusion is not sustained by the evidence. Disorganization has occurred—after a more gradual manner, to be sure—several times before—the entire composition of the body having been repeatedly changed ; and still the identity has been preserved through all these changes, and we feel assured that our existence here is ONE. We can recall the events of the past, and even in life's last hours—when the still conscious soul catches glimpses of the world beyond—the little incidents of childhood are preserved with all their freshness. Thus it is rendered evident, that there must be an internal or spiritual constitution, which is the ultimate recepticle of all the impressions made on the organic instruments of perception ; and hence the lines of individuality are not obliterated by the gradual decomposition of the living body. With these facts in view, we can not entertain the hypothesis that another and final transition, whatever may be the circumstances of its occurrence, can obliterate the record, destroy consciousness, and make an end of life.

Will it be said that this argument is unsound because the transitions between infancy and old age are unlike death, being more gradual ? This objection, specious as it may appear, can not invalidate our reasoning. If the change be *entire*, the time employed in its accomplishment can make no important difference. Whether the constituents of the body are removed in a longer or shorter period—in portions large or small—the conclusion appears to be inevitable. If there were no inward form or spiritual constitution, it is certain that the molecular eliminations would periodically destroy the identity of man, and hence memory would be limited to a brief period, and a narrow range of objects, events and ideas. Suppose the existence of a tablet, bearing a certain inscription; If you annually remove one-seventh part, either by the destruction of a particular section of the same, or by displacing one ultimate atom in every seven, it would follow that at the expiration of seven years the whole would be removed. But if, to render the illustration more complete, we suppose the places occupied by the eliminated particles to be supplied by others, we shall at last have only a *blank tablet*. Who then would be able to read the inscription? So if man, like a monument, were only formed of the substances of the physical world, the records of his personal experience would be frequently blotted out, and he would, *ex necessitate*, be obliged to commence his individual life anew.

But this point admits of a more forcible illustration. The impressions made on the sensorium—more especially through the organs of vision—very much resemble the photographic images. Baptista Porta, the inventor of the camera, must have studied the stucture of the eye, which also has its dark chamber, its double convex lens, and a membrane susceptible of the most exquisite impressions, and corresponding to the chemically prepared surface of the photographer's plate. The physical phenomena of vision result from the admission of light through the lenses of the eye into the visual chamber, and from the natural laws of refraction, the images of external objects being thus daguerreotyped on the dark surface of the choroid membrane. Now if there were no internal, spiritual depository of the images thus produced, not one of them could remain unobscured, since every new picture on the same surface would serve to disfigure and obliterate the last, producing a complete chaos of broken outlines and dissolving forms.

But time is no such iconoclast, in respect to the images that live in Memory. Instead of defaced records and dissolving views, the forms and associations of all the Past are clearly inwrought in the faculty of memory, and the events of childhood are frequently remembered with the greatest distinctness. The old man among the graves of his generation is seemingly insensible of the living tide that rises around him, and on which he is upborne like the last wreck of the storm. He seems solitary, and may not regard the presence of any one, for he is absent in spirit. I have seen the old man, and learned the cause of his abstraction.

> " Through the shadowy past,
> Like a tomb-searcher, Memory ran,
> Lifting each shroud that Time had cast
> O'er all he loved.''

If the identity is destroyed when the elements of the body are dissipated, will the materialist tell us why the old man thus dwells in the past; and by what mysterious magnetism is he consciously attracted to the absent and the dead?

The evidences of man's two-fold nature are various and apparently conclusive. Within this corporeal frame there is another body, constituted of more ethereal elements and an imperishable organization. It is a curious fact that persons who have lost a limb always have an internal consciousness that the body is still complete. Although an arm or a leg may have been amputated years before, and its decomposed elements scattered by the winds and waves, the individual yet feels that the lost member is with him and sustaining its proper relations; and his sensation extends to the very extremity, almost as perfectly as when the limb was there. This may seem incredible, but the fact is confirmed by the uniform experience of all who have suffered the loss of one or more of their members. The sphere of their conscious existence is never circumscribed by this partial destruction of the body. From this significant fact we can only infer that the individuality of man does not belong to his body, but, on the contrary, that it inheres in a supra-mortal and indestructible constitution.

It is worthy of observation that certain physicians and material philosophers have attempted to account for the important fact just noticed, by presuming that the sensation of the lost member results from *association*. Such an explanation needs to be explained; and to be fortified by some show of evidence. Indeed it is no explanation at all, but an absurd assumption. If it were possible for the senses to be so influenced, and perverted to this unaccountable degree, they would be totally unreliable. Agreeably to this hypothesis, if I have been accustomed to meet a friend—dressed in a drab coat—every morning for one year, I may expect to see the same drab coat forever after, notwithstanding my friend may have exchanged it for a black one. We are accustomed to see all people with some kind of wearing apparel, but no law of association prevents our instantly distinguishing a nude figure from those that are clothed. But (to bring the illustration nearer home) if a man who has been sick and in constant pain for ten years should at length recover, he surely would not continue to suffer—from association—the same pains during the remainder of his natural life. If, in such a case, the materialist were himself the patient, he might rationally dispute the reality of the cure, but he would surely be the last man to entertain his own hypothesis, in attempting to account for his continued sufferings.

But the man who in his youth lost a limb, even now, in his maturity, feels that he has all the members necessary to constitute a perfect manhood, and he is hourly reminded that sensation remains entire though the nervous mechanism is in part destroyed. This is a most significant proof of the existence of an internal and immortal constitution. This spiritual body can not be mutilated by such instruments and methods as may be employed to disorganize the physical structure. But if there be no spiritual organism—the ultimate receptacle of all our sensorial impressions—how can feeling remain when the sensor nerves are severed and the entire member has perished? Moreover, if these members of the body may be removed without either disturbing the original limits of sensation or circumscribing the sphere of consciousness, it must follow that the whole body may be decomposed and yet all these powers of life, and sense, and thought may remain.

But if a man be immortal in his individuality, why do the faculties of the mind seem to decay with the organs of the body? Here we meet the old Materialism in the stronghold from which it has contended with its greatest apparent success. Those whose conclusions are determined by sensuous observation of visible phenomena, know little or nothing of mind except from its outward manifestations. When these become imperfect, they infer that the mind itself is impaired, whereas the derangement is confined to the organic function. So long as the mind is restricted to the use of these physical organs, its manifestations must be rendered irregular by the varying conditions of the body, and constantly liable to interruption from the accidents and circumstances that may impair the integrity of its organic instruments. In old age the spirit manifests itself but feebly through the body. The apparent decay of the faculties must necessarily accompany the transformation whenever it occurs naturally ; for, as the vital forces are progressively withdrawn from the body, the parts most remote from the citadel of life first become cold, rigid and insensible. By degrees the soul ceases to manifest its qualities and powers through the old organic medium it is about to leave forever. When at length the deathless spirit—already arrayed in the robes of its Immortality—is prepared to depart, it may not pause to rebuke our unbelief by waking anew the slumbering tones of its broken lyre.

It was no part of the author's purpose to discuss the Relations of Man to the realities of the life beyond ; and hence, in concluding this treatise, we leave him on the boundary of another world, with a profound consciousness that he can never die, in any sense that implies the loss of his identity. I could as readily conceive of the annihilation of space and substance. It would be treason against the Divine government to entertain the thought, that the light of a single human mind will ever be finally extinguished. Not whilst these spiritual instincts remain, to intimate the existence of an incorruptible life, can we relinquish a hope that is the anchor of the world. The reason that investigates the subtile principles and eternal laws of being; those ceaseless aspirations in which we mount up to heaven; and the mysterious power of cognition whereby we lay hold of invisible things—all express the solemn affirmation of the great life to come. And then—there are chords now swept by invisible hands, whilst notes of inspiration fill the soul with unearthly music. Those chords must all be *broken*, and we must have the demonstration, that the last tone is hushed in the shock of the falling temple, or I shall yet seek for the indwelling divinity above the ruins of its mortal shrine. Till then, these amazing powers, and this conception of another life, which everywhere—in all stages of civilization, and among the savage tribes—lives and blooms in the soul, shall be recognized and cherished as the hand-writing of God and the revelation of our Eternal Life.

> I *feel* this Immortality o'ersweep
> All pains. all groans. all griefs, all fears, and peal,
> Like the eternal thunders of the deep,
> Into my soul, this truth— THOU LIV'ST FOREVER!

CPSIA information can be obtained
at www.ICGtesting.com
Printed in the USA
LVHW022023120422
716028LV00006B/148

9 783752 591112